continued . . .

"I love how Jade Lee guides her readers away from the typical romance novel, giving us more: more plot, more tragedy, and more love story to remember. A 'do NOT miss' read."
—*Fresh Fiction*

"One of the best historical romances I've read this year . . . This story of a woman yearning for respectability and the two men who want to claim her will linger with readers long after they close the cover."
—*The Romance Reader*

"Jade Lee has written an enjoyable character-driven story with style and class. It's steamy but tasteful and will be enjoyed by readers who like books where love redeems a dark and damaged hero."
—*TwoLips Reviews*

AND PRAISE FOR THE OTHER NOVELS OF *USA TODAY* BESTSELLING AUTHOR JADE LEE

"[A] refreshingly different, sexy Regency romance."
—*Chicago Tribune*

"Lovely historical romance."
—*Publishers Weekly*

"It's unflinching and unabashed in historic social and cultural detail . . . Elegant complexity and beautifully rendered."
—*Booklist* (starred review)

"Strangely hypnotic."
—*Romance Reviews Today*

"An exotic and emotional historical romantic tale."
—*ParaNormal Romance*

"I enjoyed the sensual and hot love scenes, and boy were they hot, WOW!"
—*Night Owl Reviews*

"Lee . . . [has] brought something new and intriguing to erotic romance . . . This is what places her in a class with the best."
—*RT Book Reviews*

"A highly enjoyable read."
—*All About Romance*

"Jade Lee provides a wonderful, refreshing tale."
—*Genre Go Round Reviews*

"Delightfully different." —*Midwest Book Reviews*

"An exhilarating, fast-paced tale from start to finish."
—*The Best Reviews*

Berkley Sensation Titles by Jade Lee

WICKED SURRENDER
WICKED SEDUCTION
WEDDED IN SCANDAL

Wedded in Scandal

JADE LEE

Enjoy a little scandal!

Jade Lee

BERKLEY SENSATION, NEW YORK

THE BERKLEY PUBLISHING GROUP
Published by the Penguin Group
Penguin Group (USA) Inc.
375 Hudson Street, New York, New York 10014, USA
Penguin Group (Canada), 90 Eglinton Avenue East, Suite 700, Toronto, Ontario M4P 2Y3, Canada
(a division of Pearson Penguin Canada Inc.) • Penguin Books Ltd., 80 Strand, London WC2R 0RL,
England • Penguin Group Ireland, 25 St. Stephen's Green, Dublin 2, Ireland (a division of Penguin
Books Ltd.) • Penguin Group (Australia), 250 Camberwell Road, Camberwell, Victoria 3124, Australia
(a division of Pearson Australia Group Pty. Ltd.) • Penguin Books India Pvt. Ltd., 11 Community
Centre, Panchsheel Park, New Delhi—110 017, India • Penguin Group (NZ), 67 Apollo Drive,
Rosedale, Auckland 0632, New Zealand (a division of Pearson New Zealand Ltd.) • Penguin Books
(South Africa) (Pty.) Ltd., 24 Sturdee Avenue, Rosebank, Johannesburg 2196, South Africa

Penguin Books Ltd., Registered Offices: 80 Strand, London WC2R 0RL, England

WEDDED IN SCANDAL

A Berkley Sensation Book / published by arrangement with the author

PUBLISHING HISTORY
Berkley Sensation mass-market edition / March 2012

Copyright © 2012 by Katherine Ann Grill.
Excerpt from *Wedded in Sin* by Jade Lee copyright © by Katherine Ann Grill.
Cover art by Judy York.
Cover design by George Long.
Interior text design by Kristin del Rosario.

ISBN: 978-0-425-24593-4

BERKLEY SENSATION®
Berkley Sensation Books are published by The Berkley Publishing Group,
a division of Penguin Group (USA) Inc.,
375 Hudson Street, New York, New York 10014.
BERKLEY SENSATION® is a registered trademark of Penguin Group (USA) Inc.
The "B" design is a trademark of Penguin Group (USA) Inc.

PRINTED IN THE UNITED STATES OF AMERICA

10   9   8   7   6   5   4   3   2   1

ALWAYS LEARNING   **PEARSON**

ACKNOWLEDGMENTS

Thanks go to so many people for this book: Kate Seaver, amazing editor; Pamela Harty, amazing agent; and David Grill, amazing husband and hero.

Plus thanks to my amazing friends and supporters: Elizabeth Hoyt, Cindy Dees, and Deb Miller.

But for this book and this series, Kim Castillo is the most brilliant, because the first germ of an idea came from her.

Thank you all!

Chapter 1

✕

"Yer wants to go in there? But, er, why?"

Robert Percy, Viscount Redhill, ignored the mine manager and began stripping off his coat and gloves. They were in the shack outside a coal mine that his father had purchased in a fit of drunken entrepreneurship. Sadly, the earl didn't fall down in his cups like a normal person. No, instead he bought businesses, which Robert then had to save. And given that no one in his family knew anything about coal mining, this was going to be a challenge indeed.

But the first step in a new venture—or after one of his father's drinking binges—was to inspect the new property. So he was determined to go down into the hellhole of a mine despite Mr. Hutchins's objections. He'd already pulled off his coat and folded it neatly to the side, but after one glance outside at the filthy employees all lined up near the mine entrance, he stripped off his waistcoat as well. He would have taken off his fine lawn shirt, but he couldn't greet his new employees half naked.

"It's mighty dark down there," continued Mr. Hutchins, his full whiskers twitching in agitation. Truly, the long nose and scrunched face made the man resemble a rat in some rather unfortunate ways. A rat who obviously did not like leaving his nest.

"Last I recall, the dark never hurt anybody."

"That's 'cause 'anybody' ain't been down in the mines," Mr. Hutchins groused. Then he sighed heavily and pulled his rather impressive bulk out of his chair. "I think yer daft, milord, but if yer insisting, I'll have Charlie show you about."

Robert paused, his gaze narrowing down to a few pertinent details. First of all was Mr. Hutchins's girth. His waist was just the right size if he were a draft horse. Second, everything in here was filthy, but not with coal dust. No, he could barely breathe for the stink of cigar. And third, Mr. Hutchins had a telltale wheeze when he moved even around this small office.

"When was the last time you were down in the mines, Mr. Hutchins?" he asked.

"Wot? Why jest last week, I'm sure. But it's a filthy place and beastly hot."

"I believe that a manager should see what he manages, don't you, Mr. Hutchins?"

"Oh, I do, I do!" he said as he wiped the sweat from his balding pate. "Go down there every year to inspect the new finds. Now, if you wish to see something most interesting, I can take you to inspect our carts. They're in a terrible way, milord—"

"I will definitely inspect them, Mr. Hutchins. After I see the mine." And so saying, Robert left the filthy mine office to head toward the black cave hole of an entrance. All around him, scrawny men, women, and children tugged their forelock or curtsied as he passed. He smiled at each of them, feeling the bizarre echo of when he'd last traveled to his family's Scotland estate. All the servants had lined up then as well to greet the young master of the estate. But those people had been well fed and clean. These people had coal dust encrusted in their very skin and a haunted, hollow look to their eyes.

Bloody hell, what was his father thinking buying such a place? Even half drunk, his father could have seen how very sick these people were. But his father had never actually inspected his new purchase. No, he left that to Robert to perform *after* all the papers had been signed.

Mr. Hutchins made his way to his side, his wheezing growing louder as they crossed the rocky ground. "You sure ye don't want to inspect the books? I'm an excellent bookkeeper, I assure you. You'll find everything in order. Every copper accounted for!"

Robert nodded, his gaze picking out the bleeding hands of a child standing nearby. "Who is that boy there?"

"That? That's Charlie's sis Brenda."

That was a girl? "She works in the mines?"

"Our last mine horse died a year ago from the air. Ain't good for horses, you know. Then I realized that two or three young uns can pull a cart just as well and they appreciate the work. Helps their families, you know, and is cheaper fer us. Lord Brimley said it were good thinking."

Robert didn't doubt it. Lord Brimley was a pinchpenny in all aspects of his life except for his brandy. That made him, of course, a great jolly good friend to Robert's father.

"As my family now owns this mine, Lord Brimley's opinions are of no interest to me. And I shall see that there are new horses immediately."

"Oh. Oh, dear. But what shall I tell the parents of all those dear children?"

"That their children should enjoy the fresh air while they are young. And that they shall be paid for the care of the horses instead."

Robert didn't wait to see Mr. Hutchins's reaction to that statement but bent his attention to the mine entrance. Or more accurately, he spent a moment fighting his nausea at the thought of entering that dark maw. Mr. Hutchins must have sensed his hesitation as he sidled up.

"Perhaps you'd rather see the books first."

Robert ground his teeth together and forced his stiff legs to obey him. It wasn't a maw, for God's sake. It was a mine entrance and dozens of workers went in and out of it every day. Women and children. He could go down despite the air of depressing filth that infused the entire county. An unhealthy miasma, to be sure.

"Charlie! Charlie, my boy!" called Mr. Hutchins. "Come along and show his lordship the ladders. Mind that you point out all the interesting bits."

Charlie was no more a boy than Robert was. But he was obviously younger than Mr. Hutchins and had a warm smile that included all his teeth. "Aye, sir. Right this way, milord. First ladder is jes' inside." Then he walked quick as a wink into that dark maw.

Robert squared his shoulders and followed. He only paused once, and that was to glance back at Mr. Hutchins. "You know, I'm not sure Charlie will know quite *all* the things to show me. I believe I require your expert guidance."

Mr. Hutchins had the predictable response: a grimace of distaste quickly covered. But he followed and now Robert was forced to step lively or be shown as craven as the heavyset Hutchins.

They moved slowly, Mr. Hutchins wheezing the entire way. They descended three more ladders, lit two barely flickering candles, and passed a dilapidated cart before Hutchins came to his first interesting tidbit.

"There's the bones of the first fireman killed here, over a hundred years ago. Was burning off the gas, he was, and not a very fast runner, obviously."

"My God," Robert breathed. "Why wasn't he taken up and buried?"

"Oh, well, it ain't really his bones," said Charlie. "Just the spare bits of a horse, I think, but we say it's a miner to scare the kids into taking the work serious. The little ones especially need to be kept in line. It's dangerous work down here, and we can't have them thinking it's games."

Robert frowned. "Why would anyone think it's a game?" When his father had first informed him of this mine purchase, Robert had rapidly tried to learn everything he could about coal mining. He was aware of some of the terrible dangers miners faced daily. He couldn't imagine a child in this hellhole, much less that any would consider it a game.

"Ah, well, you know children," Charlie said with a sad smile. "It's hard on them at first, but there are some that will make fun of the worst things."

Robert had no answer except that he never wanted this mine to employ a child ever again. If it were up to him, no man would have to come down here, either, but then again the nation needed its coal.

"I think that's far enough, don't you think?" asked Hutchins. Robert couldn't really see the man in the dim light, but he could smell the sweat. Or maybe that was his own, as the heat was suffocating.

"No," Robert forced out. "Show me where you're working now."

"But that's a ways further down, my lord," said Charlie, doubt lacing his tone. "And it's none too pleasant."

"Lead on," he said grimly while his gut tightened. Then, to distract himself, he began asking questions of Charlie. Mr. Hutchins didn't have the breath to answer, but Charlie had a good head and full understanding of the work being done. Robert's head was nearly bursting with information when they came to the newest cut.

Miners were there with pickaxes and shovels, all stooped over as they worked. Robert's clothing was drenched in sweat, and his head was pounding from the noise and the thick air, yet he was still compelled to greet every man and compliment his work as any noble lord should. It was his responsibility, and so he did his best though inside he was screaming to leave. And then he asked a most terrible question.

"But," said Robert, looking at the rickety wood supports in the tunnel, "can those possibly be safe? What if someone accidentally knocked it with a shovel? Or if a child drove a cart into it?"

"We take care not to," answered Charlie. That wasn't a terribly inspiring answer to Robert, who was lifting his candle to inspect the wood. To his eye, it was thin and worm-eaten.

"Keep that down!" rasped Mr. Hutchins in a gasping cry. "Do you want to kill us all?"

"There's no firedamp here, sir," said Charlie gently, as if he were talking to a child. "We bled off the gas just yesterday. That's why we's working here, if you recall. You wanted to tell his lordship about the fresh tunnel."

"Yes, yes, but you can never be too careful," said the manager. "Gas is the very plague down here, your lordship. And it hovers at the top of the cave."

Which was why all the candles were set on the floor or in low crevices, Robert realized. "I'm not so worried about the gas right now as the wood. Where did you get it?"

"Got a right nice lot in a few months ago. Found it meself. Cheap and sturdy."

Robert looked at the miners. None of them seemed to agree, but they didn't speak up. Mr. Hutchins must have seen it or perhaps he was used to defending his purchases. Either way he wheezed his way over to the largest of the support beams.

"Sturdy, I tell you. It's good wood!"

"But it's too thin, sir," inserted Charlie. "It don't hold in place and it don't hold strong."

"'Course it does. You just have to make sure it's seated right. Look here." He squatted down and brushed at the base of the beam. "Seat it solid like this, and nothing will bring it down."

Robert dutifully inspected the base of the beam. It certainly did look well braced to him, but what did he know? And how could one see by the light of a few paltry guttering candles?

"You've done a good job bracing it, Charlie," he said as he inspected the smaller wood pieces that ringed the beam.

"Thank you, sir, but—"

"Don't you worry, Charlie," interrupted Mr. Hutchins. "This here is good wood and extra safe with those braces." He pushed to his feet, or at least he tried to. But given his size, he had to grab hold of the wall to help himself. It would have been fine, but the wall crumbled a bit beneath his hand, and the falling rocks hit a candle, knocking it over. Mr. Hutchins, obviously fearing for his clothing, jumped backward. But he was not a man who could jump easily. He lost his footing and tripped over another rock. Which brought him right up against the support beam with all his terrible weight.

Robert sighed. All he saw was a fat man falling down. A man who ought to be able to maneuver better in the mine he supervised. But the mine workers understood more. They saw one of Mr. Hutchins's feet knock aside two of the bracing wood pieces before his full body slammed hard against the beam. The wood slid out of its seating with a scrape that was almost inaudible. But the men heard it and were rushing up and out of the tunnel long before Robert realized the danger.

Only Charlie stayed behind, his arms reaching up to grab the beam before it toppled completely. Robert joined him a second later, but it was too late. They had no secure hold on the beam. The thing fell to the ground, bringing down another roof support that fell squarely on the toppled Mr. Hutchins's legs.

That was when the dirt began to fall. Hard rocks, tiny pebbles, choking dust poured down. Something heavy slammed into Robert's shoulder, but didn't bring him down.

"Run!" he screamed at Charlie, but his voice was choked off by the dust. He could barely see. God only knew how some of the candles still burned in the thick air. Robert grabbed Charlie's arm and hauled him past the growing pile of debris. Then he shoved Charlie up the tunnel before squatting down to help Mr. Hutchins, who was howling like the very devil.

Going completely by feel, Robert ran his hands over Mr. Hutchins. The man was half covered in dirt, but he could find no other obvious injury. Already the man was clawing his way backward, slowly pulling himself out from the pile of rocks. But he wasn't working fast enough and would never get free in time.

Squatting down, Robert gripped the man beneath his armpits and hauled. Good God, the man must weigh fifteen stone! But he heaved. And Mr. Hutchins moved. And together, they worked him out enough that he could be dragged clear.

Charlie met them ten feet later, along with two other miners who waited beneath the more solid supports. With more hands to help, Mr. Hutchins was at last pulled to his feet. At least his screaming had stopped. The air was too thick with dust for anyone to speak.

Then they all stumbled, climbed, and hauled one another up the ladders to the blessedly clean air. Mr. Hutchins collapsed just outside the entrance. By his wheezing breath, Robert knew the man was still alive. And in the sunlight, he didn't see any blood beyond the small cuts that they all sported. Probably bruised badly and would soon hurt like the very devil, but just in case, Robert performed the medical inspection he'd been taught.

He ran his hands over the man's body, steadily, carefully probing for broken bones or unseen wounds. Nothing unexpected appeared.

"You'll live, Mr. Hutchins," he finally managed to push out through his raw throat. Then he turned to look at the other miners. "Anyone else hurt?"

"No, milord," said Charlie. "Weren't a real cave-in. Just a slide, like, and we're all faster than him."

"Good, good," said Robert as he dropped to his knees. Bloody hell, he felt weaker than a kitten. "One more thing, Mr. Hutchins."

"Yes, my lord?" the man wheezed.

"You're fired."

Helaine Talbott looked at the huge edifice before her and tried not to tremble. It was a wealthy home in an exclusive neighborhood. Five years ago, she would have sailed up the walkway, assured of her acceptance. But that was before her father had exposed himself as the Thief of the Ton. That was before his friends had cut him, his clubs had blackballed him, and he had disappeared to parts unknown. That was before his wife and daughter had sunk to the pits of penniless despair. And that was well before Helaine had discovered a strength inside her that defied even her father's terrible blunders.

That was before, and this was now. She had to remind herself that she was not coming to this establishment as a petitioner. She was offering a business deal, straight and simple. With luck and a lot of charm, she would emerge victorious. She would have to, because failing today would mean the poorhouse tomorrow.

So she steeled her spine, went up the walkway, and took the knocker firmly, though she had to work around the faded black ribbon that signified mourning. Helaine was wearing her best gown, one appropriate to her former status. And when the door pulled open on well-oiled hinges, she gave the butler her most aloof smile.

"I am here to visit with Lady Irene. Just tell her I'm an old school friend, as she won't know my current name."

Such a cavalier attitude toward name would not be allowed in a pedigreed household. But this was a cit's home, a family made wealthy through the shipping trade. Yes, Lady Irene had married down in title, but definitely up in wealth. As such, old friends from school would be rare indeed. Helaine had found that out herself when all of her childhood friends began giving her the cut direct.

"You have no card?" sneered the butler.

"Oh!" she gasped as she abruptly spun around. "My reticule!" Her reticule was safely settled on her dresser at home, but she pretended the height of despair. "I left it in the hackney! Oh, my! What am I to do now? I am visiting here and . . . oh, dear," she moaned.

It worked. The butler sighed and gestured her inside. From there it was a simple matter to smile up at the lady of the household, who was just now descending the stairs. Her name was Mrs. Knopp, and she was Irene's mother-in-law. She was also everything that the *ton* liked to decry as an encroaching cit. She was large and loud and much too wealthy.

Five years ago, Helaine would have noticed only that much and looked no deeper. But she was wiser now and took the time to see other small details about the woman. Her mourning dress was done in the most expensive fabric and style, so the household suffered no financial strain. But there was a great deal of strain in the lady's eyes and her slightly forced gestures. Despite the woman's bright smile, Helaine could see a sadness about her, as if a mantle of pain weighed her down.

It was grief, of course. The woman had lost her only son. Still, her voice was strong enough as she peered down at Helaine.

"Smithee! Who have we here?"

The butler responded in sneering tones. "She claims to be an old school friend of Lady Irene."

"Really?" A gleam of interest sparked in Mrs. Knopp's eyes. She rushed down the last few steps to Helaine's side. "A school friend, you say? Oh, it shall be ever so excellent for Irene to see you. She has been so withdrawn. She needs an old friend to bring her out of her room, take her shopping and the like. Maybe to a party or two. It's perfectly acceptable, you know, though she's not out of mourning yet. But a party or something, one where her dearest mama could remain at her side."

Irene's "dearest mama" was Mrs. Knopp. Irene's real mother had passed on more than a decade before. Obviously the cit had hopes that Irene would bring the family access to the upper echelons of the *ton*. And Irene's father had resurrected the ancient practice of a bride price so that the earldom would be well compensated for Irene's sacrifice in marrying down.

Helaine smiled as warmly as she dared without raising the lady's hopes. "I don't attend many parties these days, Mrs. Knopp, but I should dearly love to talk to Irene for a bit to see how she fares. We used to be good friends."

Mrs. Knopp took the slight well, nodding as if she expected no less. "Well, I must say the visit is most excellent nonetheless. Smithee, go tell Irene she has a friend here and order tea. We shall settle in for a nice chat in the salon."

"I am right here," returned a quiet, delicate voice. It was Irene, gliding down the hallway from the back of the house. "There is no need—Helaine! Is that you?"

Helaine felt her breath release at the warmth in her friend's voice. She had not been certain of her welcome. After all, Irene had merely married a cit. Helaine's fall had been much, much deeper.

"Yes, Irene, it's me. Will you let me sit with you for a while? I have missed our late-night whispers."

Helaine saw it all flash through her friend's expression. The memory of why they had stopped communicating. Of all that had passed in the intervening years. As girls they had bonded over poverty, both understanding the silent misery of having titled fathers who were perpetually broke. Helaine's disgrace had come first, but Irene had been pulled from school soon afterward because her father couldn't pay her tuition. And neither of them had seen each other since.

A million expressions flitted through Irene's face, but none settled long. And then her once best friend sighed and looked at her hands. "Wouldn't it be lovely to return to our beds back at school? To whisper about the new cook—"

"And her terrible cherry tarts!" Helaine felt a laugh bubble up from nowhere, free and lighthearted, as she hadn't felt in so very long. "And how I shall never learn to darn socks!"

Irene smiled, bringing a softness to a face too harsh with angles. "You did have a terrible hand."

"Still do, to tell the truth," she said.

"And I still cannot manage to dress my hair in anything but a straight braid." Irene gestured to the long thick cord of black hair that fell down her back.

They waited there a moment, both standing in the hallway staring at one another. Helaine had the impulse to hug her friend, and yet she didn't dare. By society's rules, that would be much too presumptuous. And Irene, too, looked uncomfortable.

It was Mrs. Knopp who rescued them, half escorting, half dragging Helaine into the front salon. "Come, come, we can't be gadding about in the hallway. Come into the parlor. Smithee! Tea, right away. And do we have any *tasty* tarts for Irene's dear friend?"

The butler bowed with a touch less doubt in his expression. "Right away, madam." Then he departed while the three women settled in the opulent salon.

But then once again an awkward silence descended. Once, she and Irene could not stop talking to one another. But now, they both stared at their hands. Helaine felt most awkward of all because she could not broach her business proposal with Mrs. Knopp right there. But neither could she ask to take a tour about the gardens or whatnot. Not after tea and tarts had been summoned.

Again it was Mrs. Knopp who came to the rescue. She asked about their friendship at school, about the terrible tarts, and then—of course—about her family. Helaine answered truthfully, identifying her father as the Earl of Chelmorton. Nothing would come of hiding it, but then a miracle happened! Mrs. Knopp did not know of her father's terrible crime. She did not speak to Helaine as if she were the daughter of the Thief of the Ton. She merely pressed to discover whether or not Helaine was married and if there was much good husband hunting in London now before the Season began.

It was all quite lovely, and so very normal as to be abnormal. She had not had a conversation like this in years and Irene was kind enough not to spoil it. But then the time for an afternoon visit passed. Half an hour. Forty-five minutes. Soon it would be an hour, and she could not stay longer. She had to speak to Irene alone.

She began with the most casual of inquiries. "You have such a lovely home. Does it have a back garden as well?"

"Oh, lawks, no," squealed Mrs. Knopp. "I daresay that Irene misses the gardens and the dirt, but I can't say as I do. I was born and grown in London. It's the fresh air that makes me cough!"

"But there is a park," said Irene in a quiet voice. It was disconcerting. As a girl, Irene could be amazingly shrill, but now she was beyond subdued. One might even suggest cowed. "I was thinking of going there just when you called. Would you like to join me?"

Helaine smiled her gratitude. Irene had always known just when Helaine wished to be private. "That would be lovely."

Mrs. Knopp laughed too loudly. "I am afraid I will not join you on Irene's constitutional. She looks frail, to be sure, but she has the devil's own stride!"

It worked out better than expected. While Irene left to change her clothes, Helaine was able to get Mrs. Knopp talking about her husband's business. As was true of many cits, she had a basic understanding of her husband's line of work, and was rather proud of him to boot. Helaine learned that the Knopp Family Shipping Company was extensive indeed. Better and better. And then Irene came back, they stepped outside, and suddenly everything changed.

Irene was sick. Helaine couldn't be sure why she hadn't seen it before. Perhaps it was because the lighting was never very bright inside London homes. But the moment they stepped outside into the brilliant sunshine, Helaine had to struggle to suppress her shock. Irene's skin was so pale as to be virtually translucent. And she was so thin as to be gaunt.

"Oh, Irene, is Mrs. Knopp so very terrible? She seemed rather nice in a loud sort of way."

Irene turned, her eyes widening in surprise. "What? Oh, no, she is quite sweet."

"So you are happy living there?" That was a rather blunt way to put it, but the question needed to be asked. For a multitude of reasons.

Irene merely shrugged, her face averted as they wandered down the lane. "I suppose I am as happy here as I would be anywhere." She paused and flashed Helaine a mischievous look that so resembled the girl she used to be. "And the food is much better than anything I had at home or at school."

"But do you eat it?" The words were out before Helaine could stop herself.

"What?" Irene asked, her expression slipping back to vague. "Of course I eat."

They turned a corner and, far ahead, Helaine could see

the park. Despite what Mrs. Knopp had said earlier, Helaine wondered if Irene could make it so far a distance.

"Irene," she said softly, putting a hand on her friend's arm, "forgive me, but are you well?"

Irene slowed, obviously reluctantly. "I am tired all the time," she finally confessed. "And I weep at the strangest things. A sound. A smell. I know it is grief. I know that it has become a danger to my health. I know it, and yet . . ." She shook her head. "I cannot seem to stop it."

"Grief?" Helaine asked. "For your father?" Irene's father had died a bit more than a year ago, but there hadn't been much love between them. "Or perhaps you grieve what might have been," she said, her thoughts turning to her own life. "I often wonder what would have become of me if my father hadn't been . . . well, if he hadn't been such an incredible idiot."

Irene's smile was wistful, but there was a tautness in her body that felt almost like anger. And her hands were clenched so tightly it was a wonder no bones broke.

"Irene?"

"I grieve for Jeremy," she said, her words almost clipped. And right there, Helaine saw a flash of the girl who used to be. The one who would sometimes rant about injustice and the cruelty of having a father who lived solely to hunt and eat. "I grieve for my husband and the life we never had."

"Oh!" cried Helaine, her face flooding with mortification. How ridiculous that she had never suspected such a thing. "But the nature of your engagement . . . the things that were said . . . I was well out of the social round by then, but even I heard." She bit her lip, trying to stop the flood of words. "I beg your pardon, Irene. I cannot think how stupid I sound. Please, please, forgive me."

Irene released a soft sigh, then began walking again toward the park. Her steps were fast, as if she were outrunning some demon, but then she tired and once again returned to a pace that Helaine could easily match.

"I know what was said about us," Irene said. "How Papa made Jeremy pay a bride price for me. About how terrible he was to sell me to the highest bidder. It wasn't true, you know. It was never true. But I let them say it because it was the only way Papa would let us marry."

"You loved him!" The words came out as a kind of shocked exhale.

Irene lifted her face to the sun. "I was so angry, and he made me laugh. He called me beautiful and brought me treats." She glanced at Helaine. "No one had ever brought me treats except for you and you were gone."

Now it was Helaine's turn to look away. The less said about her departure the better.

"Yes, I loved him. But he had to go on that damned boat. He had to prove himself a seaman and a captain."

Helaine glanced at her friend's face. "Was he very bad at it?"

"Oh, no. He was very good, but even a good man can die at sea. They said there were pirates, but Jeremy rallied the crew and fought them off. But he was wounded and grew ill. They even cut off his arm to try and save him, but it was too late."

"Oh, my God," Helaine whispered. "How horrible!"

"We learned of it ten months ago, but he was three months at sea before that. So a year has passed since I last saw him. A year since he held me in his arms. A year since . . ." Her voice broke and she rushed forward. They were near enough to the park now for her to reach a bench. Irene half stumbled, half collapsed onto the seat. But then she just sat there, her eyes gazing off at a nanny pushing a pram.

"Oh, Irene, was there a baby?"

She shook her head. "No child. And sometimes I wonder if that is a blessing. I do not know that I could care for a child."

"Of course you could." Helaine said firmly. "There is a strength that appears when one most needs it."

Irene's gaze shifted to Helaine. "Do you think so?"

"Of course I do." It was a ridiculous discussion since there hadn't been a babe. Still, Irene seemed to take comfort in it. Sadly, it put paid to any hope that Helaine had of success in her mission. She could not ask a grieving woman to set everything aside and . . . well, and become even lower than a woman who had married a cit for love.

So she sat there with her once best friend and looked at the nannies and their charges. They stayed there for nearly a half hour when Irene abruptly shook herself out of her reverie.

"Come now, out with it. What did you want to ask me?"

Helaine started guiltily. "I'm sorry?"

"Don't try to hide, Helaine. You forget that I watched you hide that shrew Claudia's socks. You didn't come visit me on a whim. You have something to ask."

Helaine lifted her shoulder in a shrug. "I came to make an offer to a desperate woman trapped in an unhappy home. I was wrong to assume such a thing, and I deeply apologize."

"But you weren't entirely wrong. I am unhappy. Just not for the reasons you assumed."

"Either way—"

"Either way, you shall ask me what you came to ask. And then we shall see what is to be made of it."

Helaine nodded. In truth, she had no other choice if she wanted to avoid the poorhouse. And yet it was so desperately hard to confess. How did one explain her choices to a woman who had fallen in love and married into wealth?

"Come, come, Helaine. It can't be so hard. I already know about your father's sins."

"But not my own."

Irene merely raised her eyebrows in query. In the end, Helaine gave in.

"Do you know what I became after my father died?"

Chapter 2

Helaine took a deep breath. Might as well confess it all at once.

"I'm a shopkeeper, Irene. I own a dress shop, or at least half of it. Or almost half. Never mind, the particulars don't matter. The point is that I design clothing, Irene. And my partner sews them. I am a tradeswoman and . . ." She looked up into her friend's eyes, trying to express the amazement she felt at her next words. "And I absolutely love it."

Irene's mouth dropped open, the shock obvious. "I just assumed you had married or something."

Helaine laughed, though the sound was strained. "Well, that is the usual course of things, isn't it? And I had offers, too, but not for marriage." She saw understanding flash through Irene's eyes.

"Yes, I know the type of man who comes calling when a titled girl is in trouble."

Helaine dared touch her friend's hand. "But you found love. For a time at least."

Irene's expression grew wistful. "Yes, for a marvelous time." Then she straightened to frown back at Helaine. "But we are speaking of you. Do you really own a dressmaker's shop?"

"Yes. It's called A Lady's Favor and it's not too far off Bond Street. I go by Mrs. Mortimer there."

"Really?" Irene tilted her head. "I cannot imagine you as a Mortimer."

Helaine smiled. "My mother was fond of bemoaning how mortified she was at what I was doing. Mortified, mortified, mortified! I took the name Mortimer to tweak her."

"And did it?"

"Definitely. But now I am stuck with it."

"Ah." There was something in the way she said the word that caused Helaine some concern. And then Irene's hands began to knot in the folds of her skirt. "You have come to ask me to frequent your shop, haven't you? I would, of course. Your ideas were always quite innovative even back at school—"

"Oh, no! Not those silly—"

"But you see, my mother-in-law insists on the most fashionable modiste. Silly woman, actually—the modiste, not my mother-in-law, though I suppose her, too, in some ways. In any event, she would be most upset if I transferred—"

"I'm *not* asking for your patronage, Irene!" Helaine's voice came out louder than she intended. The idea that she would come begging her old friends for their business was beyond humiliating. "We have clients aplenty!" she lied. And damn it, her friend knew she was lying. She always had.

"Do you, Helaine? Truly?"

Helaine sighed. "Yes, we do. For the moment. But not for long unless . . ." Her voice trailed away, and once again she saw how useless this whole errand was. Irene had no reason to agree, and every reason to send Helaine packing. But she could not stop now. "As I said before, I thought you were desperately unhappy. I thought you would grasp at any chance to escape." She lifted up her hands in a gesture of futility. "I came, Irene, to offer you a job."

"What?" her friend gasped.

"We cannot get the right supplies," Helaine explained.

"But your father-in-law is in shipping. He has cargo from all over the world. And I remember how good at spotting bargains you are. You found the most amazing things for no money at all!"

"It was a necessity in my household."

"Yes," Helaine drawled. "Mine, too, but you excelled at it."

"Hardly a skill I'm proud of."

"But you should be!" said Helaine. "You cannot know how desperate I am for someone to shop for us. To find bargains in silks and lace, to locate just the right baubles or ribbons. I can look at a woman and see just the right clothing for her. Wendy can sew anything I dream up and more. But neither of us can find the cloth or the baubles. Certainly not cheaply. Not like you could."

"So you want me to shop for you?"

Helaine turned to her friend, using all her persuasive skill. "You are grieving a husband. You have all the material wealth a woman could want. And yes, we were once the best of friends, but that was a long time ago. But nonetheless, that is what I am asking you to consider: be my purchaser. You cannot imagine how liberating it is to earn your own money. I know it is crass to say it, but the first time we were paid, I danced in the workroom. I bought a bottle of wine and we celebrated away all our profits. And yet, I do not regret it for one second."

Irene smiled. "I cannot imagine you dancing in a workroom."

"I have done it," said Helaine with a touch of pride. "I have done so much that I never imagined possible." She leaned forward, her voice taking on the joy of what she had done. "I support myself and my mother now. Working has given me such power, you have no idea."

Irene did not appear to be listening. Her gaze was on the water, and the longer she stayed silent, the more Helaine's heart sank.

"Perhaps," Helaine finally ventured, "you know of someone else, someone in more straitened circumstances? A widow who can argue with equal aplomb with a merchant or a ship's captain. Who is familiar with the shipping—"

"A woman who needs a reason to get up every morning," interrupted Irene. "A woman without children and without hope."

"Yes, I offer hope," Helaine pressed. "I have hope aplenty for all of us. Indeed, some days I think it is all I have."

Irene nodded, and Helaine knew from experience that her friend was thinking hard. Within a moment, Irene would have the answer. When they were children, she would produce the mathematical result or the location of the cheapest candy maker. Now, Helaine could only pray that she had a name. A woman who would save their little shop and Helaine's personal slice of heaven.

"Very well," Irene said as she abruptly pushed to her feet.

Helaine scrambled to keep up. "You know of someone?"

"Hmm? Why, certainly I do. Me! And I also know of a shipment of Brussels lace, though it won't come in for some weeks yet."

"Really? But that would be excellent!" She knew of at least three ladies who would jump at the chance to get a dress with the right type of lace on it.

Irene grinned. "And I know just how to get at least three bolts of it for a song."

"Three bolts! But how? And who—?"

Irene abruptly engulfed Helaine in a fierce hug all the more startling because of how very thin and frail the woman looked. "You leave that to me," she said when she finally released her.

"But—"

"Now listen, my dear. I shall get you the lace, and you shall pay me twenty percent more than I pay."

"We do not have much ready cash—"

"Never you mind that. You tell me what you want and how much you can pay. I shall find you what you need and make myself a tidy profit to boot."

Helaine felt her mind reel in shock. Her friend had certainly embraced the mercenary spirit quickly enough. "My goodness—"

"Do you think I learned nothing from sitting at the table every evening with my father-in-law? He speaks business all the time! I could not help but learn something. And now, finally, I have the chance to put to practice what I have learned."

"But—"

"Never fear, my dear. And thank you!"

Helaine laughed. "For what? I should be thanking you."

"Nonsense! You have given me something I have not found in over a year."

"I cannot imagine what," she said as they turned to leave the park.

"A reason to get out of bed every morning, Helaine. You cannot know how much I have wished for that. And now," she said as she released a giggle like a schoolgirl, "I shall endeavor to make us both rich, rich, rich!"

Helaine giggled, too, though not with as much unrestrained enthusiasm. She had succeeded in her task. Against all odds, Irene was to be their purchaser. God willing, she would be good at it.

But now she had to move on to her next, much more difficult task. After all, Irene had to have a shop to supply. It would do no good to have Brussels lace for a shop that no longer existed. A Lady's Favor needed to survive long enough for the lace to arrive, for the orders to be made and sewn, and then for the bills to be paid.

So after a few minutes of serious discussion and a lovely walk back to the house, Helaine took her leave. Irene promised to contact her as soon as she had word on the lace. And Helaine promised to call on her in a few days with a detailed list of the fabrics they needed. But then it was done, and Helaine hailed another hansom cab. It was time for her very next and even more clandestine task.

"Take me to Viscount Redhill's residence in Grosvenor Square."

* * *

Robert already had the bottle of brandy in hand when there was yet another knock on the library door. It was barely three in the afternoon, but after a morning such as today, brandy was the only choice to combat the headache growing behind his right eye.

"My lord?" asked Dribbs as he pushed open the library door unbidden.

"No, Dribbs," Robert said quite firmly.

"Well, yes, my lord. There is a visitor."

"No, Dribbs, there is not."

"But she is most insistent."

"No, Dribbs, she is not. Because there is not a visitor to see me." To further make the point, he dispensed with the swirling and airing of the alcohol and took a healthy swig straight from the bottle. It was almost gone anyway.

"Well, yes, my lord, there is."

"No, Dribbs, there cannot be. My father has already been here today, so he cannot have purchased another mine or an interest in a gold venture in Antarctica or discovered the secret to stuffing genies into bottles to grant his every whim."

"No, sir, it is not the earl."

Robert exhaled in relief. "Thank God—"

"It is a woman."

"No, Dribbs, it most certainly cannot be a woman. Because, you see, I have already spoken with Gwen about her upcoming nuptials just this morning. My mother is in bed where she always is at this hour. And as for all those future in-law women who have let the house next door, I have just this moment escaped from the upstairs salon where the baroness and her sister were rearranging Mama's figurines. They were arguing about whether sunlight was bad for a porcelain shepherdess. Porcelain, Dribbs. Why would anyone ever be concerned about a porcelain complexion? Especially since the damned thing has a bonnet!"

Robert forced himself to take another swig of brandy. When had his life become so dashed ridiculous?

"Very true, my lord. Most odd. But the woman who wishes to see you is not destined to be your relation."

"Thank heaven." He dropped down behind his desk, pushed aside the mountain of papers to set the bottle down, then looked up in confusion when Dribbs had still not disappeared. "You can go now."

"Well, no, sir, I cannot."

"Of course you can. Just step backward and shut the door."

"Well, yes, I could do that, my lord, but if I were to do such a thing, you would damn me for it in a day's time. Perhaps even sooner."

"Perhaps. But at least you wouldn't be damned right now."

"Excellent point, my lord. But you see, the lady in question is a Mrs. Mortimer. And she has a trifling matter for you to deal with."

Robert snorted. In his opinion, all female matters were trifling. But that didn't stop them from plaguing him with their nonsense day and night. Still, something about the name tickled the back of his brain. He knew that name, but from where?

"She is the dressmaker for your sister's wedding," supplied the butler.

Ah! There it was! Gwen had been waxing eloquent on the lady's dressmaking skill just this morning. The woman had done this and that, tucked something in or let something out. And then Gwen had blushed a deep pink. That was what stuck in Robert's mind: that his sister had blushed a deep, embarrassed pink. Because the dress made her look more attractive. In a sexual kind of way. And dashed if that was something he absolutely did *not* want to know about his sister.

He took another swig from the brandy bottle, only to discover that it was empty.

"I shall find you another bottle directly, my lord."

"Good man."

"But first you must speak with Mrs. Mortimer."

"No, Dribbs. I must not."

"But if you don't, she will inevitably tell your sister that she was denied your presence. And then your sister will commence quietly sobbing in her bedroom because this wedding is already more than she expected and you will of course hear her or notice her red eyes. And then you will find out the reason for her tears and be furious with yourself for being such a callous brother. And then, my lord, you will instruct me most specifically to not allow you to say no to visitors anymore."

"I would never say such a thing!" he said indignantly.

"You did say such a thing just last week when your mother was distraught over a lost delivery of perfumes."

"I most certainly . . ." His voice trailed away. Damnation. He most certainly had. "Bloody hell."

"It is a trifling matter, my lord. Best deal with it now and be done. Then no more tears, and you can have your brandy straightaway after it is finished."

Robert released a heavy sigh. "Damnation, Dribbs, I don't know whether to sack you or double your pay."

"Double my pay, sir. Indeed, I believe you promised me that last week."

"I most certainly did not! *That* I would remember."

Dribbs paused a rather telling moment. Then he tilted his head. "Are you sure, my lord? Are you absolutely sure you would remember?"

"Yes. I most certainly am."

Dribbs released a dramatic sigh. "Yes, I am afraid you would." Then the man straightened to his full height, stepped backward into the hallway, and pulled the library door wide. "Mrs. Mortimer to see you, my lord. She will not take more than ten minutes of your time."

That last was added with a stern look to the lady in question. The lady of course nodded sweetly in acknowledgment, but Robert saw the martial gleam in her eyes. He also saw her full cleavage, her sweetly rounded hips, and the dark red lips of a woman who obviously wanted to be kissed.

Good Lord, what had he just been thinking? She was a dressmaker, for God's sake. Who would want to kiss a dressmaker? That would be like fondling the bootblack. True, it was often done, but not by him! And yet here he was thinking of just where he would fondle her.

"My lord?"

Robert came back to himself with a start. "I beg your pardon?"

"No, I beg your pardon," she said. "You sounded as if you were choking."

"No. No. Just . . . um . . . mourning the loss of the brandy. Empty bottle, you know." He lifted the bottle and shook it about as proof. Then he sheepishly set it back down again. Really, what was he doing? One did not discuss empty brandy bottles with servants. Unless it was the servant's job, which it was definitely not for her. Damnation, he was addled! "I believe you wanted something?"

"Yes, my lord. I am afraid I require payment."

"You're afraid of payment? Well, if that's a problem for you, you needn't bother visiting."

She paused a moment, her brows lifting in surprise. Then a glimmer of a smile skated across her lips. "Er, no, my lord. I apologize deeply. I misspoke. I have no fear at all in me, and thus I am here at your door asking for payment. Now, if you please."

He sighed. Dribbs was right. Best to be done with it. The thing was, what with his father's recent investment whims and his sister's trousseau, he was rather tight on ready cash. The repairs and like at the mine alone had depleted the earldom to the point where they all must economize. Add in a bride's trousseau, and he had no idea where the funds would come from.

"Really, Mrs. Mortimer, there is a process for this. I have a man who brings the bills directly to me. You need not come visiting—"

"I have already spoken to Mr. Starkweather. He said I should speak directly to you."

He frowned. "The devil you say. Can't imagine Stark-weather doing such a thing. He is usually most officious about his place. Likes to keep the riffraff away from me, he says. Good man, that Starkweather." Robert smiled at the empty brandy bottle and wondered when ten minutes would expire. Soon, he hoped. Though he did like the view of Mrs. Mortimer's bosom, especially when seen through the exaggerating distortion of his empty brandy glass.

Then he had cause to look up from this glass. Was the woman blushing? Enough that her cleavage had turned a rosy pink? Why, she most certainly was! Extraordinary. Especially since with her figure she must be used to being ogled, and not just through a brandy glass.

He frowned. Obviously, he was missing something significant, but for the life of him he couldn't quite grasp what. He set his glass down, pulled in his feet so that he sat straight in his chair despite the way that made his temple throb, and forced himself to be serious.

"I have had a most trying morning, Mrs. Mortimer. Please tell me why I should talk with you and not with Mr. Starkweather?"

"Because I am not riffraff, my lord, and never have been." Her voice was clipped and cold despite the blush that still pinked her skin.

He blinked. Had he said that? Oh, yes, he supposed he had implied it at the very least. And yet, some devil in him could not resist tweaking her.

"Ah, well, you certainly don't appear to be riffraff, Mrs. Mortimer, but you are a bill collector attempting to circumvent my man Starkweather. At a minimum, that suggests you are Riff, if not exactly Raff."

Far from deepening her blush, it actually caused her color to cool and her eyebrows to arch. "I can see you have a love of the ridiculous, my lord."

"Well, I certainly love my family, and if that is not a love of the ridiculous, then I don't know what is."

She had no answer to that. Good thing, because he really ought not to say this sort of thing to a stranger, servant or not.

He relaxed backward in his seat, trying to decide exactly what he should do with the lady. Any other day he would have already paid her just to be rid of her. But he found himself smiling at her in an absent sort of way. She was lovely to look at, and she sat there all prim while he spouted all manner of nonsense. It was really quite fun. Until she spoke, her voice low, her manner almost soothing unless one actually listened to her words.

"Do you know how humiliating it is to come begging for honest payment, my lord? To stand hat in hand before some clerk on a high stool who curls his lip at one merely because one's birth is not as exalted as yours?"

He blinked, startled by what she said. "Starkweather does not sit on a high stool." Then he frowned. That was not at all what he meant. As far as he knew, Starkweather was a fair and honest man, but of course, he did not know that for certain. Neither did he know if the man ever curled his lip at honest tradesmen. All he knew was that the man sat at a desk like a normal person. And so that was what blathered out of his mouth.

Naturally, she took his statement as the stupidity it was. "I was speaking metaphorically, my lord."

"Were you?" he wondered aloud. "Nevertheless, it's not quite the thing to accuse a man of being high in the instep if he was not actually on a high stool. Makes me wonder if you were speaking of Starkweather at all."

Ah, he had her there! He could tell by the way her gaze canted aside and the color in her bosom flushed again. Most beautiful, he decided. And rather distracting. Thankfully, he was spared more of this odd discussion by a firm knock on the door. He didn't even need to say a word because he knew who it was. Ten minutes was up and Dribbs was pushing open the door.

"My apologies for the interruption, my lord," said Dribbs with a faint smile. "But your next visitor has arrived." He lifted the bottle of brandy into the air.

"Excellent," Robert said with a grin. "I am sorry, Mrs. Mortimer, but I am afraid I leave all matters of bill payment to Mr. Starkweather."

The lady pushed to her feet, but not to leave the room.

Instead, she stepped forward to confront him across his desk. "No, my lord, you shall not. Do you think I cannot see the bottle of brandy in his hand?"

Robert raised his eyebrows in surprise. Her back was to the door, so how could she see anything that was in Dribbs's hand?

She snorted. "The reflection, my lord." She waved airily at the polished black marble of his fireplace. From her angle, it would provide the perfect reflection of Dribbs.

"Ah. Most clever of you."

"I am not clever, my lord. Just stubborn. It will take the work of a moment for you to write me a bank draft. I insist you do so. Unless you wish it to be known that the Viscount Redhill does not pay his debts."

Now that was a serious allegation. "You would not say such a thing, Mrs. Mortimer, because I would have you ruined in a heartbeat. I pay my bills."

"Then pay this one." She stepped forward and slapped a paper down on his desk. It was a bill, neatly itemized and tabulated in a fair hand.

He picked it up with a frown, perusing the list to the best of his ability. It was his sister's trousseau, he supposed. Dresses, ribbons, underclothing, and the like. He even double-checked the math on the list and found it to be accurate. But such a total! The sum was exorbitant!

"This cannot be right," he murmured.

"I assure you it is. Would you care to summon your sister to verify it?"

God, no. He had no wish to engage Gwen in yet *another* discussion of clothing. And from the look of triumph in Mrs. Mortimer's eyes, she knew it. What was more, she chose that moment to shift into a beautiful smile. It was warm and winning, and it transformed her face from merely lovely to one of sweet seduction.

"Come now, my lord. Merely write the draft and then I shall personally pour you that glass of brandy. Mr. Dribbs's arm must be getting very tired holding that heavy bottle aloft."

My God, what a potent woman! He was already reaching for his bankbook when reason grabbed hold of him and stopped his hand. Something was very wrong about this situation. As far as he knew, Starkweather would never refuse an honest bill. And this woman was using all her wiles to get him to pay an exorbitant tab.

He looked back at the paper, his mind searching for the elusive clue. What was he missing? What . . .

"My lord?" Her voice was a distraction, a low siren song of seduction. "Your brandy awaits."

"Describe to me this dress," he said by way of stalling. "What does it look like?" He pointed at random to the most expensive single item on the list. A ball gown with pearl buttons.

She frowned. "Truly, my lord? Why ever would you wish to—"

"Humor me," he said as he folded his arms across his chest. Then, to save poor Dribbs, whose arm did appear to be shaking most dreadfully, he motioned to the sideboard. "Set it there, Dribbs. I find that Mrs. Mortimer and I have a bit more to discuss."

Dribbs did as he was told. And while the butler was setting the bottle far out of reach, Robert turned his attention back to the woman across from him.

"Do you know anything of my father, Mrs. Mortimer?" he asked.

The woman shook her head and a tendril of honey fine hair slipped from her chignon to dance about her pert chin. Adorable, he thought.

"I am not acquainted with the Earl of Willington," she said.

"Well, he is a charming fellow. Loves a good bit of brandy, a cigar, and his friends. Some say I resemble him in looks." He gestured to his hair. "Brown hair, broad forehead, and we are nearly the same height."

She nodded, obviously confused by his wandering thoughts. "Then your father must be a handsome man."

He took the compliment as his due. Many thought his

entire family had been inappropriately blessed in their looks. "Yes, well, there is something else about my father that everyone knows." He waited a moment for her to ask the obvious question. She did so with a touch of irritation.

"I am simply breathless with wonder, my lord. What could it be that everyone knows?"

"That my father is the greatest gull on earth. Yes, truly, the man could be snookered by a mentally deficient boot-black. In fact, I believe he was, just last year. Bought some magic blacking cloth, I believe. Thought he'd make a fortune with it."

A spark of interest did indeed light in Mrs. Mortimer's eyes. "Magic blacking cloth?"

"Yes. I believe it was cheesecloth soaked in the boy's spit."

She gasped. "You cannot be serious!"

"I most certainly am. My father bought it for a shilling." Then he sighed. "To be fair, the boy had been chewing to-bacco and so the cloth was rather thick and black. It did *look* like a blacking cloth."

She laughed. Not a full laugh. Indeed, because she sup-pressed it, it sounded more like a horse's snort than a lady's laugh.

"That story cannot be true."

"I assure you it is."

Then she tilted her head while her eyes danced in mer-riment. "I cry foul, my lord. I believe you are lying to me. And I believe I shall prove it to you."

"Really? Pray, how?"

"I shall make a wager with you, my lord. If I can prove that you are lying, then you will pay my bill. If not, then I shall leave without further ado."

He wasn't so sure he wanted her to leave just yet, but he was a gentleman and so he nodded. "Very well. If the bill is honest, then you shall be paid immediately."

She nodded slowly, obviously taking that as the best bar-gain she could make. "Very well, my lord. You say the story is true, that it happened exactly as you said."

"I do."

"Well, then, I submit to you that either the bootblack was *not* mentally deficient in that he gulled an earl. Or that the earl was aware of the true nature of the magic cloth and was merely being kind to a handicapped boy."

Robert frowned, wondering which could be true. Given that his father had been quite proud of his purchase, he thought it more likely that the bootblack was not nearly as deficient as he claimed. Nor, he supposed, did the boy have an ailing mother and four younger siblings to feed. Thankfully, he did not oversee his father's staff, as the man lived in rooms at his club. So long as the earl kept within his quarterly allowance, Robert didn't care if he purchased a dozen magic blacking cloths.

"Have I won our bargain, my lord?"

He smiled. "Yes, I suppose you have."

"Excellent," she said with a grin. "Then if you would—"

"I said if the bill was honest, Mrs. Mortimer. You have yet to describe this ball gown to me. Unless, of course, there is some reason why you would not."

"Don't be ridiculous. Of course I will describe it."

He smiled and shot her own words right back. "I am simply breathless with wonder."

She grimaced, her nose wrinkling in a delightful manner. "It is blue, my lord, with Belgium lace crisscrossed over the bodice. Shoulders bare, as she will be a married woman by then and can reveal a great deal more than before, and with a shawl of gauze such as will preserve her modesty if she wants or that can be draped in a variety of tantalizing poses should she not."

He blinked. My God, did she think he wished to know of his sister in tantalizing poses? "You are speaking of my baby sister," he said in irritation. "The one who wore pigtails and sported ink stains on her nose."

"No, my lord," she said gently. "I am speaking of your fully grown sister who will be a married woman within a month. And quite possibly increasing soon after that."

He shuddered at that. His baby sister with a babe of her

own. He knew it was possible. Probable, even. That is what married women did, was it not? But in his mind, she was still so young.

"It is the way of young girls, you know. They grow up and start families of their own." Then Mrs. Mortimer did something wholly unexpected. She rose in a single lithe movement and crossed to the brandy snifter. Then she poured him a glass, swirling it for him just as it ought to be done, and brought it to him. But she didn't just cross to his side; she set it in his hand, then sank to the floor before him. She looked up at him just as his sister had once done, back when she was still a hoyden running wild throughout the house. And Mrs. Mortimer smiled up at him in exactly the same way.

"Change is hard, especially when it is inevitable. But you should be proud of the woman she has become, my lord. Not fighting the purchase of her trousseau."

He swallowed. She was right. And when she sat like that before him, he could deny her nothing. Except for one thing.

"Mrs. Mortimer," he said as he reached out and stroked her cheek just as he had done with Gwen so many years ago. "I cry foul."

She blinked. "What?"

"Gwen does not have a ball gown such as you describe. It has not been made and you and your bill are false." She made to leap to her feet, but he was faster than she. Within a second, he had clamped a hand down on her arm, preventing her escape. "Oh, do remain right where you are, Mrs. Mortimer. It will no doubt take a few moments for the constable to arrive."

Chapter 3

゛ーＭＸ

"No, no, wait!" cried Helaine, as she desperately tried to free herself. She might as easily tilt with an oak tree. "I am not lying!"

Lord Redhill's dark eyes glittered down at her. "You know why I told you that story about my father and his bootblack?"

She shook her head. She had no idea except that it had lulled her into flirting with the man. Flirting! She hadn't done that since she'd been a respectable earl's daughter and not Mrs. Mortimer. She licked her lips. "My lord . . . ," she began, but he cut her off.

"Because in this one aspect, Mrs. Mortimer, I am *nothing* like my father. I cannot abide a thief no matter how charming. And you, my dear, are obviously one of the best."

"I am not!" she cried, horrified that tears were welling up. With one simple exchange, she had been transported right back to five years before, when she protested her innocence to no avail. She'd been honest her entire life, then her father committed one drunken, thieving stupidity, and she was tarred with the same feather. The humiliation of that memory pushed her to a strength she did not normally possess. She shoved him off, though her arm was nearly wrenched from its socket, and stumbled backward.

"Call your sister!" she cried. Then she did not wait for his high and mighty lordship to do it. She whirled around and bellowed. "Dribbs! Call Lady Gwen down here immediately!"

She could tell that surprised Lord Redhill. It also seemed to stun Dribbs, who opened the door with his mouth hanging ajar.

"My lord?" he asked.

"Call Lady Gwen," she ordered even though the question had not been directed at her.

Dribbs glanced anxiously between his employer and Helaine. "Lady Gwen has left with the other ladies. They have decided to buy a flock of sheep for the porcelain shepherdess."

Helaine took a moment to comprehend that statement. Then she decided there was no profit to figuring it out. The point was that Gwen was not here to help her. Meanwhile, Lord Redhill took it as another sign of her perfidy.

"How convenient for you," he drawled. "I'm sure you saw her leave before you arrived at my doorstep."

"It is not blasted convenient!" she snapped. "And you are a bloody prig for saying it is!"

If his lordship was surprised by her tone before, now he was downright flabbergasted. Or perhaps furious. It was hard to tell with his eyes glittering so brightly and his jaw tightened to granite.

"Have a care, Mrs. Mortimer. I have been indulgent up to now, but my patience is exhausted."

"Then you should not go accusing people of thievery!" To her shame, her voice broke on the word. So she forced herself to take a deep breath, to push aside all the shame her father's crimes had created, and to face Lord Redhill like the competent, accomplished and *strong* woman she was. "If you would do me the favor of *listening*, my lord, I shall explain everything."

He arched a brow then leaned back in his chair. "By all means, explain yourself," he drawled. He meant to appear casual, but she could tell that he was anything but. He meant to see her hang, so she went into her explanation as if her life depended on it. Especially since it very well might.

"I adore your sister," she began. "She is a beautiful woman with a sweet temperament. A genuinely good person, and that, my lord, recommends her to me as nothing else."

"I am well aware of my sister's accomplishments," he said, his voice just short of threatening. "And that she also, unfortunately, shares in my father's gullibility."

And there was the threat. Helaine merely glared it aside.

"If you recall, I have been making dresses for your sister for her last two Seasons." She could see by his face that he did *not* recall, and so she amended her statement. "Whether you recall or not, I have been dressing her and I'm quite proud to do it. So when she requested that I create her wedding trousseau, I was more than happy to do it."

"Of course you were," he drawled.

"I was," she continued, again glaring her fury at him. "But I most specifically informed her of my problem."

He arched his brow and for the first time did not venture an opinion.

"I am a small shop, my lord. Lady Gwen wants a large trousseau and she asked that I also dress her future in-laws as well. But it is more than my small shop can afford *on credit.*"

She paused a moment and stared at him. Obviously he did not understand the most simple financial terms. That surprised her, given that he was by all accounts skilled in financial circles.

"My lord," she began again, "I cannot afford to buy the fabrics she requires. I do not have the ready blunt. And so Lady Gwen promised that she would pay for it. In advance."

And there it was out. The unheard-of practice of *not* buying on credit. For many in her position, it was a fact of life. For his lordship? He'd probably never even imagined the idea.

She waited in taut silence, wondering if he would answer. In the end, he leaned forward, steepling his hands in front of him on the desk.

"Is that why Starkweather refused to pay you? Because it was for goods you had not yet delivered?"

She nodded. "I explained everything to Lady Gwen and she did agree to my terms."

He grimaced. "So again my relations are bent on making financial commitments that I am supposed to honor."

Helaine winced. Put like that, she did feel a bit sorry for the man. But she was not in a position to allow sympathy. "That is the usual way of things, is it not? She is your sister. You or your father pays her bills until she marries."

He snorted. "My father hasn't a groat to his name."

"Then it falls to you."

He didn't respond except to stare at her, his eyes glittering with some unnamed emotion. In truth, the sight gave her chills. "My lord," she offered gently, "if you wish to change the way of the world, I heartily support you. Give your sister charge of her financial affairs and I shall address myself to her. I can tell you that there are myriad benefits to a woman when she manages her own affairs."

He lifted his brow. "I am sure you can," he drawled.

She detected no outright condescension in his tone, but she bristled nonetheless. "You have no cause to judge me, my lord. I am merely an honest woman plying her trade like any man."

He closed his eyes in apparent weariness. "That is not a recommendation, I assure you. Men lie and cheat all the time."

How well she knew that. "But I do not."

He opened his eyes, and for a moment she wished he had not. In it, she saw pain mixed with weariness. It was stark and reminded her of her own mirror every morning.

"Very well," he said. "You have persuaded me."

His voice was so deadpan that she did not understand his words. "So, you will pay me?"

He shook his head. "Hardly. I believe your bill beyond

ridiculous. But I shall this very afternoon open an account for my sister. Then she shall have the decision of whether to pay your outrageous fee or not."

And with that he stood, turning to Dribbs, who had not left the library door. "Fetch my coat immediately. And show Mrs. Mortimer to the door." A moment later, he was gone.

"Bloody arrogant, high-handed, drunken bastard! To suggest that I was robbing them! Robbing! He was going to call the constable!"

Helaine paced the workroom of their small shop, trying to work off her fury. It didn't help. She still felt bruised and humiliated by her treatment that afternoon.

"He bloody well didn't, did he?" gasped Wendy, her seamstress, co-owner in their shop, and her best friend in the world. She was currently cutting the last of their silk fabric for a dress that would go to the bastard-in-question's sister. Sadly, if they didn't get paid soon, they wouldn't be able to purchase what they needed for any of the rest of her order. "Imagine calling the watch on you!"

"He didn't. I stopped him beforehand, but it still didn't change his attitude. He called our bill ridiculous. Outrageous and ridiculous!"

"Wot! The bloody cheek!"

"'What,' not 'wot,'" chided Helaine without thought. Wendy had grown up in a poorer neighborhood than Helaine. Much, much poorer. And her heritage often showed in her speech. But Helaine had been helping her friend better herself, most especially in terms of how she spoke. They were trying to establish themselves as dressmakers to the *ton*. It could only help if Wendy sounded more educated than she was.

As expected, Wendy grimaced but repeated the word correctly. "*What* a bloody cheek," she said firmly. "Our prices are exactly *what* they should be."

"No," said Helaine with a sigh as she leaned back against the worktable. "Our prices are high."

"As they should be! You are dressing the peers!"

Helaine shook her head. "Only a few. Maybe we should charge less. At least until we are better established among the aristocracy."

"But we cain't!" Wendy said as she made the last snip in the silk. "You yerself said they won't come to someone who charges less."

"True, but maybe I was wrong. And maybe my dresses aren't as good as—"

"Oh, enough," snapped Wendy. "I won't hear you saying things like that again. Your designs are beautiful. You see just the way a dress ought to be, and now you must shut up or I'll be sewing this dress wrong in fury."

Helaine smiled. "You'd never do that. You're too good."

"As are you, and I won't be hearing a word different."

Helaine leaned forward and pulled the scissors out of her petite friend's hands. She was done cutting anyway, but it never hurt to be safe. "Very well. You are a brilliant seamstress, and I am an excellent designer. Between the two of us we cannot fail!"

"Exactly!"

"But maybe I should relook at our prices nevertheless . . ."

"Aiee! It's like you were that first year," Wendy said. "Always worried, always questioning. I thought you'd growed out of all that. And now here you are, after one conversation with a bloody lord, right back to oh me, oh my, are we fools for doing this?"

Helaine swallowed, realizing her friend was right. Five years ago, the young seamstress had been filled with passion and hope. At seventeen years of age, Wendy had possessed the strength of a woman five times older. As an apprentice to the previous owner, she had sewn Helaine's one and only ball gown. From Helaine's dress design, Wendy had recognized Helaine's talent and begun thinking way back then. When Helaine's father had destroyed everything, it was Wendy who had sought her out and suggested the dressmaking business. She had everything arranged almost before

Helaine had known what was happening. She'd even had the wherewithal to spring Helaine and her mother out of debtors' prison, though heaven only knew how she'd managed that. Wendy had never told her how that happened, and it was the one secret that remained between them. But that one shadow could not dampen the love Helaine felt for her friend. Their current success was wholly due to Wendy's belief in both of them. And because of her, they were now owners of a dress shop with clients from the *ton*.

But it was a house built upon cards. Their most elevated client was Lady Gwendolyn and her future in-laws. It had been quite the coup to get the lady to buy just a single gown two Seasons past. And then she'd purchased a few more last Season. And now, as a miracle from the heavens, the lady wanted her entire trousseau! If this order went well, it would be the making of their little dress shop.

But if it all fell apart now because of one arrogant, high-handed brother, then there would be no stopping the disaster. There would be no more elevated clients and no more steady flow of customers. And given that they barely made it through from one week to the next now, there was nothing to keep them from the poorhouse.

"Stop it!" ordered Wendy without even looking up from her work. "I can hear your brain yapping all the way over here."

"I didn't say a word," returned Helaine stiffly. It was a pretend anger because they really were the best of friends. And because they had only each other to rely upon. If either failed, they both failed.

"But you be thinking and worrying yerself to death and I won't have it. Got the milliner's daughter Francine coming tomorrow, and we need you to design her something that will get her wed."

Helaine sighed, the sound coming from deep within her. "I'm not sure anyone can do that." The girl was fat. Not even plump, but decidedly fat, and she had a mean temper to boot. The first could be hidden. The second made any efforts at dressing moot.

"Well, if you can do it, then we'd be established for sure."

"Wendy—," Helaine began, but her friend just shook her head.

"Jus' talk to the girl. You can tell her things about how to be sweeter."

"But there are some things—"

"Tut-tut!" the girl said as she pointed her needle straight at Helaine's heart. "They can't all be like Lady Gwen. You just think on that and not our prices. Teach that fat girl how to be nice on the inside, and then she'll find her man."

Helaine plopped down by the worktable and pulled out her sketchbook. She didn't need it. She already knew what would *look* best on Francine. "It's not about being nice," she said as much to herself as to the seamstress. "It's about feeling happy inside. Then nice is easy. As is husband hunting."

"There you go," said Wendy with a grin. "You just teach her that and we'll be rich. Easy as stitching a straight line."

"Well, maybe for you," said Helaine. Her stitches had always wandered willy-nilly.

"Fine then," said Wendy. "Easy as drawing a straight line. And that I know you can do."

That she could. Now if only she could get someone to pay for their talents. Then they would be rich. Or at least not a half breath away from the poorhouse.

It was that fear that carried her through the night and into the next morning. Years ago, she and her mother had spent two nights in the poorhouse. Two nights crammed into the same bed with a rail-thin mother of three. Two nights of starting at every noise and holding her mother while the frail woman sobbed. Thankfully, they were both exhausted from a day spent doing prison labor—pounding hemp into rope—that at least they managed to sleep on the second night. And then Wendy had rescued them, offering them her home until the business turned a profit. And slowly, their life had changed.

Helaine and her mother had rooms of their own now, right above the shop. And if they didn't own anything of value anymore—it had all been sold six months after her father's disappearance—at least they each had a bed, food on the table, and a little coal for the winter. It was more than many had in London, and Helaine was grateful for it every day. And terrified it would all disappear on the morrow.

That was the fear that pulled her from her bed at dawn and sat her down at her worktable to sketch. And that was the fear that drove her to work on Lady Gwen's trousseau, sketching a new dress for her wedding that would emphasize every detail of the woman's beautiful body. And that was the fear that had her setting down six new designs before Miss Francine while the girl was munching on crumpets and spilling cream upon the paper.

"But wot 'bou' m' 'ck?"

Helaine leaned forward. "I beg your pardon?"

The girl set aside the crumpet and dusted off her fingers. "Wot about my neck? Won't it pinch?" she asked, pointing to the full collar.

"Oh, no. Not this material and not when Wendy sews it. Trust me, Francine. It shall look divine."

The girl was obviously not convinced. Her face pinched up and she reached again for the crumpet. "But it's so plain. Not a ruffle or rosette anywhere." She stuffed another full bite into her mouth. "Mama says at least with the rosettes, the men will look at the decoration and not me."

Helaine blinked, shock reverberating through her system. "Surely your mother doesn't say that! The men are *supposed* to look at you, Francine. How can you possibly think to attract a man if they are looking at the rosettes and not you?"

Francine didn't answer as she stuffed another bite into her mouth. But her eyes did, and her body. Her gaze dropped to her lap, and her body slumped in the seat. She was the picture of a depressed, downtrodden woman. Helaine knew the look. She understood the need to hide yourself any way you could. After her father was exposed as the Thief of the Ton, she had done everything but put a bag over her face as a way to hide.

"It never works, you know," she said gently. "Nothing can hide who you really are. No laces, flounces, or even the best rosette that Wendy can make will hide who you really are." Then she leaned forward and lifted the girl's chin. "And Francine, nothing should."

The girl didn't believe her. She sat there in slumped misery. "I'm fat, Helaine. No one wants a fat wife."

"No one wants a mean wife, Francine. I have seen many fat girls get married. Many ugly girls, too. Fortunately, my dear, you are not ugly and not exactly fat yet, either. And you have the advantage of something special."

Francine wrinkled her nose. "Yes. My father's money."

"No, silly!" Helaine said. "A talented dresser. Come, come. Put down that silly crumpet and let me show you the truth. Let me show you what I see when I look at you."

She didn't have to pull hard to get the girl to comply. They went to the dressing room to where Wendy waited with the first of three dresses they had made for Francine. In the back of Helaine's mind was the ever-present knowledge that the girl had to like these dresses—and pay for them—or they would have no money at all until Lady Gwen chose to pay. But she tried not to let it influence her at that moment. This time was for Francine, and she would not let anything detract from that.

Wendy began with a smile, lifting up the first of the three dresses. It was a moment that Wendy most especially treasured because the ladies always oohed and aahed over what was before them. But Francine didn't. She scrunched up her nose and made a bad face that clearly upset Wendy.

"'Ey, now . . . ," the seamstress began, but Helaine stepped forward to interrupt.

"Wendy, dearest, before we get to the gowns, perhaps you could do me a favor. Please, would you find that spare piece of muslin and cover the mirror?"

Not surprisingly, her friend looked at her in shock. "Cover the mirror—"

"Please, Wendy."

The seamstress knew better than to argue. Helaine was the one who soothed the customers and brought in business. When they were in front of a client, Helaine ruled. And so

Wendy bobbed a quick curtsy and went to the back room to find the fabric. Meanwhile Helaine turned to Francine.

"What were you looking at right then?" she asked gently.

Francine frowned. "What do you mean? I was looking at the dress."

"I don't think so. I was watching your face. You were looking in the mirror. At yourself, weren't you? That grimace was what you do every time you look in the mirror, isn't it?"

Francine shrugged, one shoulder coming up to her ear while her eyes slid away. "Nobody wants to look at your ugly dresses anyway," she snapped.

And there she was: Mean Francine. Helaine was beginning to see the problem. Mean Francine only came out when the girl felt threatened or embarrassed. And this, too, Helaine had some experience with.

"Very well, Francine, I would like you to do something for me. I would like you to turn and look at yourself from all angles in this mirror."

"What?"

"I want you to see how you look right now, really look."

"Why?"

"Please, my dear. Just leave yourself in my hands for a few minutes. And then you shall see something truly special, I promise you."

The girl was not going to leap right into trust, and who could blame her? If her mother had been telling her she was fat and ugly all her life, then of course the child was angry. Especially since Mama dressed the girl like this.

Under Helaine's instruction, Francine stared at herself in the mirror. She was dressed in puce, of all colors, a washed-out, dull brown. Flounce after flounce covered her, adding to her size and making her look like a fat lump of mashed potatoes and gravy. At least her hair didn't lie in a flat, greasy pile. The girl was clean and her brown hair was quite lovely. Except that it was pulled ruthlessly back from her face as if someone—her mother most likely—wished to pull the skin back from her nose as tightly as possible. It didn't work, of course, but created a perpetually pulled expression and most likely gave the girl a terrible headache by day's end.

As requested, Francine looked at herself in the mirror. She turned slowly around, her eyes filling with tears of misery. And in the end, she didn't even finish her perusal, but sat down in a defeated lump. She didn't even have the strength to argue but just sat there, her eyes darting this way and that, as she no doubt looked for another crumpet.

"There now, you have looked. I shall not ask you what you saw because I can see it in your face how miserable you feel right now. Ah, here is Wendy."

And there was Wendy, covering up the mirror with quick jerks of her arm. As the muslin settled over the reflection, everyone—Helaine included—sighed in relief. The girl in that mirror was the picture of dejection.

"Now, please, Francine, if you would but stand up, we shall help you into your new gown. You shall see what I see when I look at you."

Francine didn't argue. She obviously hadn't the strength, but hope did sparkle a bit in her eyes. Just a tiny flash, but one that shot to Helaine's soul. The girl wasn't lost yet.

"First off, let us change your hair." Francine didn't have the time to argue as Helaine plucked pins out of her hair. Before long a tumble of loose, lovely curls fell down and Francine was sighing in relief.

"Those hurt, don't they?"

"Terribly. But Mama says—"

"For the moment, Francine, I have no desire to know what your mother says. She may be the best of all mothers, but she does *not* know how to dress you."

At that, Francine gaped at her. It was perhaps the first time that anyone had contradicted her mother, who was, in Helaine's opinion, a narrow-minded tyrant. It wasn't that the woman was cruel. She did love her daughter. But as happened with some mothers, the woman could only see the flaws, not the beauty, in her offspring. That was why Helaine had specifically conspired to see poor Francine alone, at a time when her mother was busy with her son's tutor.

"Today, dear Francine, is about you. And what will look best on you despite what your mother says."

The girl had no response except to nod. She was obviously still in shock that someone would speak ill of her mama.

"Next, you absolutely must remove those terrible boots. You should try on this pair of silk slippers, I think." She held up a dainty pair dyed the palest of pinks.

The girl looked down at her thick half boots, designed more for a man who worked in a pigpen than for a girl. "But Mama said—" She stopped when Helaine raised her eyebrows. "Slippers wear so easily," she finally managed.

"And if you were to be traipsing about London, then you should wear those, I suppose. But we are dressing you for a London party, my dear. Come, come. Mr. Shoemaker makes the most divine slippers. If you like them, then we shall bring his daughter Penny in to show you what can be done for your feet."

Helaine didn't mention that Mr. Shoemaker had *not* made these particular slippers. That shoe shop was too pricey by half for demonstration slippers. But if Francine wanted to change her footwear, she could afford the best. Meanwhile, Francine did as she was bidden, pulling off her boots with a grimace. Truly, those boots could not have been made for her. They were much too huge.

"Whose are those?"

"My cousin's, when he grew too big for them. Papa said there was no use in throwing out perfectly good boots."

"Hmph." Helaine snorted. Even she could see where Francine's feet were rubbed sore from the ill-fitting footwear. "Then we shall put your father's feet in boots that are two inches too big and see how he likes trying to dance in them."

"I don't like how they make such noise when I walk," the girl confided.

The rest of her clothing was serviceable but nothing

refined. Cheap muslin for her shift and a corset as ill fitting as her boots. On a flash of inspiration, Helaine called for it all to be changed. A silk shift and a new corset. Indeed, Wendy had to run to the shop three doors down to obtain a corset of the right shape and fit. It was terribly expensive, but price was not the problem with Francine.

By the time Wendy returned, Helaine had already restyled the girl's hair. She was not especially skilled at it, but her years at school had taught her some things. After all, what more was there for girls to do in the evenings but play with each other's hair?

Finally they could get to the clothes. Silk shift and a corset that fit correctly went on first. Wendy had taken her cue from Helaine and brought in a pair of silk stockings as well. Pale blue slippers and then the dress, a beautiful, simple dress of midnight blue.

"But it is so dark!" Francine protested. "I thought all young misses were supposed to wear pale colors."

"Oh, the tyranny of Almack's!" Helaine huffed. "You are fortunate, my dear, that you are not constrained by those biddies. We shall fashion something exactly for a dance there when you go, but for now, be grateful that none of those harpies shall be staring at you. They chose those colors specifically because pale gowns are beneficial to *their* complexions and no one else's."

Francine nodded, completely awed that someone would criticize that hallowed dance hall of the *haut ton*. In truth, as the daughter of a milliner, Francine would never be allowed inside the doors, but it never helped to point out a person's social limitations. So Helaine spoke in "ifs" and "whens," as she helped Francine into one of her simplest but most inspired designs.

Simple, clean lines. A high back collar that plunged in front to a scandalous V neckline to show her cleavage. And best of all, a full drape of fabric to make her appear stately rather than frumpy. With her hair flowing softly about her face, she appeared like a queen emerged from her boudoir.

"One last thing," Helaine said as she carefully draped a necklace of deep amethyst about the girl's throat. It was paste, of course, and rather dull at that. But it was all that was needed to complement Francine's porcelain skin. "And now, the mirror."

Wendy waited a moment, pursing her lips. "The line ain't right," she said as she ducked forward. Wendy was lying. The line of the dress was perfect; it was Francine who was not right. She still slumped as she looked with worry down at the dark-colored fabric. "Lift up straight, else you'll be nipped by the pins," Wendy said.

Francine did as she was ordered, lifting her chin, her torso, and then her whole body into a tall, statuesque line.

"Oh, absolutely perfect," breathed Helaine.

Now came the moment of truth. Wendy stepped back and took hold of the muslin on the mirror. She paused to grin, and then she pulled off the fabric in a whoosh. Helaine held her breath. It all depended on whether Francine could see the change. Some women, she knew, would see only the ugly no matter what one did. But the girl was young, and life had not yet battered her into bitterness.

The moment her reflection appeared, the girl gasped. Then she stared. Then she stared some more, her mouth ajar with shock. "But . . . but . . ." She was so stunned she couldn't formulate the words.

"Do you see?" asked Helaine with a grin. "You're beautiful!" Then she crossed to the mirror and started pointing. "Your skin is flawless, like creamy foam. This dark color brings out that beauty. You should never wear pinks, Francine. It makes your cheeks look as if you were drunk."

"Mama loves pink," she whispered.

Helaine did not have to say anything. The girl's tone said that she knew her mother was wrong.

"Do you recall how you objected to the high collar of my designs? Do you see how it lifts and lengthens your neck? Does it hurt you at all?"

Francine twisted her head left and right. "It feels divine!"

"Especially since there is no starched lace. That, my dear, feels terrible. But this? Heavenly."

"Yes, it does."

"Now, some will say that your neckline is too low, that it should be square, and all sorts of other nonsense. Look here, my dear, the men will see this"—she outlined the dark crevasse of her cleavage—"and they will think lustful thoughts."

"Mrs. Mortimer!" the girl gasped, but it was mock outrage. Helaine could see that she was thrilled at the idea. Likely she had never thought of herself as someone who could inspire carnality in any man.

"And here is the best part of all," Helaine said. "Walk a bit. See how the light blue slippers peek out as you move? Men shall be looking to see your dainty ankles, and you do have divine ankles, my dear."

"I do?"

"Well, of course you do! Just look."

Francine did, and it was all Helaine could do not to laugh. The girl lifted her skirt enough to see her ankles in the mirror, and then she released a giggle. Twisting her foot left and right, she inspected her ankles from all different angles, her expression shifting to a happiness that seemed to suffuse her entire body. It flushed her cheeks, straightened her spine, and generally brought life to all of her.

"I do! I do!"

From beside the mirror, Wendy had folded her arms across her chest but was looking on with a grin. "Told you a good dresser was all you needed." She said the words to Francine, but her eyes were on Helaine. And in the sparkle of delight, Helaine read a satisfaction that could only come from work well done. The design, the sewing, and even the slippers and necklace all combined to create a reflection that was not perfect so much as alive with joy. And joy was so much better than perfect.

"Look at yourself, Francine," Helaine said. "Look at your face and your eyes. You are happy. You are beautiful. And that, my dear, will attract men like moths to a flame."

Francine turned, her eyes shimmering with hope. "Do you think so?"

"Of course I do! And if you don't believe me, then there is a man just on the other side of this curtain. I heard him come in just a few minutes ago. He is our bookkeeper and he has been sitting there most patiently. His name is Anthony and he is a man used to numbers. You know the type, I believe. Your father is such a man."

Francine wrinkled her nose. "Yes. He'd never lie about anything even when he should."

"Exactly. That is Anthony through and through. He will tell you exactly what he thinks." Then she stepped forward to whisper into Francine's ear, "And mind you watch his eyes. See where they go. I wager they will drop right here." She gestured to the girl's ample cleavage. "And if he blushes, then you shall know that there are lustful thoughts in his mind. Even in one so prosaic as Anthony."

Francine giggled, but she was more than excited by the idea. Helaine waited a moment to be sure all was ready. Then she called through the curtain to the workroom behind.

"Anthony, would you mind terribly? I have something I need to ask you."

She heard a rustle of a chair scraping backward. Her desk was there and she knew that, as their bookkeeper, he had no doubt been going over the accounts.

"Anthony?" she called again when there was no answer. Then, with a wink to Francine, she hauled open the curtain.

There, sitting in the center of her workroom, was *not* Anthony. It was Lord Redhill.

Chapter 4

≫⫻≪

Robert hadn't known what to expect when the curtain parted between workroom and showroom. Of course he'd heard the women's voices, even knew that the enterprising Mrs. Mortimer was one of them. But he had not expected to come eye to bosom with a young girl of a decidedly lush figure.

He leaped to his feet, as did Anthony beside him, at the very same moment that Mrs. Mortimer squeaked in alarm.

"Lord Redhill!" she gasped. "What are you doing here?"

Robert forcibly dragged his eyes away from the girl turned nymph. And not an anemic nymph as drawn in children's books, but the kind pictured on Greek vases. "My God, woman, what have you done to the girl?"

"I'm terribly sorry," Mrs. Mortimer said stiffly, obviously not sorry at all. "But you do not belong here."

"I don't belong here? No decent woman belongs here! Is that what you intend to do to my sister?"

The woman arched a brow at him, but he did not miss the way her clenched fists had landed on her hips. She was trying to control herself, but there was raw fury inside her.

"Lord Redhill, you forget yourself!"

"I most certainly do not!" he roared. "I won't have you doing *that* to my sister!"

Mrs. Mortimer was about to object. She drew in her breath, but she never got the chance to speak her mind. The girl grabbed her arm and pulled her out of the way. And then she stepped right up to Lord Redhill, her face flushed and fearful.

"What has she done to me?" she asked.

He looked down at her and, as God was his witness, he could not prevent his eyes from dropping farther. He didn't intend to, but they were right *there*. And he was a man after all.

Then the girl stomped her foot, making her bosom jiggle in the most delightfully terrible way. "Tell me! What has she done?"

He dragged his gaze up to the girl's face. He tried to modulate his voice, but his throat was choked off. "You seem like a nice young woman," he said gently, "but this . . . woman . . . has dressed you as a . . . a . . ."

"A tart?" the girl asked, her voice shaking slightly.

He shook his head even as he said, "Yes. Well, not exactly a tart. Much higher class than the usual flyer. But I'm afraid no man can look at you like that and think of anything but . . . but . . ." He felt his face heat in a blush. In desperation, he looked back at Anthony, hoping for help in explaining the situation. Sadly, the poor bookkeeper had flushed a bright crimson and his gaze was locked exactly where it ought not to be. "Oh, bloody hell," he murmured, only to belatedly realize he shouldn't be saying such words in front of ladies. "Well, you can see exactly what happens when you are dressed like that."

With a soft curse, he walked directly in front of the book-keeper, blocking his view. "Anthony, I believe I should like that tea now," he said by way of distraction. It didn't work. The boy was clearly still dazed. So Robert had to snap his fingers. "Anthony! Tea!"

The young man blinked. "Oh. Yes, my lord. Of course. Yes. Tea. Right away . . ."

Except the man didn't leave. He took a meandering route to the workroom kitchen that allowed for him to see the girl the whole way. He didn't even bother to hide his intentions, but stared slack-jawed the entire way. Fortunately, Mrs. Mortimer wasn't completely lost to propriety. She released a heavy sigh.

"Perhaps you could have my mother assist, Anthony. In the kitchen upstairs, if you would."

Anthony nodded, and finally disappeared up a staircase to the upper rooms. Only then did Robert turn back to the girl.

"You see," he said gently. "Dressing in such a way is not at all appropriate. What would your mother say?"

That was the wrong question to ask. He knew it the moment the words were out of his mouth. The girl's eyes widened. At first he thought it was in horror, but it quickly became something more like glee.

"Mama will hate this!" the girl gasped. "Hate it with a passion!" Then she leaped forward to engulf Mrs. Mortimer in a hug. The lady stumbled slightly, but quickly regained her footing, returning the hug threefold.

"Oh, Francine, you are most welcome!" she said with a laugh.

"I want three more dresses like this!" the girl said when she stepped backward. "No, ten more! I shall have my entire wardrobe redone just as you think best!"

Robert groaned. He couldn't help it. "That is not at all what you should do."

Then the girl turned to him. Her back was straight and her eyes glittered with happiness. "My lord," she said loftily, "I believe you and my mother would get along quite famously. Her dresser is down on Bond Street with all the other stuffy old people. I suggest you go there and leave the younger generation to dress as we wish."

Robert gaped at the girl, completely flabbergasted. It was bad enough that she had spoken so tartly to him—a peer of the realm. But to call him stuffy? Old? Good God! Thankfully, Mrs. Mortimer intervened before he could find the right words to blast the chit back into her place.

"Yes, well, I believe Lord Redhill's tastes have been adequately expressed. Come along, my lord. This is a place for ladies. I believe your tea awaits in the front room."

She grabbed his arm and pulled him along. She could not have budged him if he had not allowed it. But his mind was still grappling with the girl's words. Had it happened to him? Had he really turned old so young?

He stepped into the front parlor, moving easily to the settee as Mrs. Mortimer directed. Anthony appeared a moment later, the tea set rattling on the tray.

"Thank you, Anthony," said Mrs. Mortimer as she gracefully removed the tray from his hands before the china shattered. "And in the future, I believe guests should wait in this parlor, not the back workroom."

Robert looked up to see the young man blush again, his gaze going down to his feet. "Er, yes, mum. It's just that . . . er, well . . ."

"It was raining," Robert inserted, trying to rescue the man. "And I was rather forceful in pushing my way into the nearest doorway." He had, in fact, maneuvered exactly to get into the back workroom. He learned much more about a business from the back.

The lady turned to frown at him. "You bullied your way inside my workroom?"

"Er . . . yes."

Her eyes narrowed and he had the uncomfortable feeling that he was about to receive a well-deserved dressing-down. It didn't come . . . at him. She turned to poor Anthony, and he was stunned to hear how cold her voice became.

"Any number of lawbreakers and miscreants will attempt to push their way into the back. If you cannot stand proof against them, then you are of no use to me."

As expected, Anthony flushed a dark red, but he was not entirely without a spine. He lifted his chin. "I am an excellent bookkeeper, Mrs. Mortimer. I have served you extremely well in that capacity."

"Not if you allow anyone to push their way uninvited into my back room. Good God, Anthony, there are ladies there! Clients and their families, not to mention Wendy and myself. Can you imagine what could happen?"

Robert all but rolled his eyes. "Doing it a bit too brown, aren't you? I hardly think you were in any danger from me."

"Really?" she drawled as she spun around. "And how would you feel if I pushed my way past your valet to enter your bedroom, my lord?"

It was a poor choice of words, especially since he was thinking how magnificent she looked. Her clothing was perfect, emphasizing her height and her full bosom, but it was the color in her cheeks and the smudge of dirt on her forehead that he found so appealing. She appeared both statuesque and infinitely human. Which made her a *woman* in his mind, and a very appealing one.

His thoughts must have appeared on his face, because she abruptly glared at him. And that, perversely, made her more attractive to him.

"Very well, my lord. I shall remember that you find it perfectly acceptable for a stranger to bully your staff, enter your library, and rifle through your personal papers at will."

"That would be most unwise," he said, his voice dropping at the very idea.

"As it was for you to try the same with my own."

He arched his brow in outrage, but honesty forced him to keep quiet. That was *exactly* what he had been trying to do when he went into the workroom. He had wanted to know what sort of woman she was. But all he could manage was a stiff rebuke.

"Anthony was most discreet regarding your personal affairs. And he never left me alone in the back."

She huffed as she turned to face the boy. "And that, my lord, is the only reason Anthony has not been sacked."

He could see her words hit the young man, as well they should. In truth, no bookkeeper would stay employed for long if he did not live and breathe the word "discretion." But he didn't say that aloud. At least not until after Anthony had bowed stiffly and retreated. And even then, Robert waited while Mrs. Mortimer took her seat and served him tepid tea.

"Not many young men can withstand a peer, you know," he said gently.

"And I'm sure you were most forceful." She lifted her chin. "That does not endear you to me."

Far from being insulted, he was rather amused by the idea. Usually merchants tried to ingratiate themselves with him, not the other way around. He found the difference in her delightful. But that did not mean he had to be nice.

"And I find your manner of dressing women to be deplorable," he said.

She nodded. "And I agree with Francine. You should dress yourself on Bond Street. Leave the young to those who *are* young."

He arched a brow. "Are you calling me old, Mrs. Mortimer?"

"And stuffy."

"Good Lord, soon you will be offering me a cure for rheumatism."

She tilted her head. "I believe my mother has one. Would you like me to fetch her?"

He shook his head, startled to find his lips curving into a rueful smile. "I believe I have more than enough women in my life."

She dipped her chin in agreement, and he noticed that her eyes were sparkling with humor. His mood as well had lightened considerably. Then, contrary woman that she was, she had to go about and destroy his bizarre mood.

"I dress my clients as they wish to be dressed, my lord. Francine needed to see herself as desirable."

"You will not do that to my sister!" The response was automatic, the words irrational even to his own ears. And the dratted woman wasted no time in pointing that out.

"Your sister is about to be married. She is a woman grown and able to choose for herself how to dress. Obviously, you have no respect for me, but do you have none for your own sister?"

He swallowed. Did he truly have no respect for this woman? "On the contrary," he said, though the words came stiffly to his lips. "I have respect for your fearlessness. Bold business dealings are the only way for a woman to manage on her own. You impress me with your very survival."

She set her teacup down without the slightest sound. "I do not know whether to be complimented or insulted."

"Complimented, Mrs. Mortimer. Definitely complimented."

She paused, and he could tell she was thinking deeply. A tiny furrow appeared between her brows, which he found unexpectedly charming. "Does that mean you will pay in advance for your sister's trousseau?"

He released a sharp bark of a laugh. "I have told her that such a practice is ridiculous and demanded only by sharks and thieves."

"Now I am definitely insulted," she retorted coldly. Oddly, she did not sound insulted so much as resigned. She had expected his opinion to be as such.

"But I stand by my word. She has been given access to her funds. She will choose how to spend them."

The woman visibly brightened, and he couldn't help but feel pleased by the change. "You will not stop her then? You will allow her to come here?"

"It's not real freedom unless she has the right to make bad choices."

Her shoulders lowered in relief. She didn't speak at first, and he became captivated by the slow dawning of humor in her expression. Her brows lifted, her cheeks seemed to gain color, and her lips curved in the slightest of smiles.

"Thank you for your wisdom."

He blinked, his mind only slowly shifting away from the sight of her lips. "You make me sound like an old cleric sitting on a dais. You know, some women find me quite spry."

"Some women would find aged Cheddar cheese to be spry."

He blinked. "Did you just compare me to cheese?"

"I did, my lord." Then she leaned forward and touched

his hand. "But never fear. I have quite the fondness for Cheddar cheese."

He looked at her. First at where her hand touched his, then at the sparkling humor in her eyes. Never before had he imagined such a conversation. Certainly never with a woman, much less a dressmaker. But there was an ease between them, one that allowed for absurdities. And he found himself completely charmed.

"I can see why my sister likes you," he finally said.

She shook her head. "I assure you, you do not."

"Really?" He was learning to just let her have her say. No matter what nonsense she spouted, she would nevertheless manage to be both charming and interesting. "Pray enlighten me."

"Your sister likes me because I listen to what she wants, not what you or your mother or her future in-laws want her to want."

He shuddered slightly at the thought. "My sister can be too willful by half."

"Those days are long gone. You have nearly cowed the spirit out of her."

"The devil you say!"

"I do. But never fear. She is learning to assert herself again."

Now he did groan. "Reason enough to keep her far away from you."

She smiled. "Reason enough to let her have control of her own funds and make her own decisions. She will never be able to stand up to that mother-in-law without some strength of her own."

He could not argue there. And no matter what Mrs. Mortimer thought, he did wish the very best for Gwen. "Very well, then I grant that you are simply another step in her growing independence."

She took a sip of her tea. "At least you did not suggest I was a 'bad choice' again."

"The words were implied."

"Of course. How silly of me to miss that."

"But if Gwen likes you because you support her budding independence . . ." He had to suppress his shudder at that thought. "Why is it that you believe I like you?"

She set down her cup and looked at him, her expression turning serious. "Do you, my lord? Like me?"

"Like" was much too pale a word. And it wasn't even remotely accurate, though he had no substitute. "You are not repellent," he finally said.

"Damned by faint praise."

"I don't believe that was praise at all."

She snorted. "Touché. Very well, my lord. You aren't repelled by me because I do not allow you to bully me. I suspect that everyone dances to your tune at home—"

"Nothing could be further from the truth—"

"And that can be extremely exhausting, what with telling everyone what to do and seeing that it is done."

He leaned back in against the settee, dislodging a pile of dress patterns as he moved. "I tell you, no one listens to me. At home or anywhere else."

"Anthony did. Francine listened as well."

"But did exactly as she pleased."

The lady grinned even as she picked up the tumbled patterns. "Francine listened to what you thought and then made her own decision. That is an excellent thing, I believe, in a young person."

"You obviously know different young people than I do."

She smiled, but her expression was wistful. "This is fun, is it not? Trading insults, bantering back and forth about the people we know."

He grinned. It was the most fun he'd had in an age.

"That is why you don't despise me, my lord. Because there is no relationship between us, no need to please or be pleased by the other. We can be as absurd or as contentious as we wish, with no consequences."

"I could still ban Gwen from your shop."

"But you are a man of your word, my lord, and promised not to do such a thing."

He sighed loudly, adopting a most dramatic pose. "Oh, damnation, my honor!"

Her expression went from wistful to fully entertained. Exactly as he had wished. "No consequences, no relationship, not even as dressmaker to client." She took a deep breath, unconsciously drawing his attention to her beautifully formed breasts. "I vow it is a relief to me as well."

He was silent for a time, his mind on her curves, on the lightness he felt in her presence, on the delight of her conversation. The offer formed in his mind long before he voiced it. In truth, he'd had it in his thoughts after their first meeting, even knowing how improbable it was. That, perhaps, was the real reason he had come skulking about her back room, and it was not to have a look at her books.

So he waited a time, thinking once more upon the possibility. He had made some discreet inquiries after their first meeting. He had learned from Gwen what was said about the woman, and from there it was a matter of the right question in the right ear. The answer was just what he had hoped. It took a moment's more consideration but in the end, the words were inevitable.

"I should like to offer my condolences, Mrs. Mortimer."

She frowned, obviously confused by his words. "My lord?"

"On the passing of Lord Metzger. I understand you were both very . . . close." She had, in fact, been his mistress for many years. But now the man was dead—he'd died some months ago—and she was without protection.

He watched her swallow, seeing those exact thoughts whisper across her features. "His lordship was indeed a good friend," she said, caution in every word.

"So I understand. But now he is gone, and I should like—"

"No relationship, my lord. Do you not recall what I just said? *No relationship.* The delight we have in our conversations would alter drastically if we began . . . something else."

"Really?" he said as he leaned forward. Her hand was resting on her knee and it was the work of a moment to capture her wrist and thereby trap her in her seat. "Do you think so?"

"I do. I most certainly do." Her voice was high in pitch and he caught an undercurrent of panic. She knew he was drawing close to kiss her. She knew it and was panicked by the thought. Or perhaps she was simply playing the part of an ingenue to spark his interest. Whether real or feigned, he was beyond intrigued. Indeed, certain parts of him were all but demanding she surrender to him right here and now.

But he was more refined than that and so he slowed his approach. He easily flipped her hand over to press a kiss into her wrist. To his delight, he felt her shiver as he pressed his mouth to her tender flesh.

"Do you know," he said against her skin, "I believe I should like to explore something with you."

"I'm sure you would," she said somewhat tartly, though her voice trembled. Her arm did not as she whipped it backward out of his hand. She didn't know that it was exactly as he'd planned. While she drew her hand back, he pretended to be pulled forward enough that he had to catch himself on the armrests of her chair, thereby trapping her beneath the tent of his body. "My lord, this is most inappropriate."

"On the contrary," he said as he slowly lowered his face toward hers. "I believe an offer of protection is exactly appropriate between the two of us."

"My lord! I am a dressmaker!"

"Not to Lord Metzger, you weren't. And not to me."

She had drawn back to the farthest reaches of her chair, but she hadn't screamed. He saw the rapid beat of her pulse in her throat and felt the tight puff of her breath against his cheek. She was interested, of that he was certain. But how quickly could he get her to fall? Normally he enjoyed the dance of maybe yes, maybe no. But with her, he found he wanted merely to possess as quickly as possible.

"No, my lord." She put a hand to his chest to stop him. There was little strength in her words and her wrist, but it was enough to make his honor prickle.

"Don't you want to explore, Mrs. Mortimer? To find out if our delightful conversations will continue *with* the benefit of a relationship?"

She licked her lips in anxiety, and his gaze dropped from there to even lower. Her bosom was flushed rosy pink above her gown, and her beautiful breasts were tightened into hard points that made his blood crow with delight. Without even thinking it, he lifted his hand to stroke one hard nub, but she caught him before he connected.

"No, my lord. No!"

He twisted his arm around hers such that he caught her wrist again and lifted it to his mouth. Nearly a decade ago, his uncle had taught him how to seduce a woman with just his tongue. It had been the most useful lesson any relative had ever given him. He used it to its fullest extent now as he teased and stroked her wrist. And as he applied himself to her skin, he watched her face. Her mouth opened on a gasp as she made to pull her hand away. But he was already at work on her wrist, and he saw her eyes widen in shock. Obviously Lord Metzger had never been instructed by a lecherous uncle, because Mrs. Mortimer's body began to react.

Her lips darkened to a rich, wet red. Her eyes, so wide a moment ago, began to soften in a kind of daze. She shivered against his lips, and her knees, which were pressed so hard against his thighs, eased slightly apart. She probably wasn't even aware of her reaction, but he had been taught well. He knew what to look for in a woman.

And then, formidable woman that she was, she gathered her wits. She closed her eyes and stiffened her spine. When her words came, they were hard and implacable.

"No, my lord. I will not be your mistress. Pray respect my wishes and remove yourself from my person."

He lifted his head and slowly set down her arm. He watched her exhale in relief, obviously believing she had won. And cad that he was, he took advantage of that one moment of vulnerability. Before she could stop him, he closed the distance between them.

He kissed her. He more than kissed her, he used his superior position—in height, in social status, and in simple physical prowess—and he owned her mouth as only a man can own a woman.

One kiss, one moment, and she was his. Or so he believed . . . for about five seconds.

Chapter 5

❧❦❧

He was kissing her! Lord Redhill was kissing her, and it was *wonderful*!

Certainly she had been kissed before. There were any number of unscrupulous men who had tried to take advantage of her, especially after her father's perfidy was known. And in truth, she had known on some level that Lord Redhill would fall into that category eventually. He was not a man to be denied anything, and if she caught his fancy—which she knew she had—then he would of course be required to act upon the impulse. He was a man, after all, and that was what men did.

So she had expected the kiss, had seen the signs, and had her defense ready. After all, she was experienced in stopping all manner of advances. In fact, that was why she had developed the fictitious persona of Mrs. Mortimer, Lord Metzger's mistress. Lord Metzger had no more been her lover than her driver, but the widespread belief that he was her protector had helped her keep her virtue without all that unnecessary grabbing and demanding that men did. Then poor Lord Metzger had died. Lord Redhill had sauntered into her life. And now he was doing things to her mouth that she had never imagined possible.

He'd started with a simple press of lips to hers, but at her gasp of surprise, he had swept inside. One other man had done that to her, back when she was at school, and she had choked on his invasion. She had wasted no time in shoving the man so hard he landed on his backside.

But Lord Redhill didn't invade with such brute strength. Instead he teased her, coaxed her, and indeed, something about the sweep of his tongue, the nip of his teeth, even the delightful taste of his breath set her body to humming. Humming, by God, when she was absolutely *not* a woman who hummed.

She felt his hand at her neck, a single finger, then two, caressing beneath her jaw, slowly coaxing her head backward to rest cupped in his other hand. She couldn't stop herself from complying. His stroke trailed fire along her skin and, unlike anything else in her life, that heat slid beneath her flesh and into her blood. And with her surrender, Lord Redhill increased his conquest. The press of his body grew harder, the penetration of her mouth more dominant.

This could not be happening. She could not allow this! Her mind screamed at her to wake up and stop him. She had to. And so she did, though it took every ounce of her will-power. She curled her hand, the one that pressed limply against his chest, and she dug her fingernails in. Then she bit down. Not hard, just a steady closing pressure that forced him to withdraw or have his tongue cut in half.

"Trust me—," he said against her temple.

"Try that again and I shall draw blood." Then she shoved as hard as she could with her nails against his chest.

His eyes darkened, and he did not move even so much as an inch. She had to be hurting him. Or perhaps not, given the muscles she felt beneath her fingertips. But he had to see the firm determination in her eyes. He had to, because she very much doubted she could keep it up for much longer. He was so close, his scent an intoxicating mixture of sandalwood, citrus, and something else, something drugging to her senses.

Then someone screamed.

Lord Redhill stiffened, his body jerking backward. Helaine gasped and scrambled away as well, knocking over her chair as she moved. And all that happened before she even realized who had interrupted them. But once she was on the opposite side of the room, her hand pressed to her lips in shock and simple pleasure, Helaine found the presence of mind to focus.

The screecher was Lady Gwen, Lord Redhill's sister. The woman was petite, her cheeks flushed from the weather outside, but she was a virago of fury as she advanced upon her brother.

"Robert! How could you? How dare you! She's my modiste!"

"Gwen!" squeaked Lord Redhill, and it was indeed a squeak. Or at least as much of a squeak as a man with a deep voice could make. "What are you doing here?"

"She is my dresser!" snapped Lady Gwen. "Really, Robert, I expect such depravity from Father, but from you? I thought the help was safe!"

"Gwen, really, that's not—"

Lady Gwen wasn't listening. She spun around, turning her back on her brother in order to step forward to grasp Helaine's shaking hands. "I am deeply sorry, Mrs. Mortimer. I cannot imagine how horrible this must be for you."

Helaine tried to speak. She opened her mouth to say something— anything—but she hadn't the presence of mind to think of words. Her blood was still simmering with a heat that could only be described as passion. Passion! Inside her! She had long ago given up hope that any man could move her. She was *not* a passionate woman. But his kiss had stirred her. And the shock of that left her slack jawed and stupid.

"Lady Gwen," she began, stalling for time as she tried to order her thoughts.

"No, no, don't say anything. He is a beast to accost you in such a manner, but never fear. He has given me access to my funds, so you shall never have to see him again."

On the opposite side of the room, Lord Redhill snorted in derision. "Gwen, you cannot think that I forced myself anywhere. I—"

Gwen spun around. "Don't say it, Robert! Just don't! You and I have both heard that exact faradiddle from Father countless times. What was it you told me right after you demanded he find rooms elsewhere?" Gwen tapped her finger with her chin. "Oh, yes, you said that just being titled put Father in an unfair position over the maids. Willing or not, he was *forcing* himself on them and you wouldn't stand for it."

Lord Redhill's face turned a blistering shade of red. Helaine might have said he was angry, except that he shoved his hands deep into his pockets and looked more embarrassed. "She's not a maid in my household, Gwen," he said, his voice low but no less powerful.

Helaine touched Lady Gwen's arm, her sense of justice forcing her to confess part of the truth. "Please," she said as she drew the woman around. "Your brother has learned of my past. He was simply applying as a replacement protector."

It took a moment for Gwen to understand what she meant, and when the information finally processed, the woman blushed to the roots of her fine blond hair. "Oh. Oh! Oh, but does that mean—"

"I have turned him down," Helaine said.

Gwen frowned, her gaze darting between the two of them. "That was a refusal?"

Helaine sighed. "Men usually don't take 'no' on the first try. Your brother is no more and no less than any other man in that regard." She said the words and tried not to choke on them. The truth was that one kiss had shown her that Lord Redhill was a great deal more spectacular than any other man.

"Oh, well," said Gwen, her eyes flashing fire at her brother again. "Never fear. I shall be sure to emphasize that point to him in the future." Then she straightened and crossed to the door, hauling it open with a dramatic flourish. "I believe you have your answer, Robert. Good-bye."

Lord Redhill's gaze narrowed on his sister, clearly annoyed

by her high-handedness. But it was his next look—the one that rested long and heavy on Helaine—that had her squirming where she stood. It brought to mind all that they had done in the space of a few seconds, and all that might have happened had his sister not appeared precipitously. Her mouth went suddenly dry and she could not hold his gaze.

He waited an interminable minute longer, then finally spoke. "You are right, Gwen. I believe I shall take my leave. But pray, my dear, do not let my actions influence your financial decisions. Her request for early payment is not the usual course of—"

"Oh, just get out!" Gwen snapped. "You are the most pompous ass I have ever known!" And with that, the petite woman grabbed her brother's arm and shoved him out the door. Never had Helaine seen the like, and a part of her was thrilled to see that someone was capable of putting the arrogant, managing, incredibly seductive Lord Redhill in his place. Especially as the door slammed on his behind.

"I vow you are a most amazing woman," Helaine said. "How can I express my gratitude?"

"What? Oh, Mrs. Mortimer, you should be the one demanding my forgiveness. Really, Robert can be such a bully. But never you fear, I have been putting him in his place since he was in shortcoats. I shall most certainly continue to do so on your behalf."

Helaine released a halfhearted laugh. On the one hand, Lady Gwen was delightful when she spoke with such righteous indignation. On the other hand, she had no wish to come between the two siblings and certainly not about something as confusing as a kiss. "Please, my lady, you will do me the greatest favor if you just forget this entire incident."

"Of course, of course. Ring for some fresh tea, and we shall talk of something much more pleasant than my wretched brother."

Helaine did as she was bidden, grateful to settle into a discussion of clothing and dress styles. She was able to bring out the sketches for Gwen's trousseau that she'd done early that morning, and was pleased when the lady began to embellish the designs to just what she desired. Gwen was working extra hard to be pleasant, and Helaine was inordinately grateful for the respite from her feelings.

And yet, no amount of time spent in fashion discourse could completely erase the memory of Lord Redhill. It could not hide the fact that her body still heated at just the thought of the handsome man. It could not prevent her lips from tingling slightly whenever she chanced to look at the chair where he had kissed her. Nor could it completely stop her wayward thoughts from reliving every sweet sensation that he had stroked to glorious life.

There was no doubt in her mind that she had just been seduced. In the space of a few seconds, the irritating man had conquered her. It mattered not that she had only given him a kiss. The horrid man had awoken something inside her and, try as she might, she couldn't lie to herself about that simple fact.

He had seduced her, and what made it even worse was that the whole thing had nothing to do with attraction. Well, perhaps *she* was attracted to *him*, and she would go to her grave regretting that. But *he* wasn't attracted to *her*. Not in the usual way.

His offer, and consequent seduction, was simply about asserting dominance. She and Francine had bested him. They had all but called him an idiot, and they had done it in front of Anthony, another man. What was any male's reaction to humiliation? Why, sexual domination, of course. And she had succumbed! For the space of a few heartbeats, she had given in to his dominance like any weak-willed woman.

Oh, what a fool she was! After all, she wasn't a young girl, innocent to the ways of men. Her naïveté had been stripped away the moment her father's name had been destroyed. Then all manner of men had shown up, planning to take what her father could not defend. None of them had counted on her strength of character, on her resilience, or on her changing her name to become a dressmaker. She had resources beyond becoming someone's mistress!

And so she would tell him if she ever saw him again.

And God forbid he should try anything like that on her again! She was prepared now. She would put him in his place so fast, his head would be ringing for a week!

If . . . When . . . She bit her lip and tried to get hold of her raging temper. She was only angry at herself. After all, he was acting as all men did. Meanwhile, she had a customer—and one whom she desperately needed to charm.

Sadly, that was where they encountered a problem. It turned out that Lady Gwen had indeed heard her brother's warnings. She was not in the least bit inclined to pay even so much as a groat ahead of time. Or, at least, she wasn't unless Helaine agreed to a rather spectacularly bad idea.

"I-I'm sorry?" Helaine stammered. "I'm afraid I didn't hear you exactly." She had, in fact, heard everything clearly, but couldn't believe the request.

"Well, you see," Lady Gwen began, obviously embarrassed and yet excited at the same time, "my brother might be obnoxious, but he did impress upon me that proper management of money required thought and maturity. He did say—"

"Yes, I know," Helaine interrupted. "He believes that advance payment is a ridiculous notion. But we are in a special circumstance."

"I know, I know! Which is why my solution works perfectly!"

Helaine sighed. "My dear, you are a gently bred woman. Commerce requires something of a less refined nature."

"But you are a gently bred woman as well. Don't try to deny it. I can hear it in your voice."

She was right. Helaine had once traveled in the most elite circles. But that was a long time ago. "Lady Gwen—"

"No, no! My mind is quite made up. If you wish to make my trousseau, then you must simply allow me to go with you to purchase the cloth. I wish to see everything. Then I can pay the merchants directly—and on credit, I might add—and you shall have what you need to make my clothing!"

Helaine tried not to squirm in her seat. Lady Gwen had

no idea what would be involved in purchasing the items required. Especially since some of these merchants could be downright nasty. "But if you have the money, there is no reason to purchase on credit."

The girl brightened considerably at that. "Well, that is where you are wrong! Robert talked to me about interest. Said having money earns more money! Just imagine! It simply earns money because you have not spent it. Therefore, credit makes the best sense of all. I get to earn interest, and you still have the wherewithal to buy fabric and the like."

Fabric, yes. Tomorrow's dinner, no. But she couldn't say that. In truth, as a businesswoman, Helaine had learned about the miracle of interest as well. Except, of course, they never had enough money to earn interest.

"That's all very clever of you," Helaine began, "but you don't understand the locations I must go to get things. And truthfully, I have just entered an arrangement with another lady to purchase things on my behalf. She is much more capable of handling herself in the rougher locations. Lace, for example, is often negotiated right on the docks."

Far from being deterred, Lady Gwen actually clapped her hands in excitement. "Oh, my! That does sound like an adventure."

"It's not," Helaine returned with as dampening an attitude as she could manage.

"Well, it will be for me!" Gwen said happily.

Helaine stalled by drinking her tea. It had long since gone cold, but she sipped at it nonetheless. There had to be some way to dissuade the girl, but try as she might, she simply couldn't think of a thing. But one look at the girl's face and she knew Gwen would not be dissuaded easily. In the end, Helaine set down her cup with a definitive click.

"Very well," she said slowly, "on one condition. You shall not go anywhere without me. Ever. Truly, Lady Gwen, that is for your own safety."

"Of course, of course," Gwen returned happily.

"And you shall bring a footman with you. A big, burly one. Perhaps two."

The girl's eyes widened in surprise. "You truly think it is that dangerous?"

"I do," she said firmly.

"Very well then. Two footmen of extra large stature."

Helaine leaned back in her seat, her nefarious plot accomplished. There was no way that the girl could get the use of two footmen without her brother finding out. And once he did, there was absolutely no way the man would allow his sister into such a potentially dangerous situation. It was horrible of her, but she did not see another way.

Meanwhile, Lady Gwen was practically bouncing in her seat. "So? When do we go and to where?"

Helaine pretended to think hard about it. "Well," she drawled, pulling out the most reprehensible name on her list of suppliers, "as soon as you send word that you have the footmen, we shall go to Captain Johnny Bono's Excellent Mercantile. Mind that you let your butler know where you are going. Dribbs would want to know where his staff is working." And he would be sure to let his lordship know as well.

"An excellent suggestion," the girl crowed. "I shall send word tonight!"

Five hours later, Helaine discovered all her manipulations had failed. A letter arrived from Lady Gwen stating that she had obtained the necessary protection and would arrive at the shop at noon on the morrow. But it wasn't until the postscript that Helaine truly began to panic. It read:

P.S. I'm terribly sorry, but Robert has insisted on coming along as well.

Robert wasn't exactly sure what to expect when they entered Mrs. Mortimer's dress shop. He knew she would be there. He guessed she would be somewhat on guard against him. After all, he had attempted to seduce her, and frankly, he was still intent on doing the deed.

Despite the scolding from his sister, Robert did not feel

as though he was violating any ethical code of behavior. If Mrs. Mortimer were just a dressmaker, then she would naturally be off-limits. But she'd been mistress to Lord Metzger long before she became a dressmaker. As Lord Metzger was conveniently dead, Mrs. Mortimer was open game. And Robert was more than willing to be a hunter.

So he had decided to accompany his sister on her shopping expedition. He would risk a day of boredom if it meant he could continue his pursuit of the exquisite Mrs. Mortimer. At least those were his thoughts before he saw her that morning.

She was dressed all in black, as a widow, complete with bonnet and umbrella. But the dress itself was a study in contrasts. The fabric was cheap wool, but the cut was exquisite, showing off her swells and hollows in a way that made him look twice. Especially because she looked plump. He frowned, studying her more closely. The swell of her bosom looked natural. Beautifully natural, but the rest of the dress . . .

"Are you wearing padding?" he gasped. Her form had added in girth by at least an inch if not more.

She arched a brow at him, color tingeing her cheeks. "What I wear and why is none of your concern, my lord."

A well-intoned set-down, but color was still building in her cheeks. She was embarrassed, but why? Meanwhile, she had turned to his sister.

"Please, Lady Gwen, I cannot think this is wise. Even with the presence of your brother. *Especially* with his presence."

Gwen frowned, both irritation and confusion in her words. "I don't understand. You said you buy much of your supplies from this Johnny Bono."

Mrs. Mortimer bit her lip in consternation. "I do, Lady Gwen, but he is exactly the reason I hired Irene. However, Irene is not available this morning. And this is hardly the place—"

"I am sick to death of people telling me where it is and is not appropriate for me to go. If you are safe there, then

I most certainly shall be, especially with Robert and Jack along."

Jack was their burliest footman and he was waiting on the carriage seat along with their coachman. Meanwhile, Mrs. Mortimer smiled her most winning smile and touched his sister's hands.

"I know you are most brave, but believe me when I say that there are places I would certainly not go if I had no need. I spent the morning writing to other vendors, requesting a private audience for you, but none are available. I'm afraid they don't believe I've landed a client such as you."

"Private!" gasped Gwen as she rolled her eyes. "I am not so delicate that I need such exalted service. And as for their beliefs, it is their loss. You are an excellent dressmaker, Mrs. Mortimer, and I wish to begin purchasing my dresses. Now, if you please."

Mrs. Mortimer gave in. Indeed, what choice did she have with Gwen so insistent? But Robert had heard the fear underlying the woman's tone and was not so sanguine as his naive sister.

"Why 'especially' with me?" he asked.

Both ladies turned to him in confusion.

"You said you didn't want to go *especially* in my presence. Why is that?"

Mrs. Mortimer shrugged. "Johnny Bono is a man of moods, my lord. A happy mood and his goodwill shows through. He will lower his price, and I have only moderate difficulty with him. But bring in a lord, and his price triples. Bring in an arrogant, domineering lord, and he will be surly indeed."

He arched a brow. "I'm not always arrogant and domineering, you know."

"Oh, of course you are," Gwen answered before anyone else could. "But we shall bargain him down with the offer of more sales in the future."

Mrs. Mortimer obviously did not like that idea, but she tried for a conciliatory tone. "Perhaps, Lady Gwen—"

"Come, come, I insist. We shall go now and find some lovely bargains for me and my in-laws-to-be."

The dressmaker gave in with a regal nod of her head. But before they left the shop, she touched Gwen's arm. "Please do not mention future sales. I do not like being beholden to Mr. Bono, even by implication."

Gwen's eyebrows shot up at that, and she was about to argue, but Robert cut her off.

"An excellent suggestion," he said firmly. "As Mrs. Mortimer knows this Bono fellow best, I believe we should take her advice."

Mrs. Mortimer's smile of relief was reward enough. But as Robert helped his sister into his carriage, he had cause to fear. He paused as he extended his hand to the dressmaker.

"Exactly how dangerous is this place?"

The woman sighed, and the sound came from deep within her. "There is likely no danger to you or your sister, my lord."

"So why the resistance?"

"Because I must return there after you are done. Or Irene in my stead. And the situation will not be so . . . safe."

His eyebrows narrowed in anger at that. It had never occurred to him that women in London would fear for their safety on British soil. But of course, that was ridiculous. Woman were vulnerable whatever their station in life.

But there was no time to reconsider, and in truth, he had no wish to. He wanted to see this Johnny Bono and ascertain for himself if Mrs. Mortimer was simply exaggerating her fears or if there was true danger right here in his own backyard.

Some fifteen minutes later, they arrived at a location that could only be described as vile. It was a warehouse conveniently located near the docks and tucked in tight to the fish yards. The stench was overpowering and, worse, the buildings sat too close to let the air blow the scent away. Two blocks before, Mrs. Mortimer had passed his sister a sachet of sweet-smelling herbs. Both ladies had one pressed to their nose, and Robert envied them the feminine accoutrement. But if he thought the smell alone would deter his sister, he was sadly mistaken. As soon as the carriage came to a halt, she grabbed her reticule and made for the door. After a shared expression of resignation with Mrs. Mortimer, Robert assisted the ladies to disembark.

Then he met Mr. Bono and had the overwhelming desire to shove them both back inside the carriage. The man was standing at the doorway to the warehouse, a smile of welcome on his face. He was tall, dressed immaculately, and was, by any account, handsome as sin. He also had a way of looking at the women that raised Robert's every protective instinct.

"Mrs. Mortimer! How very delightful it is to see you again." He stepped forward and took her hand in greeting. The dressmaker allowed it, even seemed to smile in welcome, but Robert could see the tension in her body as the man pressed the back of her hand to his lips.

"It is always an adventure seeing you as well," she said dryly. "Allow me to present Lord Redhill and his sister, Lady Gwen."

The man immediately changed his attention to Robert's sister, clasping her hand in a nearly reverent embrace. "Exquisite, my lady. Welcome," he said as he pressed his lips to Gwen's hand. If it weren't for the gloves she wore, Robert would have had a hard time allowing even this intimacy. Which was ridiculous, since the gentleman had acted—so far—only in a most proper manner. Especially as he finally released Gwen to bow politely before Robert. "My lord."

Robert gave him the barest of nods as he looked about. "Which is your warehouse?" he asked, doing his best to keep his voice urbane. They were surrounded on all sides by the dark, ugly buildings.

"Why, all of them!" Mr. Bono said with a sweeping gesture. "Did not Mrs. Mortimer explain? I am the only place to find the most exquisite items. Unique purchases from around the world. Treasures, my lady," he said to Gwen. "Around every turn, veritable treasures from China, India, and even some countries as you have never heard of before."

"Oh, my!" Gwen gasped. "Truly?"

Before Mr. Bono could answer, Mrs. Mortimer stepped forward. "Your silks, please. We are shopping for silks today."

"Excellent choice," the man returned. "Most excellent. Come along. I shall show you what has arrived just today."

They followed docilely enough, the ladies, Robert, and Jack. The coachman would not leave the horses and knew to keep a pistol in his lap just in case. But that would not help the ladies any as they stepped into the dark interior of a massive warehouse.

"Mind your step!" Mr. Bono called as he gestured to four of his workers. They were filthy brutes who smelled terrible, but they held aloft lamps as Bono led them on a meandering path through furniture, crates of odd metal lamps, and even a pen of roosting chickens.

"Just got a parcel of them from a farmer who had too many."

The chickens, he supposed.

"But what you ladies want is back 'ere, but then you know that, don't ye, Mrs. Mortimer? She and I, we been back 'ere many a time, ain't we?" He made it sound like he and the dressmaker had been doing much more than selecting fabrics, and Robert could see Mrs. Mortimer stiffen at the innuendo. But she didn't say anything, which led Robert to believe that such suggestive banter was typical of the man. Which made Robert like him less and less.

They continued to wander through a maze of items, the pathways getting narrower and narrower. And then, abruptly, a woman appeared beside him. She was clean and had big fat curls of hair and a dark red dress cut down almost to her belly. It would take the work of a moment to rid her of that gown, as she no doubt knew.

"Oh, guv," she cooed as she stepped between him and the ladies. "There be a better cut of cloth just over there."

"No, thank you, ma'am," he said stiffly as he tried to push past her. But there was no room to move. He'd have to climb over crates of what he thought might be onions and turnips.

"Coo, gov'ner, you won't be far from yer ladies. Just over there."

There might be men who'd be tempted. She smelled good, and her charms were more than ample, but Robert wasn't in the least bit interested. And the women were moving farther away. So he did the only thing he could think of.

He smiled as warmly as he could manage. He stepped close to her and put his hands on her waist. As expected, she melted forward. Which gave him the leverage he needed to lift her high up in the air, around the crates, though she did bang her leg on one, and set her firmly down behind him.

"No, thank you, ma'am. Sorry about your leg." Then he turned and hurried forward to catch up with the others. Which was when he noticed that he wasn't the only one being trapped in the tight confines. The lanes around the bolts of fabrics were so narrow that only one person could pass at a time.

Gwen was in the lead, inspecting the various fabrics as best she could in the lamplight. Mrs. Mortimer came next, doing her best to point out flaws in the cloth where it was damaged by water or vermin. Mr. Bono stood right behind Mrs. Mortimer, protesting whatever flaws she saw, as any merchant might. It was all very civilized except for one thing. At first Robert couldn't be sure he was seeing correctly, but a minute's observation showed him the truth.

Mr. Bono was fondling Mrs. Mortimer. It might appear that he was leaning forward to point out the sumptuousness of some bit of velvet, but as he did it, his opposite hand slid down the lady's buttocks. Robert didn't for one moment think she welcomed his attention. Her attire and attitude toward Mr. Bono had been absolutely neutral. And yet, she stood there and accepted his caresses without complaint.

Or at least not without obvious objection. As Robert was maneuvering his way forward, he saw her "accidentally" elbow the bastard backward. At one point, Mr. Bono even gasped and shied his booted foot sideways, as Mrs. Mortimer must have stomped on it. But she was in a doomed position. The pathway was such that there was no room at all. Mr. Bono must, of course, touch her. And she must, of course, tolerate it if she wished to purchase his goods.

And all the while, Gwen kept a running prattle about this fabric and the other, obviously unaware of what was happening right beside her. Fortunately, Robert was not so oblivious.

He reached forward and grabbed the man by his collar. Or at least he intended to. Before he could grab hold, one of the lamp holders shoved out a billy stick and it cracked into his wrist.

"Oh, yer lordship! Begging your pardon!" cried the man. "I thought to hit a fly."

"The hell you did," Robert grumbled. Damn, his hand was numb from the wrist down. He glared around him. Everyone looked the picture of innocence, from Johnny Bono all the way through his four burly lantern carriers. Everyone, that is, except Mrs. Mortimer, who understood exactly what was happening and had turned a mortified dark red. Meanwhile, Robert turned a dark eye to his sister. "Gwen," he said sternly, "we are done with this cad. You will—"

"Aw, now, your lordship," interrupted Mr. Bono. "I expect you saw my bit o' fun with Mrs. Mortimer and took the wrong idea. Why, she and me, we be the best of friends, and she's used to a bit o' fun from me. Gets a might bit insulted, she does, if there ain't no touches between friends. And as you can see, it's close in here. Hard to avoid, but I can be seeing as how you'd get the wrong idea."

"It's close in here by your design, Mr. Bono. And I have no interest—"

"But your sis 'ere been loving the silks and velvets. Best on the docks, an' I'll give you a good price. Don't be misunderstanding me an' Mrs. Mortimer. Ain't that right, Mrs. Mort? You and me, we do this ever' time."

Robert could not clearly see the dressmaker's face. Mr. Bono was standing directly in front of her, his expression hidden. Robert didn't need to see it, though, to know exactly what was happening. The man was giving her a hard look, silently threatening her unless she complied. He almost smiled. Given the way she had spoken to Robert throughout their acquaintance, he looked forward to the set-down she was about to give the man. But it never came.

"O-of course, my lord," she stammered, her voice audible but not invested with the power he usually heard from her. "Mr. Bono and I are old friends. And friends are allowed certain liberties. In fact," she said, turning a winning smile up to Mr. Bono, "I find him most masterful. The way he manages all his domain. It quite turns my head."

Robert stared at the woman. He could not be more shocked if she had turned green and sprouted horns. Was it possible? Could he have misread the situation so drastically? She couldn't possibly want this man's attention, and yet her expression was almost . . . dreamy as she looked at Mr. Bono.

Meanwhile, the man turned back to Robert, his face all smiles. "Mrs. Mort knows that after a bit o' fun, I will give 'er—and you—the best I gots. In fact," he said as he gestured to one of the lamp bearers, "there's a few bolts I separated out jes' for her. And while we're waiting, 'haps my sweet Miriam can be getting you a drink, what? Put some fire in yer belly, it can."

Miriam was the tart dressed in red, and she immediately stepped forward from the shadows, a bottle of brandy in one hand and scotch in the other.

"Definitely fine stuff," she cooed. "An' there's more in the back."

Robert barely even looked at her. He was busy searching Mrs. Mortimer's face for a clue. In truth, he was rather disappointed in her. She seemed of a higher sort than to accept advances from the likes of Bono. But whatever the reason, the man obviously had her under his thumb. He knew it the moment she flashed him a wan smile and turned to Gwen.

"Lady Gwen, it is up to you. If you prefer, I can . . . um . . . return later and make the selections."

"Absolutely not!" snapped Robert. The last thing he wanted was for Mrs. Mortimer to return here alone. If they were to buy fabrics from this cretin, then they would do it now.

"Aw, don't be fretting, dove!" said Mr. Bono to Gwen. "And 'ere's the silk, jes' for you."

A cascade of palest yellow silk spilled out before them. Beside them Gwen gasped. Even Mrs. Mortimer couldn't seem to resist reaching out to stroke the beautiful material. But Robert was done with this fiasco. He had no understanding of what exactly was between Mrs. Mortimer and the repulsive Mr. Bono, and at the moment he didn't truly care. He just wanted done with this business.

"Gwen," he snapped, "it is time to depart. We will not be purchasing any of Mr. Bono's wares."

"But Robert!" his sister cried.

Mrs. Mortimer, too, seemed abruptly very alarmed. "Please, my lord, I know this is not what you are used to, but if you will recall I did try to tell you that the situation here was unusual."

"Mrs. Mort and I have a special relationship," began Mr. Bono, but Robert never gave him the chance to continue.

"There will be no business done here today," Robert snapped. "Gwen, he is not an honest businessman, and I'll have no truck with him."

"'Ey, now! There's no need t' be insulting! I'm an honest man."

And to his shock, even Mrs. Mortimer objected, her voice high with alarm. "Pray don't say that, Lord Redhill! Mr. Bono is the most excellent of gentlemen!" She turned to the man, panic clear in her expression. "The yellow silk, Mr. Bono. Please. Right away."

"*No!* There will be no purchase at all today," Robert said as he held out his hand to Gwen. Her mouth was set in a mulish line, but he glared her into submission. In the end, the girl huffed.

"You are the worst sort of brother, you know that?" she spat. "Generous one moment, then high-handed and obnoxious the next."

Robert didn't bother to respond. Gwen knew when he

would brook no interference. She took his hand and they began the business of leaving. Mrs. Mortimer, however, stood back, her panicked eyes going between Lord Redhill and Mr. Bono.

"Yes, there will be," she snapped. "The yellow silk!" Then she swallowed. "I shall have to purchase it on credit, you know. But I shall pay you back as soon as—"

Mr. Bono's eyes narrowed. "Yes, you will, Mrs. Mort. Ain't no cause for you to be bringing customers here who ain't customers and insulting my good name."

"I know, Mr. Bono. Please understand, they had every intention of buying—"

"Harry," he snapped at one of his men, "wrap up the silk." Then his eyes hardened as he looked back at the dressmaker. "We'll be negotiatin' the price when you return."

Her eyes widened. "Oh, no, Mr. Bono. We'll be settling this now."

"Not when it's credit, ducky."

"Then I won't be taking the silk."

The two were at a standoff, with Robert getting more impatient by the second. "We are leaving, Mrs. Mortimer," he said, his words coming out as a low growl. "I cannot think what you are about, but I have had enough. Do you wish us to leave without you?" It was an idle threat. He had no intention of abandoning her here, but he also didn't want to loiter here while she played at whatever game was going on between them.

Bono arched a brow, his expression turning to a smug superiority. "Would you prefer to stay here, Mrs. Mortimer?"

Robert watched her swallow nervously, her gaze darting between the door and Mr. Bono, but her voice came out hard and cold. "Name your price, Mr. Bono."

"Two guinea."

She gasped with horror. "That's outrageous," she cried, "and you know it!"

"That's the price."

"I won't pay—"

Robert released a curse that was not meant for ladies' ears, but he was rapidly beginning to wonder at Mrs. Mortimer's claim to that title. After all, she was standing here dickering with a man who had been molesting her person. But one glance at the "lamp bearers," and he knew they were out of time. The men surrounding them were moving in. If it came to a fight, then there was no way Robert could protect himself, much less either woman.

Loath though he was to do it, Robert pulled out his own purse. With a curse of disgust, he fished out two coins and tossed them on top of a nearby crate.

"There's your money," he all but snarled. Then he grabbed the bolt from the thug and jerked his head at Gwen. "Outside. Now."

It took them much too long to escape the warehouse, but they did. Gwen made to slow as she took a deep breath of the fish-scented air. It was foul, but it was better than what was inside the closely packed warehouse. Robert tagged her bottom with the end of the bolt. "Go!" he breathed. He had already ascertained that Mrs. Mortimer was behind them, moving just as rapidly as Robert. But none of them were faster than Mr. Bono himself. He must have some secret pathway through the warren, Robert thought uncharitably, because before they made it to the carriage, he saw the man crossing to stand before Gwen.

Urbane as ever, Mr. Bono bowed deeply over Gwen's hand. "I can see that I have offended your brother, Lady Gwen. Please let me apologize. Perhaps we can find a way to do business another day."

"I would not count on that," Robert growled as he handed off the bolt of silk to the coachman.

The man turned and executed a deep bow, but kept his eye on Gwen. "Perhaps not today, but Mrs. Mortimer and I can come to some arrangement for other silks. I believe a soft rose would be exactly your color, don't you think? As sweet as your lovely cheeks. Makes a man think of things he ought not with a lady like you."

"Oh, Mr. Bono!" said Gwen, her blush burning hotter as she looked away.

"Get back!" Robert growled as he was at last free to step forward aggressively against the bastard.

Mr. Bono backed away immediately, his bow deep and deferential. "Don't you worry, guv," he said. "I know I can't do anything but look at the likes of yer sister." He cast a wink at Gwen that had Robert growling anew. "And don't you be mad at him," he said to Gwen. "It's a man's right to protect his sister from the likes of me."

That was the moment Robert realized the man's cleverness. With one sentence, he had cast Robert in the role of overprotective brother, while Bono was the charming rogue. He laid even odds that Gwen would come back again, only this time without her bear of a brother. Damnation!

And just when he thought it couldn't get any worse, the man turned to the dressmaker.

"A pleasure as always, Mrs. Mortimer."

"Of course, Mr. Bono," she said with a smile. She made a valiant effort, but Robert could see the strain in her eyes and the pinched tightness to her smile. Then she turned toward the carriage while Bono winked at Robert.

"I won't lay a hand on yer sister, I swear. Thankfully, other women are not so exalted, what?" And with that the man abruptly swatted Mrs. Mortimer's behind. She released a squeak of alarm as she completed the climb into the carriage, but she said nothing while Mr. Bono released a hearty chuckle. "You have a good afternoon, now!" And with that he dropped into a low, mocking bow. Robert didn't know how the man could make a deep bow insolent, but somehow he did. And he had half a mind to whip the man, except of course that it would only prove him insane and overprotective. Bloody cheek.

All he could do was to climb into the carriage and slam the door shut. Lord, he was so livid, he expected to take the rest of the ride back home just to find the calm to not punch something. Sadly, he was not given a respite in which to fume. As soon as the carriage began moving, Gwen turned on him.

"Really, Robert, what did you mean by all this? How can you insist on coming and then keep me from purchasing anything? If this is what you mean by my being responsible for my own funds, then I cannot think that you are serious. Why, you—"

"Gwen, please!" he said, exasperated as he leaned forward to look earnestly at Mrs. Mortimer. "Are you all right?"

The lady's eyes narrowed and her color was high. She took a moment, as if she, too, were trying to get hold of her temper, but she obviously failed. Because a second later she was blasting him as if he had been the one to accost her. "I knew I should not have let you come. I knew it! But no, I trusted to your understanding of business, to your promise to be discreet. My God, do you know what you have done today?"

"Done?" he snapped back, his own temper slipping free. "What have I done but pay two guineas for some blasted silk? And to that bastard!"

"That bastard is the only one who will give me credit! And now his prices will be tripled! What you have done, my high-handed lord, is ruin me and my business!"

"Ruin you? I paid for the damn silk!"

"And how many dresses can I make from that? One, maybe two? What about muslin and lace, thread and buttons? Did you think about that while you were ruining me?"

"He was accosting you!"

"He was most certainly not!" she snapped back.

He slammed back against the seat, and his mind's eye unerringly repeated what he had seen. "So it's true. You are his mistress."

Crack! The slap of her hand across his face surprised him as much from the speed as the vehemence of her attack. His head shot to the side. He hadn't even seen the blow coming.

"I am no man's mistress. Not his and certainly not yours!"

He didn't move, but he felt the imprint of her hand burning on his cheek and his fury coalesced into a cold, ugly thing. "I know what I saw, Mrs. Mortimer. But of course, it is no business of mine. And," he added, his eyes narrowing into hard slits, "no business of ours will be exactly what you get."

He saw that Mrs. Mortimer understood immediately what he meant. She blanched to a ghostly white, but didn't say a word. It took Gwen a moment longer to comprehend, but when she did, she bristled with all her youthful contrariness.

"Why, you interfering, high-handed, arrogant . . . brother!" Gwen spat the last word as if it were the gravest insult. "I do not have the slightest understanding of what just happened, but I completely agree with Mrs. Mortimer. It is all your fault, Robert! All of it!" Then, to prove that she wasn't completely at a loss, she turned to Mrs. Mortimer, her expression concerned. "Am I to understand that Mr. Bono accosted you?"

Mrs. Mortimer released a sigh of frustration. "Gwen, dear, please do not be concerned. It is the sad truth that women in my position are accosted constantly. Your brother yesterday, Mr. Bono today. It is a game they play—"

"Do not think to put me in the same category as that villain," Robert snapped, but guilt was burning a dark hole in his gut.

Mrs. Mortimer went on as if she had not heard him. "It is why I wear padding when I visit Mr. Bono. He likes to . . . er . . . touch. And if I allow just a little touching, the price is better. I praise his masterly skills in front of his men, I giggle and simper, and yes, I even tease. If I could afford to go elsewhere, I would. Indeed, that is why I am working with a new woman who will hopefully solve this problem. But she has only just begun to work and was unavailable this morning."

Gwen frowned. "But you shouldn't have to do business that way."

Mrs. Mortimer reached out and touched Gwen's hand. "Should and shouldn't do not apply to some of us. Be grateful that you are protected."

"Well," huffed Gwen, "you shall not be punished because of my brother's boorishness." She shot a withering glare at Robert. "I believe, Mrs. Mortimer, that I shall double my trousseau purchase. And I think I will get all of my friends to visit you as well. It shall be a condition of attending my wedding. They must all wear a gown made by you."

Color returned to the dressmaker's cheeks, and Robert had the churlish instinct to be furious at her for impelling his sister to do such a thing. He had been trying to protect the woman, damn her. And she had somehow managed to turn him into a villain and his sister into her greatest patron.

"My God," he whispered, "you are the most brilliant businessman it has ever been my misfortune to meet."

Both women turned to look at him, but it was the dressmaker who spoke, with an arched brow, no less. "I am not a business*man* at all, my lord. In fact, I believe that is the source of our difficulties. You have no idea what to do with a woman in business."

"Because a woman ought not to be in business," he groused. And then he could have bitten off his own tongue for his stupidity. He merely meant that she ought to have a man to do her purchasing and the like. After all, if a man were to go to Mr. Bono's, then all this havy cavy nonsense would not happen. It was all perfectly logical, and yet it was absolutely *not* the thing to say to these two women. To say that they were insulted was a mild understatement. Gwen huffed and called him the type of names he had long since learned to tune out. Mrs. Mortimer simply looked at him with pity in her dark eyes. Pity! When he was the damned viscount and she was a nobody dressmaker!

Good Lord, but he was beyond grateful when they finally arrived at the shop. He leaped out immediately, simply to remove himself from the diatribe Gwen continued to level at his head.

"Gwen, my dear," he said, interrupting her in midword, "I believe I shall walk from here. Pray go home and let Mother know what has happened. I'm sure she would love to know the exact details of my perfidy."

If there was one thing his mother enjoyed, it was a lively discussion of his faults. In the meantime, he gestured to the coachman. The footman was already carrying the bolt of blasted yellow silk into the shop. If Robert had his choice, he would turn around and depart immediately. But politeness required that he open the shop door for Mrs. Mortimer. She smiled her thanks, her expression tight. And politeness also required that she invite him inside.

"It has been a long day, my lord. Would you like some tea before you depart?" Her words were no more and no less than what he expected. But some devil in his heart made him look her in the eye, waiting until she finally met his gaze. "My lord?"

"This is not done between us. I will not stay now, but I will return."

He watched understanding and dismay fill her expression. But there was a spark of excitement there. He was sure of it. Excitement, desire, all of the feminine reactions that said, Do come back. Do challenge me again. He read them in her eyes. Or so he told himself. Then he spun on his heel and walked away.

Chapter 6

~≫≪~

Robert didn't go to his home. Nor did he head for his club. He needed time to think and analyze his emotions, and so he headed for the one place he could be himself: his brothel. On the occasion of his sixteenth birthday, Robert had been summoned into his father's library and told it was time to become a man. But as his father never did anything that was less than grand, he presented his son with not just a prostitute for the night, but an entire brothel, named the Chandler, a place where any man could get his wick lit. And, as was typical with all his father's business purchases, the reality was a great deal more sordid than the presentation.

He and his father had shown up at the brothel steps, only to stand at the doorway for a terribly, terribly long time. Eventually the door was opened by the only standing "candle" in the house, the rest having been stricken by fever.

His father had taken one whiff of the stench and started to back away. Robert was doing the same, except that the "candle" fainted straight into his arms. At that point, he had no choice. He half carried, half dragged the girl to the nearest settee, then sent his father to fetch a doctor. His father didn't return, of course, but the doctor did. And together, the two men toiled as no heir to the Earl of Willington had done in generations.

Ten days later, nearly half the candles had survived. And when Robert collapsed, it was the madame of the house who, settling him in her own bed, nursed him as his own mother had never done. From that moment on, Robert and Chandelle were fast friends. And the brothel became something else entirely, though with the same name. It was a hospital of sorts for working girls. A place where the women could heal or die with dignity. If some of its former trade continued, Robert wasn't aware of it. And he certainly didn't take a cut of the profit.

What he did take was a back room that was wholly his. In it, he read, relaxed, and dabbled in the one thing he had once wanted to do above everything else: medicine. He kept track of the treatments the girls received, the concoctions and the potions that helped and those that did not. He had visitors of a sort, too. Men of medicine he consulted on one case or another. But mostly, he and Chandelle managed alone, doing their best for the girls who knocked upon their door.

He told no one what he was doing. It was perfectly acceptable for an earl's son to own a brothel. It was absolutely unacceptable for him to be housing them to no profit and be treating them as human beings, caring for their diseases, and seeing that their children grew up in a wholly different life.

And if his father ever found out that this was the reason there weren't enough funds to make his disaster of a mine immediately profitable, then there would be the devil to pay for sure. Chandelle and her patients would be safe, Robert would see to that. But the earl would demand a reckoning— and a good deal of money—to recompense what had gone into the Chandler. And sadly, Robert just didn't have the money in his own right to do that. Not in one lump sum. So he kept his passion secret, and he went there only when he was assured no one would miss him.

Chandelle met him at the door, opening it quickly and ushering him inside. When he would have spoken, she pressed a finger to his lips, then gestured him to her bedroom. He followed her quietly enough to where three children sat completely enraptured by the sight of a mama cat licking clean her new litter of kittens.

"She wandered in and set up right by my fire," whispered Chandelle. "What was I to do but call in the little ones to watch? It has given their mothers three hours' worth of peace!"

He smiled as he looked down at the mangy mama cat. Her fur was burned in patches and uneven in others. One eye was gone, and if he wasn't mistaken, her tail was bent at an odd angle. But the animal was alive and caring for her kittens with all the devotion of the Madonna.

"Well, she looks like she'd be a good mouser." The cat looked nothing of the sort. But then, he'd learned not to judge people—or animals—by their appearance.

"She'll teach her kits well, you mark my words. Then you'll see. Not a rat would dare show its face here."

"At least not the four-footed kind," he drawled. They still had problems with men of one ilk or another come looking for a woman or her children. That was why he kept a couple of large guards in the house and paid them well. Mostly they fetched and carried whatever was needed. But other times, they kept the human vermin outside.

With a wry smile, she gestured him out of her room again. He stepped out and headed for the upper floor of patients. She accompanied him, and he slowed to match her pace. Chandelle had once been a great beauty, or so he'd been told. But now she was in her fifties—an ancient age in her profession—and the sickness that had brought them together so many years ago had yet to leave her joints. That made her stiff as she moved, slow and unsteady with the paint box whenever she bothered, and mostly unfit to do the day-to-day nursing some of the patients required. But nursing had never been Chandelle's strength. She had an eye for people—their talents and their failings—and she had no reservations about using that knowledge for the good of her charges. As a madame, she'd been a deft hand at blackmail. As the head of a home for sick women, she knew whom to accept and whom to toss from her steps like bad meat. Every one of her charges had helped out in one way or another. And neither she nor Robert would have it any other way.

Today, however, she turned that keen eye on him. Or rather, her keen nose. She sniffed the air as they walked and curled her lip. "You 'ave the smell of the docks on you."

He nodded. "Spent an extremely unpleasant hour at Mr. Johnny Bono's Mercantile."

"Johnny Bono! That bastard! Tell me you won't have no truck with the likes of him."

Robert smiled. "No truck, I swear. But I'd be grateful for news of him, especially as it concerns my sister's dressmaker."

She stopped halfway up the stairs, pausing to draw breath. Or perhaps it was to eye him with an all-too-clear gaze. "A dressmaker, you say?"

"Mrs. Mortimer. Her shop is—"

"I know it. And I know 'er." She waited another moment, chewing her lip as she looked at him. Finally she frowned at him. "So you be looking at the lower orders now for your girls? Fed up, are you, with the society women?"

He considered lying for a moment. He could pretend that Gwen's dressmaker meant nothing to him. But this was the one place in the world where he did not need to pretend, and so he tucked away the urge and opted for honesty. "I don't precisely know what my interest is."

"But you are interested. In Mrs. Mortimer, and not the pretty seamstress."

He smiled. "Not the pretty seamstress, whomever she may be."

"But the lady?"

He shrugged, turning away to climb the stairs when he grew uncomfortable with Chandelle's stare. What he felt for Mrs. Mortimer wasn't up for discussion. At least not until he had an understanding of his own motives. But then again, that was exactly why he came to this place, wasn't it? To sort out his thoughts. That usually meant talking with Chandelle.

"She makes me think," he finally said.

Chandelle surprised him with a burst of laughter. "More thinking ain't wot you need, Robert. Swiving is more like it."

He grinned. "Well, she makes me think of swiving, too. Does that help?"

Chandelle blew out a low whistle. "So you found 'er."

Robert slowed as he topped the stairs. "Found who?"

"A woman to match yer brains and yer brawn." She thumped his arm. "But does she match yer heart? She'd have to have an awful big heart to meet you there."

He frowned as he shook his head. "I don't know," he finally admitted. "She's a businessman . . . er . . . woman. Reminds me of you in that. I admire her strength."

Chandelle snorted. "She ain't the one for you, then. Strength is one thing, boy, but a heart is something else. Your woman gots to 'ave heart. A right big one."

He grimaced, wondering if she was right. Not about wanting a woman with heart. Of course he did, whatever that meant. But about whether the dressmaker lacked something essential. He had no idea. "I asked her to be my mistress."

Chandelle let out a low whistle. "She turned you down, eh?"

He gave her a wry look. "Down flat."

"So you came 'ere to lick yer wounds. Want to do some doctoring for women who'd be grateful."

He raised his eyebrows. Was that what he was doing? Salvaging his wounded pride?

"Ain't nothing to be ashamed of. No one likes the word 'no,' least of all you lords."

"But—"

"Tut-tut," she said as she grabbed his arm and hauled him toward the main ward. "We got a whole house full o' women who'll say yes to you. And there's a couple bedpans to be cleaned and that would make me right grateful."

"Bedpans?" he said in his most haughty tone. "I am a lord, you know."

"And a right good one, you are," she said, knowing his protest was halfhearted at best. "Hard work will fix what ails ye. But first off, I want you to 'ave a look at little Steve. He's the new baby. Ain't been taking the breast like he were meant to."

Three hours later, he was grateful for Chandelle's wisdom. Hard work had indeed cleared his thoughts. He'd looked at nine patients in all, only sending for the doctor on one—Steve's mother. The babe likely sensed that his mother was dying and wouldn't drink from her. So he'd tasked Chandelle with finding a wet nurse. And while Chandelle had done that, he'd changed bed linens, made the special foods that two of his patients required, and yes, he'd even taken care of the bedpans. After three hours, he felt refreshed and productive, as if he'd fought a hard battle and won. It didn't matter that the fight would continue tomorrow or that by week's end, he'd need to find a new mother for little Steve. For now, he felt good. So he was whistling as he left the Chandler, his mind emptied of everything but the tasks he had performed this day.

Sadly, other tasks would hit him the moment he returned home. He was due for another visit to his father's thrice-cursed mine. He had to study the latest suggestions from the steward at the seat of the earldom. And who knew what sort of scolding would come from Gwen and his mother the moment he walked in the door. Which meant now was the perfect time *not* to go home, but to begin his seduction of one feisty dressmaker.

He looked at his watch and realized he would arrive at the dress shop just in time for a late tea. It never occurred to him that she would have customers. As a rule, ladies shopped during the morning, not the afternoon hours. But then he crossed the street to the shop door and was nearly bowled over by a thin woman with a pinched nose and a worried expression.

"Oh! Excuse me, sir!" the woman gasped as she veered out of his path.

He recovered easily, grasping her bony elbow when she

might have fallen in a puddle. "Entirely my fault," he said, because that was what a gentleman said even though she was the one who had run into him. "Careful of your step!"

"Lord Redhill!" cried Mrs. Mortimer from the doorway. She had obviously been showing her customer out, only to be startled by his presence. He smiled at her, his gaze taking in her new attire. No longer was she dressed in padded black, but in a flowing gown of soft green. She looked like a young tree right before its first full season. Her figure was mature, but her body and her face still had some youthful innocence. Her curves were not so much ripe as modestly covered and yet ready to burst free with just the right touch. It was an odd thought to have about a woman, but he could not shake the impression. Nor could he stop imagining how he would undress her slowly, peeling away the bark, so to speak, until he reached the tender, sweet wonder beneath.

"M-my l-lord?" stammered the customer, who was still caught in his grip.

He forced his attention back to the unknown woman. "Have you found your feet then? I am sorry I startled you."

The woman gaped at him as he gently let go of her arm. Meanwhile, Mrs. Mortimer stepped into the conversational breach. "Mrs. Richards, may I present to you Viscount Redhill."

Mrs. Richards's eyes widened even farther. "G-good afternoon, my lord. I-I hadn't realized . . ." Her voice trailed away as she looked at the dressmaker with dawning speculation.

"His sister is Lady Gwen, one of my customers," she said rather coldly. "He is no doubt stopping by on an errand from her."

A lie, of course, because Mrs. Mortimer obviously wanted to make clear that he was not visiting for any salacious reason. And since he saw no reason to broadcast his private affairs, he cheerfully agreed. "Some bother about yellow silk," he drawled. "It shall just take a moment."

"Of course, my lord," she answered.

Meanwhile, Mrs. Richards curtsied to him. "I have met your sister," she said. "A lovely woman."

"Thank you," Robert murmured, uninterested in prolonging the conversation.

Thank God the woman took the hint. "Well, thank you for your time, Mrs. Mortimer," she said. "I shall return next Tuesday with Francine for our fitting."

"We will be ready."

Given the dismissal, the woman had no choice but to nod and depart, though her gaze lingered as long as possible on him. But eventually she disappeared around the corner, and at that moment, Mrs. Mortimer released her breath in a long, heavy sigh.

"She will think the worst of me. Indeed, I believe you have merely locked in her poor opinion of my morals."

"But why?" he asked. "I am merely here about the yellow silk."

She snorted. "You are a terrible liar, you know. You should have made demands regarding a bill or the like. That she might have believed. But to discuss fabric? A viscount on behalf of his sister? Never."

He pursed his lips. She had a point. He would never have come here on a task from his sister. "Why does she already think the worst of you?"

"That was Francine's mother." When he didn't readily place the name, she gestured with her hands, indicating a large woman. "You remember, the girl with the lush figure."

Robert finally placed the girl in his memory, but then he compared her to the stick-thin, prune-shaped woman he'd just met. "That can't be her mother!"

She laughed. "Francine takes after her father in her body's size."

"He must be—"

"Have a care, my lord," she warned before he could finish his thought. "Francine is my friend and I dislike certain words, especially when applied to my friends."

He immediately moderated his tone. "Of course. I merely

meant that Francine's father is likely a man of some stature."

She snorted. "He is at that. Tall and broad and fair-minded. It is her mother who is less charitable in all aspects."

"She doesn't like how you have dressed Francine." He couldn't blame the woman. Her daughter had been gowned in an entirely inappropriate fashion, in his opinion. Too lush by half.

"She will come around," Mrs. Mortimer returned calmly. "She loves her daughter and wants her to be happy. The right clothes can only help with that."

He didn't argue with her because what she said was correct in principle. And as she already knew his opinion of the gown—he'd made that quite clear before—he saw no reason to be contentious. So, feeling very virtuous, he simply nodded and gestured to the inside of her shop.

"May I come in? I'd like a moment of your time, please."

She didn't budge from her position in the doorway. "My lord, it has been a long and tiring day."

"Tea will be the perfect restorative."

"My lord . . ."

"Please. I owe you an apology, and I would prefer not to deliver it on the street." She had no choice but to let him inside now. Good manners demanded as much, and so she gave in. She dipped her chin and stepped aside. He followed as close as he could manage, lifting her arm and escorting her to a chair. He gave her no time and no space to thwart him, and in a moment, she was exactly where he wanted her to be.

Helaine was beginning to resent Lord Redhill's very high-handed ways. He all but forced her into her own shop, shut the door, and half guided, half pushed her onto the settee. Then he sat across from her and dropped his hands on his knees before frowning at the table between them.

"First, allow me to apologize. I did not understand the

situation at the warehouse, and I fear I have made things worse for you."

She didn't answer. She had no desire to think about the disaster that awaited her if she ever returned to Johnny Bono's warehouse. And she had no idea where else she could buy fabrics. Irene was a miracle worker—or had been as a girl—but she had never tried to purchase things on the scale of what a dressmaker's shop would need. And she had already sent around a note saying the task was harder than she expected and would take more time. Perhaps after Lady Gwen bought clothing at other establishments, things would be easier. Merchants would advance her some small amount of credit. Or perhaps Francine's payment would help, assuming her mother could be convinced to approve the dresses . . . Her mind spun on with possibilities and dangers, and all of it stopped cold at his lordship's question.

"Tell me what I can do to make up for the problem I have caused."

She didn't have to think long about that. The words came quickly. "Never, ever interfere in the running of my shop again. And that includes your sister's choices."

"Done."

She shook her head, almost laughing at the ease with which he said it. She already knew that he was much too high-handed to do as he promised. It wasn't that he was malicious, just unthinking. He would interfere without remembering his past promises or any future consequences.

"Swear it, my lord. Upon your honor, upon your family's honor."

He reared back, startled by her demand. But she was the daughter of a drunken earl. She knew that the only thing an aristocrat valued above his brandy was his family's good name. In the end, her father had valued his drink more than his name, but she didn't think Lord Redhill was the same sort. So this oath would bind him as securely as anything.

"Your oath, my lord. Or you may leave my shop now."

His eyes narrowed in anger, but he complied. "You have my oath as Viscount Redhill, as the future Earl of Willington, and as a man of honor that I will not interfere in your business again. Not unless you ask."

"I shall never ask."

He arched a brow. "That remains to be seen. Now, am I forgiven? Will you accept my apology?"

She exhaled, relieved that one of her difficulties had been solved. "Yes, you are forgiven. Now if you please, it has been a long day." She started to stand, but he forestalled the movement by touching her arm.

"We spoke of tea. Would you still like some?"

She felt her shoulders slump with weariness. Really, would she never be rid of the man? Did he not understand that his very presence added more work to her life? "Tea has to be made and served, my lord. Will you do that for me? Or will you snap your fingers and demand that my partner leave off her work to wait upon us?"

His frown deepened. "I had thought I would get it myself. I was still in shortcoats when I learned how to make tea and slice a loaf of bread."

She bit her lip. She was being churlish, and he was acting rather kind. More kind, in fact, than her own father had ever been. She wished she could tell him to go to the devil. But he was Lady Gwen's brother and she needed the man's good-will. And even worse, she rather liked that he had offered her tea. Though she very much doubted he would actually rise and make it himself. And right there was the solution to her problems. All she need do was keep demanding things from him. First tea, then something more improbable. Then more. Eventually he would tire of the game and leave her alone. And in the meantime, she could amuse herself by watching the man try to serve her tea in her own establishment.

She leaned back against the settee and released a long breath. "Tea would be lovely, Lord Redhill. The tray is over there. Pray do make us a pot." She waved languidly in the direction of the kitchen.

He smiled at her, as if he knew exactly what she was doing, then immediately grabbed the tray. A moment later he disappeared into the kitchen, which was really part of the back workroom. Helaine waited, listening to the bang of pots and the like. What was he doing back there? And where was Wendy? Wouldn't they be talking or something? Unless his lordship refused to speak to someone so low in status as a seamstress. But that couldn't be true, could it? And really, it was rather bad of her to send the man back there and *not* warn Wendy. What if he upset Wendy somehow?

So it was that within a minute of resolving to have him serve her, Helaine pushed to her feet to see exactly what disaster he was creating in her ordered kitchen. She moved quickly but silently, the instinct to keep invisible well in-grained from her childhood. Which meant she was able to observe him as he scooped filtered water from the bucket and into the pot. His movements were efficient, his bearing easy, as if he had indeed made tea for himself many a time. But how could that be? He was the son of an earl!

He set the kettle to boil then went about searching for the tea tin. He found the fancy tea, the one purchased for clients, and was already pulling it down when she stepped forward. "Not that one. Behind it. That is what I drink."

He frowned then peered into the cupboard, finally bringing out the cheap tin. As she expected, he opened the lid and wrinkled his nose at what was inside. "Surely you don't prefer this."

She arched a brow. "It is what I drink. You may of course take from whatever tin you choose." But that would require two different pots of tea. She waited for him to refuse or simply make the expensive tea and convince her to share it with him. But he didn't. He put away the expensive stuff and waited with her for the kettle to boil.

Meanwhile, Helaine glanced at the rest of the workroom. Wendy was nowhere in sight. Her work was laid out, but the room was empty. It wasn't like her to waste daylight when she could be sewing. "I wonder what happened," she said to herself as she moved through the back room.

He followed her as she meandered among the tables. Then she saw it: a box opened on the chair Wendy usually used. Out from the box spilled the most gorgeous scarf she had ever seen. Blue, black, and gold danced about on fabric almost too delicate to touch. The design was paisley, but that in no way described the elaborate, shimmery display.

Behind her, Lord Redhill whistled in appreciation. "Your seamstress is most fortunate in her lover."

Helaine turned around. Trust a man to leap to the most scandalous conclusion. "A lover! No, no, this is from Wendy's brother. He's a seaman and sends her the most beautiful things from wherever he visits. This must be from China."

"India, I believe. And I assure you, this is not a gift a brother sends." He lifted the piece up from the box. The scarf was larger than she'd thought; indeed, the sheer fabric went beyond the length of his arms and down almost to her knees.

"Do you know what a man thinks when he sees something like this?" He did not wait for her to answer, but stepped up to her and slowly draped it across her body.

"We shouldn't touch that. It's Wendy's," she said even as she was marveling at the smooth caress of the fabric against her cheek.

He didn't listen but slipped the scarf around her shoulders. "He imagines her naked and wearing just this. He sees the pink blush of her skin as it mixes with the gold threads, and he wonders what part of the pattern will touch the dark rose of her nipples. He thinks of slowly unwrapping her like a present on his birthday, one that is revealed in the sweet privacy of his bedroom. And he dreams of laying her down on top of this as he gently settles between her thighs."

"Lord Redhill!" Helaine squeaked, her face burning in embarrassment. "That is a most inappropriate conversation—"

"If you would consent to be my lover, I would buy you the most amazing fabrics from India, China, and even the Americas. We will dress you up in them and I will stroke the fabrics across your flesh so that you can feel every exquisite caress. And as the colors skate across your skin, I will kiss every inch. Silk, velvet, even soft wool shall float across you until you are delirious from the sensations. And then, when you can take no more, I will lay you down and show you even more."

Helaine stared at him, her thoughts whirling with the images he described. They were not even all that graphic. He spoke of skin and kisses, and every inch of her body responded. Her insides went liquid from the intensity of his gaze, and when he stroked his thumb beneath her jaw she gasped as a tremble seized her. It was a quiet sensation, like a shimmer just under her skin, and it frightened her almost as much as it intrigued her.

Never before had a man's words stirred her so effectively. And never before had a man looked at her with such sensual promise in his eyes. Other men had wanted her, but it had been for their pleasure, their amusement. Lord Redhill talked of what she would enjoy: pleasure such as she had only imagined.

Then he leaned forward to take her lips. She wanted to deny him. She knew she ought to turn away, but she could not. She wanted to feel what he promised, to know what women with good lovers experienced in their beds.

She let him kiss her. She lifted her mouth to his and let him tease the edge of her lips with his tongue. Her flesh swelled beneath his stroke, and she closed her eyes to better experience it. She felt his teeth, nibbling along the edges until his tongue thrust inside. He was not bold in his possession, but careful and so very thorough. She did not know what to do. And yet, apparently she did. Without conscious understanding, her tongue dueled with his. Her neck arched and her head angled, and soon she was taking part in a kiss as never before.

Then his hand found her left nipple. He cupped her breast and rubbed a thumb back and forth across her bodice. The shimmer beneath her skin caught fire, and her nipple was like a flashpoint of heat. And still his thumb continued back and forth, back and forth, like kindling added to the fire. Her breast swelled, her breath caught, and it became too much. Too hot, too hungry, too . . . too much.

She gasped and spun away, her forearms clutched against her breasts. She felt the hard center of her nipples and the ache that they had become. Her breath still came in stuttering gasps and she half stepped, half stumbled backward. He caught her, of course, beneath the elbow with his warm, strong support. He held her up effortlessly while his eyes narrowed and his expression tightened with confusion.

And into that long moment came a whistle. The teakettle, finally ready. Perhaps it had been singing for a while. She did not know. But at least it gave her something to focus on rather than her thudding heart. She straightened, meaning to go to it, but he was faster. As she supported her own weight, he released her arm and crossed to the kettle. Not seeing the rag, he used his own jacket sleeve to pick it up. He'd already set the leaves in the pot, and so he poured. The leaves were steeping in less than a minute, and then he finally turned to stare at her.

She swallowed. Surely an independent woman such as herself would have something to say. But her body was still not her own. The overwhelming feelings were beginning to fade, but they were replaced with a keen yearning to be touched like that again.

"So," he said slowly. "You were never Lord Metzger's mistress."

Chapter 7

Helaine felt a flare of panic choke through her. "N-no. Of course I was Lord Metzger's—"

"In name, of course," he interrupted. "But his mistress in fact? You were never that."

She tried to read his expression, but couldn't, perhaps because she was still struggling to manage her own tempestuous emotions. All she could tell was that there was no point in further lies.

"How did you know?" she asked.

"Your kiss, though beyond delightful, was not the kiss of a seasoned courtesan."

She had a flash of illogical jealousy that he should know these things and she should not. How many courtesans had he kissed? How many innocents? Meanwhile, he folded his arms across his chest and gazed at her.

"How did this happen? Did Metzger lie? Were you not able to defend your reputation?" There was anger in his tone.

"No!" she gasped. "No. He was an old family friend and . . ." How to explain this without revealing too much? "He had cause to feel sorry for me. So one day, he suggested the ruse. He was a powerful man at the time. I went to a few balls on his sleeve and once kissed him beneath the mistletoe when we were sure we were observed."

"But it never went further." A statement, not a question.

"He was a good man. I was sorry for his passing."

She saw him wince and understood too late that her words implied that Lord Redhill was *not* a good man. After all, he had just pushed for a great deal more than a kiss. She had no answer to that. He had done nothing more than what all men did. They saw a woman they wanted and took steps to own her. At least he had stopped when she pulled away. Many men would have pursued her. They would have pushed her up against the worktable and done as they willed. And damn her traitorous blood for wondering what that would be like with Lord Redhill.

But she could not allow herself to be tempted back into his arms. This man was no aging statesman like her former protector. There would be no lie between them. He would own her as a man owns a mistress. And so she forced herself to move away from him. She unwound Wendy's scarf and folded it neatly back into the box. She kept her back to him, though her body prickled with awareness. And when she finally forced herself to look at him, he stood in the kitchen with the tea tray in his hands. It was such an odd sight that she stared. Never did she think to see him standing there like a butler holding a tray.

"I thought we would have the tea in the front room," he said, his voice a low rumble that she felt in her belly.

She nodded, unable to speak. Then it became clear that he was waiting for her to precede him, so she rushed ahead, nearly tripping over her own feet in her haste to move. She collapsed back into the settee, barely holding on to her dignity as he set the tray down. His movements were smooth, his expression blank. One would think he had spent years as a butler, so impassive was his expression. But then he sat down in the chair again and looked at her.

"Should I pour?"

"Oh! No!" Damn her scattered wits. She needed to think.

"Cream? Sugar?" she asked, grateful that her voice had regained some strength.

"Just sugar."

She finished pouring, then offered it to him. He took it without touching her fingertips, and she stupidly mourned the lack of his caress even though she had expressly set her hand such that he would not touch her. Then she poured for herself and was soon able to take a fortifying sip of the plain tea. He had made it strong, which bolstered her even more. There was no subtlety in the flavor, no fruity or floral notes. Simple English tea, and it reminded her more than anything that she was meant for plain things. Expensive teas, sheer scarves, and silk sheets were the distractions men used to get what they wanted. And as intriguing as the idea was, she had no room in her life for such things. The cost was too high.

She was still settling her nerves when he spoke, his words gentle and wholly unexpected.

"What is your Christian name?" he asked. The question was so surprising that she lifted her eyes in surprise.

"Helaine," she said, forgetting herself enough to give him her real name. When pressed, Mrs. Mortimer told everyone her name was Helen.

"A beautiful name. Mine is Robert."

She nodded in acknowledgment, though she would never call him that.

"I have handled this incorrectly, Helaine, but the desire remains. I should like you to be my mistress."

"And I desire to be an honest dressmaker who isn't constantly accosted." She did not invest her words with anger. She simply stated it and prayed he would hear her.

He did understand her implication. His wince was proof of that. But that didn't stop him from pleading his case. "I am a slow lover, Helaine, patient and generally considerate. And though I have never taken a virgin, I would make an exception for you. I would introduce you correctly to this business. And would pay handsomely for the privilege."

He paused, but when she didn't speak, he leaned forward.

She could tell he meant to touch her hands, but she kept herself firmly away. Despite her aloof position, his words were tempting her, especially as he continued to speak in that low, throaty voice that seemed to settle into her bones.

"We could make whatever arrangements you desire, though I do ask that my sister not find out."

"Oh, no!" she gasped, horrified by the very idea.

He gave her a wry look. "I see we are in agreement on that. My demands would not be heavy, and I can let rooms nearby for our use. It might take me a bit to get all arranged. The financials can be slow sometimes, but I will pay. Forgive me for being blunt, Helaine, but are you a virgin?"

Her cheeks flamed at that, but she managed to nod.

"Do not be embarrassed. Virginity is an excellent thing. And the usual price for it is rather exorbitant." He named a figure that would easily cover her expenses for months. One that would pay for enough fabric for a dozen trousseaus. "I would give that to you on our first night. Then you would have a monthly allowance afterward. And when we separate, that money plus any gifts would be yours to keep."

She knew she was staring at him, the shock apparent in every line of her body. This was the strangest conversation she'd ever had. Did all men simply arrange their sexual affairs in such a businesslike fashion? Apparently so. Probably because plain speaking was best for this sort of thing. But she couldn't help wishing for some pretty phrases, some wooing before the deed was done.

He must have taken her silence as agreement. He must have believed he had accomplished his task, because he smiled at her then. The expression transformed him from cool aristocrat to a satisfied man, much like her father after a really excellent night of drinking.

"What say you, Helaine? Have we made a bargain?" From his tone, she could tell he expected her to say yes. She didn't.

She shook her head. "I am a dressmaker, my lord. I am afraid my skills for anything else are sorely lacking."

His eyes seemed to glitter at that, and she couldn't tell if it was laughter or anticipation. Either way, it added to the feel of a man very content with his lot. "I assure you, a lack of skill is expected in a virgin. And you may be a dressmaker, but you are also a beautiful woman. One, I might add, who has advertised herself as a man's mistress for quite some time. You lose nothing by becoming one in truth and have much to gain."

"What do I gain, my lord? Money? A protector?"

"All of those things."

"And what if I don't want them?"

He arched a single eyebrow. "But you do need them. Money most certainly, but also a protector. Otherwise you would not have played the game with Lord Metzger."

He had her there. "But what if I don't *want* it?"

"That also is patently false. Do you deny it?"

She couldn't deny it, but her pride made her press her lips together. She'd be damned if she admitted it. He was becoming much too sure of himself, too certain of her, and she didn't like it. So she leaned back on the settee and crossed her arms. She was well aware of what the action did to her breasts, lifting them up such that her cleavage was on display. As expected, his gaze dropped straight to her chest. But of course, she was equally the fool here because at his intense stare, her blood heated, her nipples tightened, and she began to think of saying yes. So she forced the denial out quickly before she could change her mind.

"My life is different now than when I made my bargain with Lord Metzger. I am not alone anymore. I have a shop that I love, people who care for me—"

"And Johnny Bono fondling you between a bolt of muslin and a crate of onions. Do not think I have forgotten about that. Indeed, just say yes and your difficulties with that character will end."

"I would be simply trading one man for another. One type of abuse for another."

Her words were a challenge to him, but she never anticipated how much. His mouth tightened and his eyes glittered cold with fury. "Never suggest he and I are of the same cloth, Helaine."

Honesty forced her to admit the truth, but her pride kept her from making it an apology. "Not of the same cloth certainly, but of the same intent."

"I will never force you."

"You merely point out my vulnerabilities, and offer to save me from them one by one."

He nodded. "That is what men do, is it not? They save their women from danger."

There it was. The last piece she needed to strengthen her spine and convince her to say no. He had no idea how hard she had fought for her independence. For her room above the shop, for a purpose and profession that brought money to her. Money that was hers and hers alone. She still feared debtors' prison, but for now, she would not trade her independence away.

"You forget that I have no need of rescuing. Ladies come to my door every day asking for my dresses. And as for Mr. Bono, I have handled his attentions for years now; I shall undoubtedly continue to manage for many years to come. So you may keep your money and your rooms. I am quite content as I am."

"Really?" he drawled, the word a sensuous caress that throbbed deep in her belly. "And what of pleasure?"

"Do you know," she said, feigning a cheerfulness she did not feel, "I believe that men derive a great deal more satisfaction from carnal pleasures than women. I assure you," she lied, "I will rub along quite nicely without it."

"That, sweet Helaine, would be a crying shame."

She had no answer to that. She had little understanding of the pleasures of the flesh. Many a night she had slept in her cold bed and wondered about them. What did married women know that she did not? And would she ever learn?

Apparently not, because she pushed to her feet. "Thank you for your offer, my lord, but I am not interested."

He stood because she'd forced him to. The man was too polite to stay seated before a woman, even a woman who had just refused him. "I have not finished, Helaine. I still need to know what Johnny Bono holds over you."

She shook her head. "Nothing except that he is the only one who will sell me fabric on credit."

"That, at least, I can change. Name the best fabric merchant in London. I shall contact him directly and tell him my sister has engaged you to make her trousseau. He should extend you credit immediately."

She blinked, the magnitude of what he was offering hitting her broadside. "You would do that even though I refused you?"

"Of course," he said, sounding vaguely insulted. "I cannot have my sister or her dressmaker subjected to a scene like that one again. And as for your refusal, let us say that the matter has been tabled for the moment. I am not a man to be put off so easily."

Excitement shivered down her spine, and she did her best to suppress it. "Years ago, I would have swooned at the idea. I would have lain awake nights wondering if you would ask me to dance or bring me a posy." She sighed and let her thoughts turn to the intervening years. The daily struggle against starvation, the nightly fight against despair. The girl she'd once been was long gone. In her place stood a woman who had learned to be cautious. Thrills were never worth the risk. And men, no matter how charming, were liars.

"What are you thinking, Helaine?" he asked. "You look so sad. I assure you, what I offer will not turn out badly."

She laughed at that, though there was little humor in the sound. "There is always a cost for pleasure, my lord. And it is always the woman who pays."

He reared back at that, but he did not step away. Indeed, a moment later, he was beside her, his hand reaching for her face. "It is not always so, Helaine—"

"It is." She grabbed his fingers and forced them back. He didn't fight her. She could not have done it if he had. Instead, he twined his fingers around hers and stroked his thumb into her palm. "I can see that you will take some convincing."

"My maidenhead is not for sale."

"I was not speaking of your virginity, Helaine. Merely

of my intentions. I have underestimated you. I see that now. I look forward to the chase."

Alarm beat equal pace with excitement in her heart. "My lord—," she began, but he cut her off.

"The name of the best fabric merchant, Mrs. Mortimer. You have not told me what it is."

She blinked, too startled by his change of topic to think clearly. "Wolferman's," she answered.

"You should hear from them by tomorrow morning." He flashed her a smile. "And from me some day—or night—after that."

Then he bowed over her hand and showed himself out. He moved slowly enough that she could have stopped him. She had time to say something haughty or dismissive or even polite. But he had confused her. In truth, he had excited her, nearly seduced her, tempted her, and reassured her, all in the space of an hour. She had no words left in her, much less any wit.

And then it came to her. Just before the door closed behind him, she rushed to the opening to call after him. "My lord!"

He stopped and turned back to her. "Helaine?"

"You caught me unprepared today." She took a step outside into the sunlight. She straightened to her full height and mentally wrapped herself in all the good things she had done since her father had doomed them all. She was a strong woman, and no man could take that from her. "I was surprised and confused. But no longer. You will not find me so malleable ever again."

He arched his brows. "I hardly think you malleable, Helaine."

She shrugged. "Nevertheless."

He bent in the most courtly of bows. "Then let the games begin."

Chapter 8

❧❧❦

"Tea, Wendy. He sent me tea!"

Wendy didn't look away from where she was expertly threading a needle even in the evening's poor light. "Well, what of it?"

"He sent me *cheap* tea!"

Now Wendy did look up from her stitching. "Really? But he's a viscount. Would he even know where to find cheap tea?"

"Yes!" She set the tea tin down on the worktable and glared at it. "It's the exact tea from the exact shop where I usually buy it. He must have read the tin."

"Blimey, but how could he even find it? It can't possibly be on any of his usual routes." Wendy did the unheard-of act of setting down her sewing to cross to the far side of the worktable where the tin rested. "There's a note here."

"Yes, I know."

Wendy peered down at it, turning it this way and that. "What does it say? I can't make out all the words." In her spare time, Wendy was paying Helaine's mother to teach her to read. She was absolutely determined to better herself and that included being literate. Plus, it had the added benefit of giving Helaine's mother something to do.

Helaine picked it up and pointed to the words one by one, though she'd already memorized the entire note. "To Mrs. Mortimer. I greatly enjoyed our tea, but I fear we finished your tin. Please accept this replacement as a token of my esteem. I have duplicated exactly the blend you prefer, but should you wish for something different, something that gives more pleasure, simply tell the proprietor of this establishment. He has already been directed to provide you with whatever blend of sweet or spicy that most satisfies your heart. In fact, if I might be so bold, there is an oriental blend that I particularly enjoy as it seems to surprise me every time I drink it. I think it might suit you perfectly."

"But what's this letter 'R' here for?"

"That's his signature. It stands for Robert, his Christian name."

"Coo," said Wendy, her eyes huge. "Using a lord's Christian name, are you now? Even if he is an odd one."

"He's odd like a fox," she said as she plopped down morosely onto her desk chair. The note was a ploy to intrigue her, to tempt her, to get her to *think* about him and about each and every bizarre word in the letter. And it was working! She hadn't stopped thinking about him since the damn gift arrived. What should she do? Should she accept the terrible cheap tea or go back and select the most special, most expensive blend she could imagine? Would he learn of what she did? Of course he would. But how would he interpret it?

And if that weren't enough, she had a dozen or more questions about the wording of the letter itself. She'd examined everything from his unusual signature to the word "pleasure," which had indeed sent a very unwelcome shiver of delight down her spine. And what about the part about an oriental blend that surprised him? Why did he think it would suit her? Was he suggesting that she surprised him?

Or that she liked being surprised, which she didn't. She absolutely did not!

And most important of all, how did she respond to a letter like this? It was most improper, that was to be sure. Or it would be, if she were still Lady Helaine. But she wasn't that girl anymore; she was Mrs. Mortimer, a supposed courtesan. But she was also a woman who had just received her first gift from an admirer in nearly five years. That alone made her cherish it, if it weren't so blasted aggravating!

"Tea!" she huffed. "What am I to say to tea?"

Wendy had returned to her stitching. "What is there to respond? Go buy that oriental stuff and say thank you, all sweet like, so that he'll give you some more."

Helaine sighed. If only it were that simple. "He will think I accept everything else about him then. Everything else he *wants*."

Wendy didn't even spare her a glance. "He wants what he wants. All men do. More fool him if he thinks accepting some tea is the same as saying yes to everything else."

"True," she said, knowing her friend's logic was sound. Except that she couldn't shake the feeling that she needed to be more careful in her response. Exactly how would he interpret it if she went ahead and picked out new tea? Or, more dangerous yet, the tea he suggested?

"Unless . . . ," said Wendy, her voice taking on a sly tone that made Helaine glance up. "Unless you want the same thing 'e wants. Then I'd be much more careful in what I pick. Then I'd be choosing a tea that was sweet and spicy, jes' like he said."

"But that is exactly the kind of tea I like! The oriental kind that tastes exotic and special. He will never believe that I picked it out because it is just what I want and not because he suggested it. Ugh!"

Wendy burst out laughing at Helaine's disgusted sound. "You are thinking too much about it. Buy the tea. Enjoy it! And maybe you'll enjoy a mite more at the same time."

"I cannot," Helaine said, regret dragging at her every word. "I simply cannot."

Wendy shrugged. "Suit yourself. But if it were me, I'd get the oriental blend."

"If it were you, you'd pick up your mum's favorite black tea and not think two snips about it." That was because Wendy was of a practical mindset. And usually Helaine was, too. But not now. Not when it came to the devilishly handsome and vastly intriguing Lord Redhill.

She was still thinking about the problem the next morning when the first of three messengers arrived. Not letters, not notes, but actual messengers from the top three fabric merchants in London. All of them sent senior clerks who informed her most solicitously that they would welcome her business on credit. One even told her that his firm had set aside a special blue silk just for her perusal.

Unlike the tea, this was a gift she could not afford to refuse. She instructed each clerk that her agent would be contacting them shortly, then she dashed off a note to Irene. With this type of leverage, her friend would be able to negotiate incredible deals. Finally, their little shop had hope of success. So she decided to express her gratitude to his lordship. But how? Perhaps at her favorite tea shop.

She found the proprietor of the tea and medicine shop to be in an excellent mood. Mr. Withers was a generally pinched and tiny man, worn down by the day-to-day difficulties of trying to survive. His shop generally serviced struggling workers, and he was besieged daily by desperate people hoping to get miracle medicines for cheap. To have someone of Lord Redhill's status visit him was exactly the boon everyone in business prayed for. And she could tell by the width of his smile that he had no intention of letting any link to Lord Redhill disappear. Which meant, of course, that he was intent on maximizing his connection with her.

"Mrs. Mortimer! How pleased I am that you came to visit today! Do you know I have been mixing a new special blend? Pray try it. I had you in mind when I began it, you know. You have always been such a delight whenever you visit. Why, just the other day . . ."

"Please stop," she said. Once she had expected such immediate attention as her due, but now she found it unsettling. She had been walking into this shop for years now and rarely exchanged more than the most cursory pleasantries. Such overflowing of words from him left her distinctly uncomfortable. "I have merely come for some tea."

"Yes, yes, the oriental blend."

"No. Please."

"Oh, dear," he moaned, his face positively drooping with dismay. "He told me you might be difficult. He said I should insist, though. Indeed, he told me if you didn't come here today that I was to send on the blend anyway to your shop. Please don't make me do that, Mrs. Mortimer. My dear Millie would have to make the delivery, and you know how her feet ail her so."

His dear Millie did indeed have aching feet, as did everyone else in this area of London. "Mr. Withers, I wish to purchase some tea to send to his lordship. By way of thanks."

"Of course, of course! I was just mixing a special blend, as I said. One especially for lovers," he added with a wink.

"What? No!" She should have expected this. She'd forgotten that she was no longer the daughter of an earl, one who could receive a gift from an admirer without people assuming the worst. But not now. Not as Mrs. Mortimer. Her gift of tea meant something else entirely. "His lordship and I are merely acquaintances."

"Of course, of course," he said, nodding his bald pate. "Discretion is always important."

Obviously he didn't understand that discretion meant going about business as usual. Not scraping and fawning over her.

"My purchase, Mr. Withers?"

"Yes, yes. As I said, my special blend."

"Absolutely not! I wish something else. A dark tea, I believe."

"An Earl Grey, perhaps? That's very masculine."

She nodded. But it needed something else. Something

that was reminiscent of his lordship. "What if you add extra bergamot? To make it especially strong."

"Yes, yes, but a bit overpowering, don't you think?"

Exactly like his lordship, in her opinion. But Mr. Withers had a better idea.

"Perhaps we could soften the brew a bit. Add a touch of lightness, perhaps? A fruit or a spice?"

She didn't want to admit that Lord Redhill had a lighter side, but she knew he must. He had a sister who adored him, and by all accounts he was the strength behind the title. "Raspberry," she abruptly said. She had no idea why she thought a small bumpy fruit was appropriate for his lordship, but it just seemed to fit.

"An excellent choice!" Mr. Withers crowed.

"How much will a small tin cost?" she asked.

"Oh, my, I'm sure you don't want a small tin."

"I'm sure I do," she returned firmly, knowing she would have to bargain quite sternly from now on. Once the local merchants heard that she was sending and receiving presents from Lord Redhill, the price for everything would soar.

Sure enough, Mr. Withers quoted an exorbitant price. She countered, and the bargaining went on tediously. In the end, she had to threaten to find another shop before he came to a reasonable cost. Eventually it was done, and "poor Millie" was thrilled to deliver the package herself despite her aching feet. All it took was for Helaine to seal the note that was to accompany the gift; then she added another missive for Lady Gwen and a third for Dribbs. She handed over the last of her meager coins. Fortunately, they were expecting payment from Francine's father at any moment, so they wouldn't starve for long. Or so she hoped. In the meantime, she needed to maximize the business she already had.

It was time to start discussing Gwen's wedding shoes. A dress was just a dress, after all, even if one did get married in it. Most brides wore their dress again every Sunday afterward to church. But what the newly married truly cherished, what lay on the mantel for their daughters to exclaim over, were the wedding shoes. There would have to be ample room on the sole for the minister to write the bride and groom's name, along with the date. The fabric would have to be delicate enough for a beautiful bride, but sturdy enough to be worn all day if need be. And the color had to exactly match the gown.

Which is why she headed directly for the Shoemakers' shop. But when she arrived at their door, she received quite a shock. The store was closed. Helaine was a breath away from leaving when she heard the babe.

A child was wailing, and from the desperation in the sound, she guessed he had been crying for some time. Helaine could not go in through the store, but she knew the right stairs and climbed to knock on the door to the rooms above. No one answered, but when she tried the latch, it opened easily. Surely the Shoemakers would not have simply gone out and left the babe alone, would they? Surely not.

She walked through the narrow hallway, wrinkling her nose in the fetid air. No smell of sick, but the babe was surely messy. Where was everyone? Growing more alarmed by the second, Helaine found the child. He was perhaps eight months, old enough to stand in his crib and wail, but not old enough to climb down and make free about the home.

Helaine was not skilled with children, but she knew enough to hand him a toy and change his diaper. After that, she was at a loss.

"Let's say we find you some bread, shall we?" she murmured as she carried him to the kitchen. She found nothing, not even a bit of cheese or moldy bread. What had happened here? Everything seemed in order, but no one was here. Then she heard a light tread on the stair. A moment later Penny appeared, her face as worn as Helaine had ever seen. What the boy saw, however, was the loaf of black bread in the girl's hands and he immediately began wiggling to be free.

"Oh! Oh, my!" Penny cried when she saw Helaine. "Whatever are you—ach, yes, yes, Tommy. Here's your dinner." The girl ripped off a hunk of the bread, then quickly peeled the hard crust away. She gave the child the soft center and he immediately stuffed it in his mouth. "I only stepped to the baker's just down the way," the girl said. "Just a moment because he was asleep. There was nothing in the house and we needed the food."

"But where are your parents, Penny? What has happened?"

The girl started to respond. She opened her mouth, she tried to speak, but no sound came out. And then the tears began to flow. Without noise. And without an interruption in movement of bread to the child. Tears just leaked from her eyes in a steady stream.

"Oh, no," whispered Helaine. It had been awhile since she'd come by their shop. Lady Gwen was Helaine's first wealthy bride, and so the first customer who required shoes. "Oh, Penny," she asked, "is it just you and the boy now?"

The girl nodded miserably, doing her best to wipe away her tears and still feed the boy. Helaine reached out and gave the girl a hug. In truth, it was unfair of her to think of Penny as so young. Though still small, almost pixielike, Penny had to be in her early twenties by now.

With sudden resolve, Helaine took the bread from the girl's hand. "Here, I'll feed your son. You pack a bag. For tonight, at least, you will stay with me. I won't hear a word against it. Honestly, you will be doing me a favor. Mama has nothing to do all day but sit and mourn everything she has lost. So, quick now. Before it gets dark."

Penny released the bread to Helaine, but she didn't move. Her eyes were huge and so full of sorrow that it broke Helaine's heart. "But I cannot, Lady Helaine. It wouldn't be right."

It had been so long since anyone had used her true name that the words actually gave her a start. It sounded so foreign. "I am Mrs. Mortimer now. While you are packing, you must tell me how you came to have this handsome boy here for a son."

Penny gave in. She grabbed a satchel and put in spare cloths for the child and some very worn clothes for them both. Then the three of them began the walk to the dress shop, though God only knew how Helaine would house them. There was barely enough room for herself and her mother above the shop. As for food, there was some soup left. Enough for two, but not for four. And Helaine had just spent her last coin on Lord Redhill's tea.

But perhaps there was something she could manage. She was still thinking about what she would do when Penny finally found the voice to talk.

"He's not my son, Mrs. Mortimer," she said. "He's my brother now, but he was my cousin. Mama's sister died of childbed fever. We don't know where his father is. He's a seaman and like as not won't be coming back. So he came to be with us. Papa declared him the son he never had, and so he's my brother now."

Helaine arched a brow and looked down at the girl. "Of course. How terrible," she said. She didn't believe a word of it. Many a girl had gotten pregnant and disappeared for a while, only to return with a new "cousin" come to stay. But given her own sordid history, Helaine had no right poking holes in anyone else's tale. "That must have been very hard on your mother."

"Mama cried on and off for the first month. But only when Tommy slept. Then after that, she was too busy to cry. And Papa was too happy to finally have a boy to learn the trade."

"Your father made beautiful shoes. I still remember the pair my father bought himself for Christmas one year. They were perfect, and he said they fit like a dream."

Penny didn't answer, and too late Helaine realized that it had been a mistake to mention her father. Penny was one of the few people who knew the truth of her past, knew exactly who her father had been. She couldn't risk that information getting out. She couldn't allow any of her customers to know her real name. They would frequent the shop of a known courtesan, but would never come to one owned by the daughter of the Thief of the Ton.

"Penny," she began, hoping the panic didn't show in her voice. "Penny, if you are to stay with me, you must remember: I'm Mrs. Helen Mortimer now. A dressmaker. Anything

I might have been before, *anyone* I might have known before, is gone. Dead and gone. Do you understand?"

Penny finally lifted her chin, her eyes round with surprise and then a slow understanding. "That wasn't your fault, what your father did. Everyone knows that."

"No, my dear, they don't." Helaine stopped walking. They were at the top of an alley underneath a single large maple that had somehow survived the growth of the city around it. Tommy had finished his bread and was squirming to get down. Though it saddened her to do it, Helaine passed the boy back to Penny. She had to make the girl understand. "Surely you know about mistakes, Penny? About wanting to start again fresh and new?" She glanced significantly at the child. "My other life, my other name, is gone. You cannot tell a soul about it."

An odd expression flicked over Penny's face, a deep hurt as if Helaine had wounded her. "I understand, Mrs. Mortimer. I won't tell a soul."

Helaine released a breath, relieved all the way down to her toes. She remembered Penny as a quiet girl with large eyes and a clever mind. She didn't think the girl would be one to gossip. "That's good. If you can manage, the shop is not far from here."

They started walking again in silence. It might have been awkward except that it was filled with babbling sounds from little Tommy. They were nearly there when Helaine at last found the words to break the silence between them.

"My mother will ask, you know. She was never one for discretion, not when you are to stay in our home with us. Will you tell us what happened to your family? Or shall I make something up?"

Penny lifted up the boy in her arms, tucking his head against her shoulder. She rubbed her cheek against the curly mop of his hair as if for comfort. But when she spoke, her words were clear and calm and filled with such anger that it stunned Helaine.

"My parents were murdered. Nearly six weeks ago. The creditors came and took everything they could. I have only our home, no money, and no one to care for Tommy while I look for work." Then she lifted her head off the boy and looked Helaine in the eye. "So if you want me to keep your secret, you must make a bargain with me. Or I shall tell everyone who you are and what your father did."

Chapter 9

➤✦◄

Robert frowned at his desk, not at all pleased with the correspondence lying before him. There were the usual three piles. The first was a to-do pile of decisions regarding the family investments. It included letters from his stewards, management reports, articles, and a variety of scientific discussions regarding everything from mining to fishing rights. It was a very large pile and it sat at the top of his desk.

At the far left where he really didn't want to look was the pile he called "family melancholia." This included his father's latest ideas, reports about his younger brother's Grand Tour of debauchery through Europe, and finally the doctor's missive on his mother's ailment. She had chronic pain, or so she claimed. Mostly, the woman just sat in the dark and stared at the fire. Some days she didn't even get out of bed. The pile was dubbed "melancholia" because, despite his best efforts, he had been singularly unable to affect any aspect of that pile. His father had more wild ideas every day; his brother, Jack, obviously planned to seduce every female on the Continent; and his mother would not step out of her room. So whenever he looked at that pile, he was buried beneath a tide of sadness mixed with futility. It had gotten so bad lately that he'd ordered Dribbs to put a full, bushy plant on top of the pile. The man never did, of course, but he did keep a full bottle of brandy nearby.

The third pile was easier to deal with, but no less small. It was simply bills. And his family had a lot of bills.

But none of those piles were the subject of his current disgust. No, what lay before him dead center was two notes. One from the delectable Helaine and another from Charlie, the new mine manager. Helaine's note held his attention the most. He smiled at the rough linen paper, held it to his nose to detect the faint sprinkling of lemon, and even traced his fingertip over her soft curving letters. Very feminine, to his mind, and also unusually fine penmanship for a girl of the middle classes, even a courtesan. So she must have had a decent education. All of that made him smile. Her words, however, did not.

> *To Lord Redhill,*
>
> *Three vendors visited me this morning with offers of credit. Thanks to your efforts, I have hopes of establishing my little shop as a premier dressmaker to the* ton. *Words cannot adequately express my thanks. All I can do is to offer this humble token of tea for your enjoyment as it reminds me of you. Please know that my deepest expression of gratitude will come to you through your sister. I shall work tirelessly so that she is the most beautiful bride any woman could hope to be.*
>
> > *With humble thanks,*
> > *Mrs. H. Mortimer*

Robert snorted as he read it through again. He did not want her gratitude, and he certainly did not want it expressed *through his sister.* The very idea made him slightly queasy. Of course that was clearly the point. It was rather repulsive to think of his mistress also being his sister's dressmaker.

Only a madman would pursue such a thing, especially against both ladies' wishes.

And yet he could not stop himself. Helaine drew him. She challenged his mind, she roused his protective instincts, and she made him harder than granite. No woman of his acquaintance had ever done all three things. He had barely spent more than a couple hours in her presence and yet he'd spent the better part of the last two days thinking of more ways to intrigue her. Intrigue her, tempt her, then seduce her. That was his plan, and he was spending an inordinate amount of time thinking of ways to do it.

The other letter on his desk was not nearly so enticing. It was from Charlie, the young man who had shown such strength of character down in the mines that one benighted day. After firing the old manager, Robert had promoted Charlie to the job. The boy wrote that the sacked Mr. Hutchins was stirring up the workers. He said that men who had not one month ago cursed Hutchins's name were now following him as he fostered a revolt. It was all because Robert had shut down the mine for repairs. He would not allow one man, woman, or child inside the damn place until it was safe to do so. But men out of work had little to do but curse the people in charge. And Robert's other decree, that he would hire no woman and no child under the age of twelve, had hit some families hard. They needed the extra income. Which meant that the whole area was a powder keg of unrest.

Damn. It would take more money and more time to settle this peacefully. And that would take him away from London when he really wished to be with Helaine. Enough dithering, he told himself sternly. It was time for action. So thinking, he grabbed his own stationery and pen. Two minutes later he had invited the lady to share tea with him at a small, intimate café. If she wanted to express her gratitude, then she could do so in person. Where he could persuade her to be more demonstrative of her thanks. A minute later, he rang his bell for Dribbs.

"Dribbs, I need you to send a footman to deliver a note for me, if you would."

There was a deafening silence as his butler hesitated at the door, neither coming closer to grab the letter nor stepping outside to call for a footman.

Robert looked up with a frown. "Dribbs?"

"Er, might I inquire, my lord, is that perhaps a missive for Mrs. Mortimer, the dressmaker?"

Robert straightened up with a frown. "My correspondence is none of your concern, Dribbs, just the delivery. Any competent butler would know that."

The man colored a dark red to the tips of his ears, but he did not back down. "Of course, my lord," he said. "But it may interest you to know that I also received a note from Mrs. Mortimer."

Robert felt his eyebrows rise almost into his hairline. "Did you?" he asked, his voice deceptively low. "I can't imagine what about."

"Well, my lord, she bade me to make a pot of your new tea directly, and . . . um . . ."

"Spit it out, man."

He didn't spit it out. In fact, he dashed out of the room only to return a second later with the tea tray. On it was a steaming pot of tea, presumably with the leaves already brewing. The tea, he recalled, that Helaine had sent. The tea that reminded her of him. He took a tentative sniff and felt his sinuses clear. Good Lord, but that was strong stuff. Meanwhile, Dribbs finished setting out the tray, but he didn't leave. Instead he stood there, still flushed a dark red, and with a clear apology in his eye.

"She said something else, didn't she?" Robert asked.

"Yes, my lord. She said if you were to write her a letter or in any way try to contact her, I was supposed to give you something. And say something."

Robert leaned back, surprise and pleasure slipping through his mind. "Go on."

"She said that she hopes you enjoy this rather strong,

almost overbearing brew. And that while you are drinking, you might enjoy some reading material." At which point, Dribbs held out a political pamphlet.

Robert took it, frowning as he saw an unfamiliar woman's name as the author. A quick glance, however, had him bursting out with laughter. The opening lines asked these questions: *Why can't women have productive careers? Why are we forced to choose between becoming a wife or a whore with nothing in between?* It went on to claim that a woman without a man was perforce expected to become a mistress. She was barred from most legitimate trades and occupations. And even the lower orders such as maids and cooks were subjected to the lewd and unwanted advances of their employers. Almost as if the men believed that if a woman had no protector, she must wish to be a whore.

The message from Helaine was obvious. Coupled with her statement that this overbearing tea reminded her of him, she was sending him a well-deserved slap. After all, she had refused him. And when he thought to ignore her refusal, she turned his own butler against him.

"Clever woman," he said as he continued to scan the pamphlet. Sadly, he did indeed recognize the attitudes described in the treatise. Other men of his set, and certainly his own father, believed the female staff existed to serve his needs—sexual and otherwise. He had not until this moment put himself in that category.

Meanwhile, Dribbs was shifting awkwardly from foot to foot, obviously nervous about his employer's reaction. Robert barely spared him a glance.

"Never fear, Dribbs. You are not about to be punished, but do try to recall that you work for me and not Mrs. Mortimer."

"Of course, my lord. Did you . . . would you still like me to call a footman for your letter?"

"No, no. I shall have to write something else now." Then, while Dribbs was bowing himself out, Robert took his first sip of the tea, which surprised him by being rather delightful. It was bold, strong, and with a hint of something sweet underneath that kept it from being crass. In truth, it reminded him of her.

He continued to sip his tea and think of her. He also read her pamphlet from cover to cover, then, when that was done, he turned his attention back to Charlie and the difficulties at the mine. It was another hour before he realized he was stuck. And another hour beyond that before he was rescued and from a most unusual source: Gwen's fiancé.

The boy was of a lanky build and quiet demeanor and had the rather prosaic name of Edward. His father had died of a fever some years back, so he had inherited the baronetcy as well as a parcel of domineering women in his mother and an aunt who had been a stern schoolteacher. He had a younger brother who was off at school and a sister who was growing up to resemble the mother, more's the pity. And yet, this quiet, henpecked boy, who looked just like an Edward ought, had somehow captivated the vivacious Lady Gwen.

Exactly how he had done it was a mystery Robert wanted to solve. And given that Robert was doing nothing more than sipping cold tea and staring at correspondence that annoyed him, the sound of Edward's voice in the hallway was a welcome distraction. When the boy requested a moment of his time, it seemed like a gift from heaven. When Dribbs opened the door, Robert bade the boy to please sit down, by God. He ordered something stronger than tea, too, though, given this tea, he wasn't sure anything but a stiff brandy would qualify.

"Hello, hello, Edward," Robert began with a warm smile. "What brings you here this afternoon?"

"Escaping my mother and aunt, of course," said the boy as he dropped into the leather chair by the fire. "Must tell you how sorry I am that we rented the house next door. You're not used to having all those women squawking about, and I've talked to them about making too free with your door, but they don't listen. Not yet, at least. But if you want them barred, I'll see to it."

Robert took a moment to stare at the boy. Edward wasn't

fidgeting, just sitting there with an open-eyed honesty. "You're asking me if I want to bar your mother from my doorstep a few weeks before your wedding?"

"My mother, my aunt, and my sister. Yes, my lord. And myself, too, if you wish, though I'd be sad 'bout that, you understand."

"But you're about to marry my sister."

The boy grinned. "Exactly. I'm stuck with my kin, you see, but you aren't. And I can't see the point of upsetting my future brother-in-law just because my mother likes to poke around where she's not wanted."

Robert tried to think back. "Has she poked herself somewhere she wasn't wanted?"

"Well, she did rearrange your mother's thingy-bobs."

Robert raised his eyebrows. "Thingy-bobs?"

"A shepherdess and her flock, I believe. In the salon."

Oh, that. He remembered now.

"And she bought your mother perfume, too, I believe."

Robert was busy unstopping the brandy bottle but he did manage to raise an eyebrow. "Why would I be insulted by a gift of perfume?"

"Well, she gave it to your mum by way of saying that the lady smelled and this would sweeten her up."

Robert released a snort of amusement. "My mother does smell badly at times. So maybe she will take the hint."

"And then she forced your mum to take a walk. All but abducted her. I doubt Mum could have done it alone, but she had my aunt and sis with her. To hear them tell it, they grabbed both of your mum's arms and just lifted. Then didn't stop until they were blocks away."

Robert set the brandy down, his mouth slack with astonishment. "They forced my mother to walk with them?"

"Yes, my lord."

"But she hasn't been out of the house in . . . in three years."

"So I was given to understand. Which was the final straw, you see. I don't listen to half what they say, but that was too much. If your mother's of a delicate constitution, she won't be proof against the women of my family. They're too much for most men, you see. And, well, I wouldn't want to overset something you had placed in balance. But that's what my mum does, you see. Oversets things that are in balance. Which leaves the rest of us to put everything back in order."

"You mean you do it," Robert said. "You put everything back in balance."

"Well, I am the man of the household. It is my duty, and all."

"By asking me if I want to bar your family from my door."

"Yes, my lord."

Robert just stared at the boy. The man wasn't more than twenty-two years old. He hadn't even fully grown into his adult stature yet. He was too lanky by half, too much arms and legs and ears. And he did have rather large ears. Yet here he was, talking to a future earl about balance and barring his mother and the like.

"My God, that's how you caught her," he breathed, shock in every syllable.

"My lord?"

"That's how you caught Gwen. You . . . you balanced her."

Edward's mouth dropped a measure, and his face colored up to his ears. "I can't say that I would ever manage your sister as such. That's not at all—"

"Of course it is!" Robert cried as he set down the brandy to lean forward onto his knees. "Tell me what you did. Gwen is lively, she likes to dance, and she—forgive me, Edward— she never would have noticed you in the usual way. You don't dress well enough, you aren't even in London for most of the Season, and she even told me you hate dancing."

Edward nodded his head. "Got no sense of timing. Been told that since I was a boy."

"Well, then, what in God's name did you do to stop my sister in her tracks?"

"Oh, she did walk right on past me, my lord. Time and time again."

"Come on, out with it, boy. How'd you stop her?"

"I asked her to help me get a wallflower some dances. A particular friend of my sister's, actually. Very shy gel."

Robert leaned back in his chair. "But isn't that a gentleman's job?"

"Of course it is, and I had already danced with all the wallflowers. But as you said, I don't come to town that often. I had no influence over the other men at the dances . . ."

"But she did. My sister knows everyone and was courted by just about everyone."

The boy grinned. "She does and she was. Up until I spilled some lemonade on both ladies . . ." He paused, his ears once again coloring. "Begging your pardon, but that is exactly what I did. Splashed it everywhere, I fear, and then I . . . well, I convinced her to help out Debra. Find a man for the girl. But of course, she didn't really know Debra or what kind of man she needed."

"But you did?"

Edward shrugged. "She's a friend of my sister's from school. Came to stay with us one summer. Two years older than Connie but painfully shy."

He frowned, thinking back. "Was that the wedding of a Debra Smythe to Sir Henry Barnes? Good Lord, you arranged that? Gwen talked of nothing else for months!"

Edward raised his hands in denial. "I did nothing of the sort! That was all Gwen's doing. I just pointed out the girl." When Robert obviously didn't understand, Edward set down his own glass of brandy—untouched—and attempted to explain. "They've all got good hearts, you know. My mother and aunt, too. They just can't see how someone would want to sit in one's room for years on end."

He was talking about Robert's mother. "I don't understand it, either, but it's what she says she wants."

Edward nodded. "And you and I respect that, but not them. They think that deep down she wants to go out, so they force her to whether she thinks she wants it or not."

And maybe it was all to the good. Maybe that was exactly what his mother needed. Robert resolved to visit her later today to see if she had improved or was worsened by the interference. "But that still doesn't tell me how it got you engaged to Gwen."

"Gwen was bored, and Debra was terrified. All I needed to do was point out the imbalance to them both and they worked to solve it by themselves."

Robert remembered that Season, what little of it he paid attention to. Debra was Gwen's project. Debra seemed to be ever so grateful for the help, and eventually true love blossomed for Miss Smythe. "But how does that win you Gwen?"

"Well, once she was in balance, her good sense was restored. And there I was, being the humble progenitor of her success. So long as I didn't interfere in whatever she was doing, she and I got along famously."

"Famously," Robert echoed. "That's not what I remember." Actually the courtship had been rather tempestuous, but no one had expected anything less from Gwen. In fact, Robert had sometimes wondered if all of his mother's spirit had been poured into Gwen at an early age.

"Well," Edward said as he ducked his head to take a sip of his brandy, "you asked how I got her attention. Not how I kept it."

But Robert already knew the answer to that. Edward was an extraordinarily levelheaded young man. And that was exactly what Gwen needed. "All you did was point out a problem."

"And step back out of the way. That's most important."

"Yes, with Gwen that certainly would be." And could that, perhaps, be the solution to not one but two of his own problems? After all, what he needed was an innovative business approach to satisfy the miners and still allow the mine to be profitable. Sadly, he was fresh out of ideas, as were all of his usual confidants. There was only one other person he could think of who had already demonstrated an ability to think of different solutions and had the boldness to see them through.

Helaine, of course. After all, she was the one who'd made the unheard-of request for him to pay in advance of service. She was also the one to suggest that Gwen—an unwed girl—be allowed to make her own decisions regarding her funds. Could it be as simple as pointing Helaine at a problem and seeing if she had a solution? He had nothing to lose, especially as he had already exhausted all his other choices. Even if she had no new ideas, he would still count it a success if it got him deeper into her confidence.

"Point them at a problem," he said.

"And then step out of the way," said Edward.

"Well, of course," said Robert, not really listening. He was thinking instead of exactly what he would do once he got deep into Helaine's confidence. Of all the things he could do to her. And that she would do to him. "I'm not really the interfering sort."

"Er, that's not exactly how Gwen describes you."

"What?" Edward started to respond, but Robert waved him to silence. He didn't really want to hear what Gwen thought of him. "Look, I won't bar the door to your relations. To my mind, I've been spectacularly unable to help my mum, so if your mum can do what I can't, then I shan't interfere. But I do have one request."

"Name it."

"Have Gwen bring all the women here to get their dresses made. She can set up the dressmaker in one of the upstairs rooms. We've got women up to the rafters. Don't see why we can't have them all involved in the project. And if it gets my mum bathed and out of her bedroom, then all the better."

Edward frowned, obviously stunned. "You cannot wish to have all those women running around your home."

Robert grinned because he didn't much care about *all* the women. Just one. One beautiful dressmaker who would sleep a staircase away. "Nonsense," he said. "I'll just hole up in here or at my club. Won't make a bit of difference to me."

So it was done. Between that and asking for Helaine's advice, she was sure to tumble into his arms inside a week.

Chapter 10

❦

"*I am offering my home to you, and you're trying to* blackmail me?" Helaine could hardly credit the cheek. And yet, looking at the pale, gaunt Penny, she knew only desperation had forced the girl to do this. Desperation and a child. But that didn't make it acceptable. Or something that Helaine could simply forgive.

"No, no!" Penny gasped, obviously horrified. "I just want you to listen! I just . . . I want a chance and no one will give it to me."

"Little wonder, if you've been trying to blackmail—"

"Please!" Penny was visibly trembling. Enough that little Tommy looked up from inspecting a beetle to stare at his sister. A moment later he was crawling back. "Just listen. For a moment."

Helaine sighed. She remembered being this desperate once. She had a mother to feed, not a babe, but it amounted to the same thing. "What do you want?" she asked, her tone softening against her will.

"I know how to make shoes," she said. "I've been working with my father for years. His hands didn't work so well sometimes, and I always did for him when he couldn't."

Helaine frowned, wondering where this was going. "Then you should get an apprenticeship with one of the other shoemakers. I'm sure—"

"I tried. They won't talk to me. There are boys aplenty and no one thinks shoes made by a girl will be sturdy enough."

"But you're skilled. Your father was an artist."

Penny nodded. "They say that was my father; no one wants *me*." She blinked back the tears that Helaine knew were equal parts humiliation and desperation. But she had to be honest. Some of the work of being a cobbler was taxing. There was strength involved. Would she be inclined to buy a pair of boots if she knew they were made by a woman? Probably not. She'd be too afraid the shoes would fall apart. It didn't make sense, but her own prejudice made her understand Penny's problem.

"What about ladies' slippers?" Helaine asked. "Certainly you could do that."

"But the boys do it. The ones who don't have the strength. I could have worked with my father for years and no one would know the difference. I *was* doing his work. But now . . ." Her voice trailed away on a sob. She didn't have to finish because Helaine knew what she was saying. Now no one would hire her. Now she was a girl alone trying to support a baby.

"But what can I do about it?"

"You have a dress shop where ladies come to buy clothing."

Helaine nodded. "Yes, that's what . . ." It took her less than a moment to understand. "You think to sell shoes there. To women."

"No one need know and even if they did find out eventually, I would be a woman selling to women. Dancing shoes and the like." Penny picked up Tommy with more strength and animation than Helaine had seen from her all afternoon.

"Think what you could sell when the slippers are made of the same material and color to match the dress."

"But ladies already do that."

"But they go to different shops, different people. You could promise them excellent shoes without ever leaving your store. They would not have to walk in bad weather. I could fit them right there."

"But then they would know you are a woman."

Penny shook her head. "I would merely be helping someone else. I would be taking the sizes for the shoemaker. We shall make up a name." She lifted up the boy. "We will say it is Tommy's father."

Helaine hesitated. "The shoes would have to be of the finest quality. It is my reputation at stake here. If the shoes fall apart, then no one will come back to my store."

"But they won't. I swear it!" She stepped forward. "Please, Lady . . . Mrs. Mortimer. You know what it is like to be alone and starving. This is what I know how to do. And I am very good at it. I have all my father's tools. Please, please, help me."

Helaine didn't like the way the girl had gone about asking, and she certainly didn't like the idea of bringing on yet another two mouths to feed. Yet she couldn't deny the business possibility. If Penny really was as good as her father, then this was a boon she couldn't pass up. But if the slippers fell apart or looked horrible, then it could damage her reputation at a critical time.

"Penny, I will have to think about it. And I will need to see you make a pair of shoes. I must know if you can do the work."

"Of course, of course. And I swear I shall never tell anyone about your past. I swear it, Mrs. Mortimer. I just needed you to listen."

She needed a great deal more than a willing ear, but Helaine was apparently in a generous mood today. With a twist of her wrist, she indicated that it was time to keep walking. They didn't speak the rest of the way to the shop.

Helaine was too busy wondering at herself. She was not in a position to expand the shop. And yet here she was, taking in a girl and her baby without anything beyond a prayer.

"I make no promises," she said sternly as they made it to the shop. "I have a partner who must agree. And if your work is terrible—"

"It isn't."

Helaine continued as if she hadn't heard. "—or if you are rude to the customers, then I can't have you here. I won't."

"I have waited on all manner of customers all my life."

Helaine knew it was true. It would simply be a matter of the craftsmanship. If Penny truly was as good as she said, then perhaps they could work out an arrangement. Perhaps.

She was so busy thinking that she completely missed the man who stood by the doorway until she was almost right upon him. He was lounging there as if waiting just for her. And when his chocolate eyes danced with joy at seeing her—or at catching her unawares—she was hard-pressed to think of anything at all. Lord, was there anyone more of a ninny than her?

"Good afternoon, Mrs. Mortimer," he said, his voice as smooth and rich as everything else about him.

She swallowed and tried to gather her wits. "Good afternoon, Lord Redhill. I don't believe I have anything for your sister right now, but if you could step aside a moment, I shall check."

He obliged her by stepping a good half inch aside. She glared at him because she knew he wanted to crowd her, to have his body close to hers. And as she undid the lock on the shop door, her entire right side tingled at his proximity. But that wasn't what sent shivers down her spine. No, that came the moment she heard his voice all soothing and warm as he spoke to Tommy.

"Well, hello, young man. I see you are most fortunate, held aloft in the company of two beautiful women."

Helaine pushed open the door and turned around just in time to see the boy grab hold of his lordship's gloved finger and try to draw it to his mouth. He didn't succeed, of course. The babe hadn't the strength, but he did manage to play a game of tug back and forth with Lord Redhill, drawing the finger close only to have it slide down to chuck him under the chin. And all the while Helaine watched in horror as Lord Redhill's expensive calfskin glove got covered in baby drool.

She would have said something. Indeed, she shared a shocked look with Penny. But there was nothing to do, as Lord Redhill appeared completely enthralled by his play with the child.

"He's a handsome boy," he said without pausing in his game.

"Thank you, your lordship," said Penny with a soft-spoken deference in her tone. "His name is Tommy. I'm afraid he's cutting teeth and your glove—"

"Teething, are you?" he said. "Well, that's a painful process. What have you done to help him?"

Helaine looked to Penny for an answer. She was too flabbergasted to say anything. Imagine a man asking about the care of a baby! Most men would have dismissed the child from their thoughts within seconds of registering the annoyance. Meanwhile it was left to Penny to answer.

"I give him something hard to chew on. Bread if we have it. Papa used to let him chew on an old wood foot measure."

Lord Redhill's eyes raised. "A foot measure?"

"Miss Shoemaker and her brother are children of a rather famous, er, shoemaker, obviously. She's come to visit my mother and me for a time."

"So I have interrupted an afternoon visit," he said as he walked into the shop. He moved slowly because Tommy still had hold of his finger and Penny had to follow at an equal pace. Then they were all inside and Helaine could shut the door. "But perhaps I could beg a moment of your time, Mrs. Mortimer. I do have something I wish to discuss with you."

Helaine nodded. What else could she do? He was the brother of her most prestigious client, and truthfully, she was rather intrigued by his cheery mood. "Penny, if you would but follow me, I will show you upstairs. Your lordship, if you would disentangle yourself from Tommy?"

Lord Redhill grinned as he looked down at the boy. "Well, old chum, it's time for the women to whisk you away. Here, why not keep my gloves? They're clean and tough enough. Chew on them all you like. Much better than an old wooden tool, don't you think?" So saying, he stripped off his gloves and left them clutched in the boy's hands.

"Oh, your lordship!" gasped Penny. "They're too fine for a baby to use!"

"Nonsense. I have another pair, and Tommy likes them."

Helaine shook her head, both appalled and warmed by his generous act. Did he truly not understand the worth of his gloves? What man casually gave up fine leather gloves to a teething child? One who was too rich to understand their value or one who truly had a soft spot for children. Looking at Lord Redhill's face, she knew the answer. He gazed at the boy with the same kind of wistful hunger she sometimes saw in her own mirror. He wanted a child, but despaired of ever having one.

Which was a ridiculous thought. Of course he would have children. He would marry a high society wife and start begetting children. It was only herself who would likely never marry, never have children. She was the daughter of a disgraced earl. No man of her set would have her, and even the tradesmen kept their distance. They sensed her education and upbringing even if no one knew of it. Besides, she had set herself up as a mistress to Lord Metzger. No decent man would have her now.

So rather than comment, she turned away and began climbing the stairs to the upper rooms. Her mother was there, dozing in a chair, but was soon roused, and her eyes gleamed with interest when she learned from Penny who waited below. Both ladies then shooed Helaine back downstairs, and she was all too willing to abandon them. But she didn't burst in on him. Instead, she slowed to a stop just out of sight so that she could watch him.

He was sitting on the settee, paging through one of her sketchbooks of dress designs. All in all, he was of a rather normal sort for an aristocratic male in his prime. As was typical, he was slightly taller than the general public, with strong hands, broad shoulders, and clothing to emphasize his power. His hair was dark brown and wavy, and his eyes were a soft chocolate brown that reminded her of her favorite morning drink, once upon a time. His skin was clear, his teeth well placed, and even his nose wasn't too pronounced. In short, he was normal and nothing about him explained the fluttering in her stomach whenever she saw him.

He looked up as she neared, and his expression warmed with delight. Maybe that was the reason. She could recall no other gentleman who seemed genuinely happy to see her. Not even her father, though he could be delightful for short periods of time. Or maybe it was the way Lord Redhill simply looked at her, his eyes steady and clear. What did he see when he stared at her like that? She saw a man who did not drink to excess, who had a clear understanding of himself and the world, and who—apparently for this moment—wanted to spend his time with her.

She was powerless to refuse him. But that didn't mean she couldn't tweak him a bit.

"Looking for something in tulle, perhaps?" she asked gesturing to the book. "I don't recommend flounces on someone as tall as you. But perhaps a dash of lace somewhere around the bodice, perhaps?"

His eyes lightened in merriment. The edges crinkled a little, and she would swear they shifted to a honey brown. "I'm afraid I'm not much interested in lace. Itches too much, you know. My valet is forever starching my collars until they are hard enough to cut wood. Or my chin. I shudder to think what would happen to my tender skin should he get hold of lace."

Helaine laughed. "Well, then I would definitely steer away from that. Perhaps a lovely ribbon or two."

"For my hair, you think? A big bow, perhaps, to bring out my eyes."

"Definitely."

They were joking, of course, and about a silly thing. Lord Redhill generally dressed in simple lines, clean masculine attire that was serviceable, casually fashionable, and wholly himself. The idea of him as a dandy just made her smile. That they could joke about something like this was completely unheard-of in her experience. Certainly she teased her female friends, but never a man, and never with someone as unsettling as him.

"Would you care for some tea, my lord? I have recently acquired a rather unusual oriental blend. Imagine, but it just appeared in my cabinet the other day."

"How odd," he said. "Shall we repair to the kitchen to try it out?"

Helaine felt her skin heat at his words. The intimacy of the idea, not to mention what they had done the last time they went to the kitchen, made her fingers tighten and her thoughts scatter. When had she become this silly girl, distracted by the slightest memory of him, unable to form a coherent statement?

"Helaine?"

"Um, I believe my mother is heating tea for Penny upstairs. We have a small cookstove up there as well. She will make extra for us, I am sure."

"And the special tea blend?"

"I believe that is Wendy's, as she is the one who opened the door to the messenger who brought it. Mama will make something from upstairs. Unless you wish me to go tell her specifically—"

"No, no!" he cried. "Pray don't leave. I have a need to talk with you." Then he gestured to the chair opposite the settee. "Please, won't you sit?"

He was inviting her to sit in her own salon, but somehow the gesture felt right. Or as right as anything this afternoon had been. Truthfully, Lord Redhill possessed the quiet confidence that would allow him to command in whatever location. But oddly enough, he wasn't commanding her to sit, merely asking. And looking a little flushed himself as he did it.

She settled into the chair, using the motion to cover her nervousness. And when that did not ease the quivering in her belly, she glanced back at him. "This is most odd, you know. I cannot imagine what you would like to discuss with me."

"Actually, Helaine, I came seeking your advice."

She frowned. "My advice? I don't understand."

"Pray let me explain. My father purchased a coal mine that is having some problems. Not the mine itself, though that is difficult enough. I had to shut it down for some much-needed repairs. You cannot imagine the danger those people endure every day. I went down there once and was caught in a collapse. It was horrible."

"You were caught in a collapse?"

"I was on the good side of it, if there is such a thing. Not hurt at all, though I have suffered a nightmare or two."

"I can imagine," she said with a shudder of her own.

"I really ought to tell you how I made a heroic rescue of the miners and the like, risking my neck in feats of derring-do, but truthfully, it happened so fast. I simply reacted, and then when the dust settled, we grabbed on to each other and ran for our lives. It wasn't until everything was over that I started shaking. And then, let me tell you, I was terrified."

"We? So there were others with you?"

"The former manager, whom I promptly fired. The new manager, who had helped me escape. But none of that happened until afterward."

She scanned his face. He wasn't even pale, and he certainly wasn't crowing about what he'd done. He was simply relaying what had happened as if it were incidental to what he wanted to talk about. And yet, she kept thinking of it. This man could have been killed in a mine collapse. Possibly a few feet difference and he would have died.

"That is horrifying," she whispered. She felt chilled to the bone.

"The conditions in that mine were horrifying," he returned. "Which is why my problem right now is so very baffling."

She was about to ask what he meant, when they were interrupted. As she expected, her mother had made tea. She was coming downstairs with the tea tray, her eyes sparkling with interest. Helaine leaped up to help her. The woman had never been one for lifting anything, much less a full tea tray while coming down stairs. And while Helaine was taking command of the tray, her mother beamed at Lord Redhill. Helaine had only a moment to look at her mother and realize that she was in trouble. The lady was dressed in her best gown, her hair obviously brushed and rapidly pinned up in a style from ten or more years ago. While Helaine was busy settling the tea things, her mother was extending her hand like the countess she was.

Except she was *not* a countess anymore. Their identities were hidden, their names changed. But one look at her mother and she knew the lady wouldn't be able to keep it a secret. Not when this was the first lord in years to make anything resembling a social call. Even if it was in the salon of a dressmaker's shop.

"Good afternoon, Lord Redhill," her mother began. "I trust my daughter is making you comfortable? So kind of you to send her that oriental tea. I had it made up especially for this afternoon so that you could taste some. An excellent choice, I must say. Quite stimulating."

Her mother paused for a breath, which gave Helaine time to rush in with the "correct" introductions. "Lord Redhill, please allow me to introduce my mother, Mrs. Appleton." Appleton was her maiden name, and Helaine hoped that by speaking it so clearly, the woman would remember that she was no longer Lady Chelmorton. Sadly, it had no obvious effect. Her mother simply smiled and sat down in the chair Helaine had just vacated. That, of course, forced Helaine to sit beside his lordship on the settee, which had no doubt been exactly her design.

"It is a lovely day, is it not, my lord?" her mother began as she waved for Helaine to serve the tea. "I vow the summer will be here before we know it. Why, Helaine was remarking on that just the other day."

Lord Redhill answered exactly as one would expect, moving smoothly into the polite social banter one exchanges with a debutante's mother. Helaine tried to participate. She even managed to comment once or twice, but the whole time she was on pins and needles praying that her mother didn't slip up, that Lord Redhill remained blissfully ignorant of how bizarre it was to take tea with a dressmaker's mother, and yet all the while secretly pleased that her mother could have this one moment of her former glory. One afternoon's tea wherein she got to be the lady of the manor again. One short twenty minutes of what should have been her life.

And then, thank God, it was done. Her mother gasped in mock horror at the time and pushed to her feet. "I'm terribly sorry, my lord, but I must beg your indulgence. Penny has been upstairs with that rapscallion all this time, and she really needs help with the boy. Please, do excuse me."

Lord Redhill stood and bowed over her hand. "It has been a pleasure, Mrs. Appleton. I hope that I may call more often."

"Of course, of course! And now you really must excuse me. That boy, you know." And off she went. She even left the door to the back staircase open just as any good chaperone would do if she were stepping out of a parlor for a moment.

Helaine released a sigh of relief. Her mother had enjoyed her moment of remembered glory and no harm had come of it. Or so she thought, until she turned to look back at Lord Redhill. She should have realized he was too intelligent to be fooled. She should have barred her mother from joining them, because one look at his thoughtful face told her that he was seconds from figuring it out. Not exactly who she was, but that her parentage was much more elevated than any dressmaker's.

"My lord," she began, not even knowing what she wanted to say but she had to distract him somehow.

He turned his chocolate eyes her way and all her words disappeared. He knew. She could see it in the way he kept his expression extremely neutral, and yet his eyes seemed to sparkle with a secret understanding. He didn't say anything and neither did she. She was too busy fighting panic to formulate any thought at all. Finally he spoke, his words confirming her fears.

"Your mother is lovely, but sad. As if she has suffered a great loss." He tilted his head. "If I might ask, what happened to your father?"

"Gone," she said, the words choking her. "Many years now."

"I'm sorry. How did he die?"

Helaine shook her head. "Not dead. Just gone. We don't even know where. Just . . . gone."

His eyes widened as he worked through the implications of that. "But what of his money? His employer or . . . or other income?"

Like from his lands? Unlike most earldoms, the land had not been entailed, as Helaine's grandfather had been as irresponsible as her father. The paperwork had never been filed, which meant the land was free to sell. And it had been, shortly before Helaine's fourteenth birthday. At the time, it had been great fun. They left the moldering old estate for a set of rooms in London. But without any income at all, the money steadily disappeared. A year after her father had disappeared, there was nothing left and creditors were banging on the door.

"We had nothing, my lord, except what I could manage here."

His eyes roved the small shop, taking in the wallpaper that was beginning to yellow, the cheapness of the furnishing. He was likely remembering that the mirror in the back required resilvering and that she usually kept the very cheap tea for herself.

"You've had a difficult time of it, haven't you?"

She looked at her hands, ashamed of the tears that burned her eyes. Things were going well for them. Lady Gwen's order alone would see them through much of the winter, or so she hoped. This was not the time or place to become weepy.

She felt his hand caressing her cheek, the slow stroke of his thumb across a tear that had escaped. She pulled away.

"Forgive me," she said. "I'm afraid it has been a long day."

He did not pursue her, but neither did he pull away. He simply let his hand drop from her face to land on the settee near hers. Not touching, but the merest shift would bring them into contact.

"No," he said softly. "Forgive me. I believe I have upset your life more than I realized. You have a business to run, and yet I am here taking up your time with tea and chats with your mother."

Helaine released a sad snort at that statement. "As you can see, we are overflowing with customers right now. They are lined up around the block." Obviously it was a lie. Sadly, they had no more appointments for another few days. It had all been a downward spiral the moment the fabric sellers had refused them credit. From then, they'd needed to request prepayment from their customers, which had many of them fleeing to other dressmakers. Helaine's only hope was for Lady Gwen to look so excellent that she pulled in more customers from her references.

"Then let me pay you for your advice. Please, allow me to take you to dinner somewhere. We can talk as we eat."

She shook her head. "My lord, that is not appropriate—"

"I can hardly discuss what I want with your mother upstairs and more people in the back likely to walk in at any moment."

Strangely enough, Wendy was *not* in the back, which was highly unusual. But it was true that they had been interrupted at every turn.

"Please, I really could use your advice," he said.

"I can't imagine that I could be of any assistance. You were speaking about mining."

He nodded. "Well, yes, this is rather unusual. Which is why I should like our discussion to be discreet."

She looked at him then, studying his face for clues. Obviously this was yet another attempt at seduction, but in a most unusual manner. He had come discussing coal mining.

"A meal at an inn I know. Excellent fare, quiet conversation, that is all. I shall return you home by ten."

"It hardly seems appropriate."

"Of course it's not appropriate. A future earl asking the advice of a dressmaker? Good God, I would be the laughing-stock of London. If it got out, I would be banned from my clubs, even spit on in the streets."

He sounded so aggrieved that she couldn't keep from smiling. "My goodness. Put like that, it's a wonder you did not appear at the door with a bag over your head."

"I considered it, believe me. Though more because I thought you would bar the door to me than any other reason."

"Yes, well, that was a reasonable fear. Fortunately for you, Tommy had a firm grip on your finger and dragged you inside against my will."

"Thank God for Tommy."

"Yes—"

"And thank God that you are an understanding sort, kind and compassionate. You will not tell a soul of what I am asking. And you will allow me to pay for your excellent advice with a meal of very hearty stew."

"But—"

"Please, Helaine, do not make me beg. My grandfather is already rolling over in his grave as it is."

It was his expression that finally swayed her. Part teasing, part desperate, and wholly delightful. He was not commanding her, he was charming her. And he had just given quite a gift to her mother in that twenty minutes of polite tea. The two combined made for a potent package. Plus, she had to admit to a great deal of curiosity about what advice he could possibly want from her. But she couldn't give in yet.

"I have a great deal to do this evening," she said. "I am learning to keep my own books, and that takes time and diligence. There is also correspondence to manage, and Penny has come for a visit."

He paused, hope still shining in his eyes. Then he reached out and squeezed her hand. "What time should my carriage come by? You can finish your bookkeeping and reward yourself with an excellent meal with a delightful companion."

She bit her lip, trying to sort through the evening. She would need time to finish the accounting, then bathe and dress her hair. Time as well for some light cosmetics and to air out her best gown. It was not a ball gown or anything like that. Simply a dress that was more appropriate to evening and . . .

And seduction.

She paused, trying to examine the situation logically. But try as she might, she couldn't force herself to say no. She wanted a lovely dinner. She wanted to be pursued. She wanted to laugh and tease and discuss mining with this man. And even if he meant to bed her for the pleasure, she did not have to say yes. He was not the sort to force her when she refused. Her virtue would be absolutely safe, provided she maintained her own discipline.

"Three hours," she suddenly said.

He raised his eyebrows. "Three hours?"

"I have a lot of accounting to do."

He nodded. "Of course. Then I shall endeavor to be sure that the dinner is an appropriate reward for such diligent work."

He stood to leave, taking the time to bend over her hand. She allowed him to do so, reveling in the feel of being courted as if she were Lady Helaine again.

"Three hours, Helaine. Not a moment more."

"Not a single second."

Then he left. She waited a few seconds, reliving the

afternoon's events, anticipating the evening to come, and relishing the excitement that was tingling through her blood. And when good sense started to surface, she roughly pushed it aside. A minute later she was buried in her books, using the steady march of numbers to obliterate all rational, *moral* considerations.

Chapter 11

❧❦

Robert walked blindly away from her shop, his mind in a whirl. He knew who she was! Robert knew her real identity and that changed everything. She was Lady Helaine, daughter of Reginald Talbott, Earl of Chelmorton, aka the Thief of the Ton. The scandal might be five years old, but he remembered. It had been all the talk for a Season at least.

The man had stolen from the military troops. The exact details escaped him, but the crime was heinous enough. Stealing from English boys so far from home? Many people cried for the man's blood. But Talbott was an earl and not a smart one. Robert's father had once called the man a buffoon, and considering the source, that was an insult indeed.

There had been quite the debate about what was to be done. It went without saying that the entire family was banned from society. Now Robert felt cruel for joking about being tossed from his clubs and spit on in the street. Her father had certainly suffered that fate. Herself as well, most likely, though he could not remember specific events.

So much was clear now. She'd been educated as the

daughter of an earl, so of course she would speak and move as a lady born. As did her mother. No wonder the woman seemed so sad. She'd lost everything just because she'd married a fool.

He hadn't heard how the debacle was settled. The earl disappeared from society, the discussion of his punishment was overtaken by another matter, and nothing was heard of the Chelmortons again. Until now. Half a decade later, he'd found the daughter, Helaine. She was a talented dressmaker who barely survived above her shop. And her poor mother obviously lived as such women did, playing with children and reliving past glories. She couldn't even marry again because her husband had disappeared, not died.

But the sacrifices they had made! With no means of support, the daughter becomes a dressmaker. She cannot go out as herself. No one would frequent her shop. So she invents a fictitious name. Then, to avoid the likes of Johnny Bono, she invents a protector as well. Lord Metzger had been close friends with the missing earl. He'd obviously done what he could for the girl, claiming her as his own so that she need not succumb to other more difficult protectors. But at what cost? She could never marry decently, and yet she was obviously not trained as a courtesan, either. At least she had a talent for dresses.

His admiration for Helaine soared. She was resourceful and strong as few women of her set could possibly imagine. And he wanted her now with a passion bordering on insanity.

How awkward that the more he learned about her, the more desperately he wanted to bed her. And yet his honor declared her off-limits. It made no sense, but she was the daughter of an earl. How could he set himself to seduce her? He would be debauching an innocent.

The answer didn't really matter. No matter how much he told himself that he should back away, he couldn't force himself to behave. He ought to allow the woman to build a life, but he could not. If Helaine could not marry, then perforce she must either live chaste or become some man's mistress. She had obviously intended to be chaste, but that was a cold and empty life. Why not become a mistress in fact? His mistress. She could do much worse than what he offered.

Yes, he told himself. Despite her identity, despite the fact that she'd been raised a woman of his own set, her circumstances had not changed. And that gave him an opening to possess her. An honorable man would walk away. Apparently he was more like his father than he'd thought. Because honorable or not, he intended to bed her. Tonight.

Helaine dressed with as much care for this evening as she had for her first ball. She'd only attended one. It had been the come-out ball of one of her school friends, and both she and her mother had scrimped to buy the gown. It had been one of her own designs, the materials purchased on the cheap, with the actual stitches sewn by a very young Wendy, though they hadn't known it at the time. It was the ball gown that had started Wendy thinking along the lines that eventually led to their dress shop. But Helaine hadn't known it at the time. That night, all she knew was that her mother had dressed her curls perfectly, her father had escorted them like a proper gentleman should, and Helaine had danced the night away.

It was the best night of her life, and yet tonight she felt more excited, more daring, and more on edge than even then. Perhaps it was the hint of despair that touched her. After all, she knew she was taking an irretrievable step. Tonight, whether or not she became a mistress in fact—and she was resolved that it would be *not*—she was losing her virtue in her own mind. She was going to share an evening alone with a gentleman. Without a chaperone, without a good reason beyond his company, and with a great deal of titillating excitement simmering in her blood.

What she was doing was beyond the pale, and Helaine desperately feared that everyone would know it. She didn't even dare look at her mother, so she asked Penny to help her style her hair and then escaped as soon as it was possible. And when his lordship's carriage arrived outside the shop, she rushed out without so much as a good-bye.

He was waiting for her, opening the carriage door even before the footman made it down from his perch. She climbed in, her nerves making her breathless. But the moment she saw his face—his expression pulled wide in an excited grin—she knew she couldn't regret her choice. He was filled with the same giddy kind of excitement that she was. It was as if they were two kids sneaking downstairs for a treat from the kitchen, and not a man and woman in search of something a great deal more mature. That image helped her relax back into the squabs, which in turn allowed her to notice something other than him.

The carriage was beautiful. The interior was spacious and smelled of cedar. The squabs were made of rich velvet, and it was warm inside. He had a brick for her feet and a rug for her lap and even offered her a cup of spiced wine as she took in her surroundings.

"The inn has good wine, but this is better," he said as he offered her a glass. "I have stronger stuff as well—"

"No, no. This is excellent. Thank you," she said as she took the glass. Their hands were gloved. They were both dressed as if for a ball. He looked excellent, of course. The fit of his coat set off his broad shoulders. The color was dark chocolate, a perfect match for his hair and eyes. It was kept from being dull by the white of his lawn shirt and a brilliant emerald in the center of his silk cravat.

He looked handsome and every inch the viscount he was. She bit her lip, feeling the world peel backward to her girlish fantasies. How many nights had she spent dreaming of just this moment—herself in a carriage with a handsome aristocrat? Of course, in her pretend world, they were on their way to something respectable, but it didn't matter. This moment did. So she took a sip of her wine, closing her eyes to appreciate the taste and the delightful fulfillment of her dreams.

"Do you like it?" he asked.

It took a moment for her to realize he was asking about the wine. "It's perfect. Where are we going?"

"To the Black Horse Inn. I have, once or twice, stayed there when I can't stand my family anymore."

Her eyes widened. "You have not!"

"I have. The first time, I'd just turned seventeen. I was returning from endless hours with the steward at our family seat and knew I would face another pile of correspondence when I arrived in London. So I decided to stop at the inn instead. It was the most heavenly night!"

"What did you do?"

"I read. I took a hot bath. I dreamed of gorgeous women, and I fell asleep."

She shook her head. "I don't believe it. At seventeen, you would still have been in school."

"I was."

"So how could you be seeing the steward and managing the bills? You were much too young."

"On the contrary, beginning at the age of twelve, every Boxing Day, my father pulled me into his library and gave me a new responsibility. At first it was overseeing the wine cellar. He said the butler was stealing him blind, and he wanted me to end the nonsense."

"And was the butler to blame?"

"God, no. That was my father, forgetting how much he drank every night. But my mother praised me for the excellent vintages I purchased and even Dribbs said I was being very clever. I think he was just grateful that my father stopped cursing him as a thief."

"But you were only twelve! You must have shown quite the skill with management."

He laughed, the sound filling the carriage. "Not then, I assure you. But my father was remarkably bad at management, so it wasn't hard to make an improvement."

"What did you get the next year?"

Even in the darkness of the carriage, she could see him frown, trying to remember. "The sheep, I believe. Or was that the next year?"

"But so much work. And you were still in school?"

"Yes, but I didn't mind at first. It was kind of fun. I felt important stomping around the estate giving orders. But by the time I was seventeen, the novelty had worn off."

"Did you come to hate Boxing Day?"

"Despised it with a passion." Then he leaned back in the carriage and smiled at her. "What did you do for Boxing Day while I was locked in my father's study?"

"Oh, nothing exciting. Sketched mostly. I spent much of my childhood with dirty fingers. I would draw the most elaborate things."

"Landscapes? People?"

"Oh, no. Clothing. Dresses much too impractical to ever be possible. My favorite was a court gown. Flounces weren't even the half of it. Lace, jewels, feathers from exotic birds. You name it, I'd drawn a dress that featured it. I did one that was made of sheets of flattened gold."

"Gold! Can you imagine how heavy that would be? Like walking around carrying plates on your body. I doubt you could even breathe."

She smiled, but didn't answer. Was gold particularly heavy? She'd never held enough in her hand to know. But come to think of it, she remembered a guinea she'd once played with. She recalled how solid it had felt in her hand. A whole dress of coins would indeed have weighed her down to the floor.

He must have understood her embarrassment. When she didn't respond, he chuckled, filling the darkness with the sound of good humor. "But that's what youthful dreams are all about, I suppose. I used to dream of running a hospital where every illness was cured within the space of an hour. Sliced open your leg? Here's a bandage that seals it within seconds. Birthing fever? Just drink this and you'll be right as rain in a twinkling. Even wasting diseases were no proof against my miracle cures."

"Did you see yourself as the brilliant doctor saving all? Or as the recipient of all those grateful hugs and kisses when all was made well?"

"Ah, well, that depended on my age. I began as the brilliant doctor admired by all. By the time I was a teenager, however, I must admit to a few grateful-daughter fantasies."

"Sounds normal enough."

"Not what I envisioned doing. I was not only brilliant, but I had the brawn and stamina of a Greek god."

She laughed. She couldn't help it. He was being so forthright about his young fantasies that she was charmed. Thank God this wasn't a proper excursion. They could never discuss these things in the presence of a chaperone. "The Greeks were a lusty lot, as I recall."

"Gods and goddesses alike. I remember trying to compare Athena and Aphrodite to my mother. Couldn't see the similarity anywhere."

"Your mother is not warlike or passionate? That surprises me, given how lively Gwen is."

"My mother is not much of anything at all, I'm afraid. She has trouble facing the day, sometimes doesn't even get out of bed."

"Get her a grandchild or two. Then you'll see how she changes."

He snorted. "Well, that shall be Gwen's job. I've had enough tasks gifted to me over the years. I cannot stand another." It was a lie, of course. She remembered how he had played with Thomas. There had been longing for a child in his face. She was sure of it.

"But you will have children eventually. The honor of the earldom and all that."

"Yes," he sighed. "Yes, all that."

She'd gone and spoiled it, she realized. She hadn't meant her comment as anything more than the inevitable future of a man such as him. Marriage, children, and more little aristocrats to replace the old ones. The line continued.

But with that statement, she brought to mind his future wife. A woman who, obviously, would never be her. That soured her mood immediately. But that did not explain his silence. She didn't dare ask. It was too forward, but he saved her by speaking in his mellow voice, the tones low and yet so intimate.

"Can I tell you a secret, Helaine?"

"Of course."

"Whenever I think of children, I recall those Boxing Day mornings. I remember looking at the stacks of responsibilities added to my little desk in the corner of my father's library. There was so much work there that I never had room to write unless I put the papers on the floor."

"You were too young for all that. You wouldn't do that to your own son."

He sighed. "But it would be his eventually. More and more, in a never-ending stack. Sometimes I fear I will die beneath those piles and no one would notice for months."

"Don't be silly. The servants would notice the smell within a few days."

It took him a moment to process her tease. And then he released an abrupt bark of laughter. "Yes, I suppose you are right. It would only be a few days."

"A week at the very most."

"At the most." He chuckled, the sound like a slow caress. "That is what I most like about you, Helaine. You make me laugh at the oddest times."

He said her name, and her whole body warmed. "And perhaps your son will take to management, as you have."

"Is that what I have done? And here I thought I was simply standing up to my responsibilities."

She could tell by the way he spoke that he had no joy in his tasks. She understood the idea in principle. After all, she had no love of washing the laundry or learning bookkeeping. They were tasks that had to be accomplished and she had no servants to do them anymore. What if his entire day, every day, were filled with such things? Then being an earl would be no boon but a horrible life of drudgery no better than what the lowest footman or maid had.

She reached forward and touched his hand. They were both gloved, and yet the warmth seeped through as if she were touching a flame. "You paint a very bleak picture, my lord. Surely your life cannot be so terrible."

His hand flipped over to clasp hers. It was too intimate a gesture and she ought to pull back. But she didn't. She liked the feel of his large hand surrounding hers.

"No, no," he said. "It is not so terrible. Certainly not now when I have a beautiful woman with whom to discuss it. And excellent food ahead as well." At his words, the carriage slowed. They had arrived at the inn. She looked through the window to see a quaint building on the outskirts of London. And though it wasn't a coaching inn, their carriage had plenty of room.

She waited as she knew she ought, and within a moment the footman opened the door and handed her out. She descended as she always imagined she would: with a liveried footman before her and a handsome man behind. She stepped out into the darkness, feeling her curls bob about her ears in the breeze. She shivered as it was not yet spring and her gown was too thin. But Lord Redhill was beside her in a moment, helping her adjust her wrap while shielding her from the wind with his body. And then together they stepped into the inn as stately as any couple could walk into a ballroom.

They were greeted at the door by the innkeeper, who did not look at all like a majordomo. He was of middle years and middle girth, but his smile was all welcome as he bowed before Lord Redhill.

"Everything is prepared, my lord. Even found the almonds, just like you said."

Helaine felt her excitement surge. "Almonds? Truly? I've never had them, but my father said they were delightful. They're from India, aren't they? He discovered them at . . . oh." Her voice trailed away when she finally remembered what her father had said about them. Almonds were an aphrodisiac, and he had learned about them in a brothel. She wasn't supposed to know that, of course, but her father had been so far into his cups he hadn't realized he was speaking to his young daughter.

"They are just a nut, my dear," said his lordship, his voice and his words designed to soothe her. "A particular favorite of mine and delicious when roasted. I shall be pleased to see your very first taste."

She flushed and looked away. Of course he was lying. Almonds must cost a fortune, and no man bought such a thing without hoping to make good use of their other properties. But she was spared the necessity of answering as they were ushered into a cozy room with a cheerful fire, a table laid out for two, and a long couch with large pillows. The innkeeper took her gloves and wrap and set them on the table nearby. Lord Redhill shed his outdoor attire as well, and then took her hand flesh to flesh while the innkeeper slipped discreetly away.

She knew she was trembling. Seeing the very cozy nature of this room, she knew she would end up in his arms before the evening's end. But even as the idea shook her, a part of her was already justifying it. What harm would a kiss be? Or a few more? She was already ruined, so no harm at all, and nothing more than they had already done.

He escorted her to a seat by the fire. He did nothing untoward, not even stroking her palm, and yet her heart was beating so fast. She found it hard to catch her breath.

"Would you care for some more wine?" he asked as she made a valiant attempt to gather her wits.

"Yes, that would be lovely."

He poured and brought them both glasses. He sat beside her on the couch and took a drink, closing his eyes as he appreciated the taste.

"Not exquisite, but not so bad either." He opened his eyes to look at her, so she hastily took her own sip.

"Lovely," she said, though she hadn't tasted a thing.

He looked at her a long moment, then he sighed. "You are nervous, Helaine, and I don't wish you to be. What can I do to help?"

He understood! She smiled warmly at him and took another long sip from her wine. And when she was done, she managed to look at his face and not think of much beyond his beauty. He was a very handsome man in a very ordinary way. Nothing stood out, nothing made any part of his face more patrician or very angular. His nose was perfect for his face. His jawline firm without being harsh. And there was enough softness to make him appear relaxed, saving him from being too stern.

"You remind me of a stag I once saw," she said abruptly. "He was in the distance, standing there looking out while his family grazed nearby. He had antlers out to . . ." She couldn't even bridge the gap with her arms. "Well, anyway, they were huge. There was nothing unusual about the sight. We were forever seeing deer, so he was just the papa watching while his family ate. But he was stately, you understand, and powerful. I vow they were the happiest deer family in England. That is what you remind me of."

He blinked at her words, obviously stunned. "I am at a loss," he said. Then when she went to drink some more, he stopped her. His hand came around hers and he held the glass away from her mouth. "And I believe we should eat some dinner soon."

She looked down at his hand, so large and so warm. He surrounded her wrist. He could likely break it just by squeezing his fingers. And yet, she never feared him. She could say that of no other man, not even her father. Sometimes when he got drunk, he could be violent. Not against people, but against the furniture, certainly. He used to throw the empty bottles. She'd learned early not to go anywhere near after he called for the third bottle.

"Do you ever drink to excess?" she asked as she looked at his hand.

"Depends on what you mean by excess. There were a few times when I was a stumbling drunk," he said, "but that was many years ago now. Mostly it has been my sad task to call the carriages for my friends and to hold their heads while they . . ." He cleared his throat. "Well, you understand."

She giggled. "Yes, I certainly understand. My father's valet had that terrible task until he quit. My mother after that. Then no one at all."

"Because he left?"

She nodded. "Because he left. But he was forever leaving, then turning up at the oddest times. I sometimes think I shall walk upstairs and find him sitting there, easy as you please, with a glass of brandy in his hand."

"He sounds like an unsteady fellow."

She snorted. "He was that and more. But he was charming, too, and he could always make me laugh."

He smiled as if he understood. Too late, she realized that she was speaking too much, too freely. What dressmaker's father had a valet? But then he was speaking and she became caught up in his words again.

"It's easy to make little girls laugh," he said. "When I came home from school, I used to spin my sister around such that her legs went flying. Or sometimes I'd wrap her in a bear hug of a greeting. She used to try to wriggle free, but I held on tight until she complained that she couldn't breathe. But in truth, it was I who was breathless. Gwen doesn't look it, but she has strength in her arms. I used to tell her she had muscles like a sailor."

"You did not!"

"I most certainly did. I think that is why she has picked that baron of hers. He's tall, but still scrawny. I think she could best him in a fight."

Helaine recoiled in mock horror. "That's terrible! To say such a thing of your sister."

"Oh, but she'll say it herself, you know. My sister is no shrinking violet, and caring for my mother is no easy task."

"Is she bedridden, then?"

He nodded. "Sometimes. When the headaches are bad."

"I'm sorry."

He shrugged. "It has been this way since I was a child. My mother is frail; my sister is not."

"Your father is a charming rogue, but you are not."

He arched his brows. "Are you saying I am not charming?"

"I am saying you are not a rogue." When he didn't respond, she answered his unspoken question. "Yes, I have learned a little about your father, the Earl of Willington. A jolly good fellow, by all accounts. Has the devil's own luck turning investments around. Which means, I believe, that he buys terribly stupid things and yet you manage to make them profitable."

He looked at her a long moment. "You are very well informed."

"You told me as much when we first met. Plus, I am very good at listening to your sister. She is very fond of you."

"Even if she calls me harsh and dictatorial."

"Even so."

"Humph," he returned. And then there was no more talk as the innkeeper brought them their dinner. He laid it out: quail with a sweet glaze, potatoes split and swimming in butter, and winter apples cooked with a covering of sugar. It was a feast the likes of which she had only heard about but never seen, much less tasted. And when she looked back at Lord Redhill, he merely smiled as if he knew how much of a treat this meal would be for her.

"You said simple stew."

He gestured to another bowl as the innkeeper set it on the table. He lifted the lid and the scent of a savory beef stew filled the room.

"Of course," she laughed. "I should not have doubted you."

The innkeeper ducked away while Lord Redhill took her hand and escorted her the two steps to the table. He held out her chair for her, poured her more wine, and then seated himself across from her.

"But where are the almonds?" she asked. Truly she didn't really care. There was more than enough here to delight her for years to come. But she had to say something, and that was what came to mind.

"That is for after dinner," he said. "For a snack if you are still hungry. If we talk for a very long time."

"Ah," she said, her gaze going to the fire. There was a very large space set out before the fireplace. Easy enough to set the pillows on the floor and lounge there. She had seen her father do so once. With a woman who should not have been in their home. Her gaze returned to Lord Redhill.

Could she do that with him? Lie in front of the fire and speak in low murmurs? Would he kiss her then? Would he caress her face? Would he touch something more?

"You have it all planned," she said.

"I'm told that's what I do best."

"Yes," she said, knowing that fear was not what was making her body flush with heat. "I'm sure it's one of the very many things you do well."

He opened his mouth as if to answer, but no words came out. A moment later he addressed himself to serving her food, dishing out one delicacy after another. He chatted companionably about this and that. He spoke of how he liked this dish prepared, he told her an amusing story of Gwen's first introduction to quail, and he even delighted her with horrible tales of his food at school. In truth, she spent as much time laughing as she did eating.

Then the meal was done, the dishes removed, and Lord Redhill was taking her hand as he led her from the table. But they did not return to the couch. No, instead, he grabbed hold of two of the very large pillows and tossed them on the floor right in front of the fire.

"Do you mind?" he asked. "I find this much more comfortable. Lets me stretch out my legs after a large meal."

"Of course not," she said because that was what she ought to say. She did not want him to be uncomfortable.

"You needn't join me," he said as he leaned back against the table and stretched out his legs. "But I do find it much easier to roast the almonds from here rather than over there." So saying, he gestured to a bucket of the nuts sitting next to a roasting frame beside the fire.

"But I am so full. I couldn't possibly eat another thing."

"Ah," he said with a laugh. "But we have not yet even begun to talk. Who knows how you will feel in an hour or more?"

"An hour! My goodness, what could we possibly talk about for an hour?"

He shrugged. "Anything you like, Helaine. But do just

come sit here beside me. Save me from having to crane my neck."

What could she say to that? She didn't want him to hurt his neck. "Of course, my lord."

"You must call me Robert."

She nodded. Of course she would use the Christian name of the man who was helping her settle down beside him.

"Say it, Helaine. Please say it."

She gazed into the warm depths of his chocolate eyes. They were seated hip to hip, the pillows braced behind them, the fire before them. His arm was behind her, gently encouraging her to lean against his chest. And his face was a few inches away, his mouth even less.

"Say what? Your name?"

"Say yes."

Chapter 12

❧

It nearly killed Robert to wait for her answer. He knew she wanted to say yes. Her body was already straining for him, her sweet perfume making him half crazed with lust. Her gaze held his, and in it, he read desire, excitement, and a sweet regret.

"N—"

He kissed her. Whatever word was on her lips was erased beneath his onslaught, his gentle domination as he moved his mouth across hers. Then he invaded her as a man ought, with steady pressure and thorough command. She was untutored, so he instructed, he teased, and he thrust himself inside.

She gasped and might have pulled back, but there was nowhere for her to go. He had positioned her with her back against a chair. And besides, he had his arm behind her, the bulk of his body to her side, and his other hand slowly wrapping across her front. When she was fully inside his embrace, he would ease her to the floor. There was a pillow there, conveniently placed. And once he had her on her back, everything would proceed exactly as it ought.

That was his plan, and he knew it would work. She was already arching into his kiss, her body stretching for him, her arm slowly wrapping around his back. But why was she reaching high? She should be clutching him as he over-whelmed her senses, not stretching up so she could reach . . .

She grabbed hold of his hair and yanked. His head jerked back with a cry.

"Ow!"

Her expression was the ultimate in innocence. "I'm sorry, my lord. Did your head get caught on something? Perhaps it was my word. I believe I said *no*."

She released his hair and folded her hands primly in her lap. Meanwhile, he was feeling to see if she'd left any hair on his head. Clearly she was a woman who took things at her own pace. He would just have to go slower. And while he was thinking this, she was trying to put them on a more equal footing.

"You said you wanted to talk to me about something? About your mine?"

He sighed, his thoughts immediately wandering to the problems he had there. It would be good for him to talk it out. It would clear his mind and fill the time before he tried to kiss her again.

"I received yet another letter from the man I promoted to manager. Charlie is his name. Good man, but young. Maybe that was my mistake. The other men don't re-spect him."

She sniffed. "I find that reasons like youth are just ex-cuses. Men invariably do what they intend and damn the circumstances."

He frowned. "That's a hell of a cynical attitude." Too late he realized he had cursed in front of her, but she merely shrugged.

"Johnny Bono will take advantage of whoever comes along if he can. Male, female, young or old, his intention is to feed his appearance of power and virility."

"Swear to me that you will never do business with that bastard again."

She shrugged. "I certainly hope I won't have to. As for your miners, look to their actions. What are their intentions? Then find some way to either use that intention or fire them. You really have no other choice."

He frowned, startled by her logical thinking. If he weren't staring right at her, he would swear the advice came from a man. Meanwhile, he was trying to follow her words to their logical conclusion.

"Charlie writes that the previous manager has been stirring up the men. I understand Hutchins well enough. He wants his job back. But I am making the mine better, safer for these men. Why would they turn on me?"

"They're not turning on you," she snorted. "You are a viscount and perforce believe that everything relates to you. You make logical steps toward the improvement of their lives, and you don't understand why everyone doesn't fall into line with your ideas."

He sighed. "It has certainly worked before."

"Or you have merely had the money and the distance to do what you deemed necessary and didn't look any closer." She tilted her head and the firelight caught on the delicate tracery of veins in her neck. Her skin was so fine, it seemed almost transparent. Clean and clear. He vowed he'd never seen so beautiful a neck. "What has changed, my lord? Why are you struggling with this business venture and not the others?"

He was so caught up in the sight of her flawless skin that he didn't at first catch her words. But she was looking at him so frankly, as if expecting an answer.

"My lord?"

"Robert," he admonished, though the word was automatic. His mind was caught on the shocking realization that she was figuring out the one thing that he kept carefully hidden.

"Very well, Robert. Tell me the truth. Are you really worried about the mine? Or was this just a ruse to get me alone?"

"Yes, I am worried," he said.

"And yes, it was a ruse. That part I already knew. But if you are truly worried about the miners, then perhaps you should be a bit more specific. What exactly are they doing that is so worrisome?"

He sighed. "Someone has vandalized the equipment. I purchased new carts and ponies to pull them, but someone has destroyed the new ones." Normally he would just buy new carts and post guards for as long as was needed, and thereby enforce his plans for long enough that the people accepted the new status quo. That was what he had done for his father's other investments. Eventually the people saw that their lives were better off and accepted the changes. But he hadn't the money to do such a thing right then. And so he was in the awkward position of having to try to appease vandals and worse.

"Have you posted guards?"

"I have instructed Charlie to do so, but what if those that work as guards are the very ones doing the damage?"

"Can Charlie hire from outside the town? Or would that just be seen as outsiders trying to step in where they aren't wanted?"

He nodded, impressed again. "You understand my dilemma."

"I understand stepping into a new place, a new business, and trying to learn the rules. Fortunately I had Wendy to teach me, just as you have Charlie. What does he suggest?"

He grimaced. "That we hire the children again. He believes that is why the carts were destroyed, so that I would be forced to hire the children again."

"Then I think you should listen to him."

He straightened. "Did you not hear me talk about the horrendous conditions there? Would you send your child into that pit? Never seeing the sun, in constant danger of fire or gas or cave-in? I have a hard enough time allowing the women to work, but to use children is monstrous!"

She didn't answer. She was looking at him with her head tilted, her hair slipping free to dangle about her shoulder.

He saw the beauty of her skin again, and his eyes were drawn to it, as well as to lower down where the soft mounds of her breasts were revealed.

"How tight is your money, Robert? Do you have the funds to force your opinion on these people? To pay the children to go to school?"

He grimaced. Yes, she had figured him out exactly. "No," he snapped. "No, I do not."

"Then I am afraid you will have to compromise your ethics in favor of slow change, slow growth. You can work to fire the children, one by one, later. But not just yet."

He looked at her and knew she had come to the exact crux of the problem. He was not a man who compromised easily, and certainly not on the welfare of children. He couldn't erase the sight of those bones in the tunnel, the ones placed specifically to frighten the children.

"I hate the idea of a child going down in that hole." So saying, he flopped onto his back. The place where he had meant to lay her down ended up being the pillow for his own head. He stared up at the ceiling and he tried not to see those bones again.

He didn't. He saw her face as she leaned over him. She touched his cheek, her hand warm, her expression filled with beauty. "You are an overbearing, pompous, opinionated man, my lord. But you are also a good man."

He waited a moment, deciding whether he would be insulted by her words or not. In the end, he decided she was too beautiful to be at odds with.

"Will you kiss me now?" he asked. "To make me feel better about stealing the sun from little children?"

She laughed. "Of course." Then she leaned down and planted a quick kiss to his forehead. He was prepared, though. Once she was close, he slid his hand behind her neck. And when she would have pulled away, he did not release her.

"You know," he said right next to her ear, "you have offended my lordly sensibilities."

"Have I?" she asked. Her voice was breathy, but no less clear. "By calling you overbearing?"

"And pompous and opinionated."

"Do you deny the charge?"

"Of course not. It is part of my aristocratic heritage. I would not be allowed the title were I not."

She arched her brow. "There is overbearing, and then there is *overbearing*."

"Kiss me again."

"See, there you are, ordering me—"

He did not allow her more time. He pulled her close and used all his skill. She was in the superior position, so he could not dominate her as was his usual method. Instead, he tried to tempt, to ask, and to cling. This ended up working much too well. Usually when he took his pleasure from a woman, he controlled the pace, making sure they both ended up satisfied.

But in this position, he was forced to please and not take. But it made him crazy with lust. If he allowed it to continue, he would go too fast. He would forget her and take what he wanted. This time, it was he who broke away.

"Helaine," he gasped. And when he had no more words, he looked back at her, traced her swollen lips with his thumb, and calculated the force he would need to flip her on her back.

She must have read his intention. She must have seen that he was on the edge of his control, because she pulled back, her eyes wide with alarm. It should have cooled his lust, but with distance he could see more of her. He saw how her skin was flushed and her nipples were tightly pressed against her dress. He caught her wrist, holding her beside him when she would have run. "You must know this is why I asked you here today."

"Yes," she whispered.

"So why do you run?"

She bit her lip, and he found the sight too gamine. She was not a woman who gave in to games. She was clearly torn, her desire at war with her good sense. He wanted her to cease this indecision and choose him. Choose the pleasure they could share.

"I will not hurt you, Helaine," he said. "Though I have never done it before, I know how to initiate a virgin."

She blanched at that, her gaze slipping from his face to his chest, but stopping there. At that point, he realized that perhaps she was not *acting* gamine. Perhaps she really did not know what he was about.

He needed to be more blunt. She was a woman who would be nervous where she did not understand. So he took her hand. She was trembling, resisting his caress, so he simply held her such that her palm pressed against his heart.

"Do you feel that?" he asked. "That is what you do to me. My heart is pounding for you."

She swallowed, but didn't speak. Then he slowly drew her hand downward. If she was reluctant before, now she was downright alarmed. But he didn't release her, and in time her curiosity overcame her fear. Plus, he was relentless, pushing her hand down until she felt the full length and girth of him beneath his clothing.

"Oh!" she gasped. "It's so hot!"

He didn't speak. His eyes were rolling back from the pleasure. God, what he wouldn't give to strip out of his clothing right this instant, to feel her flesh stroking him, kissing him, taking his whole length between her thighs. He wanted that almost as much as he wanted to never move, to never end the sweet torment of her hand on him.

"I know the mechanics," she said. "Mama explained it to me years ago. I just . . . I don't understand how it can happen."

She was petting him slowly, measuring the size of him, and he was breathless from the exquisiteness of her exploration.

"We will fit," he managed, though he had precious little control of his reason. "This I swear to you. We will fit beautifully."

She did not remove her hand, but her touch slowed, her strokes stopped. A moment later, he was able to open his eyes and look at her.

"Don't you understand?" she said softly. "Lying with you is such an irretrievable step. I know my reputation is already damned. I know it, and yet, someday there might be a man who loves me. I would want to go to our wedding night a virgin."

He nodded. He understood her words, but they were at distinct odds with her actions. "Why did you come here tonight?"

She laughed, and he heard desperation in the sound. "Do you know how long it has been since someone talked to me about anything but clothing and money? Since a . . . a man touched me the way I wanted to be touched?" She shook her head. "I could not force myself to give up this treat. But that does not mean I wish to be deflowered, either."

She removed her hand from his body and placed it neatly in her lap. Her face held regret and longing, but nothing compared to the anguish he felt at the loss of her caress.

He cleared his throat, struggling to gather his wits. "As to deflowering, Helaine, there is much that can be done without loss of virginity."

Her eyes widened and he could tell he'd surprised her. "Something beyond kissing?"

He groaned. "Did you imagine that there was nothing else? A kiss or the full deed?"

She bit her lip and looked toward the fire. "I had wondered, but there seemed little point in speculating."

He pushed up onto his elbow so he could face her more closely. And then he stroked her cheek. He went slowly, their gazes locked, letting her stop him when he went too fast. She barely moved, and so he caressed her cheek, then rolled his thumb over her lips. Her mouth was open slightly and he could feel the moist curl of her breath around his thumb. Without breaking the connection of their gazes, he trailed his fingers down her neck and across her bodice. Her breath caught and held, but she did not stop him. And soon he was able to cup her breast in his palm and stroke his thumb across her tight nipple.

Her mouth opened even more, and her eyelids fluttered. She probably didn't even realize it, but she also lifted her chest the tiniest bit so that she settled more fully into his palm.

"There is so much that can be done without the loss of virginity," he said. "Will you trust me to be careful? To show you pleasure without taking your innocence?"

She grabbed his wrist, stilling his movements. "I believe my innocence is in tatters at my feet right now."

Now he did smile. "There are different levels of innocence, don't you think? How old are you, Helaine?"

"Twenty-eight."

"Much too old for naïveté. Any man who loves you will expect that you have experienced something of life."

She pulled his hand away from her breast, but kept it between her palms as she rested them in her lap. She did not know what he could do to her with just a simple shift of his fingers.

"That's not true, and you know it."

He paused, wondering what he really did believe. "I think that there are more choices for women beyond wife and mistress. You are proof of that. You are a dressmaker and a business owner. And I think that if you choose to experience all that life can offer, then no man should damn you for it."

"Just me," she whispered. "And the man I might one day marry."

"Is there a man?" He could scarce believe the alarm that shot through him at that thought. What if she had already selected someone? What if she knew—

"No one," she said. "But I would like to think I could find love." Her lips curved in a soft smile. "That is the wonder of not being the child of an earl. I have the luxury of marrying who I want. I can choose a man for love."

He knew that she was in truth the daughter of an earl,

but that an honorable marriage among his set was impossible. So perhaps she had the right of it. As plain Mrs. Mortimer, she did have options that he did not. She could marry any man she chose with no one to say she was marrying down.

"*Mrs.* Mortimer is not a virgin. Perhaps you should embrace your identity completely."

She laughed at that, a sweet shimmer of sound that was real humor. "Surely you have better arguments than that, my lord."

He smiled. "Only one. So much has been taken from you, Helaine. Allow me to give you an evening's pleasure. That is why you came here, is it not? To have one evening of joy? I swear I will not take your virginity, my dear. Do you trust my word of honor?"

"Yes," she said, though the word was barely more than a breath of air.

"Then kiss me again, Helaine. Place your hands here, on my chest." He guided her palms to rest just below his shoulders. When the feelings became too intense, she could raise her arms to grip his shoulders or lower them to do what he had already taught her. "And let me give you something special."

He kissed her. He went slowly because he had more respect for her now, and more awareness of her needs. He teased her lips, he stroked his tongue across the seam, and he slipped inside. He didn't dominate, but he played with her. And when she relaxed into his kiss, he slid his hands around behind her back.

His fingers were deft as they slid the buttons from their holes. Her gown began to open, the shoulders slipping down. He felt her awareness of the change. Felt her tremble in anxiety, so he renewed his efforts with the kiss. And he slid his hands up from her buttons to stroke her bare flesh revealed. The base of her neck, the elegant curve of her shoulders, and the long sweep of her arms as he pushed her dress down.

Her chemise was in the way. It was a thin piece of cheap cotton, and he mentally decided to buy her a new one of sheerest silk. Especially since he had no patience with the thing. There were no straps, and he had no desire to break their kiss to lift it off her head.

He tore it, the flinch in his conscience eased by the decision to buy her a dozen new chemises. But it was nothing compared to her reaction. The low rasp as the fabric tore had her pulling back, her eyes wide and her lips wet from his kiss.

"What did you do?"

"Only this," he said as he gently, slowly, and deliberately pulled her torn chemise from her body. It was still trapped beneath her gown, so the steady tug caressed her skin the way he wanted to. It abraded her nipples and made her shiver in delight. Or so he hoped.

"Trust me," he whispered as he tossed the thing away. Her dress was barely held up, the neckline caught on the swell of her breasts. Her skin was flushed and her body taut. She was like a young deer torn between immobility and a full-out bolt. So he petted her as he would a terrified animal. He stroked his fingers gently along her shoulder, his thumb brushing the prominent line of her collarbone. Her skin was flushed, and her breath suspended, so he continued talking just to reassure her.

"Some nakedness is required, Helaine. But you can trust me."

Then he leaned forward and began kissing along her neck. The position was awkward as she was sitting before him, her legs tucked to the side. But he managed to do what he needed. He pressed tiny kisses along her collarbone, to her sternum, then eventually to the top of her breast, where the gown restrained him.

He felt her relax into his attention, her breath easing out on a long sigh of delight. So he decided to be bolder. He lifted his hands, cupped a breast with one hand while the other tugged her gown down to her waist. Then, before she could react, he caught one pert nipple in his mouth and began to suck.

He could tell no one had done such a thing to her ever

before. She perhaps had never even conceived that a man could do this. Her body arched as if it had been struck by lightning. Her hands rose immediately to his shoulders, holding him tightly.

He did not stop, did not release her. He began to suck in rhythmic timing that had her swaying forward and back in time to his motions. While one hand lifted her breast into the better position for his mouth, the other boldly gripped her free nipple and began to squeeze it.

She began to shake, her body coming alive beneath his mouth and hand. It was the work of a moment to ease her down to the floor, though he had to scramble at the last moment to cushion her head with the pillow. Now he had full movement with her reclined and him on his knees above her. There was so much he could do to her from this vantage point. But instead of pursuing her down, he took a moment to look at her.

She was naked from the waist up, and the fire continued to touch her skin with golden light. The rosy blush of her skin, the lifted puckering of her nipples, and the slightly dazed look in her eyes had his blood demanding more.

"Lift your hips," he said, his hands going to where her dress pooled about her hips. "Let me see you naked."

Her eyes widened, the dazed confusion rapidly shifting to alarm. "Robert . . . ," she began, but he wasn't listening. He had the strength and the leverage he needed. He knew how to do this. His work with the patients at the Chandler had long since taught him how to quickly and efficiently strip a woman. So he did.

He pushed his hands beneath her slender body, looped his thumbs into the curve of her gown, and stripped the thing away. Between one breath and the next, her dress was gone. Except for her stockings and shoes, she was naked and laid out before him for the taking.

Chapter 13

❧❦

Helaine knew the moment she was in trouble. Up until now, she had seen passion in Robert's eyes. Desire, humor, even frustration had slipped across his features. But never had she seen that dark possessive glint in him. Not until he had looked down at her half-naked body and decided he wanted more. At that moment he had switched from friend and possible lover to a man bending the world to his will. Then he had stripped off the rest of her gown and she had gone from slightly dazed to frightened in the space of a heartbeat.

She scrambled backward, but wasn't fast enough. He clamped a hand on her ankle, and his dark eyes widened in surprise.

"Helaine?" he asked, his voice frighteningly soft. "Where are you going?"

"No," she said as she struggled futilely to free her foot. "No, you have gone too far."

His nostrils flared and his hand tightened on her ankle. "Too far? I have done nothing you did not want or allow."

She frowned, damning herself for daring to believe this was possible. That she could enjoy the company of a man without it turning ugly. "Not me, you dolt," she snapped. "You have lost control of yourself; you have gone too far in your own mind. Now let go!"

She kicked hard with her foot. She meant to simply jerk her ankle out of his hand, but she connected with his hip in the process. Her toes crumpled against his bone, and he grunted at the impact. Sadly, it did nothing to help her escape. If anything, his hand gripped even tighter.

"What are you talking about?" he demanded. "I am no different than I was a moment before. If you will just relax, then you will see."

She grimaced. His tone, his touch, even the tight grip to her fingers told her he'd lost patience. He'd forgotten about her entirely and the thought made her infinitely sad. Furious, too, but sad as well. For a while there, she had thought they could be friends.

"You have forgotten yourself, Robert," she said slowly. Gently. As one would talk to a rabid dog because, in her mind, that was exactly what he had become. "I am sorry for what has happened, but you need to release me." She straightened up, all too conscious that she was virtually naked. "Let go of my ankle or I shall scream."

He reared back. "The devil you say!"

"And if you hit me, I shall have bruises that your sister will see. I might even now have them on my ankle."

That hit him far more than anything else. His hand jerked back as if she burned him, and then he gazed hard at where his fingers had wrapped around her body. There were no marks, except perhaps a reddened imprint. She was sturdier than that. But it gave her enough freedom to scoot backward and grab her shift. The dress was behind him and out of her reach.

"Helaine," he said, the word half plea, half apology, but she knew better than to believe him now.

She lifted her shift, damning her hands for how they shook. It took her a moment to sort through the fabric, and then she nearly cried. The shift was ripped and would never be worn again. It was old and meant for the rag bin anyway, but she had precious few of them and mourned the loss of even this.

How had she allowed herself to be so seduced? He had ripped her clothing and tossed aside her dress, and he hadn't done anything more than pull off his cravat. That alone showed her how far outside of her depth she had gone. What had she been thinking to come to him like this? To lie with him even a little?

"God, I am such a fool," she said. She balled up her shift into one hand, then gestured to her gown. She had learned from experience with her father that a firm, calm hand was needed when he was deeply in his cups. "Hand me my gown, please, Robert."

He complied, passing over her clothing with a slow hand. His expression was serious, though, and he appeared to be thinking furiously.

"I don't understand what just happened," he said.

She was on her feet already, quickly pulling the gown over her head. The buttons down the back were another problem altogether, but she could manage a few of them. The rest would have to be covered beneath her wrap.

"Turn around. I can do them for you." His words were simple, his expression calm. He was back in control of himself. She saw that now, but she didn't trust that it would last.

He must have seen that hesitation because he sighed and shook his head even as he pushed to his feet.

"I assure you, I can restrain myself from ravishing you for the time it takes to fasten a few buttons."

Yes, he could, but she was not at all sure she wanted to get that close to him. After all, her skin still shimmered with an awareness of him that was wholly unwelcome at the moment. But neither did she want to leave with her gown half done. So she slowly approached him and turned around.

Her back muscles twitched when he put his fingers to her skin. He didn't work the buttons at all, just set the pads of three fingers against her spine.

"Passion demands some loss of control. Indeed, I believe that is the point. To be swept away."

"You promised to sweep me away, my lord," she returned. "One of us had to remain in control. You lost yours, therefore—"

"That is not how passion works."

She thought about it a moment and had to admit he was probably right. Meanwhile, he lifted his fingers from her skin and made quick work of her buttons. And when he was done, she stepped away to look at him. She fought with her words, but finally expressed them in an awkward way.

"I do not trust men who are not in control of themselves."

His expression darkened. "So you have been hurt before."

"No, not like you mean. But even a child knows there is nothing more frightening than someone who is larger, stronger, and more powerful who has lost control. Who gets hurt in that situation, my lord? The powerful aristocrat? Or the weak woman?"

"You are many things, Helaine, but weak is not one of them."

Oh, how she wished that were true. She was vulnerable in so many ways. Financially, she risked everything, and he had no understanding of what it was like to teeter on the edge of poverty. Personally, she felt more and more vulnerable to Robert, even after this debacle. He was charming, smart, and titled. Everything she had once wanted in a husband.

"Then call me a coward, my lord, because you frighten me."

He leaned back against the mantel, his expression hooded, his arms crossed over his chest. "You are no coward, either."

She shrugged. She had no answer to that. She felt like the smallest thing next to him. An egg, perhaps, or a tiny seedling about to be crushed beneath his boot heel. Not because he was cruel, but simply because he wouldn't notice what he was doing.

"I should stick to my own kind, I think," she said softly. "There should be a man among the merchants of this world. Someone who will understand what it takes to survive the whims of the aristocracy."

He snorted. "You have hidden your birth, but not your breeding. Even your own kind, as you put it, knows that you were born the daughter of an earl."

She gasped, needing to run his words over again in her mind. They didn't change, and neither did the truth.

"You know who I am," she whispered. He knew what her father had done. Now she really was at his mercy. He could destroy her at any moment. All it would take would be a word, a comment to his sister or mother. He might not even do it intentionally, but what about one day in his cups? What about—

"I will be your mistress," she suddenly said. "I will spread myself before you, do whatever you want. I will—"

His arms dropped to his sides in shock. "Good God, Helaine, I do not mean to blackmail you! What kind of monster do you think I am?"

Her knees went out from beneath her and she sank to the couch in terror. "What do you want?" she said. "There are so many lives dependent upon me. I pray you remember that. Not only my mother, but now Penny and the boy. Wendy would survive. Dressmakers always need a talented seamstress. But the rest of us . . ." Her voice trailed away. What would she do if he turned against her? He touched her shoulder then. She had seen him move forward, had steeled herself for his caress. What demands would he make?

He stroked her cheek just once, and then let his hand fall away. "I shall call for my coach. I will stay here, Helaine, and he will return you to your home."

She looked up at him, feared that he was merely delaying the inevitable. Eventually he would call on her and demand something. Men always did. How many times had her father done something nice for her? Out of guilt or charity or simply because he had won at the gaming tables that night. He would gift her with something, say it was because he loved her, but then weeks or months later he would turn it on her. He would point to his gift, whether it be a necklace or the food on the table. He would rail that he had done that for them, and he'd demand that they repay him in some way.

"I am not a monster," Robert repeated, though it was clear he didn't expect her to believe him. "I will never tell."

"And will you never lose control? Never become angry with me and wish revenge? Never—"

"Helaine!" he snapped, clearly offended. "You have no reason to fear me!" Then he huffed, his gaze going to the ceiling. "How can I convince you? I have already sworn that I will do nothing to interfere with your business. My sister has decided to make your shop fashionable. I stand here like a monk, though God knows that's not what I want. I still find you beyond beautiful. What else can I do?"

She had no answer. He could promise her the moon right now, but she wouldn't believe him. "There is nothing," she whispered, wondering how it had all changed so fast. "I have no faith in men's promises. I should have remembered that before I began this night."

"So we are all villains merely because of our biology?"

She lifted her hand in a gesture of futility. "Biology, rearing, education, I don't know. But no man has ever proved himself true to me. None have looked to my thoughts before theirs, to their family before their lusts."

He frowned and shook his head. "I have never betrayed you like that."

"You were about to."

"You cannot know that. You damn me without ever giving me a chance."

She bit her lip. Was that what she had done? She didn't know, and she hadn't the focus now to figure it out. So she straightened to her feet. "Thank you, my lord," she said with as much dignity as she could muster. "I can honestly say that I will never forget this night."

He nodded, his gaze still searching her face. "Nor I." Then he crossed to the door, opened it, and called for the innkeeper, instructing the man to have his carriage readied immediately. When that was done, he turned back to her, gently holding up her wrap and gloves.

"You will wish these," he said neutrally.

She nodded and forced herself to step up to him. It wasn't that hard. Indeed, now that she was leaving, she found herself wanting to go back to the moment before. What if she'd closed her eyes when he stripped her of her gown? What if she'd clung to the oblivion of passion? Would she even now be experiencing pleasure the likes of which she could only imagine? She doubted the end would be any different, but the memory would be. The knowledge would change as well. She would finally know what women experienced in their marriage bed.

"I am sorry that I couldn't be different," she said as much to herself as to him. "I am sorry that I cannot find a way to give us both what we want."

The side of his mouth quirked up in a rueful smile. "Your fears are natural, Helaine. I have handled this badly."

She shook her head. "You are a man used to getting what he wants when he wants. I should never have thought otherwise."

He had been putting her wrap on her shoulders when she spoke, but at her words, she felt him shift. He laid his hands flat on her shoulders and gently turned her around. "So that is my excuse, you think? I am a man and an aristocrat, so I must by definition hurt you? I have no control of it at all?"

"You didn't tonight," she said, her chin lifting as she challenged him. "Your every intention was to charm me, to pleasure me, to make this a night when everything was perfect. And yet I will leave here more unsettled, more afraid, and more uncertain than ever before."

He grimaced. "I will not reveal your identity, Helaine. To anyone. I swear it!"

"And what is my forfeit when you do?"

He threw up his hands. "What do you want?"

"A livelihood, my lord. Promise that if you ruin me, then you will give me the means to start anew."

He nodded. "Done."

She searched his eyes, reading his intention in every line of his body. He meant what he said, and he was generally believed to be a man who honored his debts. She felt her breath ease out in relief. She no longer feared total disaster. If he destroyed her, he would do what he could to make amends. It wasn't much, she reminded herself. A dozen things could change between now and then. A passionate promise today could mean nothing at all tomorrow. But it was the most reassurance she could have right at the moment.

"Thank you," she said. Then there was no more time. The innkeeper returned to say the carriage was ready.

She left then, her gaze lingering as long as possible on his face. She wanted to memorize the texture and the colors to hold close to her at night. Perhaps she would damn him someday, but for tonight, she simply felt a longing for what could have been. If only things were very different, they could have had something wonderful together.

If only . . .

"Good-bye, my lord."

"Good-bye, Mrs. Mortimer."

Then she walked away.

Robert stayed in the inn for hours after she left. He ate roasted almonds, stared into the fire, and thought. First he cataloged his emotions. He felt everything from anger that all his plans had been for naught and elation that he had escaped a viper-tongued, inconsistent harpy. That was a childish fit of pique, but he indulged it for a few moments. It was allowed in the privacy of this little room.

Eventually he admitted that he was to blame. She had told him they would not lie together, that she would not be his mistress. He was merely angry that his plans to circumvent her morals had failed.

Which led him to shame. Deep and penetrating shame. He recalled in detail all those times when he had felt superior to his father, more levelheaded than his younger brother, more morally upright than most of his peers. Did he not care for sick prostitutes? Had he not thrown his father out of the house for accosting a maid? While his peers were drinking and whoring throughout London, he was the one working, trying to salvage his brother's tuition money from his father's latest business inspiration. He was a prince among men, the most constant, *moral* man of character in London.

Until Helaine. The moment she'd stepped into his sights, he'd planned her seduction with the same force of character that he'd applied to managing the family estate, disciplining his father, and raising his younger siblings. In short, the only reason he was accounted a man of good character was because the right temptation had not yet crossed his path. Once Helaine had appeared, all his virtue had flown away and he'd become as depraved as all the rest.

Quite a sobering thought. More sobering was that he was still thinking about her, lusting after her, and if he let his mind wander at all, he was still planning just how he could seduce her. The very idea was appalling, and yet he could not stop himself. He wanted her with a passion bordering on insanity. It wasn't just simple lust. If that were the problem, he could sate himself with any number of women. But tonight he had enjoyed her company, her humor, and yes, even her good advice.

Never had he thought a woman could be so amazing, and never had he expected that he couldn't have her. That he couldn't devise some stratagem to make her his. Or that, even worse, it would be immoral for him to do so.

But it was. Because she had refused him. Completely and utterly this time, despite his careful seduction techniques.

Which led him to one inescapable choice. He could continue down this path to ruin—hers and his own—or he could give in to her wishes and leave her alone. Obviously a good man would choose the latter. It was sobering just how hard it was to make that choice. But eventually ethics won over. Sadly, he had no faith in his own constancy now. He had to leave London or risk going back on his decision. He needed to return to the coal mine anyway. He had clothing for the night, as he'd planned to stay with Helaine. He could leave in the morning without ever driving through London, without risking a change of heart, without finding some excuse to see Helaine again.

So it was decided. He would leave her alone by way of leaving London. Once committed to the choice, he dashed off notes to the relevant people and then sought a cold and lonely bed upstairs.

Chapter 14

✦

A week later, Robert was feeling almost back to normal. He had labored hard at the mine, which was now running more smoothly. Charlie had been a good choice, and together they had stopped most of the grumbling. Yes, he now employed children, much though he hated the idea. But only boys fourteen years or older. There were new ponies and new carts for the other children to tend in the sunshine, and he had toyed with the idea of school if he could hire a teacher.

What he couldn't do was make money appear out of thin air. It would be a long while yet before he recouped his latest expenditures, but at least everything was on the right track. So he turned his horse toward London and rode steadily home. Sadly, the minute the day no longer held constant work, his mind wandered straight back to Helaine. Their evening together had taken on a rosy hue this last week. He was constantly remembering the laughter they'd shared. New things struck him every day that he wanted to share with her. And yes, he nightly tortured himself with the glorious softness of her skin, the sweet gasps she made when he touched her nipples, and the sight of her naked and dazed as he slowly penetrated her exquisite body. That last part hadn't actually happened, but he had lived it a thousand times in his fantasies.

Fortunately, he was finally home. Soon he could revel in his dreams in the privacy of his own bedroom. He stabled his horse and began trudging up the steps. He could see there were still lights on downstairs, so he knew someone was awake, most likely his sister. He rapidly readjusted his thoughts, picturing the way Gwen would squeal when she saw him and run into his arms. That was a dream he had experienced in reality hundreds of times, but it never got old. So his step was lively as he entered his home, barely giving Dribbs time to take his hat and coat.

"Where's Gwen?" he asked.

"In the back parlor, my lord, with her fiancé."

Robert felt his eyebrows raise. "Please tell me that my mother is acting as chaperone."

"Your mother retired some hours ago."

"His mother, then. Or sister. Or that aunt."

"I'm sorry, my lord. But I do believe the door has remained open."

Robert didn't wait to hear any more. He was tromping through the house to the back parlor, growing more furious the moment he saw that the back parlor door was *not* in fact open, but firmly shut. He grasped the doorknob and threw the barrier open, only to wish he had banged loudly on the door. He had not, not, not wanted to see his sister wrapped in Edward's passionate embrace, her hair askew, her lips swollen, and his hands . . . damn his hands! They were on her breasts!

They gasped and flew apart, but that didn't stop him from slamming the door hard enough to shake the rafters. "Out!" he roared at Edward.

Sadly, the boy didn't leave. He stood slowly, his expression grave even as he adjusted his pants. Good Lord, Robert did not want to see that the man had an erection!

"Welcome home, my lord," Edward stated calmly. There wasn't even a trace of anxiety in his tone, damn his eyes.

Robert glared at him. "This is not a welcome home, Edward. This is a crime."

"Oh, good God!" exclaimed Gwen as she straightened to stand beside her fiancé. "We're engaged! And you cannot be home!"

"Go to your room, Gwen. I shall see to it that Edward remembers that until the 'I dos' are spoken, he shall remain at a proper distance from your person at all times."

Gwen gasped in outrage and folded her arms across her chest. Sadly, it only served to emphasize to his mind that her nipples were tight and, again, he did *not* want to know that! "I am not a child to be sent to my room, Robert. And you must leave immediately!"

He gaped at her. Did she really think he was going to just go upstairs and ignore what they'd been doing down here? "Have you taken leave of your senses?"

It appeared that she had, because she waved at him with both hands, shooing him out the door. "Go to your club. You cannot be here. I have promised."

"I don't have a club."

"Then go to Father's club. I don't care. But you can't be here!"

It took him a moment to understand that she didn't mean he couldn't be in the back parlor where Edward was debauching her, but in the house at all. "This is my home! And you!" He rounded on the debaucher in question. "You can take yourself—"

"I cannot abandon the love of my life, my lord. Not when you are in such a state."

"What!"

"Shhh!" That was Gwen. "You'll wake the house!"

"They should be awake!" he roared back. "They should be chaperoning you. Does no one think in this house? Dribbs!"

"My lord," Edward began, "I take full responsibility for this terrible lapse in judgment. I—"

"You will not!" snapped Gwen. "If you recall, I was the one who climbed atop you, who kissed you first, who—"

"*Stop!*" bellowed Robert as he jerked open the door. "Dribbs!"

"Here, my lord," said the butler, who appeared to be cowering—yes, cowering—in the hallway. "I was just going to find your brandy."

"I don't want brandy, I want a chaperone right here, right now! Better yet, two footmen to stand guard—"

"Fine, then!" huffed Gwen as she grabbed hold of the boy's arm. "We shall simply go to his house. In fact, forget the downstairs parlor. Edward, take me to your bedroom. Lay me down on your bed. We shall have our wedding night now!"

"The devil you will! Dribbs! My sister is under guard. Three footmen at all times! Until the moment she walks down that aisle, she is never to be left alone, not even in her bedroom. They will stand there and stare at her and make sure she doesn't climb out of the window!"

He wasn't nearly done with his tirade. He had merely stopped to draw breath, but in that moment of silence, a quiet voice cut through the room. It was stern and calm, and very, very female. It was, in fact, the one voice he had never expected to hear again: Helaine's. And that was why his tirade stopped in midbreath. Because he couldn't credit that he had heard her at all.

"Goodness, you do have a way of making sure everyone knows you are about, don't you?"

Robert stood still, his mouth hanging open as he spun around to stare at Helaine. She was dressed in a simple gown that was obviously hastily pulled on. He knew that because the buttons in the front were mismatched around the belly and because her hair was tumbling loose about her shoulders. Honey brown hair flowed freely down her back.

He didn't know what to say. Indeed, he didn't know anything at all. What was she doing here? Meanwhile, Gwen rushed forward, all heartfelt embarrassment as she apologized, not to Robert for creating such a scene in the first place, but to Helaine.

"I am so, so sorry, Mrs. Mortimer. He came home unexpectedly. He said he would be away two weeks at the least. That's what he told Dribbs. Two weeks! But as you can see, he came back unexpectedly. But he's leaving straightaway. Just getting some clothes and repairing to an inn or some such thing." Gwen twisted slightly to pin him with an evil glare. "Tell her, Robert. Tell her that you're leaving straightaway."

"I finished early," he said, knowing that he wasn't speaking to anything at all. "I came home. I thought you would squeal and hug me."

Gwen scoffed as only a younger sibling can do. "I haven't done that in ages. Really, Robert, can you not open your eyes and see that I am a woman?"

That was exactly what he didn't want to see! Swollen lips? Pert breasts? Good God, he was her *brother*! "Please just go to your room, Gwen."

"No, I won't! You must—"

"Actually, my dear," interrupted Edward in low, rational tones, "I believe it has been a long day." He grabbed her hands and lifted them together to his mouth. Gwen huffed, her anger fading as a softness entered her body.

"You don't have to go," she said, her tone a great deal more moderate.

Robert opened his mouth to say he bloody well did, but Helaine's hand jerked upright, distracting him enough that the moment—and his words—were lost. Edward finished pressing a kiss to Gwen's knuckles, then executed a respectful bow to all before he nimbly dashed around Robert for the door.

"I'll see you to the door," Gwen said as she scampered with him.

Dribbs, of course, stayed well out of their way. The only reason he wasn't sacked at that very moment was because he did indeed have a bottle of brandy in his hand. But it didn't stop Robert from snapping one last insult.

"Three footmen," he called. "And bars on your window."

"That's fine, brother dear," Gwen called back. "I'll just sleep at his house tonight."

"Gwen!"

"Oh stop it," Helaine said as she neatly cut off his pathway to the front door. "She's just poking for the fun of it. And you respond like a bear with a sore paw every time."

"You don't know what they were doing when I walked in."

"And what were you doing bursting in on an engaged couple? I would say you got exactly what you deserved."

He threw out a hand to point in fury down the hall. "They are not married yet!"

"And you are tilting at windmills, my lord. Young, happy, lustful windmills."

He stared at her, his mind grappling with what she had just said. "That makes no sense!"

"Then it is a perfect match for you because you don't, either. Goodness, Robert, sit down, drink your brandy, and leave the lovers to their—"

"Don't say it!"

"To their good-byes," she finished. Then she crossed her arms and shook her head. "I cannot fathom how you have managed to raise such a delightful sister acting this way. How is it that she hasn't murdered you in your sleep?"

"She's tried. Believe me."

"I do believe you. And I also believe that she is an intelligent woman about to marry an extraordinarily levelheaded young man. You should be happy for their passion, my lord. So few have it in their marriage beds."

"Only if they *wait* for their marriage bed," he grumbled. But his rancor was fading, his ill temper slowly replaced by the joy of talking to her again.

"Never fear, my lord. Gwen told me that he has French letters. You know. To prevent pregnancy."

"Oh, my God—" The boy had purchased condoms. And told his sister about them? Meanwhile, Helaine kept talking, keeping him from saying any of the furious words that were leaping through his mind.

"Gwen said it was because they do not wish for children

right away. He has the letters so that they can enjoy being just the two of them for a while before adding children. I can tell you that she was much relieved and thought it especially touching of him. So never fear. If they have been enjoying themselves before their vows, no one will be the wiser."

But he knew. He knew bloody well too much now. "Bars," he murmured. "Bars on the windows and guards outside her door. Maybe I'll even chain her to the bedpost."

Helaine laughed, the sweet sound cutting through his ill humor like a light through the fog. "And then unchain her the moment her eyes tear up. She has told me, you know, that all she has to do to bend you to her will is to cry. Just one tear, and you melt like butter."

"The devil she did."

"She did. And I believe her. Now sit down, drink your brandy, and stop yelling. It will wake your mother and she has had a full day."

His mind was immediately distracted from how his sister bragged about manipulating him. "My mother? Is she ill?"

"No, no. But she has been up all day without her nap, helping with the dress designs and the like. Edward's relations are certainly overpowering, but they seem to be exactly what she needs right now."

"Truly?" he mused. "Perhaps I should have been more forceful with her over the years."

Helaine snorted. "No, Robert. Your type of forcefulness and a woman's type are two different things. I believe she just needed a woman's hand."

He frowned. "But what is the difference between the two?"

Her head tilted as she looked at him. "Can you not see it? Truly?"

He shook his head, finding his ill humor returning. "I would not have asked if I already knew."

She dipped her head. "Of course, my lord. My apology—"

"Just say it, Helaine. Pray do not go stiff after all this time."

She paused a moment to study his face. He kept his

expression neutral, almost bland. But he was keenly interested in her thoughts and so he waited in stillness for her perspective. In time, she realized he was being honest and answered. "You wanted your mother to get out of bed because you and your siblings needed a mother, your father needed a wife, and the household needed a mistress. The more forceful you might be with your needs, the more she would withdraw into her bedroom."

"But we did need her."

She sighed. "Yes, I know." She stepped forward and lightly placed her hand on his arm. "Robert, I am terribly sorry that she failed you. You deserved a mother who could help you against your father, against all the tasks that were thrust too young on your shoulders."

"But these other women, Edward's relations. What have they done to help her?"

"They want her to be happy, Robert. To play with the dresses if she likes, to go on a walk and breathe the fresh air if she desires. They look to what she wants and take all of the burden on themselves. Truly, your mother did nothing all day but sit and have people bustle about her showing her things. And we left her alone when she tired, though she never left the room."

"I want her to be happy, too." He hated that he sounded so ridiculous. That Helaine thought he had no care for his mother, that he did not wish her to be as joyful as she could possibly be. "I did everything I could for her."

He saw understanding light in her eyes. "Of course you did, Robert. Of course you *do.* But you are her son. If you are forceful with her, then she feels burdened by your needs. If you ignore her, she feels guilty for her lacks. If you beg her to be happy, she tries to do it for you and fails, which makes her feel worse than before."

"But she does not feel that way with Edward's family?"

"Of course not. She does not love them like she loves you."

Robert turned, his eyes widening at the impact of her words. She spoke so casually, as if all of this were obvious. Perhaps it was to her. But to him, the statement that his mother loved him reached deep inside. It touched a well of misery he hadn't even realized was there. Not until her words healed them.

His mother loved him. Despite the way she shut herself away from him, despite the whimpers and misery whenever she stepped outside of her bedroom door. Despite it all, she loved him. He tugged the words close to his heart and held them there like a precious toy. And when he feared he would unman himself by crying in front of her, he reached for the bottle of brandy that Dribbs had so conveniently left on the sideboard. He crossed to it and poured a glass with a shaking hand. When the globe was filled, he lifted it up but didn't drink.

His mother loved him. When Helaine said it, he believed it. And the knowledge was pure joy.

Eventually he found his voice, though he had to push the words through a thick throat. "If dresses and Edward's women are what she needs, then they shall have the run of the house."

"Well, I shouldn't go overboard with that, if I were you. Perhaps every other day or every third."

He turned back to her, finding he could smile now without losing his dignity. "Whatever you think best. I shall tell Dribbs to open and close the door solely upon your decision."

Her brows shot up at that. "At the direction of a dressmaker? Surely you jest."

"Surely I don't." He swirled the brandy about in his glass. He looked at the dark liquid, smelled the aroma of the rich brew, but his mind was on her. Helaine. Eventually he looked at her and asked the two questions that had been in his mind from the moment he'd seen her. "Why are you here, Helaine? And how can I make you stay?"

She smiled and stepped closer. He was within a breath of taking her into his arms when she lifted the glass out of his hands. Then she was walking away with it, sipping the brew as cheekily as if he had offered it to her. And he should have, he realized. He just hadn't thought she would drink brandy.

Meanwhile she settled onto the settee, kicked off her slippers, and curled her feet up behind her. He had to blink at the sight. How many times had he seen Gwen do just the same thing? And yet, the idea of Gwen and Helaine in the same thought, the same breath, as the same two mature women made him distinctly uncomfortable.

He cleared his throat by way of ordering his thoughts. Then he gestured to the bar behind him. "Would you care for something else?"

She shook her head. "Brandy was my father's love. I grew up stealing sips from his glass."

"Ah. Then please enjoy as much as you like."

"Just a sip," she said, taking just one before setting the glass aside. "I do not care for how a whole glass makes me feel."

"Out of control?" he guessed.

She nodded, watching him carefully as he crossed to sit beside her. They were not touching. Indeed, he sat as far away from her as he could possibly manage and still be on the settee. But he angled his face and his body to her. He did not want anything to interfere with his sight of her and these precious moments of accord.

"Helaine—"

"I am here because you asked Edward to ask Gwen to install me in the house so that I could design everyone's gowns for the Season."

Ah, yes. He had done that, hadn't he? One of his best ideas ever.

"I only agreed to come because Gwen promised me that you were not at home."

"I wasn't then."

"Yes, I'd noticed you'd returned."

"I always knew you were a perceptive woman."

She snorted, but her eyes crinkled at the corners when she did it. If he looked closely, he might say she was smiling. Then he said something that startled even himself.

"I will leave if you wish it. I do not want to make you uncomfortable."

She sighed and looked at her hands. "I am a dressmaker, my lord. I would not dream of ousting a viscount from his home."

He had the strongest urge to tap her chin, to stroke her cheek, to do anything to bring her gaze back to his. But he knew that doing such a thing would make her bolt. So he stayed exactly where he was and prayed his words would do what his body could not. "Even so, Helaine. I will leave if you wish it."

She didn't answer for a long moment, and he found himself holding his breath, waiting for her response. In the end, she shook her head. "I think in a house this size, we can manage to stay out of each other's way."

He didn't want to stay out of her way, but he didn't argue. "Thank you, Helaine," he finally said.

"For letting you stay in your own home?"

"For giving me a second chance."

Her eyebrows shot up almost to her hairline. "I said nothing about a second chance, my lord."

"A second chance to do this," he said, gesturing to the two of them sitting companionably on a settee. "A second chance to be friends."

Her mouth slipped open as if she wanted to say something but then found no words. She simply stared at him, and no wonder. Him? Friends with a dressmaker? The idea was ludicrous, and yet he desperately wanted it to be true. And truthfully, the idea was not so far-fetched, he realized. He was friends with Chandelle, wasn't he? A madame at a former house of prostitution. Why could he not be friends with a dressmaker as well? Especially one who was insightful regarding his family, smart about business, and beautiful enough to make him ache with longing.

"Is it possible, Helaine? Could you trust me enough to be friends?"

She nodded slowly, her words coming out even more reluctantly. "Yes, my lord, I believe it is possible. Not probable, but definitely possible."

He would take that as a boon and be grateful. "Then you must swear to call me Robert."

"You know I cannot do that!"

"When we are alone, Helaine. Only when we are alone."

She ducked her head, but a moment later she was looking back at him. "Very well, Robert. But only on the very unlikely occasions when we are alone together."

He grinned. "Excellent! Now—"

"Now I shall be going to bed, Robert." She straightened her legs and bent slightly to put on her slippers. He entertained himself by looking boldly at her trim ankles as he scrambled for a way to entice her to stay.

"Of course you should go rest. I'll wager it has been a very long day for you."

"Yes, it most certainly has."

"Too bad, too, because I very much wanted to tell you about what happened at the mine. That's where I was, you know. This whole long, exhausting, frustrating week. I was at the mine working hand in dirty hand with Charlie." He lifted his gaze to hers. "Would you like to hear what happened?"

She did. He could see it in her eyes and the way she bit her lip in consternation. "Did you have trouble with more vandals?"

"We did."

"But you think it settled now?"

He shrugged. "As to that, who can tell? But you were going up to bed, and I shouldn't ask you to tarry."

She hovered, both feet on the ground and her hands poised to help her stand. But she didn't move.

"Or you could stay up with me for a few moments longer. Just until I finish my brandy. I have ridden a very long way, you know. I'm quite tired as well. So it will just be the one brandy." He took a healthy sip just to prove that it wouldn't take him long at all.

She chuckled, knowing exactly what he was doing but caught nonetheless. "Very well," she said as she leaned back against the couch. "Just for a little bit. Tell me what happened with the vandals."

So he did. And he told her what changes he'd implemented, what course Charlie recommended, and what he thought about it. And he asked her opinion. And he made his brandy last for more than three hours.

Chapter 15

❦

Helaine suppressed a yawn and nearly fell down the back staircase as she did so. Lord, why had she stayed up so late talking with Robert? Why hadn't she remembered that she was *not* a lady of leisure anymore? She could not sleep until noon. In fact, if she wanted breakfast, she needed to be in the servants' hall in time to be fed. And that was over an hour ago.

But that was the whole problem when she was with Robert. She forgot who she was, even who she'd been. She was simply Helaine sitting and talking with Robert and it was *wonderful*. This morning, however, was horrible. She was so bleary-eyed she doubted she could draw a straight line, much less sketch gowns for Lady Gwen's approval.

Perhaps a bun would help. Cook kept a few handy for those who had tasks during the morning meal. She stepped into the kitchen and reached for the stack, only to be stopped cold.

"Mrs. Mortimer!" cried the tall, hook-nosed woman. She was the cook and was brilliant at the task. But she also had a way of glaring at a person just like a hawk eyeing a scurrying mouse.

"Er, yes?"

"Dribbs has asked to see you. Right away."

Helaine nodded as she tried again to reach for a bun. "Of course, of course. I'll see him directly after—"

Cook slapped her hand away. "You'll see him *now*."

"Er, yes. Right away." Helaine slunk away. She'd known that the household kept a strict schedule. No laze-abouts tolerated. Anyone who slept past morning meal would go hungry. She'd known it, and so she wasn't very surprised at her rebuff. She would just have to befriend one of the maids so that she could be woken in time tomorrow. And there would be no more late-night discussions with his lordship.

She pushed through the door that separated the main house from the servants' domain. Dribbs was there at his usual position, half an eye on the house, half an eye on who and what came through that door. He smiled immediately upon seeing her and crossed to her side.

"Mrs. Mortimer. I trust you are well this morning?"

She smiled and managed a wry twist to her lips. "As well as I deserve, Mr. Dribbs. Cook mentioned that you wished to speak with me?"

"Yes, ma'am. If you would step in here, please?" He crossed to what was usually called the butler's closet, but in this home, it was very much larger than the typical closet. He had a small room that included a desk plus a small settee and table, which was currently set with a breakfast of tea, jam, and hot buns. She couldn't see the steam rising from the hot bread, but she could absolutely smell the delightful scent and her stomach rumbled in hunger.

She glanced nervously at Dribbs, who arched a brow at her. "Is something amiss?" he asked, his voice excruciatingly dry.

She glanced at him. Something in his tone or attitude was different. As if there were an undercurrent of humor in everything he said, but that couldn't possibly be true. Whereas Dribbs was known to be rather familiar with the earl's family—downright cheeky, if truth be told—he was known belowstairs as a man with a stern hand. He would not be overly familiar with a dressmaker, even if she had spent the night talking with the earl. If anything he would be more stern, just so he could enforce his authority over her.

Keeping that in mind, she forced her eyes away from the breakfast and folded her hands together to keep from reaching for it. "Nothing's wrong, Mr. Dribbs. How can I help you this morning?"

"I understand you have been keeping irregular hours, Mrs. Mortimer," he said in a cold tone. "Are you perhaps a bit hungry?"

Helaine glanced up in surprise as she realized what was happening. She feared she was about to receive a very stern dressing-down from a butler. That would be a first in her life, but again, no more than she deserved. Still, she tried to head it off.

"I know I missed morning meal, Mr. Dribbs, and my hunger is appropriate punishment for that. But I have not in any way shorted my duties toward the family."

"I should think not!" he snapped. Then he gestured to the settee. "Pray sit down."

She did as he bade, though she moved slowly. He had indicated that she sit directly in front of the food. Was he torturing her? Setting out food when he knew she couldn't eat it?

She watched as he sat down in the chair across from her, his expression almost bland. Except for a tiny flash of . . . something. Was he laughing at her?

"Mr. Dribbs?"

"I received a note from his lordship this morning. It was there waiting for me when I arose. It concerned you, Mrs. Mortimer." He paused, looking down his nose at her in the most imperious manner.

"Er, what did it say?" she asked. Or she tried to ask. Sadly, her mouth was salivating enough that it came out more like "shay."

"He requested that you share breakfast with the family."

It took a moment for her to understand his words, and

even then she still didn't know how to respond. "I'm sorry," she finally managed. "That's, er, most unusual."

"This can be an unusual household. But his lordship was most specific. Said he wished to speak with you over his morning breakfast."

She brightened, immeasurably relieved. Robert didn't wish her to share breakfast with him. He wanted to *talk* to her at breakfast. As a master speaks to his servants. "I'll report to him right away." She made to straighten off the settee, but was stopped by Dribbs's soft cough. She froze in a half crouch.

"Was there more?"

"With Master Robert? Always. Perhaps I should just show you his request." So saying, he reached over to his desk and pulled out a crisp sheet of linen. Helaine sat back down on the settee, then gingerly took the paper. She read it twice, her heart pounding harder and harder with each word.

Dribbs: I would like Mrs. Mortimer to dine with the family beginning immediately.

She looked up at the butler, her mind blanked of anything but dismay. "He couldn't," she whispered.

Dribbs nodded, his expression grave. "Yes, ma'am, he did."

"But I'm just a dressmaker. I'm not—"

"I will remind you that in this household, we follow his lordship's requests to the letter."

Helaine stared at Dribbs, at a complete loss. First of all, she absolutely knew that he did not follow his lordship's requests to the *exact* letter. Second of all, servants did not dine with the masters, even in unusual households. And third . . . third was Dribbs himself. He was acting so completely strange. She could not get a handle on his mood. One moment she thought he was laughing at her; the next moment he seemed beyond stern.

"Mr. Dribbs, I don't know what to say."

"Say nothing then," he quipped. "As you are to dine with

the family, I have brought you here to make sure you do not disgrace my table."

She did not quibble with his claim that it was *his* table. She knew that servants often felt more pride of ownership than the masters themselves did.

"I will do my best not to shame you," she managed.

"Well, you must have some instruction. If you are to dine with the family, you must make sure to do so as a lady who deserves to be there, always cognizant that you are eating with the children of an earl."

She didn't know how to answer that. After all, she was the daughter of an earl herself. She knew how to act like a lady. If anything, she had to remember to add a coarseness to her manners so as not to expose herself.

"I, um, I shall try to remember," she said.

"Good. Now pray pick up that bun."

She looked at the man, her mind stuttering. He wanted her to pick up the roll? And *not* eat it? He waited, his eyebrow lifted, as she slowly reached out and gently lifted up the bun.

"Do not grab it as if you were handling meat. Touch it gently, delicately between two fingers."

Two fingers? But it was a rather large bun. Still, she did as he bade.

"And raise the smaller fingers like so." He fluted his fingers, holding them up before her eyes so that she could mimic him.

She glanced at him and managed a slow nod as she grasped the bun between thumb and forefinger then extended the smaller of her digits. It was incredibly awkward, and her fingers were growing stiff, but she managed it.

"Excellent. Now take a bite. Mind, not a meat pie type of bite, but delicate little nips—like a lady—along the edge. And don't forget to keep your other fingers extended."

She frowned. Did he truly think ladies ate like this? Tiny nips and bizarre hand positions? She'd never done anything so ridiculous in her entire life. But she was starving and he was asking that she eat—or nip—at some food, so she tried to do it. She opened her mouth to bite. It really was a large bun.

"Not so wide! You're not a cow. Lips closed. Lips closed, I say!"

Lips closed? How did one eat with one's lips closed? She narrowed her mouth.

"Smaller! Smaller! You are a lady, and ladies don't really eat."

She couldn't stop herself from glaring at him. Damn it, she was hungry! She was trying to do what he wanted and still get some food, but it was impossible. She thought she had it. Indeed, she managed to get the bun all the way to her lips without dropping it. But then before she could take the smallest bite, he abruptly reached forward and pulled the bun from her hand. It was easy for him, of course, because she was only holding on to it with two fingers.

"Excellent!" he said. "Now on to the tea."

Her stomach grumbled in response, and it was all she could do not to snatch the thing back in her fist and shove it into her mouth. Meanwhile, he was gesturing to the tea as he poured her a steaming cup.

She inhaled the stiff brew with gratitude. A bracing drink of that would indeed help her enormously. Without thinking, she reached for the cup.

"Tut-tut-tut! You are a lady, remember? Ladies do not pick up their teacups."

"What?" Of course ladies picked up their teacups.

"They lift them with the power of their beauty and their poise. A cup does not rest in their hands so much as float there."

"I beg your pardon?"

"It's true!" he cried.

"Of course it's not!" she snapped.

She had meant to be circumspect. She had meant to keep her eyes lowered and stick to her place as a servant in this household. But to be instructed like this by the butler was beyond humiliating. Especially since everything he said was utter claptrap! And whereas Mrs. Mortimer knew to nod and keep her mouth shut, Lady Helaine was not so easily subdued. And it was the lady she once was who snatched the teacup from the table and all but threw it at Dribbs.

"Ladies do not float their food into their mouths!" she said as she stood, teacup in hand. "With their lips shut! They are human just like you and I. Have you never met Lady Cassandra? The only lovely thing about her is her name. And she eats like her barbarian father. With her fist, like this!"

So saying, she grabbed hold of the bun and held it aloft like a palmed apple, which she then shoved straight at her open lips. She bit down on a huge mouthful and was promptly rewarded with the taste of Cook's wonderful baking. Her eyes slid to half closed and she was so enthralled with the taste that she nearly missed Dribbs's next words.

"Well, then! Can I presume that you are uninterested in learning the proper grip for a spoon?"

She almost answered what she would like to do to him with her spoon. And the knife, too, but at that moment, something sparked in her brain. Perhaps it was finally getting some food, perhaps it was the way Dribbs's eyes were crinkled at the edges. Crinkled as if he were smiling. Or perhaps holding back laughter. Her hand with the bun slipped away from her mouth.

"Good God, you are teasing me," she whispered.

"Of course I am, Lady Helaine. Forgive me, but I couldn't resist."

Lady Helaine? Her knees went out and she collapsed back onto the settee. He knew who she was. Meanwhile, Dribbs pulled the teacup from her hand and set it back on the table to refill it, as she had spilled most of it during her tirade.

"You cannot know," she whispered. "Robert would not have told you!"

Dribbs pressed the hot teacup into her trembling hands before she completely lost herself to panic. "His lordship did not say a word, but your breeding shines through. And if I might explain: your father and the current earl were sometimes companions. They both love the brandy, you see."

She closed her eyes, all too afraid of what was coming.

"This was back when the earl resided here, you understand. Before Lord Redhill asked him to remove to his club."

Yes, she knew Robert had thrown his father out of the house. How many times had she wished she could do the same to her own father? And yet a moment later, she would desperately long to see him again.

"One evening, your father was part of an impromptu party thrown by the earl. It went on quite late."

"I'm sure it went on until you poured my father into a carriage and sent him home."

"Well, yes. But did you know that your father could be quite maudlin in his cups?"

She nodded. "Yes. He would declare love for the most ridiculous things."

"Not so, my lady. He would declare his love for *you*. He had a miniature he kept in his pocket. Of you. He would draw it out and call you the best of all possible daughters. Patient, kind, and smart as a whip."

Helaine stared at the butler, her heart in her throat. "I never . . . he never . . ." She closed her eyes. Ridiculous to feel touched by words from a drunken fool. "He had so little care of us. It's . . . um . . . nice to know that he did love us."

"Drunkards are a sad lot, my lady. They love, my lady. Just like the rest of us. They love a great deal. But they just can't bring themselves to act as they ought. But never doubt the feeling."

"Thank you, Dribbs," she whispered. "Thank you for that."

"It is nothing but the honest truth. Now eat up, my lady. I know you're hungry, and Lady Gwen's new relations are running everyone ragged."

Helaine nodded, using the time to sort through the swirling emotions inside her. The feelings toward her father were complicated enough, but she had no idea how to handle Dribbs now. Bloody hell, *he knew who she was.*

"Please, Dribbs, I am especially thick this morning. I'm not sure how to proceed."

"Well, exactly as a lady ought."

She bit down into the bun with animal-like ferocity. She

thought that was the better choice than to rip the man's head off. Act as a lady ought. My God, what did that mean? "Dribbs—"

"You have suffered a great wrong, Lady Helaine, and that's a crying shame. So you're Mrs. Mortimer now, a right fine dressmaker, hiding in the shadows, skulking around the house, praying that no one notices you."

She straightened. "I do not skulk!"

"You hunch your shoulders and try to hide your face when you're not talking dresses and the like."

Did she? "That's not skulking."

"It is, because it's just when you're here. Wendy remarked on it to me just the other day. Said you don't do that at your shop. Just here."

He'd been talking to Wendy. "Dribbs, I am not ashamed of who I've become."

"'Course not. But seems to me, you're ashamed of Lady Helaine. But, begging your pardon, you're the daughter of an earl. Shameful father or not, you shouldn't be hiding yourself. Ain't no one here will think less of you. I'll see to it."

"I beg of you, Dribbs. Please do not speak of this to anyone."

"Of course not!" He reared back, obviously insulted, but a moment later, he was leaning forward to impress his point on her. "But that's just what I'm trying to tell you, my lady. There's no need to skulk."

"I don't skulk!"

"Well, whatever you're doing, the maids are beginning to remark on it. Calling you odd, and that's just not right. Blood will out, Lady Helaine. You may be Mrs. Mortimer, but people can see you're better. Trying to hide it just raises more questions."

"But they can't know—"

"No one will know. If you hold your head up and stop hiding your face, then they just think that you're somebody who used to be more. Someone facing a bit of hard times. There's no shame in that. It's only when you skul—er, hide your face—that they begin to question. Why would she hide? Who did she used to be?"

Helaine nodded slowly. She had been especially nervous here. It wasn't just that Robert was here. It was being back among the elite. What if someone recognized her? What if someone used to be a servant to someone she'd known in school? She knew the odds weren't high, but she couldn't help worrying. And indeed, her fears were justified, because Dribbs did know her identity.

"It would be disastrous if word got out."

"And it won't, if you stop acting like you've got something to be ashamed of."

Helaine swallowed. "But should I eat meals with the family, then? Isn't that more odd?"

Dribbs snorted. "You spent most of the night closeted with his lordship. Won't be the first mistress to be sat at the breakfast table."

"We were just talking!" Helaine cried.

Dribbs only shrugged. "Doesn't matter what you were doing. Just matters that you act the part. Mistress, dressmaker, daughter of an earl. None of them would be skulking about my halls."

"I am *not* his mistress!"

"As you wish," he said.

There was nothing more to be said at that point. Besides, Robert was no doubt waiting for her at the breakfast table. She still wasn't sure it was a good idea to go. After all, it only increased the idea that she was his mistress. But that was better than the truth of her identity, so she supposed she had to do what was required. Besides, it was only a couple days more. It would be nice to sit at a table again, to be served food, and to talk over dinner. Like a little taste of what might have been.

Still uneasy with the idea, she left Dribbs to go to the breakfast area. She didn't burst into the room as if she was born to it, but was mindful that she didn't skulk either. She stepped boldly forward and pushed open the door.

Two people sat at table—Robert and Gwen—and both

looked up and smiled at her. Robert's expression, of course, was a good deal warmer than Gwen's, but it was nice to see that both welcomed her.

"There you are, Mrs. Mortimer. I was beginning to wonder if you had succumbed to some ailment."

"Uh, no, my lord," she managed, as she belatedly remembered to curtsy. "Mr. Dribbs has just now informed me of your request."

Robert raised his eyebrows at her tone, which had been a tad bit snippy. He likely took it to mean she was angry with him, which she was, she supposed. After all, because of him she'd stayed up most of the night talking with him and now everyone thought her his mistress. She completely dismissed her own culpability. Guilt was one emotion she didn't have room for just then. Not with all the feelings that Dribbs had just stirred up.

In short, she was confused and disoriented, and now she had to sit at table with the man who had directly or indirectly caused all of it!

Bloody hell, she was tired. And still hungry. She decided she could understand things better with tea. But before she could move, Robert tilted his head and spoke in his usual imperious tone.

"Mrs. Mortimer? Is something amiss?"

A very great deal, but she couldn't say that. "Amiss? No, my lord. I don't believe so. Why do you ask?"

"Because you're standing there glowering, and I find it most irritating to my digestion."

"I am not glowering!" she responded before she could stop herself.

"I believe you were."

"I most certainly—"

"Actually, you were," interrupted Gwen. "Come, come, Helen. Please sit down. Have you eaten?" She gestured to the waiting footman. "Jeremy, please get Mrs. Mortimer a full plate." Then she looked back at Helaine. "We have a proposal to make to you, and I believe you shall want a full stomach before we embark upon it."

"On the proposal? Or the action?" She only asked because it was clear brother and sister were cut from the same cloth. Whatever this proposal was, asking for her assistance was merely a formality. She would participate in whatever it was because she was a servant and that was what servants did. Of course, that didn't stop her from enjoying the excitement in Gwen's face.

"Oh, don't let my brother put you in an ill humor, especially when he is working so hard to please me right now."

Helaine turned a dramatically exaggerated look at Robert. "Pleasing? Your brother?" Oh, dear. Helaine realized too late that such was not the response of a servant. Fortunately, Gwen did not notice, as she went into a peal of laughter. Then she clapped her hands in merriment.

"That is why I like you so, Helen. You have just the right understanding of my brother. You don't mind me calling you Helen, do you?"

"Of course not." She had given the girl leave to use it earlier in the week. She just hadn't realized how intimate and friendly it would feel, especially with Robert sitting directly beside them. It felt as if she were one of the family or a friend visiting from school.

"Well, in any event, to my shock Robert is indeed being most pleasant today. I was telling him that he had to remove himself to Father's club, and he was telling me that he would do no such thing—"

"I must agree," Helaine put in. "I wouldn't dream of ousting him from his home."

"Pshaw! I made a promise to you, and I meant to keep it. But then he made the most delicious proposal!"

The proposal had to wait a moment as Jeremy served Helaine a full plate. A stronger woman would refuse it. It really wasn't done to eat with the family if one was simply a dressmaker. But she really was hungry. In the end, she gave in and dipped her fork into the most heavenly eggs. Then she shamed herself by moaning aloud in delight.

Robert burst out laughing. "And here I was afraid you would refuse to eat."

"You have the most divine cook, my lord. I'm afraid my principles are no match when faced with such temptation." Then she sobered and met his gaze. "But this is rather awkward, you know. And not well done of you."

He swallowed, his skin paling slightly as he understood her message. "I am an aristocrat," he said stiffly. "I am allowed my peccadillos." Then, when she didn't answer, he softened his pose. "I simply wanted the pleasure of your company, Mrs. Mortimer. I know it is unusual, but it is not unheard-of. I can name any number of eccentrics who have all manner of people to dine."

"Are you styling yourself as an eccentric, then?" she asked.

He dipped his head, then covered the movement by grabbing his tea. "I believe I am."

Beside them, Gwen released an unladylike snort. "Of course he is!" she crowed. "He has decided to accompany us on a trip to Bond Street! All of us. Me, all my future in-laws, Edward if he will come, though he said something about a missive about sheep or hens or . . . I don't know. Anyway, and you. You must come because we can't buy our bangles and ribbons and the like without your eagle eye helping us."

Helaine stared, her food forgotten for the moment. "We are to go to Bond Street today?"

"And shop as much as our hearts desire—Robert's treat! In fact, he has become so eccentric as to say that he would seek your advice before he visits his tailor! Imagine that! I never thought I would see the day that Robert wanted to join me in a shopping expedition. And moreover, that he wanted anyone's advice but his own!"

"Unfair!" Robert cried. "I often seek other people's opinion. Just not yours, brat."

Gwen waved his comment aside and turned back to Helaine. "Is that not the most marvelous idea ever? And Robert says that not a groat shall come out of my account. My in-laws will have to foot their own bill, of course. Edward will insist upon it. But for me, I shall buy the most expensive things I can find!"

"Oh, no!" cut in Robert. "Mrs. Mortimer, promise me that you shall instill some sense into my sister. You are to teach her how to economize. How to find excellent things on a small budget."

"Oh, no!" Gwen returned. "You cannot add stipulations now. You said you would pay for whatever I bought!"

"And I will, but—"

"So are you game, Mrs. Mortimer? Will you help me spend my brother's money on the most exquisite items we can find?"

Helaine laughed as she reached for her tea. Indeed, how could she not when both brother and sister were acting so delightful? "Of course. I shall endeavor to find you the most beautiful items at a price that shall not damage the earldom. After all," she added with a wink to Gwen, "he needs enough funds to buy you the most exquisite wedding present."

Robert's groan was comical indeed. Gwen laughed and began itemizing expensive gifts her brother could purchase. Helaine found herself quickly caught up in the siblings' banter. Soon she was trading quips as easily as them and was eagerly looking forward to the shopping.

It wasn't until much later that she realized how easily she had been manipulated. She had kept herself apart for the last week in this household. She had maintained her place as neither completely a servant but certainly not one of the masters. And then Robert had come back to London. Less than twelve hours later, she had stayed up most of the night with him, the staff assumed she was his lover, and now she was embarking upon a shopping expedition just as if she were one of the family. She couldn't be any further from a servant if she'd stepped into the house as Lady Helaine.

So that made her wonder. In another twenty-four hours, just how much more of her life would change?

Chapter 16

~~✶~~

Robert hated shopping. He despised it with the passion born of a desk covered in things he ought to be doing. He despised it like he despised standing still for twenty minutes while his tailor measured or pinned or generally annoyed him while he thought of all the things he wasn't doing. He hated everything about it, and yet he thoroughly enjoyed the day.

He had never been on a shopping expedition with his sister. Not since he was in shortcoats, and what he remembered from that was boredom. Crushing, horrible boredom. So he had never been an adult watching women buy things, listening as they debated fabrics, accessories, or styles. And he had certainly never done it while appreciating the care that went into a female's appearance.

They actually thought about which colors looked best on their skin, which ribbons would highlight their hair, and whether a reticule with pearls was more feminine than one with lace. And even more bizarre, he actually understood what they were talking about. Not because he cared, but because Helaine was so good at explaining things. With examples.

She spoke in undertones, as was proper, but as they moved from shop to shop, she would explain the tenets of good dressing to Gwen, pointing out those women who succeeded and those who failed. He had never spent more time looking at women in their clothing than he did that day, and he found it fascinating. He also wondered what clothing blunders he had been making every day of his life.

It wasn't until teatime at Gunter's that he dared ask the question. And then he got his answer from everyone but the one woman he wanted to ask.

Gwen started. "You have been a fashion blunder all your life, brother dear. But at least Father introduced you to a good tailor."

"Really, Gwen!" exclaimed her future aunt-in-law. "Your brother is a very handsome man in his own way. You should not say such things. And certainly not in public."

Robert would have been reassured if it were not for the words "in his own way." He was about to ask what that meant when the mother-in-law cut in while the sister-in-law giggled into her ice.

"You are just as you ought to be, your lordship. Your aim is to be imposing, severe—"

"Pompous and overbearing," inserted Gwen.

"Stately," her mother-in-law corrected firmly.

When it looked like the discussion would degenerate further, Robert set down his teacup with a frown, his gaze trained on Helaine. "Do you agree, Mrs. Mortimer? Do I dress to—"

"Intimidate?" interrupted Gwen. "Yes."

"Well, future earls should be imposing," said the mother-in-law. "But it would be nice if you added a little bit of style to all that stateliness."

Robert raised his eyebrows in shock. "Are you saying I dress without style?"

"Oh, no!" the woman gasped, but lest he feel better about himself, Gwen was there to insert her own set-down.

"You dress boring, brother dear. Imposing, arrogant, and boring."

"Very boring," echoed the sister-in-law.

His eyes found Helaine's. "Really?"

She hedged. "Your style is reserved, my lord. It is your manner that is imposing."

"And overbearing and—"

"Yes, Gwen. Thank you, but I know your opinion." He looked down at himself. He wore brown today, a more casual change from his usual black. Plus a cream shirt and cravat beneath a brown waistcoat. He supposed, he realized with some shock, that he must appear rather drab. When he looked up, his gaze caught Helaine's. "What would you recommend?"

She tilted her head, obviously thinking hard. "A waistcoat with some color." Gwen opened her mouth to add a comment, but Helaine rushed on, cutting off his sister, thank God. "Nothing outlandish. Just a thread or two of color—red or gold, I think—to relieve the brown. And it should match your cravat, of course."

"My cravat should match my waistcoat?" He'd always matched it to his shirt.

"Just the contrast color, my lord."

He nodded as if he understood what that meant.

"And, if I might be so bold . . . ," she began, obviously hesitating.

This time Gwen would not be denied. "Pray don't stop now!" she cried. "Not when he's finally listening!"

Helaine waited, and when he nodded, she continued. "Jewelry, my lord."

"The devil you say!" he exploded. "I'll not be a dandy—" His words trailed off as the ladies burst out in giggles. Apparently the idea of him as a dandy was vastly amusing.

Fortunately for his pride, Helaine was not laughing. "A single pin for your cravat will not make you a dandy. The emerald stone looked very handsome."

He frowned, taking a moment to remember when she had seen his emerald. Oh, the night at the inn. His eyes brightened—as did Helaine's color—as she rushed on to cover.

"Perhaps you should get a gold design resembling the family crest? Something relatively small, but very unique. It would be stylish without—"

"Making me feel like a trussed-up popinjay?"

She raised her eyebrows, her expression half teasing. His sister was not so restrained and neither were her new in-laws, as those ladies began laughing in earnest. But that didn't seem to matter. The other women were as noise to him, whereas Helaine's eyes, her expression, her very being seemed to shine. With laughter, with joy, with everything that was essentially her: strength and delight. Certainly she did not always express her joy, but it was there, peeking out beneath her otherwise restrained demeanor. Delight in who she was and what she was doing. If only life would allow her enough space and breath for her to express herself more fully.

Oh, he wanted to give her that space. He wanted to take away her cares, to lift off her burdens, and to share every moment of the carefree woman that she would become. He wanted it with an ache that burned.

His desires must have shone on his face. It must have been obvious to everyone, because their laughter faded, and the delight in Helaine's expression became hidden again behind a mask of wariness. He'd done it again, he realized with a start. He'd frightened her, and that was the last thing he wanted to do. Indeed, he had arranged for this outing just so he could prove to her that they could be together without danger, without damage to her reputation or her business.

Gwen cleared her throat, obviously trying to gain his attention. From the sound of it, she'd been trying for some time. Finally he gathered his wits, ripped his gaze from Helaine's, and turned on his sister.

"Are you quite well, Gwen? It sounds as if you are coming down with an illness."

"I think," she said slowly, her words carefully enunciated, "I believe you need to visit your hideout."

"Whatever are you talking about?"

"The Chandler, you idiot. I think you need to take an afternoon to recover your wits."

Robert felt his jaw go slack in astonishment, his mind working furiously. However had she learned about that place? It was absolutely certain that no one of his acquaintance would speak of it. Certainly not to her. Meanwhile Gwen was prattling on, directing her words toward her in-laws and Helaine.

"He has this place. I heard the coachman tell Dribbs about it. A ramshackle building where he goes to think and be by himself. As if we are such a bother to him that he needs to escape us. It's quite the other way around, you know. We need the rest from him. And so I am telling you, brother dear, go away. Return when you are thinking more clearly."

Robert released a slow breath. Clearly his sister didn't know the Chandler's sordid history. She was babbling on as if it were nothing more than a dreary gentlemen's club. That was a relief, of course, until he chanced to look at Helaine.

She knew. He could see it in her tightened lips and downcast eyes. She knew exactly what the Chandler used to be. And she naturally came to the wrong conclusion about what he did when he went there.

"Let me explain—" He didn't get a chance to continue.

"By all means, my lord," Helaine said stiffly. "You have been most generous in sharing your time with us. Pray do not let us detain you."

"It's not what you think," he said firmly. Then he was stuck, because all the women were looking at him, waiting for him to explain. But he couldn't. Not in front of Gwen, who was completely ignorant of the whole of it. Certainly not in front of his future in-laws. As for Helaine, he wanted to be alone with her when he told her about that part of his life. He wanted her to know the real him, the man who did indeed love every minute he spent at the Chandler the way it was now.

But he couldn't say it now. "Very well," he said with as

much dignity as he could muster. "I can see that you ladies wish to be rid of me. But I beg of you, Mrs. Mortimer, please spare me some time this evening after I return. I should like a word with you."

"I'm sure that's not necessary—"

"On the contrary, I insist. Directly after dinner, if you would." Then he belatedly realized that he sounded as if he were giving her an order. "It is a request, you know, not a demand, but I would be exceedingly grateful for your time."

He waited for her to dip her chin in acknowledgment. It took awhile, but she finally did, so he took his leave. He had plans for tonight. Big plans. And precious little time to prepare.

It was with true dismay that Helaine realized she was an illogical, contrary creature. Not so long ago, she had walked out of an inn room intending never to speak again to Lord Redhill. And yet, not more than two days later, she had gone to stay at his house. And now, one week later, she had not only spent a very late night in conversation with him, but then proceeded to spend a lovely day shopping with him as well. And when he left them—to go to a brothel, no less— she found herself missing him quite dreadfully. He had a keen mind and actually listened to what she said. He could be quite funny when he put his mind to it and, all in all, was a delightful companion even for such a female thing as shopping.

So when he left after tea, she told herself she was glad of his absence. After all, any man who had to go to a brothel to restore his good humor was not an ideal companion. And yet, no matter how stern she was with herself, she could not keep her mind from wandering back to him. If she saw a fabric, she wondered what it would look like on him. If someone said something particularly witty, she listened for his low chuckle. And worst of all, she kept turning around to share this or that with him, only to realize he wasn't there.

Illogical and foolish! And yet she couldn't stop herself.

Nor could she keep herself from speculating on what he could possibly want to discuss with her after dinner. But she had a job to do now, and so she continued to shop with the women until they were all dropping with fatigue.

Then a miracle happened that solved all her immediate problems: Gwen asked about dancing slippers. Helaine suggested they all retire to her shop, where she was trying out a new shoemaker. It was Penny, of course, who was still staying with Helaine's mother. The girl had made a couple pairs of delightfully feminine shoes for Francine and so Helaine had decided to promote her work more extensively. Plus, the ladies wanted to see Irene's shipment of Brussels lace. Irene had apparently been able to use their new lines of credit with the cloth merchants as leverage against the ship captains. What that meant was beyond Helaine's understanding, except to know that Irene had brought the lace plus a few more bolts of silk to the shop just yesterday. And now that Francine's father had paid her bill—the girl was apparently enjoying her new wardrobe to the fullest— Helaine could afford to buy the bolts from Irene and send the woman out for more purchases.

Success was within sight—or at least disaster was stepping farther and farther away—and that was a miracle all in itself. Now she just had to build on everything she'd put in place and make sure nothing untoward happened to disrupt it. Something unsettling and unexpected—like an evening's discussion with a frustrating viscount. But that was tonight's problem. For right now, everyone was in good spirits as they tromped the short distance to her shop. And while all the ladies were fitted, Helaine wrote a note to Lord Redhill delaying their after-dinner meeting. She would be staying the night at her home here, she wrote, and so would be pleased to speak with him on the morrow.

She knew she was only delaying the inevitable, but she hoped with a good night's sleep she would have better control over her emotional state. Then she waved the ladies good-bye, spoke a few brief words with Penny, who was departing for her father's workshop so that she could get started on the work, and then kissed her mother before disappearing into her bedroom for a well-deserved nap. Sweet heaven, it was lovely to sink into oblivion without fear of handsome men with brown coats and warm chocolate eyes. No bookkeeping, no whisper of poverty, not even hunger kept her awake. And for a few hours, she was completely ignorant of the world.

Until her mother came tapping at the door. Helaine had already been stirring. She was not a woman accustomed to naps, so a few hours of sleep had both refreshed her and left her disturbingly out of sorts. She had been thinking of Robert, of course, her mind wandering over some of their most pleasant moments, when her mother interrupted.

Helaine immediately climbed out of bed and opened the door. "Yes?"

"Oh dear, oh dear, oh dear!" her mother exclaimed as she looked at her.

"What?"

"Your dress. Your hair! Oh, even your cheeks are creased!"

Helaine was hard put to make sense of her mother. Of course she was creased from head to toe. She'd just woken up. Although she did manage to look down and see how badly she had damaged her dress. "I suppose I should have undressed before I lay down, but—"

"Never mind that now! Come, come. Let's get you into something more suitable right away."

Helaine was rubbing her eyes when her mother all but shoved her back into the bedroom, efficiently stripping off her gown.

"What—ow!"

Never had she met a woman who could both strip her of her clothing and brush her hair at once. Her mother was a miracle of efficiency, if only she'd managed to pull out the pins from her hair first.

"Oh, bother!" Her mother pressed the brush into Helaine's hand. "You finish with your hair. I'll get you a better gown."

"But—"

"Brush!"

Helaine did as she was commanded, quickly unpinning her hair. "Why am I rushing to look acceptable?" she asked. She had planned a quiet evening at home.

"Because *he* is here. Said you had an appointment."

No need to think who "he" was. It was Robert, of course, and she released her breath in a huff. "I told him I would speak to him tomorrow."

"Brush! And step into this." Her mother was holding out the very same dress she'd worn the week before to the inn.

"I can't wear that! I wore it the last time he was here."

"Oh! Oh, yes." Her mother quickly spun around, dropping the dress as she rushed out of the room. She returned a moment later with a winter gown of deepest blue velvet. "You shall just have to wear one of mine, then."

"But you're smaller—"

"Ssst! You cannot refuse him, Helaine, no matter what you told him. You began this path. You cannot turn him away so rudely now. And if this is a little tight on you, then all the better."

"But—"

"Brush! Step!"

Rather than follow orders, Helaine put down the brush and turned to look her mother in the eye. "I have not done anything of which to be ashamed, Mother. There is no path, as you put it. Merely a . . ." How to put it? "A friendship. Nothing more."

Her mother dropped into a crouch so that Helaine could step into the gown. When Helaine didn't move, she looked up with a sigh. "It doesn't matter what has and has not happened. Everyone believes it of you."

"But—"

"And I do not blame you for it."

That froze Helaine in her tracks. A week ago, she'd feared her mother would be sobbing her eyes out at Helaine's fall from grace. But now the woman was pushing her into a liaison with Robert? It made no sense. And yet, as she looked into her mother's eyes, she saw an acceptance she'd never seen before. Could it be that her mother was finally ready to face the world again? Not as the ghost of the countess she once was, but as a whole woman? Someone who accepted life as it was and not how it used to be?

Impossible. It was too far a step for the woman to take. And yet, apparently, sometime during Helaine's nap, the world had changed. It was but a moment more before she realized what had happened. Or more accurately *who* had happened.

"What did he say to you?"

"Ssst! Nothing! Now step into the dress."

She did, if only to get her mother to stand. And then she was tucked and pushed and tied into place with such vehemence that Helaine knew she had guessed the truth. So when the gown was settled, she took both her mother's hands and forced the woman to look her in the eye.

"What did he say to you?"

"Ssst—"

"Do not hiss at me! I deserve an answer, Mama. What did he say?"

The woman grimaced but finally answered. "Just that . . . just that he admired your strength."

"What?"

"We were talking about you because that's what mothers do when they meet an eligible man of their daughter's age."

"Mama, you cannot think he intends marriage—"

"I know! I don't! But listen to me. He started talking to me about you, about how strong you are. That he admires everything you have done with the shop, and that I must be so proud. And I am, Helaine. I really am. You have saved us when I hadn't the strength to rise from my bed."

Helaine felt her face flush as she looked away. She hadn't even realized how much she'd longed to hear those words until they were spoken aloud. Her mother was proud of her. "Thank you, Mama. But what has that to do with all this?" She gestured to the lush gown and her hair, which was flying willy-nilly about her face.

"Oh, sit down. Let me do something with your hair." Helaine obeyed, and while her mother began to stroke it to a glossy sheen, she began to speak. "He cares for you," she said. "I can see it in his eyes. It's not Spanish coin to a girl's mother."

Helaine sighed. "Mama, you cannot believe what a charming man says. I would think you would have learned that lesson by now." *From my father.* She didn't need to say the words to make them heard. Both women knew how sweet Helaine's father could be when it suited him.

"Lord Redhill is not a drunkard," her mother snapped. "He is solid, stable, and good *ton*."

Helaine couldn't disagree with that, so she held her tongue. And then her mother caught her eyes, holding her gaze steady in the mirror. "He promised to make you happy, Helaine. He said he would do all in his power to make sure of it. And I believed him. He is not a man to make promises lightly."

"But he does not mean marriage, Mama. You know that."

The woman sighed, her shoulders slumping with the movement. "Of course I know that. But joy is something precious. You should embrace it while you can."

"Even if it means compromising . . . everything?" She didn't have to state it out loud. She didn't have to say, Even if it meant losing her virginity to a man who would not marry her.

Her mother's expression turned wistful. "I first met your father at a garden party. He made me laugh and later sent me posies. Then he followed me around from ball to theater, even to a musical evening, though he hated those things. He was charming and I never laughed so much as in that first year. Our wedding was wonderful and the night afterward out of a fairy tale. He was a terrible lover, I believe, as these things go, but he made it so much fun. We were two children stumbling about and I was so happy. Until he began drinking to excess, I was over-the-moon happy."

Helaine searched her mother's face. The words had come out in a rush, but they were no less heartfelt. Her mother was speaking the truth, and that thought stunned Helaine. "Mama, you have always said he was a wastrel and a fool."

Her mother shrugged. "Well, he is that, too. But in the beginning, it was different. We had such fun. I think that is why I now hate him, because it was so different those first few years." Her mother's eyes were distant, her thoughts far away. But a moment later, she returned to pinning up the sides of Helaine's hair while the rest fell in loose waves behind her. "You have already lost so much. I want you to feel some of the joy, too. As much as you can, if you can."

Helaine's thoughts were in turmoil, and her heart beat triple time. Was her mother truly giving her permission to lie with a man not her husband? "I cannot do something so easily, Mama. Not just for joy."

"Darling," her mother said as she patted the last curl in place, "there is nothing *just* about joy. Not true joy that comes from the heart."

Helaine shook her head. "Even so, Mama."

Her mother looked at her a long time and then finally nodded. "That is why you are smarter than I. And yet, even after everything, I wonder if I would make a different choice with your father. Those first years were the very best. A life without such wonderful times would be very dull indeed."

"But he left us, Mama. With nothing. No food, no protection, not even our reputations. He destroyed us and then he disappeared."

"I know. But, darling, because of you, we have food. We are safe. And as for our reputations, they are long gone. Royal courtesans have not so terrible a lot. They have the joy and are not trapped once it is gone."

Helaine rocked back on her heels. She had never thought of herself as a courtesan, royal or otherwise. The idea simply did not fit with her image of herself. Meanwhile, her mother was pinching her cheeks for color, then stopping to give one last piece of advice.

"If you have a chance to find joy, if only for a while, you should take it. We are safe. The shop is doing marvelously. So if he makes you happy, then take it. Take *him*."

Helaine closed her eyes, trying to sort out this bizarre world where her mother spoke sense. What she hit instead was a wall of fear. "We are not so safe as you might think. Everything could topple tomorrow."

"All the more reason to be happy now if you can." Then she pulled Helaine to her feet, inspected her from head to toe, and pronounced her acceptable before practically pushing her down the stairs. A moment later, Helaine was once again alone with Robert. And from the way his gaze heated her blood, she knew she was very close to the edge of a very large cliff. But which way should she move?

Chapter 17

᷇᷇᷇

Robert felt his mouth go dry. She was dressed in midnight blue, her bodice plumped, her skirt flowing, and her hair in a beautiful tumble down her back. Normally he might have compared her to a queen from her boudoir, Venus at night, or any other extraordinarily beautiful woman. But he had no words at that moment. Only the full, incredible vision of her.

"Robert?"

"You look spectacular," he finally managed.

"Oh. It was my mother's. You've already seen my best dress. Sorry it took me so long to come down."

He didn't care whose dress it was, he was looking at her as if he'd never really seen her before. Ridiculous, he knew, but something about her was different. "What happened?"

She started. "What?"

"You're different somehow. Less determined. Softer. More womanly."

She arched a brow and a teasing glint entered her eyes. "Are you saying I wasn't a woman before?"

He let his lips curve in a smile because she was teasing

him. She knew exactly what he was talking about, but trying to dodge the issue. "I'm saying that you were handsome before, but now you're stunning. I like your hair down."

She touched it almost nervously. "I didn't have time to style it."

"Then I hope you are rushed every time I see you." Then his expression slipped as he studied her face. "What has happened, Helaine?"

"Nothing. I have just had a busy day and a confusing conversation with my mother. And now . . ." She gestured toward him. "What is so urgent, my lord, that you had to come to my home rather than wait until tomorrow?"

"I didn't think you'd really see me tomorrow."

She lifted her chin. "I am not so inconsistent. I told you I would speak with you tomorrow and I would have."

He nodded. "I know. But something else might have happened. Perhaps Gwen would have an emergency need for a new ribbon. Or one of her new relations would absolutely insist on your attention until you fainted from the tedium of it all—"

"They are not tedious. And you should speak better of your new relations."

He barely resisted rolling his eyes at that. "They are women intent on fashion and the coming Season."

"As am I."

"But you are so much more." He took a breath, unexpectedly nervous. So to cover, he stepped forward and took her hands. He wasn't sure if she would allow it, but she was strangely accepting as she lifted her eyes to his. "Helaine, I have something I wish to show you. Something about myself that would ruin me almost as deeply as you would be if your identity were revealed."

She started at his words. He felt the jolt through their joined hands. "Surely you exaggerate."

He lifted a shoulder. "I would still have money, still become an earl in due course, but my reputation would always be tarnished, my motives suspect. I would be considered rather depraved by many and become a target of reformers and conservatives alike. Any political aspirations after that would become extremely difficult."

She lifted her chin. "I do not believe you."

He couldn't help smiling. That was exactly the response he wanted. "Then let me show you the truth of it."

She hesitated, and then she slowly withdrew her hands from his. "But why? Why would you wish to expose yourself thus to me?"

He wasn't prepared to answer that, wasn't ready to examine his motives so closely. So he opted for a portion of the truth. "I want you to think well of me."

She arched her brow. "This thing that would have you scorned by liberals and conservatives alike? This will have me think well of you?"

"I hope so. Helaine, I cannot adequately explain it. I wish to show you."

"I—" She cut off her words, turning away in confusion. "The world has gone upside down."

He crossed to her and gently set his hands on her shoulders. Her back was to him and he felt her tighten. But not for long. In time she exhaled and her shoulders eased down. He longed to pull her into his arms, to hold her while they both sorted out their thoughts, but he didn't dare. Instead he waited and prayed she would choose to trust him.

She did, but he had to wait an eternity for it. In the end, she stepped away from his hands and said, "I will get a wrap." She meant to step away from him, but he touched her arm lightly to stop her. She paused, looking at him in inquiry.

"What decided you in my favor?"

"There was no real decision, my lord. I am too weak around you. No matter that my common sense says being around you is too dangerous, I cannot force myself to listen. I enjoy your company, and . . . and I suppose that is reason enough for me to ignore everything else."

He smiled. He couldn't help himself. He liked that she would ignore all else to trust him. "Then let us say you are just weak enough. After all, a woman of too much strength is frightening to us poor men."

Her lips curved in response, and he saw a delightful twinkle enter her eyes. "And then there is the other reason."

"Yes?" he prompted when she didn't continue.

"I very much want to know what could hurt you, my lord. I shall not use it, but I should like to know this thing."

He tilted his head, wondering at her logic. "But if you won't use it, then what good will it be to you?"

"You will know that I know, and that I could go back on my word at any moment. I find I like the idea of you being afraid of me. Not a lot. Just enough so you understand how I feel every day."

His smile slid away. "Do you truly feel that afraid? Every day?"

She nodded. She didn't even say the word, but he could read it in her face. She was afraid constantly. That was expected, he supposed, with her world teetering on the financial edge as it did.

"I could relieve that fear, you know. As my mistress, you would have ample money to support yourself and your friends." He said the words, but they tasted bad in his mouth. And in his heart, he flinched. He did not like thinking of her as his mistress. And yet, the idea of lying with her was a constant desire. Even now he was hard with lust, though he took pains to hide it.

And while he was struggling with his conflicting emotions, she simply shrugged. "Fear is not so bad. It keeps my thinking clear." Then she flashed a rueful smile at him. "Most of the time, at least."

Then she disappeared upstairs, presumably to get her wrap. He heard her kiss her mother good night, then her light tread as she came down the stairs. As she alighted from the last step, he held out his hand to her. She didn't even hesitate. In fact, there was a smile on her lips as he escorted her to the waiting hansom cab.

She faltered just a moment when she saw the conveyance. "You didn't bring your carriage?"

"Not for where we are going. My servants talk enough as it is."

She seemed to understand that, and so allowed him to hand her into the cab. He gave the driver instructions and then joined her inside. And because it was cold, he settled beside her on the seat and tucked her close. Finally, amazingly, she was in his arms again.

Helaine closed her eyes and allowed the world to spin, spin, spin out of control. How many unbelievable things had happened since she had woken up not more than an hour ago? First her mother had all but said, Go and become Lord Redhill's mistress. Second, Robert had a secret that he was going to share with her. And most incredible of all: her mother didn't hate her father. It seemed like such a silly little thing, and yet, that was what kept whirling about her brain. She didn't hate him.

"What has you looking so lost?" Robert asked.

She bit her lip and guiltily lifted out of his arms. He resisted at first, but she persisted. Friends didn't press themselves so tightly together. "I'm sorry. I did not mean to sour the mood."

His hand flowed over the top of hers, and she felt his warmth seep into her even through their gloves. "I want to know what you are thinking, not change the atmosphere, Helaine. Surely you know that by now."

"Yes, of course. But . . ." She didn't know how to begin. "It will sound stupid."

"Then by all means, I must hear it now!"

She chuckled because he meant her to. And then, because it was so easy to talk with him, she found herself answering without measuring her words. She just spoke, and it felt good to work it out with another person. With him.

"My mother told me something shocking before I went down to see you. I daresay it doesn't seem very shocking, but you must understand. I spent my childhood listening to her revile my father."

"What did she say?"

"That even now, she would not change a thing. She would still marry him."

She felt him stiffen, pulling back with surprise. "Truly? She would still . . . After what he did?"

Helaine nodded, relieved that she could finally speak openly with someone about her father. "His theft was the least of it, you know. He was a drunkard, pure and simple."

He squeezed her hand, and she realized belatedly that somehow she had reversed her position. They were now holding hands palm to palm, and she could not bring herself to let him go. Meanwhile, he shifted slightly in his seat. "Don't feel as if you need to explain if it's too painful, but I wondered exactly—"

"You wish to know the details of what my father did?"

Robert nodded. "I only know that he stole from the military supplies."

She laughed, the sound bitter to her own ears. "That at least I could understand. If he stole supplies to sell to pay our rent or something like that. But no. He had a good friend. A drinking friend, of course, who was in charge of certain military shipments to Spain." Then she paused to look into his eyes. "Do you know what he stole, my lord? What my father, the Earl of Chelmorton, took from our boys fighting so far away?"

He shook his head.

"Expensive brandy. Wealthy families would ship excellent spirits across the ocean to their officer sons. Half the bottles never made it. Sailors, dockworkers, and the doctors were always nabbing one bottle or another. The doctors at least were taking it for anesthetic. The others . . ." She shrugged.

"Yes, I understand there is a great deal of theft in military supplies."

"Yes, well, my father is just one of a long list of thieves in that supply chain. Except he did not steal a single bottle here or there. He stole an entire case. And not just any case, but one meant for the Earl of Bedford's son."

Robert released a low whistle. "Bedford is not a man who tolerates theft lightly. And certainly not anything meant for his son."

"Yes, so we came to realize."

"But how did Bedford find out? Especially if the case had already entered military shipping?"

Helaine laughed. "My father is a talkative drunk, my lord. Having grabbed such an excellent brandy, he immediately had a party. And when asked by his drinking companions where he'd found such wonderful vintage, he told them. He just . . . told them. And there were likely servants there, too."

"Good Lord."

"In any event, Bedford found out and cried foul . . ."

"And your father was soon banned from society and you along with him."

She let her head lean back against Robert's arm and wondered how she could possibly be about to cry. She hadn't cried about this in so very long. "My father was a drunk and a fool, and because of that—"

"Because of him, you and your mother have had to fend for yourselves from almost the very start." He sighed. "Which means, of course, that you have been the one doing it."

"Oh, no! At first my mother was quite the wizard at keeping us together. At finding the way to get us a free meal or new clothing on the sly. But most of that was dependent upon society. Upon friends who invited us to their homes for tea or the like. Once, I believe, one of her oldest friends paid my tuition at school."

"But some scandals cannot be overcome, even by old and very dear friends."

She sighed, mourning more for all that her mother had lost rather than herself. "Mama had married for love, you see. I knew that, of course. Papa could be so much fun."

"No wonder you take a dim view of passion, Helaine. You have seen how very costly it can be."

She nodded, seeing that he was right. Perhaps that was why she was so shocked by her mother's revelation. "She hates him, though. She has said so often. She said it tonight as well, almost in the very same breath that she said she would do it all over again. It makes no sense."

"But isn't that the point of love? To not make sense?"

"But she hates him. I know she does."

"And she still loves him. The two are not so incompatible."

She twisted so that she could look him in the eye. "Of course they are. Hate and love are opposites. My mother is simply confused."

He laughed then. A low, rich sound that rumbled through his body into hers. It was so delightful a sensation that she could not be angry with him for laughing at her. "You would rather believe your mother insane than in love?"

"I would rather the world made sense again. My father is a cad and a fool. My mother would be better off having never met him, never loved him, never married him."

"And yet she said tonight that she still loves him. And that bothers you."

"How would you like proof positive that your mother is insane?"

He snorted. "We shall leave my mother and her ailments out of this, hm? We are speaking of your parents. I, for one, find it reassuring that love can withstand even the most terrible things. Yes, you suffered horribly because of your father's mistakes, but the heart does not adhere to logic. And it can love despite someone's faults." He twisted slightly and she could see his eyes squint at her in the darkness. "Is that why you have never married? Never found a lover?"

"What?"

"Because you are looking for someone without faults. Someone who will not disappoint you as your father has done."

"Don't be ridiculous. No one is without faults."

"Exactly. And so you are alone."

She didn't know what to say to that. She wanted to dismiss his idea out of hand, but inside she quailed. Was it true? Had she locked herself away because no man could possibly be perfect enough to not hurt her? "Then why am I here with you?" she said aloud, the question more for herself than for him.

He tweaked her chin. "Perhaps because I am as perfect as you can find?"

She snorted. "Hardly that."

"And yet, I am not so bad, either."

"What you are, my lord, is extraordinarily persistent. How many times have I rebuffed you? And yet you show up at my doorway and demand to see me."

"I made no demands," he said with pretend hauteur. "I merely asked."

"It is one and the same with you."

"You did not need to come down."

She shrugged. "My mother insisted."

"Now, that is a bald-faced lie!"

"She did!"

"And you could have easily refused. But instead you put on a gown, brushed your hair, and are now here with me. Why, Helaine? I'm grateful, of course, but why?"

She shook her head. "I told you before. Because I want to see this secret of yours."

"Ah, yes," he said, though she could tell by his tone that he didn't really believe her. "Then I suppose it is fortunate that we are here."

She straightened up from his side. She hadn't even noticed the cab slowing down, but a moment later the door was opened and the driver was handing her down. She stepped out and looked around, recognizing the district if not their actual location.

"Why would you bring me here?" she gasped. They were in the center of a row of large houses pressed tightly together. Farther down the street, a barely dressed woman stood at a doorway gesturing men inside. They were in an area known for its houses of prostitution, and he had brought her here!

She was turning around to get right back into the carriage when he pulled her wrap over her head to shield her face. "Cover your head," he said, "and keep tight to me until we are inside."

"But—"

"Trust me!" he hissed as he grabbed her elbow and half walked, half marched her to a door. Had she been thinking more clearly, she would have resisted. There could be no good reason for him to take her to a place like this. But she was always muddleheaded around him, and so she went with him, ducking quickly inside when the door opened. Fortunately her madness never lasted for long. Once inside, she rounded on him immediately, her mouth open to blast him for whatever he thought he was doing. But her words were stopped in midbreath.

They were standing in the middle of a large entry overdone in velvets and gilt. There were candles everywhere, or their stubs at least, and an open, spacious feel that she couldn't help but appreciate. It was exactly as she might expect from a house of prostitution, except that she didn't see any. No prostitutes. And even more confusing, she didn't hear any. What she heard was children laughing. Three, if she had to guess—two girls and boy—but she wasn't sure.

"They're playing with the kittens," said the woman who had opened the door. "An' jes' like I said, that mama cat's the best mouser I ever seen."

Helaine didn't know what to say. Nothing made sense. Meanwhile, Robert was pushing the door closed and latching it with long familiarity. As he turned back, he touched Helaine's elbow. "Mrs. Mortimer, may I present to you Chandelle of the Chandler."

The woman dropped into a neat curtsy, though her knees cracked as she did it. "Right pleased I am to meet any friend of Robert's. I heard tell of your shop. Supposed to be right lovely designs."

"Uh—thank you," Helaine responded, her gaze now taking in the woman before her. She was dressed practically, in warm wool of a common design. Her eyes were lined with wrinkles, not kohl, and she wore no jewels or anything, for that matter, that was designed to attract a man. She was as far from a working girl as Helaine could imagine, and that confused her even more.

"Chandelle used to be a madame of a house of prostitution called the Chandler," he began.

"But we ain't been doing that since 'is sixteenth birthday," cut in Chandelle. "Now we're jes' a home for rest. Plus then there's the kids." At her gesture, they walked around a corner of the large room. There, rolling about on the floor, were three children and five kittens. The children were on their feet in a moment, all crowding around Robert. They were so thick that Helaine almost missed the younger woman sitting nearby. Her face was sallow, her eyes dull, but she smiled when she saw them and she greeted them in a whisper.

"Evenin', sir, miss."

Robert spent a few moments with each child, speaking to them by name and asking over this or that. Helaine could tell he was well known and trusted by each child. Then he detached himself from the group to kneel before the young woman, his gaze intent on her face. "Good evening, Nettie. You shouldn't be out of bed."

"Ain't no bleeding or swelling," she said. For proof, she took his hand and pressed it to her left side. Robert's eyes narrowed as he poked lightly. She winced with every touch.

"It's still tender."

"'Course it be," Nettie answered as she pushed his hand away. "What with you prodding at it. You leave it alone. I'm watching the children."

He stood up with a smile. "Very well, but not too long, mind."

Chandelle stepped in. "She'll go to bed in five minutes, along with the children."

A chorus of dissent rose up from that statement, but Chandelle gave them all a stern eye. She didn't even have to say a word, and within a minute, every one of them said a soft "Yes, ma'am." Helaine couldn't help but be impressed. Clearly Chandelle was the law around here. Meanwhile, Robert took her elbow and steered her back toward the main entranceway.

"My father gave me the Chandler on my sixteenth birthday not knowing, of course, that all the women here were sick with a fever. He left, but I stayed on, helping to nurse them. We've been a hospital of sorts ever since then, but the name remains."

She stopped dead in her tracks, her mind working too slowly. "So I wasn't wrong. This is . . . It was . . ."

"Yep," inserted Chandelle as she came forward. "It were, but it ain't been that for a long time now. Go on," she said as she gestured them upstairs. "Go on and show 'er what you really do when you come here." Then she released a cackle. "Well, that's when I ain't got him doing bedpans."

Helaine gasped. "You . . . you empty bedpans?"

He gave her a rueful look. "On occasion."

"Ha!" Chandelle inserted. "I makes sure 'e does 'em once a week just to keep 'im humble."

Helaine felt a smile curve her lips. "I'm afraid it's not working very well, then. Perhaps you should increase the frequency."

Robert groaned. "Lord, Helaine, I didn't bring you here to get me in trouble."

"Twice a week it is," confirmed Chandelle. "Now go on up! Afore the rats get yer dinner."

Robert arched a brow in mock challenge. "I thought you said the mama cat was a great mouser."

"She's only one cat!" Chandelle exclaimed. "She can't get them all. Now shoo! You know the children won't go to bed if yer around to play with."

At that Robert extended his hand to Helaine. She took it and they began to climb. It wasn't a long way to the upper floor, but she spent the whole time sorting through what she'd seen and what she'd guessed. It started with Gwen. "Your sister has no idea about this, does she? Not what the Chandler was or what you've made of it."

"It mortifies me to think that she's heard of this. I will have to explain it to her, so she knows not to be blurting it out."

"Why haven't you already?"

He grimaced as they topped the last step. "Because it is none of her business!" he groused. "This is my place. Every gentleman should have a place to go for some peace. This is mine."

"Most men pick gaming clubs."

He snorted. "Betting on a roll of the dice has always seemed singularly useless to me. The stakes are too low. Money, pshaw! Trying to find the cure for the pox or a bad knife wound, now that is a puzzle for a man."

Helaine had no answer for that, and while she sorted through those words, he squeezed her fingers. "Forgive me, but I really need to check on the baby. His mother died a few days ago. We've found a wet nurse, but one can never tell if the babe will take." So saying, he knocked lightly on the nearest door, waiting until it opened. There stood a woman with full breasts and a milk-stained gown.

"Just got them both down, sir. Sleeping like a dream."

Robert tiptoed inside to look down at two cribs, the first with a girl who had the nurse's light brown hair. But the second was a tiny boy with dark hair and the tiniest little face Helaine had ever seen. He couldn't be more than a couple weeks old at most.

"So he's feeding?" Robert asked the woman.

"Oh, yes, poor mite. Took a bit o' coaxing, but he's all right and tight wi' it now."

"Thank you, Nan. You make sure to tell Chandelle if you need anything."

"We be right perfect, we is. I can't thank you enough for letting us stay here. We were in a right poor way, me and my Missy."

Robert held up his hand to stop the effusive thanks. "That was Chandelle's doing, not mine."

"But you paid fer the doctor—"

"Chandelle did. Good night, Nan." And with that, he backed out of the room.

Helaine snorted. "Liar," she whispered after he had shut the door.

He spun around. "What?"

"You are paying for this. For everything."

His lips quirked, but he shook his head. "Chandelle manages it all. I merely visit from time to time."

"To clean bedpans."

"Yes. And to . . . I'm sorry. One moment more." He tapped on another door, opening it when a quavering voice bade him enter. Inside was an old woman, clearly bedridden, but with eyes that warmed to light honey when she saw him.

"Sir!" she cried, then she descended into a bout of coughing that left her weak and pale.

He crossed to her quickly, supporting her body as she gasped for breath, then helping her drink from a glass of water when she was done. "It is not helping, is it?" he asked when she was finally back against her pillows, her breath shallow but steady.

"It's my time, sir. Ain't no medicine . . . can stop it now."

"No, Miss Mary, it isn't. We shall find—"

"Stop!" she said with as much force as she could muster. "This your woman?"

"I—," he began, but his words were cut off as Miss Mary waved Helaine forward.

"Come, come. Let me see . . . who ye finally picked."

Helaine stepped in. "Hello. My name is Mrs. Mortimer, and yes, I am certainly a friend of—"

"Sir," he said quickly, cutting her off. "I am simply 'Sir' here."

She arched her brow, but showed her understanding with a slight nod. "We are friends, he and I. Besides, I begin to think you ladies are his real love."

The woman laughed at that, her mouth opening to a toothless grin, but she hadn't enough breath for a real laugh. In the end, she settled with a pat on Robert's hand as she caught her breath. "He ain't brought . . . no one here. Nor took . . . any woman. We all offered."

"You took sick," said Robert as he pressed a kiss to the back of Miss Mary's hand. "Otherwise I would have tumbled madly in love with you."

Miss Mary smiled, but her eyes were on Helaine. "Hurt

'im," she said, "an' I'll haunt you. Your hair'll go white. Teeth rot. Haunt you—"

"I shall not hurt him," Helaine said.

"Swear it."

Robert patted the woman's hand, trying to distract her. "There's no need—"

"I swear I shall do everything I can to see him happy," she said, surprising herself with her words. But even as she said them, there was a rightness to it. Whatever else Lord Redhill was, he was a good man. Any man who could create a place like this—a home where women and children lived in happiness—was a worthy man in her eyes. His Grosvenor Square home showed the privilege of his rank. But this place, with the poor and the dying, was something else entirely. This showed his true heart.

Miss Mary held her gaze for a long while, impressing her will upon Helaine. It was odd getting this steely a gaze from a dying woman, but there was strength in Miss Mary despite her frail body, and Helaine had no doubt she could make good on her threat to haunt anyone who hurt her "Sir."

In the end, the woman was satisfied. Miss Mary let her eyes drift closed as she patted Robert's hand. "Go. Be young. Make babies."

"I shall talk to the doctor tomorrow about your medicine. We shall find something to help."

Miss Mary didn't answer except to wave him away. He nodded to her, though she couldn't see it, and tiptoed out. Helaine followed a half step behind. He didn't speak again until after the door was pulled tightly shut.

"She was Chandelle's madame, once upon a time. Quite a beauty, too. Used to run three houses with twenty girls each."

Helaine gasped, her eyes going back to the shut door. "She pulled girls into this life? Into—"

"Don't judge," he said quickly. "The girls would be taking men either way. Best they do it in a clean, safe place where they're paid for their service." He turned to her, and in his eyes she could see that he wanted her to understand, to see the women beneath the job.

"Of course," she said slowly. She well knew the desperate straits a woman could face. She would not judge any woman who chose that path. But what about the woman who paved the road? Who trapped others into the life? In her mind, they were all like Johnny Bono, taking advantage where they could in service to their own base needs.

She felt his hand on her chin, encouraging her to look him in the eye. "This is a place for women to come and die with dignity. Or to heal from wounds, like Nettie. She was stabbed by her customer because he didn't want to pay. Chandelle mans the door, and only she can ask what happened to bring them here. I don't care. Can you understand that, Helaine? I don't care who they were. Only what I see before me: sick women who need a little care."

Helaine swallowed, ashamed of her own prejudices. She never would have thought that Robert would have a better understanding of the poor and the weak than she. She never would have thought he would prove to be kinder than she. But he was. This place proved it.

"Show me the rest, Robert. Let me see it all."

His smile showed relief and joy, and before long, she was peeking in on ten ladies, plus Chandelle and the children. And then on the topmost floor was one last room, which he proclaimed his sanctuary. Pushing it open, she saw a ratty desk piled high with notes, another table of bottles containing what must be medicines, a plate of cold chicken and wine—their dinner, she presumed—and a large, comfortable bed stacked high with pillows.

"Please come in, Helaine," he said. "There is but one thing more, and then you shall know it all."

"All, my lord? Everything there is about you? If there is one thing I have learned this evening, it is that there are always more layers to you than I imagine."

He shrugged. "My heart, then, Helaine. You shall learn my true heart."

Chapter 18

Robert swung the door wide and watched as she crossed the threshold into his sanctuary. No woman had ever come in here. Doctors and apothecaries aplenty, but they were always men. Even Chandelle never dared breach this place. In truth, he had needed all that time this afternoon just to clean up the room to make it habitable for her.

And now she was here. His Helaine, looking about with wide eyes. "I don't understand," she said softly, turning back to him with an apology in her eyes.

"Of course not. I haven't explained." He took her hand and drew her forward to his desk. He pulled out a large ledger and opened it up to a random page. "This is my recording of all the patients who have passed through these doors. Their ailments, their medications, and how they fared."

She reached forward, gently turning page after page. "There are so many."

"I have been doing this since I was sixteen." He flipped the pages back to the beginning. At sixteen his handwriting was less neat, more rushed. Some lines weren't even straight, but it was undeniably his hand. "Half of the women died in that terrible time, but half did not. Many of those who survived have gone on to other employment, other lives. See here. Martha became a maid and eventually married a footman she met there. They have children now. One of them is apprenticed as a clerk at the Home Office."

"Truly? That's remarkable!"

He nodded. He was especially pleased with how well Martha had done. "She's one of my favorites. Others have not been as strong."

He was flipping through pages, remembering the women who had come through these doors. He had treated them all, tried to help them all. But he stopped when Helaine's fingers touched his. "Did you pay for his education? Martha's boy?"

"Some." It was a lie. He had paid for all of it and counted it money well spent.

"And all these women who became maids. That was off of your recommendation, wasn't it?"

"God, no! I am just 'Sir' here. I couldn't give them recommendations, but I could coach them. I could tell them what to say, how to appear, and . . . um . . ."

"How to forge recommendations?"

He shrugged. "Perhaps. I have a friend in an employment office. He understands the nature of what we do here and has been willing to help."

She shook her head. "That was quite a risk. What if one of them had begun thieving? What if a woman went back to her old life? Your friend would not help you anymore."

"There have been some bad choices," he said slowly. "But Chandelle tells me when the girl is ready, *if* she is ready. Truthfully, that is more her work than mine." Then he grabbed Helaine's hand and took her to his array of herbs and medicines. "*This* is my work. Teas, herbs, medicines. I have discovered some wonderful things for coughs. This herb when mixed with butter is amazingly soothing on lesions. It doesn't cure them, of course, but it calms the itch and that helps it heal."

He continued to point out bottles, even showing her the ledger where he recorded recipes that he had discovered. He was about to show her a grimoire he had found in an old bookshop. He hadn't cared for all the magical occult things, but the tracts on tinctures were most interesting. But as he was reaching for the book, she started to laugh. It started as a chuckle that she tried to cover but failed. Within a moment, she was chortling while he straightened with a look of mock affront.

"Are you laughing at me, Helaine?"

"No, Robert, actually I am laughing at . . . well, at this place, at these ledgers, all this study. And yes, I suppose I am laughing at you, but only in the best possible way. My God, Robert, you do realize that I understand almost nothing of this."

He frowned. "But it's simple really."

"As is stitching a straight line, but I cannot seem to do it." And when he just looked at her, she took his hands and drew them to her heart. "I don't understand it, Robert, but I think it's wonderful. You are like a little boy here, excited, focused, and so happy you can barely contain it."

He smiled, trying to see the room as she might. It was a wonder she did not think him a madman. "I love this," he said honestly. "If I were born a laborer, I would have apprenticed myself to a surgeon. I would have learned medicine from him, and then—"

"But surely you could do so now. There are lectures and the like for other men of science, aren't there?"

"Yes, yes, and I attend as often as I can. But you don't understand. As a boy, I was already trailing about after the surgeon. I helped with the cattle, you know, and had even begun following him to the village and the like. But my father didn't think that was appropriate work for an earl. And besides, there was so much else to do. The family finances were a mess. I didn't realize the extent of it at first, but I learned. Quickly. And the more I did, the more my father handed over to me."

"Oh," she said, and he could tell she was beginning to

understand. "So you turned your mind to your responsibilities."

"To management, Helaine. That's all this is," he said as he gestured about the room. "Management of medicine. Records and experiments. How do you know why one crofter is doing better than another? Why does this cow produce more milk than that one? Why does this mine prosper over another? You don't know unless you keep records, Helaine. And from the records, you can glean the answer. Maybe the crofter is lazy or maybe he is using the wrong manure. Maybe the cow is sick and maybe the manager of the mine is a self-aggrandizing fool."

She looked around. "You are keeping records, then. Of medicine."

"What better thing to manage than humanity's ailments?"

She smiled at him, her eyes going soft and her body shifting closer to his. She touched his cheek. "Your mind is amazing, Robert. It takes my breath away."

He shifted his face to press a kiss into her palm. "So you understand? Do you see why I brought you here?"

She remained silent, but he was so absorbed in the feel and smell of her hand that it took him a moment to realize it. Then when he did, he lifted his head to look at her. "You don't understand, do you? Not yet."

"Robert, this place is amazing. And I can see that it is indeed where your heart lies. But why—"

"I watched you today," he said. "I watched how you ordered clothing, how you discussed laces and reticules and hats. Good God, I thought I would go mad from all the details surrounding hats!"

She chuckled, and he could feel her laughter against his skin. "Well, hats are rather complicated."

"They're beyond complicated. They're diabolic. And yet you know just what will suit and what will not."

"But—"

"Don't you see, Helaine? You are doing your passion. I never really comprehended it until I saw you this afternoon. Your father was a damned idiot and your life has been very hard. But in this one thing, he gave you a blessing. You are doing your passion, Helaine. Dress design, hats and ribbons, it is all what you love and you are doing it every day."

He watched as her expression went from confusion to awareness then to clarity. "You envy me," she gasped. "You envy my life! Oh, sweet heaven, you are an idiot!"

"No," he said as he pulled her into his arms. She went willingly, and for that he was grateful. He needed to hold her as he explained. He needed to touch her skin and feel her close as no one had ever been this close to him before. "Well, yes, I envy you. That you can do the work of your heart every day."

"I do it because I need to pay for my supper."

"But you love it, too."

She smiled. "Yes, I love it."

"Which makes your life enviable."

She shook her head. "It's not all perfect, you know."

"It never is. The point is that I see it now. I see how good you are at fashion and how much you love it. Just like I love all of this." He twisted her in his arms to indicate the room. "And I would never do anything to stop that. I could never interfere with someone's love like that."

She laughed, the humor shimmering from her into him. Or maybe it was the other way around. He didn't know anything except that she was smiling at him. "And that makes you one big idiot. Robert, this is what you had to show me? This is your heart?"

He sobered, his mind stuttering over the plans he'd made, the thoughts he'd had. Suddenly it didn't seem so important, so urgent. "I—uh—yes, I thought so."

Her laughter bubbled up again, but it didn't last long. Not when she was looking at his very sober face. "Robert?"

"I'd give it up," he whispered. "I'd give it up for you."

"What?"

"I had to show you this. I had to take you in here to show you everything that I am. And I guess I had to realize that I want you more."

She pulled back, but his arms tightened around her. "Robert, you're not making sense."

"I know I'm not. It's because I just now figured it out. I haven't been in here for a long while, not because I didn't want to, but because I . . . I was thinking about you. And even when I was here, it was because of you. I . . . You're more important to me than this."

"Don't be ridiculous. I can't be."

He frowned, his mind still churning with his thoughts, his emotions. But in the end, he straightened up enough to look her in the eye. "Helaine, you are as important to me as all of this. More even, though that thought terrifies me in a way you can't even imagine. A woman more important than what I have wanted my whole life?" He shook his head. "Inconceivable."

"Robert—"

"But it's true. I swear to you, it's true."

She pulled backward, not quite out of his arms, but she put more distance between them. "You're getting carried away."

"I know!" he cried, half alarmed, half incredulous. "And I never get carried away! Helaine, what have you done to me?"

She threw up her hands. "I have done nothing but tell you no. Over and over."

He laughed. "You know that's not the reason. Scores of women have refused me over the years."

She released her own sharp bark of laughter. "Scores? I hardly think that's likely."

"Well, dozens at least. At least one dozen."

"Robert, you are being foolish. Come now," she said as she pushed at his shoulders. "Release me."

He shook his head and slowly tightened his grip. He didn't have to force her. She was reluctant, not refusing. "I don't want to let you go, Helaine." Her head was down, but he could put his mouth next to her cheek. He coaxed her gently to lift her face to his. "I want to keep you close forever."

"I never thought you one for pretty lies, Robert."

"That's just the thing," he said as he closed his eyes. He stopped trying to tempt her and just held her, breathing in her essence and feeling her glorious warmth. "They're not lies."

"Of course they're lies," she said. "Even if you mean them right now."

"What if they're not? What if I will feel like this forever? I'm not an inconsistent man, Helaine. What I feel for you is . . . is . . ."

"A fleeting fantasy?" She lifted her head to look into his eyes. "A passing desire?"

"Love. What if it is love?"

She gasped, her whole body tightening in his arms. She made to push him away, but he did not open his arms. He did not want her running, not yet. Not until they had worked this through. He was careful not to pull her close, but he could not release her. Not yet. Nor could he speak. The idea was too new, the feeling too special. So he held her and in time she stilled.

"You must let me go, Robert."

"In a moment. Just . . . a moment."

He felt her breath, warm and moist against his cheek. It was acceptance. She would not run, and so he slowly drew her the rest of the way into his arms. Good Lord, she felt amazing there. All soft and womanly, and yet he knew the strength she had in her. And the goodness. How he wanted to possess her. He wanted her beneath him, penetrated by him, and touched by no other. He wanted it like a territorial animal wants to stake a claim. And he wanted it the way a man wants to own a woman.

But he was not an animal nor was he ruled by his passions. He wanted her, maybe even loved her. But he would let her go if that was what she wished. So he did it. He took one last breath of her scent and then opened his arms. She stepped back slowly, confusion and a myriad of emotions crossing her face.

"Robert," she whispered, "I do not know what to think. You take my reason away."

His lips twisted in a rueful kind of smile. "You have been doing that for me since the very beginning."

"This can't last. And when it ends, where will I be?"

He arched a brow. "Are you sure? What if it is better than anything? Better than everything!"

She looked away from him, her eyes going to the bed. It wasn't large by a viscount's standards, but it was large enough for them. Just a man and a woman. He reached out to stroke her cheek. He couldn't stop himself, especially when she closed her eyes and rested her cheek against his palm.

"You know me now," he said softly. "You know you can trust me." He gently pulled her gaze back to his. "I won't lose control this time, Helaine." He rolled his thumb across her lips. "Let me love you."

She held his gaze for a long moment and he could see the indecision in her eyes. He didn't say anything. He had already said more than he could credit. So when her body slowly released and her eyes drifted shut, he knew that her decision was made and he had not influenced it.

"Yes," she whispered. "Please, Robert, please love me."

Chapter 19

❧

What if it's love? Robert's words reverberated in He-
laine's mind, echoing over and over until she could think of
nothing else. What if he loved her? What if Robert, Viscount
Redhill, future Earl of Willington, was in love with her?
This man who had tortured her, threatened her business,
and ultimately revealed his heart to her in a brothel might
indeed love her. He was arrogant, opinionated, and flawed.
And yet he was also brilliant, kind, and generous to a fault.
She knew better than most how much a place like this would
cost. But he supported it out of his own pocket. He worried
about the children of the miners. And he worried about her.

What if it's love? The idea seduced her as much as his
hands on her body, his mouth on her flesh. Because she so
wanted to be loved. By any man, but most especially by him.

Love . . .

"Yes," she said again because that was the only word she
could manage.

His hands were trembling as he caressed her face. "I'll
be careful," he whispered as he rained kisses across her
cheeks, eyes, and nose. "I swear it, Helaine. I'll be—"

She stopped his words. She didn't want to hear about careful. So she lifted her face and met his lips, her mouth open, her tongue questing for his. She felt his gasp of surprise, quickly followed by a shift in his body. She didn't understand what he was doing at first, but then she felt her legs swept out from beneath her. He lifted her up, carrying her effortlessly to the bed. And as he moved, she kept their mouths joined, their tongues intertwined.

A moment later, they were at the bed, but he didn't release her. He just stood there holding her while his mouth played with hers. Oh, sweet heaven, how could any man kiss so beautifully? All thrusting power one second, then teasing withdrawal followed by tiny nips next before he rushed inside again. It was fun, and she found herself smiling from the sheer joy of it.

He took that moment to break away from her with a gasp. He bent down, slowly setting her on the bed, but he stayed with her, his forehead pressed to hers. Her arms were wrapped around his neck, pulling him closer, and soon he was sitting beside her on the bed. Thankfully, his hands were deliciously busy. They slid down her back and were undoing her buttons, loosening her gown even as she was the one now to kiss his mouth, his cheeks, his very strong nose.

"I love your nose," she said as she skated her lips across it. Would his fingers never finish? Her gown was too tight. She could barely breathe.

"My nose?" he asked. "Why ever would you love that?"

"Because it is strong. It is aristocratic. I even love the bump right on the end."

He pulled back and tried to stare cross-eyed at his nose. "A bump?"

"Absolutely," she lied. In truth, there was no bump, but her heart was beating so fast, her body so alive, she had to say something to calm herself down. Some nonsense to cool her fire or she swore she would burn up.

"Truly?" he asked as finally, wonderfully, he finished with the buttons of her gown.

"No, silly. It is perfect." And just to prove it, she pressed a kiss right on the tip. She would have done more except at that moment he pulled back, his eyes dark with mischief.

"So you think to tease me, do you? Then perhaps I should tell you what about you that I like." He leaned forward and began kissing her cheek, his tongue making little swirls along her skin as he drew lower on her body. Her cheek became her jaw, then her neck, and soon he was pulling her gown forward and off so he could kiss her shoulder.

"You're not talking," she gasped. It was silly of her, but she wanted to know. What about her did he find so attractive?

"I haven't gotten there yet," he said. The gown she wore was one of her own designs with the shift sewn into the bodice. That meant there was nothing to stop him as he pulled it away from her torso, nothing to interrupt his gaze of her now bared breasts.

"Oh," she whispered as her skin heated. All men loved breasts, she supposed. But he wasn't looking at her there. He was drawing the gown off her arms and she was torn between covering herself back up or just closing her eyes to feel the soft caress of the air on her sensitive skin. She did neither, her gaze going to his dark eyes. Never had she seen him look so intensely. He hadn't lost control like before. This time, he was just looking, his expression adoring rather than possessive.

"Robert?"

"I love your shoulder," he said as he stroked a single finger from her neck down across the top of one shoulder. "The line is so elegant."

"My what?"

"Specifically, this little mole right here." He leaned forward to her left shoulder and stroked his tongue over a dark dot just beside her collarbone. She barely remembered that it was there. She never thought a man would like it, much less stroke his tongue across it in a way that made her blood sing.

"Oh, my!" she gasped.

"You have been tormenting me with that mole all evening long, you know," he said against her skin. "It kept taunting me from your skin. All that creamy expanse of flesh and one mischievous mole begging me to kiss it."

He was pressing her backward into the pillows, following her down as he continued to press kisses to her mole and collarbone. She giggled, her happiness coming out in the odd sound. "How can a mole be mischievous? That doesn't even make sense."

"I don't know," he said. "But yours is." He straightened up to look at her with mock seriousness. "From now on, you cannot wear gowns that reveal your shoulders or I shall be forced to strip you naked and ravish you."

He meant the words as a tease. She knew that, but her mood began to fade as fear crept in. "Is that what you are going to do to me? Am I to be ravished?"

He sobered as well, though the hunger burned in his eyes. It hadn't taken over, but it was there. "I shall do only what you want, Helaine. You shall keep your virginity."

She wasn't sure she wanted to keep it. Not now, with her body bare to him while he spoke so honestly to her. But she didn't say that. Instead, she nodded. A tiny dip of her chin while his hand stroked from her shoulder down across the swell of her breast until he cupped her boldly. She opened her mouth on a gasp, and then shuddered as his thumb stroked back and forth over her tightened nipple.

"You have the sweetest nipples ever," he said as his gaze left her face to look at what he was doing. "Tight, dusky, and they make you do the most wonderful things."

She licked her lips, trying to focus while her nipple seemed to tingle with fire under his strokes. "What things?" she asked.

"This," he said. Then he grabbed her nipple between two fingers and rolled it back and forth.

She cried out in surprise. The tingling fire had abruptly shot flames straight to her core. Her head pressed backward and her back arched more fully into his hand.

"Exactly that!" he said as his other hand cupped her and began its own ministrations.

Good Lord, she had never realized how very wonderful

her breasts could feel. As she lay there, her body burning, he stroked her breasts, shaping them, holding them, and yes, tweaking her nipples in the most amazing ways.

"No man has ever done this to you before me," Robert said, his words half question, half statement. "Every time I touch you, it is like you are surprised by the pleasure."

"No one," she gasped.

He grinned, the possessive glint flashing briefly before he lowered his head. "Then let me show you more." He put his mouth on her nipple and began to suck, pulling it deeply—rhythmically—into his mouth, where he stroked it with his tongue.

She lost herself to the sensations. Had he done this to her before? In the inn? She didn't remember. She did know, however, that he'd never brought her to this place before. A sea of sensation where her body became a needful thing.

She felt his hands on her waist, pulling her gown down. She lifted her hips joyfully, helping him strip away the layers of velvet that only suffocated her. A moment later she kicked it aside such that she wore only her best stockings tied to her thighs and her half boots. His mouth continued on her breasts, one then the other, while his hands stroked over her belly and across her hips. Over and over he touched the edge of her stockings, toying with the ties, touching the edge where fabric met flesh.

Then his mouth left her nipple to press kisses to the underside of her breast, then lower and lower. Her belly shivered as the slight stubble of his chin rubbed against her. But it wasn't unpleasant. In truth, it made a delightful contrast to his lips and his tongue.

"We are well above everyone up here," he said against her belly button. "You may scream if you like."

Scream? She never screamed. But she didn't have the breath to speak as his fingers shifted on her legs. He was lying down beside her as he moved, but in the reverse. His legs were by her shoulder, his mouth traveling farther down her belly. She wanted to touch him, but his clothing was in the way.

"Stop, stop!" she gasped. "At least take off your boots!"

He paused what he was doing, pushing up enough to look at her. "Yes, of course," he said. "But only the boots. I shan't risk more."

She didn't understand what he meant. Or perhaps it was more accurate to say that she didn't want to know what he meant so she blocked it from her mind. Meanwhile, he was drawing off his boots while the fire in her blood began to cool. She didn't move, though. She was too afraid of disturbing the glorious mindlessness of what was happening. So she watched him, seeing the powerful lines of his body even through the covering of his clothes.

"Take off more, Robert," she said. "Please let me see you as you are seeing me."

He looked at her, and her body flushed again at the hunger in his gaze. "I am not so lovely, you know."

She smiled. "Let me be the judge of that." She began to push herself upright, but he stroked a hand across her shoulder. "Don't move, Helaine. Not even an inch."

"But—"

"I love looking at you."

She had no answer to that. She had never thought herself to be ugly, but neither had she believed herself a beauty. There had never been a belief that her looks could catch her a husband even before her father had made his ridiculous blunder. But when Robert looked at her like that, she felt stunningly powerful. As if she were a goddess and he her worshipper. She hadn't expected that. Not with a man as powerful as Robert. But that was how he made her feel.

"Your shirt, Robert," she said, liking the way her voice sounded deep and commanding. "Let me see you."

His brow arched at her tone, but he did as she bade. He held her gaze as he stripped, pulling off jacket, cravat, waistcoat, and then shirt. One by one he pulled them off, but his gaze never left her face. She, however, looked her full as bit by bit his muscular torso was revealed. Now she believed that he sometimes helped with the farmwork, the mine work, and the day-to-day difficulties with patients. She could see it in his body.

"No wonder you are handsome even in dull brown clothing," she breathed. "Imagine what could be done if you made the tiniest effort in your attire."

His lips quirked. "I believe my tailor said just that the last time I saw him. But truthfully, I have never thought about it before you."

She lifted up from the bed despite his order not to move. She rolled to an elbow so she could reach him with her other hand, so she could stroke his golden skin. She even pressed a kiss to his shoulder. Then she gave him a devilish glance and abruptly shifted her position. Within a second, she was stroking her tongue across the tight nub of his nipple. After all, anatomy was not so different between man and woman. If she enjoyed it, she reasoned, he might also. A moment later she was rewarded with his gasp of surprise. Then his hand went to the back of her head, holding her against him as his body trembled beneath her ministrations.

"You learn fast," he said, his breath shallow.

She smiled against his body, loving his scent and the slight dusting of his hair against her cheek. "A student is only as good as her teacher," she said. Then she began to kiss along his torso as he had done for her.

And as she moved, so did he. He let her caress his skin while his hands once again returned to her. His fingers traced lines along her hip and over her thigh. And as she was stretching for his far nipple, his fingers slid between her legs.

She stiffened in surprise, but it was too late to stop him. His long index finger was pushing slowly, deeply between her folds and she was stunned by the pleasure she felt by his invasion. She wanted to say something. She wanted to form words or at least return to what she was doing for him. But she couldn't manage anything more than a high squeak.

"Lie back, Helaine. Let me show you." Then he didn't wait for her response, but slowly pressed her shoulder backward. She didn't have the coordination to fight him, and she didn't really want to anyway. He was in control here, which left her free to feel, to enjoy, and to let her legs tremble as her knees rolled outward.

He had more room to move now, his finger slipping down before sliding back out. Her body arched with his slide, and her eyes drifted shut while tension coiled in her belly.

"How do you feel, Helaine?" he asked. His finger continued to stroke her below while, above, his free hand began to play once again with her breast.

"So much," she gasped. "So wonderful."

He grinned at her, his attention to her nipple making her gasp anew. "Trust me, Helaine. Trust me. I will not fail you." So saying, he bent down to kiss her belly. He had to leave off what he did with her breast, but it didn't matter. Her skin was so sensitive now that any touch, any sensation, whether the roughness of his beard or the soothing swirl of his tongue, heightened her pleasure.

She felt his hand on her thigh, pulling her leg a little higher and more open. She complied because she would do anything he wanted at that moment. And as she moved, she felt his finger slip inside her. A single press, deep, then deeper still. Her body tightened in surprise. Nothing had ever invaded her there, and yet she liked it. He pulled it out, then pushed back inside again. Two fingers, and she felt her body stretch around him.

His mouth was lower now, pressing into her curls. She didn't understand what he intended until it was done. And once it was done, she did not want him to stop. He was kissing her deep down at that place that was so wonderful. She had no words then, nothing but a cry of astonishment.

A wave engulfed her, her whole body arching and contracting with the stroke of his tongue. Then more waves came, one on top of the other. Her body tightened and released, again and again. She arched in wonder and rushed into bliss.

Such bliss!

It lasted a long time and not nearly long enough. The waves faded to trembles, which left behind a sweet happiness that suffused her entire body. She lay there, feeling her breathing ease and watching Robert as he watched her. He had a silly grin on his face and if she had any strength she might have teased him about it. As it was, she could only grin back.

"How do you feel?" he asked as he stroked his hand across her belly.

She gasped at the tingles that followed his fingertips. Then she batted his hand away. "You know very well that I feel wonderful."

"I just like hearing you say it."

She released a happy sigh. "Is it always like that? Does it feel the same for you?"

He laughed, the sound almost as light and happy as she felt. "I cannot say. Perhaps we should try it again and see if there is any change."

"Oh, yes!" she cried as she spread her arms wide. "I cannot believe I have waited this long to experience that! It was wonderful!" Then she shot him an arch look. "Even if it was so very, very scandalous."

He was still, lying in the opposite direction, his bare chest pressing delightfully against her thigh. At her look, he pressed a kiss to the top of her leg and she gasped in surprise. It was almost a perfunctory kiss, and yet her body still reacted as if he were doing something a great deal more intimate.

"I think you should rest a moment before we begin again."

She knew he was right but she just shook her head. "A moment, a day, an aeon more, doesn't matter. I think I have been sensitive to your touch from the very beginning."

"I like the sound of that," he said as he pushed himself upright. She scooted sideways to allow him more room. Truthfully, she was beginning to feel cold, so she reached around to gather the covers. Then, of course, she remembered she still had her half boots on.

"Of all the ridiculous things!" She leaned forward to unhook her boots, then immediately felt self-conscious as her breasts swung with her movements. She pulled her arms tight to her chest as embarrassment heated her face. But when she glanced at him, she saw that he was far from horrified by the sight. If anything, he seemed disappointed when she covered herself up.

"I like the way you look," he said softly. "Every single part of you."

She didn't know what to say to that, so she busied herself with her shoes. But of course her fingers got tangled, and she released a very unladylike curse. He chuckled as he put his hands over hers—large and soothing.

"Let me help. You may not realize this, but it is common to feel some embarrassment afterward. Please do not. This is new to you, and I can tell you that everything about it was perfect."

She waited as he gently pulled off her boots. Then she untied her stockings, allowing him to draw them off of her until she was fully naked and could at last slip under the covers. It was bizarre that she was now completely undressed but felt more comfortable because she was fully covered. Only when she felt the warmth of the heavy blanket around her did she finally dare to say what was on her mind.

"You say it was perfect?"

"Absolutely."

"But isn't it usually more, um, shared?"

He arched his brows, humor shimmering in his eyes. But he didn't laugh at her, thank heaven. "You told me before you understand the mechanics?"

He asked it as a question, so she nodded. "Schoolgirls talk, you know, after some of them have gotten married. And some of my friends were raised in the country. Between the two, I believe I have gleaned what happens."

"Do you also know that the first time can be painful?"

She nodded.

"But there are ways to prevent that or at least minimize the pain. Helaine, are you now thinking that we can . . . that I can . . ." He looked so hopeful even as he struggled with his words.

"Yes, Robert, I am considering it." She was smiling as she said the words, another silly blush heating her cheeks.

"It is very wicked of me, but after what we just did"—she shrugged—"I want to learn more. I want to do more."

He grinned and she could tell that he was very, very pleased with himself. "I am at your command, my lady. Whenever and whatever your heart desires."

He meant it as a joke. He was teasing her as he sat there, all golden skinned and beautiful. But he used the words "my lady." As a *joke*. But she was a lady in truth. Lady Helaine. And she had just shamed her heritage terribly. The thought had her burying her face in her arms, her shoulders stiffening as she imagined what her grandmother would say of a woman like her.

"Oh, no," she heard Robert say. "Helaine, what happened? What are you thinking?"

He put his hand on her bare shoulder, large and warm where neither blanket nor pillows touched. She wanted to sink into his heat. Instead, she lifted her head and looked him in the eye.

"What would you think of Gwen if she were to do this?"

His hand remained on her shoulder, but the rest of him recoiled in horror. "Pray do not make me think of my sister in these terms."

"Because it is wrong?"

"Because she is my *sister*."

Her lips quirked a bit at his tone, but she quickly sobered. "Don't misunderstand," she said as much to herself as to him. "I would not choose differently, Robert. Tonight has been wonderful."

"It is not done yet."

She couldn't help smiling a bit at that, but still her conscience pricked her. It was silly, of course. She had made her choice and did not regret it. Plus, no matter what title she'd been born with, her situation was vastly different from Gwen's. And yet, it still bothered her. She had fallen. "We are both daughters of earls. And by all accounts, our fathers are similarly . . . er, flawed."

Robert snorted. "Yes, though my father tends to make his mistakes a little more privately than yours."

"He could hardly be more public."

He nodded, and his hand squeezed her shoulder. "Helaine, it is merely a word. Mistress. Lover. Woman."

"Tart."

He winced. "No one will damn you for what we've done."

She knew that. Her mother had all but thrown her into his arms. Her best friend, Wendy, would clap her hands and demand details. And as for her grandmother and even her father, they were all long gone. Their opinions mattered nothing. And yet . . .

"I feel as if I have cheapened myself somehow. And shamed my family name."

He sighed and his hand went to her face to stroke a finger across her cheek. "Do you want me to take you home?"

She bit her lip, taking less than a second to decide. "No," she said firmly. "I don't regret what we've done, Robert. I really don't. It's just so hard to understand. It was wonderful, and now I'm . . ."

"As beautiful and wonderful as you were an hour ago."

She snorted. "I doubt my priest would say that."

He flashed her a rueful look. "If we are to look to the priests for our judgment, then I, for one, was damned a long time ago."

She had no answer to that. They both knew as a titled lord, no priest would say a word against him. But she, on the other hand, could be cursed as a whore from many a pulpit. Not that it would happen. The priests had no interest in her at all. But it stung a little that as a titled man, he was given grace, whereas she would have to beg for forgiveness.

He searched her face, but she had no answers for him. So he shifted on the bed, putting his back to the wall before gathering her into his arms. She went easily. There was no place in the world that felt better to her than right here. She pressed her face to his chest and rubbed her cheek against his flesh while he held her tight.

And she did her best to hide her tears.

Chapter 20

❧

Robert felt her tears wet his skin. He knew she was trying to hide it, and so he didn't comment. But that didn't stop his mind from spinning. *What would you think of Gwen if she were to do this?* Those were her words, and he was hard put not to shudder as his mind replayed the question over and over.

The two women were completely different, of course. Their situations, their stations in life, were in vastly different places. He did mark some obvious similarities in strength of character, but that made them both formidable women. He liked that about them both.

I don't regret what we've done. Neither did he. And yet, he couldn't stop the moral squirm that he had just debauched an innocent. In fact, he was still painfully hard with the hunger to complete what they had started.

Which brought him to the obvious question: What did she regret? What was she crying for? He guessed it was her lost childhood and the titled woman she should have become. She wasn't mourning what they'd done, only the things she'd lost the minute her father had proved himself an ass.

"I know about lost possibilities," he said to her hair.

"Nothing like what you lost, but in my mind it was everything. At least for a while."

She straightened off his chest. At his urging, she realigned herself against him. She was still settled in his arms, but could now watch his face while he talked. And he in turn could be tortured by the full length of her glorious legs along his.

"It must have been a woman," she guessed.

"It was," he confirmed. "My mother. I remember a time when she laughed. There was a day when I was just a boy when we had a picnic outdoors. I went swimming and Gwen sat on the blanket and smeared jam all over herself. Jack hadn't been born yet. Mother looked at Gwen and laughed. She'd pressed her hands to her mouth but we could hear it." He closed his eyes, pretending he could remember the sound of it. He couldn't, but he imagined it. "She's beautiful when she's happy. Really, really beautiful."

"Of course she is. Do you know what happened? Why she changed?"

He shook his head. He dropped his cheek on the top of her head, needing the support as he spoke. "I didn't even notice at first. She's never been a loud woman and if she spent most of her time indoors, I didn't care. I was a boy. I wanted to run around without my mother, not have her trail around behind me."

Helaine shifted against him, twisting slightly while his body thrilled to the sweet torture. When she looked him in the eye, he stole a kiss from her lips. It was sweet and stirring. And she ended it much too soon.

"Your mother seems sad to me. Just . . . well, desperately sad."

"I know," he said as he dropped his back against the wall. "As I said, I didn't realize it at first. I was a boy and then I was at school. But one summer I spent a month at my friend's home. His mother was never still, always busy, always expressing herself."

"Expressing herself?"

"Well, she had five children plus guests. It was like a house party but for children. Jamie's mother would be laughing at one of us while chiding another child to stay out of the tarts. Meanwhile, she ordered the household and helped teach the younger kids while the tutor worked with the older ones. Every day we went outside for hours, probably just to save the furniture, but it was never ending. And it was the best month of my life."

"Until you went home and compared that woman to your mother," she said, proving that she understood exactly what had happened.

"I tried to help her. I did everything I could to please her, to make her smile. I tried to get her to go on walks, to sing, anything that might work. Over the years, I've begged, teased, coaxed, even yelled."

"And none of it worked?"

"Oh, it all worked for a short while. As it is working now with Gwen's future in-laws. She'll make the effort for a bit, pretend that she is feeling better, but eventually it stops. In time, she returns to her bed worse than before."

She pressed a kiss to his neck and stroked her fingers idly across his chest. "How awful. What a terrible thing to grow up, see your mother suffering, and not be able to do anything about it."

"It never stops, Helaine, but I can't help hoping. Each time, I can't . . . not hope."

"Of course not. She's your mother."

"There was a day back when I was in my twenties. Gwen was about to come out and Mother had to help with that. She went to the dressmaker's, attended parties and routs, I even saw her smile when she watched Gwen dancing at a ball. I thought that finally we had broken through. Finally . . ."

"The Season was too much for her?"

"Right before Gwen's court presentation, Mother took to her bed and would not come out. Wouldn't eat, wouldn't bathe, wouldn't do anything. Gwen and I both tried to help. Even my father took a stand, but it was like she wasn't there. A body without a soul. It was terrible."

She was silent with her arms wrapped around him and

her head on his shoulder. She lay there thinking. He knew she was thinking, but about what?

"It was at the presentation that I realized the truth. I looked at all the court ladies in their gowns, I looked at Gwen practically shaking in her excitement, and I finally knew that Mother would not change. She would never be a woman fully alive the way other women were. I had to accept that, do what I could for her, and not spend my days worrying after her."

"You had plenty to do with a sister coming out, a younger brother in school, and the management of the earldom."

"That was also when I barred my father from the house. The maids lived in terror of him, and the footmen had no love of his drunken tirades."

She shuddered against him, and he knew she was much too familiar with drunken exploits.

"The point is that everything crashed about me that Season. What had started out as a delightful time with Gwen's coming out ended in a home in total disarray."

"You cannot think that was your fault."

"Of course not. But it didn't change the disaster."

"So what did you do?"

He lifted his head off hers, shame making him look away. "I left it all to Gwen," he finally confessed. "The finances were in order. That much I had seen to. And Jack was at school, so he was fine. But I had reached my limit, so I packed up and came here."

"Here?"

"Here, where I saw patients, made notes in my books, and consulted with doctors. Here, where I had more than a dozen women grateful for my attention, and Chandelle, who managed the running of the household. And here is where I got blind drunk one night, sought out Chandelle's bed, only to be refused, and ended up passed out on the floor outside her door."

Helaine's hand stilled on his chest. "She refused you?"

"Of course she did. If I had been anyone else, she would have thrown me out on the street. And in the morning, when

I had a splitting head and a foul temper, she kicked me upright and handed me a mop and a bucket. I was to clean up the mess I'd made and, while I was at it, to mop or sweep the rest of the house. And if I didn't like it, then I could leave."

"She would have tossed you out? You were her benefactor!"

"And my father is the earl, but I also barred the door to him. Rules have a purpose. Father had violated the rules of the house in accosting the maids. And I had violated the rules of this house. Rules that I myself had established. No drinking. At all. Not in this house." He chuckled as he recalled that time. "I spent a week cleaning bedpans and mopping floors. Every dirty, disgusting job she could find, she gave to me."

"And you did it?" He could hear the surprise in her voice.

"I did. And at the end of a week she said something to me that I'll never forget." He remembered the moment. He had been wringing out a filthy mop, and sweat was stinging his eyes.

"Don't stop there!" Helaine cried. "What did she say?"

He smiled at her eagerness. "She pointed at the bucket of foul water and told me, 'That's yesterday. Looking at that will just get you more sick. And thinking about what might have been if someone didn't get sick is a waste of time.' Then she picked up the bucket and tossed the foul water outside. Then she handed me the empty bucket and said, 'This is now. Look at now. Deal with the sick you got now.' If I wanted to think about tomorrow, then I could. But only if I started with now. Not with yesterday, because that was gone."

He watched her eyebrows contract as she sorted through the words. Eventually she nodded. "So you listened and went back home?"

He laughed. "No. I thought she was a bloody idiot. It took me a long while, but I realized she was right. My parents were my parents. Life has given me so many good things, it stood to reason that something else would be off. No one can have a perfect life." He touched her chin and gazed into her beautiful eyes. "I look at the moment right now and think I am blessed."

She smiled and he saw tenderness in her eyes. "That's a lovely story, Robert, but I'm afraid I don't understand what you're trying to tell me. That I should think of only now and not yesterday? I have been living from moment to moment since the day my father first forgot to pay the rent."

He nodded, seeing that she had indeed learned, younger than he, that the past can't be changed. "But you fear you have cheapened your name. You worry what your grandmother would say. Helaine, your father destroyed your family name long before you had a chance. If things were different, then we would not be here now. But we are here now. And I can offer you so much. Do you really want to say no to that?"

She shook her head. "I haven't said no, Robert."

He brushed his thumb along her jaw. "And yet you cried, Helaine. What can I do to fix that?"

"Promise me that my business will not suffer because of this. Promise me that I will still have food for my mother and a home to live in. Promise me that what is between us will remain just us."

He smiled. "This is my sanctuary here, Helaine. Only Chandelle knows my real name."

"They know my name, Robert. They—"

"No one will speak of it. You are safe. Now and in the future. I promise."

She released a slow exhale that heated the air between them. And as her breath released, her body relaxed as well. "You are right," she said. "The past is long gone. Whatever might have been or might be thought is also long gone. I am not the girl I once was."

"I like the woman better anyway."

"Good," she said as she lifted her mouth to his. "Then make me your mistress."

He paused to search her face. "We could wait a bit. This is still very new."

She wrapped her arm around his neck and drew his mouth down to hers. "Now," she said.

He grinned. "As you command."

* * *

Helaine slid her hands down his back until she came to the barrier of his pants. Slipping her fingers underneath, she slowly worked her way around to the front button clasp. He had gone absolutely still except to lift up enough to let her work. His breath was a hot caress on her neck, but her mind was on her fingers. Could she get him undone?

She managed it, able at last to push the fabric away. She had never touched a man's body before. Not his bare skin anywhere but his hands. To stroke Robert's flat stomach was like a special treat all in itself. But to touch lower was beyond anything she had ever dreamed before. Her fingers explored his wiry hair and then touched his upthrust organ. He sucked in his breath and she felt the muscles of his stomach ripple against her hand. But he did not move away. If anything, he pushed harder against her hand.

"This is good?" she asked.

"Yes," he said, his voice tight.

She rolled her thumb along the tip, surprised at the moisture there. Meanwhile, he returned to kissing her neck, to nipping lightly at her flesh before soothing it with his tongue.

"Robert," she said, frustrated because she could not touch more of him.

"Yes?"

"Take off all your clothes."

"Hmm. Yes."

He spent one last moment kissing her neck, and then abruptly he was gone. He leaped off the bed onto his feet and then was stripping out of the last of his clothes. She lay there, watching him closely. It wasn't just his organ, which was so large and thick to her mind. It was all of him. She loved the play of light and shadow on his muscles. The glow from the fire cast his skin in a golden red tone. But most of all, she saw him as he slowly straightened to his full height. To her shock, he dipped his head in an awkward movement and his hands twitched at his sides.

"Are you embarrassed?" she asked, her surprise clear in her tone.

"A little. You are staring so intensely."

"I have never seen—"

"I know. That's why I'm standing . . . I'm letting . . ." He cleared his throat, obviously working hard to stay calm. "I know you want to see, but it's a little unnerving. I don't know what I look like to you."

"You look like you," she said as she pushed up from the bed. "Strong and proud." The sheet moved with her, but soon pooled about her waist as she reached for him. He was near enough to touch, so she did. She stroked his chest, watching her fingers outline his muscles, the narrow tapering of hair down his belly, and even lower. She touched him gently, finally able to stroke his length, curl her fingers around, and even shift to touch the sac beneath.

She watched as his thighs bunched beneath her strokes, and she heard his breath grow ragged. "Should I kiss you? The way you did me?"

"Sweet God," he muttered as she moved to do just that. But he stopped her with a hand on her shoulder. "If you do, I shall explode. Helaine, you don't know what you do to me."

She looked up at his face. "Only what you do to me."

"Lie back, Helaine. Let me love you."

She nodded, a little afraid of what was to come. And yet, one look into his heated eyes and her fear drained away. He was hungry for her, but he was not out of control. She could trust him. So she slowly lay back, the sheet still covering her from the hips down, but her torso bared for his view.

He didn't look. He touched. He stroked her breasts, lifting the nipples for his thumb and mouth. He was a master at what he did, caressing her until she was mad from heat and desire. Her breasts came alive under his mouth. Her body arched, giving him better access and relieving some of the heat that he built. But it wasn't enough and she grew restless. She wanted a return of what he had done before. Of that wave of pleasure, and so her thighs slipped open in invitation.

He didn't disappoint her. His hand slid down, stroking her. His touch invaded every part of her. He pushed his fingers inside, stretching her again while his thumb circled the place that was so hungry for him.

The wave was building; the tension made her belly taut and arched her back. She was losing control of her body in a way that was wholly amazing. And still he stroked her, rolling his thumb up and down, up and down.

And then, just as she neared the precipice, he stopped. He stripped away the last of the sheet and moved so that he was poised above her. She didn't bear his weight. There was room between them, and she was so startled that she opened her eyes.

She had begun to ask what he was doing when she felt him. His organ, thick and hard as he placed it at her opening. It felt right, pressing against her. But he did not stop there. Slowly, while her eyes widened in surprise, he pushed inside. She felt every inch of his invasion, every excruciatingly slow push. Every time she thought she had him all, there was a little more. A little more, until he stopped.

She looked at his eyes, seeing that his jaw was tight and his breath came in tight pants.

"Robert?"

He met her gaze and held it. "Lift your knees, sweetheart."

She did, feeling herself open even more to him. She knew his weight was on his arms, and she could see the fine tremors that shook his shoulders. But her attention was below on where he was so thick inside her.

"Rob—"

He thrust hard and true.

"—oh!"

The pain was not so bad. She felt it, but only as part of the whole. His hips had dropped down onto hers and his weight was now fully seated. Her knees were wide enough to grip him and as his face lowered to hers, she lifted her mouth to his kiss. He started slowly, for which she was grateful. Tiny kisses along her lips while below she simply absorbed the size of him inside her.

But in a moment she was kissing him back greedily. Opening to him above, dueling tongues, press of teeth, and the slow slide of him out below. She was gripping his back, holding his smooth skin tightly. She used that leverage now to break away from his mouth, to gasp for air while below he slid back out before another slow press inside.

"Oh," she whispered, enamored of the sensation of fullness in and out. Of his weight pressing her down as she rose up to meet him. Of everything about what he was doing. "Again."

He did as she bade, drawing out, then pushing back in. But it wasn't enough.

"Harder?" he asked.

She nodded, her breath held suspended.

He withdrew, then slammed against her. She gasped, liking the impact. Glancing at his face, she saw he was grinning. Clearly he knew how she'd react. Smiling up at him, she lifted her legs and wrapped them around his bottom. Then she lifted herself up into him, grinding against him as best she could. She watched his eyes darken and his nostrils flare. He liked what she was doing, almost as much as she did.

Then the moment changed. One second he was gasping, his eyes turning dark with hunger, and the next he was moving with a power she hadn't felt before. Her legs were still wrapped around him, gripping as tightly as she could, but he was unstoppable.

He began slamming into her, again and again, his breath rasping harsh in his throat while her blood seemed to burn hotter with each impact. Hard. Hot.

Her back arched.

Her belly tightened.

He thrust.

Yes!

She cried out, feeling her whole body tumble into bliss.

He was right with her, his body jerking, but his face alight with happiness.

And in that moment she felt it. Not bliss, not joy, but something even sweeter.

Love.

Chapter 21

~≫≪~

Helaine woke slowly, her body unfamiliar only because it felt so content. Usually her mind was working furiously before she opened her eyes, planning the day, thinking of dress designs, and worrying about countless little details. This morning was marked by a complete absence of those thoughts, and it made her smile with pleasure. More than that, it made her stretch like a well-fed cat.

"Now, that's a sight to wake with." Robert's voice rumbled through her consciousness, the perfect complement to her very delightful morning.

She opened her eyes. He was looking at her, his face creased by the pillow but his chocolate eyes heating as he smiled a lazy grin. The covers only came to midbelly on him, so she got to look at his bare shoulders and chest as sunlight turned his skin to gold.

"Mmm," she said as she reached out to stroke him from shoulder down to lean, narrow hip.

His grin turned wicked, but he didn't move. He just watched her, his gaze roving over her body. It took her a moment to realize that she, too, was naked, her upper body exposed to his view. And as the thought registered, she also felt her nipples tighten, her belly go liquid, and that sweet hunger stir her blood. Meanwhile, her stroke had reached his hip and was about to wander deeper beneath the covers, except he caught her hand. He drew it to his mouth, pressing his lips to her palm.

"How do you feel?" he asked.

"Happy," she answered.

"Sore?"

She frowned. There were aches in places that were new, but they were minor. Something else was bothering her, something that lingered on the edge of her awareness but she held off by sheer force of will.

"The past is gone," she said to that part of her that wanted to ruin this moment. "The future is for tomorrow." He raised his eyebrows, wondering at her bizarre comment. So she smiled and pulled him close enough to kiss. But just before their mouths connected she whispered an explanation. "Right now is all that matters. And right now, I want you."

He needed no more prompting. They kissed, he conquered, and after an exquisite interlude, they were again building toward that sea of bliss. No, not bliss. It was love. Sweet, joyous love. And at that moment, the fear hovering on the edge of her mind crashed through.

She loved Robert. Finally, she was in love. It was a state that she'd all but given up on, and now here it was. Love from the innermost, secret part of her soul. For the man who was her protector and would never, ever be her husband.

Pain from that thought cut through her. He was deep inside her, still pressing her heavily into the mattress, so she was able to grip him both inside and out, holding on to him like an anchor as a storm of emotion blew through her. It merged with the sensations he built as he thrust into her. And soon she lost all fear as she tumbled over the cliff.

But when the bliss faded, she was left with a melancholy kind of joy. After all, she was with him. He was kindness itself for the moment. And she was sure he cared for her, perhaps even deeply. Nothing else mattered, or so she told herself over and over while he collapsed onto his side, pulling out as he fell.

"My God," he breathed, "this has been the best night of my life."

"Mine, too," she said, pleased that the words were true. Then she let him tug her tight to his side and gratefully closed her eyes. She would sleep with the man she loved. For an hour, perhaps. Maybe more.

He was asleep within five minutes. She lay awake for a good deal longer. In the end, she slipped out of his arms. Unlike him, she really couldn't waste the day in bed. She had responsibilities to Gwen, if no one else.

She dressed quickly, careful not to make a sound. Or so she thought. But as she was struggling to fasten her gown, she heard his voice, a low rumble that heated her blood.

"Come here. I'll get it."

She looked up, seeing that his hair was tousled, his eyes sleepy, but his expression was anything but. Did he really want to make love again? And was her body heating again?

"You're insatiable," she said, speaking as much to him as to her.

"Only with you," he answered.

She nodded, dismissing his comment as the usual flattery. But as she neared the bed so he could fasten her gown, he touched her arm and waited until she looked into his eyes.

"It's true, Helaine. I cannot look at you without wanting you. And that has never happened to me before. Why do you think I pursued you so vehemently?"

"Because that is who you are. Doggedly persistent."

He shook his head. "Because of you, Helaine. Because you are worth everything."

She smiled, but the gesture was forced. In the end, she gave in to the whisper of sadness and asked the question. "But you have me now," she said. "How long will you still want me?"

He lifted her hand and pressed his lips to her palm. She shivered in delight at the feel, but that did not stop her from waiting for an answer. Eventually it came. He looked up at her and shrugged.

"I cannot imagine a time when I won't want you."

She had no answer to that. Common sense told her that whatever he felt now, eventually their time would end. But common sense was hurting her mood, so she forced the thought away. She bent down, gave him a searing kiss, then straightened up and presented him with her back.

"Tease," he said without heat. Then she felt him slowly button up her gown, taking his time as he stroked her skin before covering it up. By the time she was dressed, she wanted to strip it all off again.

But she really needed to get her day started. She needed to be buried in dress designs and fabrics and Gwen's happiness. And maybe if she managed it, she would also find time to sit and talk to Wendy about everything that had happened. More than anyone else, Wendy understood the different roles she juggled in her life.

So she stepped away, shooting Robert an arch look. "You're calling me a tease? When you lie there in bed looking like that?"

He spread his arms wide, inviting her to join him. "It's only a tease if you say yes then leave. I am not going anywhere."

"But I am. I have to think of something for Gwen's new mother-in-law to wear to the wedding, and I have to approve the shoe ideas. Penny's good, but it all must match. Irene wants me to inspect a shipment of velvet to see if it will suit, and Mama . . . well, Mama will want to talk to me about something. Always something."

He listened, his eyes never leaving her face. "Is there any amount of money that would induce you to give up the shop and stay in my bed forever?"

She bit her lip, part of her wondering if she would give up the shop for a wedding ring. But that was not what he'd asked. His question was about money.

"No, Robert. There isn't."

He shrugged. "I didn't think so. Forgive me for wishing it anyway."

She smiled. "Forgiven. And now I really must go." So

she did. She turned her back on him and the haven he'd created in this room. She walked steadily down the hallway past the women who looked at her. They all knew she had spent the night. They knew what she was now, and she was startled to see envy on their faces. And an undercurrent of warning. They were protective of their "Sir."

She smiled as best she could, acknowledging their message. Only Chandelle greeted her with any warmth. Then Helaine made it outside to hail a waiting cab. To her shame there were many hansoms loitering here, ready to take the lords back from the brothels. Twenty minutes later she would thankfully, blessedly be back at home where she could bathe, dress in her normal clothes, and finally start her day at well after noon.

Robert felt the world go flat after Helaine departed. He busied himself as he always did at the Chandler. He dealt with patients, shared a meal with Chandelle, and generally occupied himself with whatever he wanted. Except what he wanted was Helaine.

So he began planning. He wanted to let rooms for them. Something close to her shop and near the Chandler. She would need a staff, of course. Butler, maid, cook, all very discreet. He wasn't truly certain that he could afford to support both the Chandler and another household. Certainly not the kind he envisioned for Helaine. But he would find the money. She deserved that much at least.

It was midafternoon when the thought struck him. He was reading an article about cowpox and its similarity to smallpox. He wanted to make a note to contact the author of the article and reached into his desk to find paper. What he touched instead was his tin of French letters.

French letters. Condoms. The bulwark against pregnancy and disease that he purchased in large quantities for Chandelle to give away. He had her lecture the women ad nauseam about how these simple devices could quite literally save their lives. But only if they used them.

And he hadn't.

Helaine could right now be pregnant.

Helaine slipped inside the shop and tried to dash upstairs. It didn't work. Her mother saw her. In fact, the woman was probably hovering about the doorway waiting for just this moment. Either way she was right there, her expression anxious.

Helaine didn't even speak. She just gave her mother a warm kiss on her cheek. "I'm fine. It was wonderful. And . . ." Dare she say it? No, she couldn't quite confess it all right then. So she went for the easier truth. "I think I'm happy, Mama."

Her mother released a breath in relief, then gestured to the workroom. "Wendy and Penny are in there. They need to talk with you, but I'll delay them." Then she quickly spun Helaine around and undid her dress fastening. "Go and change. We will talk more later."

Would they? She wasn't sure. This was all so new to her. She wanted to hold it tight inside, savoring each second before she shared it with anyone. But she took the excuse while she could, rushing upstairs. She came down twenty minutes later, as clean and pressed as she could manage. Then she pushed her way into the workroom, ready to tackle whatever problem presented.

Wendy and Penny were bent over a table discussing which fabrics would match best between shoes and gowns of different colors and textures. A quick glance told her they were working on Francine's newest order. The girl had ordered three new party gowns and was happier than Helaine had ever seen her. To the opposite side of the workroom sat her mother, playing a drop and catch game with Tommy. It looked to Helaine to be an exhausting game where the boy dropped something and her mother picked it up. But the two were laughing in delight, and so she supposed it was a good game. Thank goodness she wasn't a mother. She didn't know what she'd do if she had to add rearing a child into the mix. But at least that was one thing that . . .

One worry . . .

Oh, God.

She stopped dead in her tracks, her mouth dropping open as she stared at Tommy. For the first time ever in her life she *did* have to worry about having a baby out of wedlock. She could have gotten pregnant last night.

Her knees went out from beneath her and she stumbled, barely catching herself on the table. Everyone looked up, but her mind was still in the grips of terror. A child? She could have a child.

The idea of having Robert's baby was not so awful. She could imagine an impish little boy with his chocolate eyes and the devil's own determination to get into mischief. The idea was not so repellent. In truth, she rather liked it. But they weren't married. They'd never be married. And the idea of raising a baby alone had her looking over to Penny in horror.

How many days lately had she looked at the girl and shaken her head, wondering how she would survive? A woman alone with a baby? At least she was getting work now with Helaine, but that was precious little income at the moment. Barely enough for food, but not for anything else. Now that could be Helaine. Increasing while she tried to speak with clients. Trying to nurse a child while sketching dress designs. It couldn't work.

"'Ey, now! Sit down. Sit down." That was Wendy, her long fingers catching her arm. Penny rushed to her other side, and soon they guided her to a chair. She collapsed into it, her body unable to do more than stare at the floor. What was she going to do?

"Mrs. Mortimer?" Penny crouched down in front of her. "Do you need some water? Are you dizzy? What's—"

Helaine gripped the girl's arm. "How do you do it? A babe and no family? How do you face the day?"

Penny blinked, her expression shifting from concern through confusion only to end with a resigned shrug. "I have you," she answered honestly. "This work and your mother."

"But we're not enough." She looked to her mother. "Not nearly enough."

Her mother understood. Helaine could see it in her eyes, the fear and the confidence all mixed together. But in the end, she appeared resolved as she lifted Tommy into her arms. "Of course we're enough," she said firmly. "Right here, we're four strong women with a place of business. Of course we're enough."

"But—"

"No buts, Helaine. We are enough. *You* are enough."

It was then that Wendy caught on. Her eyes widened, and she touched Helaine's arm. "Coo, you went and did it."

Helaine nodded.

"And was it everthing you thought?"

Her mouth curved into a smile as she remembered. "More. It was so much more."

And then Penny figured it out. "With his lordship? Redhill?" She let out a low whistle. "He's a handsome one. And he'll take good care of you and a babe."

"At the time, I wasn't thinking about a child," she whispered. Truthfully, she hadn't been thinking much at all except that it all felt so wonderful.

Meanwhile, her mother patted her hand. "We're looking too far ahead. There isn't any baby yet."

"But what if there is?"

Penny released a light trill of laughter. It was surprising really how carefree the sound was. Given everything she faced in life, she sounded so lighthearted. Enough that it caught Helaine's attention. But before she could ask what was so funny, Penny answered.

"Never ask that."

"What?"

"That's how I get by. I never ask, 'what if.' I always ask, 'what is.'" She smiled. "So are you pregnant now?"

"I don't know."

"Then don't ask. Ask what is the problem today."

It sounded like ridiculous advice to Helaine, but a

moment later it was clear that Penny hadn't intended it as advice. One look at Wendy's face and she saw that there was a problem today.

"What happened?"

Wendy snorted. "That baroness and her sister happened, that's what."

Helaine frowned. "Lady Gwen's future in-laws?"

Penny nodded. "They've changed their minds on everything. Different colors, different styles, different shoes. Everything." She pointed to a different side of the workroom where a pile of fabrics and sketches lay scattered about. It was the baroness's pile and apparently it had all changed.

Helaine pushed up to her feet, her mind wholly distracted. "Why would they do that?"

"We don't know," said Penny. "That's today's problem—"

"And wot we need you to find out," said Wendy. Then she corrected herself before anyone else could. "*What* you need to find out."

Helaine frowned, mentally working through the different dress designs that had already been selected. "They want more frills, more bows, don't they? Brighter colors—"

"And gems and lace everywhere."

Helaine groaned. "That will look awful on them."

"We know!" said both Wendy and Penny at the exact same time.

"All right," Helaine said as she pushed to her feet. Her fears had lost their grip. Penny was right. As far as she knew, she wasn't pregnant now. So she would deal with today's problem. And that meant heading off certain fashion disasters before they happened. "Do you have any of their gowns ready?"

"One each."

"And how long for you to make five big bows of loud colors?"

Penny and Wendy glanced at each other. "Fifteen minutes," they said almost at the same instant.

"Do it. And I'll wrap up the dresses. I will do what we

did with Francine. Dress them up how they want, then do it how I want."

"Will it work, you think?"

Helaine bit her lip, running over all her experiences with the entire party, including Gwen. "I think so," she finally said. "I think they are bored and looking for fun wherever they can."

"So you'll set them to rights?" asked her mother. "Before they drive all of us to distraction?"

Helaine shrugged. "I can certainly try."

And then after it was done, she would have a long conversation with Robert. Whether or not she was pregnant, they had to make provisions for the future. Or take measures to prevent it. Either way, it required a quiet tête-à-tête with him. And given the way the last one ended, she was abruptly very interested in getting on with her day. The sooner she finished with Gwen's relations, the sooner she could find some very private time with Robert.

Chapter 22

꙳⚬꙳

By the time Robert made it home, he almost wished he hadn't. Dribbs met him at the door with a look of long suffering. Robert was about to ask what the problem was when he heard the noise. Women's chatter. Loud, continuous, and on the edge of contentious. A gaggle of geese made less noise.

"What happened?" he asked. Good Lord, he had to raise his voice just so Dribbs could hear him.

"Wardrobe adjustments were requested. Designs have been altered. Colors discussed. And every maid in the house has been commandeered to assist."

"Really?"

Dribbs took care as he set Robert's gloves and hat on the stand. "All the maids from next door have joined as well." Then there was the sound of running feet down the back staircase. "I believe that is Lady Westland's dresser."

Robert frowned. "Lady Westland? From down the street?"

"Indeed."

"That's a lot of women."

Dribbs didn't need to answer. His expression was more than enough to convey his opinion.

"Never fear," Robert said as much to reassure himself as Dribbs. "The wedding is two weeks away. They shall all be gone after that."

"Really?" Dribbs returned. "I thought they intended to stay for the Season."

Robert thought back. Oh, yes, that was true. "Well, yes, but they won't be in this house."

"I believe they mentioned parties with your mother. I believe," he added, giving Robert a baleful eye, "that you encouraged the idea."

Oh, right. That was also true. "Er, well, yes. But the Season won't last forever. It'll be over in . . . in . . ."

"Seven weeks and three days. Unless it rains on the day of their departure. The baroness has declared she despises traveling on rainy days."

"Ah. Well, then I suppose I will pray for sun."

"As will we all, my lord."

Robert hid his grin as he moved down the hallway. Usually he would head straight for the library, but today he paused, then headed up the stairs instead. He couldn't actually hear Helaine's voice amid the general noise, but he had to see her. The need was growing stronger every second that he waited.

He never made it to the door. There were too many women peering inside the upstairs parlor. Maids he'd never seen before, all talking. It reminded him of a cockfight with everyone shoving and straining to see. Except that it was inside his house and everyone was female. And presumably, at the very center were not two aggressive birds, but his relations and Helaine.

Fortunately, his status as owner of the house bought him some breathing room. The onlookers magically melted away from him, though he did detect a few resentful glares. Eventually he made it through the door, though not much farther before Gwen hissed at him.

"Robert! Mind your step!"

He froze with one foot raised then looked down. There wasn't a bare space of floor or furniture in sight. He slowly set his foot backward, forcing him to stand with one foot inside the room and the other outside. But it was enough to give him a good look around.

He counted no less than seven women with perhaps a half dozen others who appeared to be women, though it was hard to tell given that they were buried under mounds of fabric. All he could see was a few mobcaps and round eyes. In the middle of it all stood the dowager baroness, Gwen's future mother-in-law. She wore a gown that might have been dark red, except that it was buried beneath the drape of three huge black bows. They were so huge, they looked like crows. And on top of it all, the woman wore a monstrosity of a hat.

"My lord!" the woman trilled. "I am so glad you are here! What we need is a man's opinion."

Gwen groaned, the sound carrying loudly despite the muffling effect of so much fabric. "Pray not Robert. He hasn't—"

"No, I think a man's point of view is just what we need," came a voice. A beautiful voice. Helaine's voice.

Robert scanned the room, searching desperately for her in this blinding mess of fabrics. He saw the aunt and the younger sister and more maids, but no Helaine. Until finally she appeared, popping out from behind the huge hat. "Over here, my lord."

He finally saw her, and his heart swelled. Good Lord, she was beautiful. But tired. He could see it in her eyes. She was tired. And no wonder, given what they had been doing at all hours last night and this morning.

"Mrs. Mortimer," he said, doing his best to keep his voice neutral. But it was so hard when all he wanted to do was sweep her into his arms and carry her back to bed. "I didn't see you behind that . . . behind the . . . I didn't see you there."

"Well, yes. Here I am, and I believe we desperately need your opinion." Then she turned to the dowager baroness, forcing the woman around to face Robert. "There you go. Now, Lord Redhill, what do you think of this gown?"

He arched a brow. He was supposed to give a polite answer to that? "Um, I am not really counted a leader in fashion."

"Nonsense!" snapped Helaine from where she stood behind the baroness. "You can give your honest opinion of this."

He looked back at the gown, then up to Helaine. It took him a moment to realize she was grimacing at him. Trying to tell him something. But what? Oh! She was grimacing. He was supposed to say it looked ugly? But how could he say that about a woman's gown?

"Well," he began, "I do think . . . I mean . . . it is not really to my tastes."

"It is the bows, isn't it?" asked the baroness.

He glanced at Helaine, who was nodding. "Oh, yes," he said. "The bows are—"

"The wrong color, aren't they? Too dark. What about an orange? Would that be better?"

Behind her, Helaine was shaking her head.

"Er, no," he said. "I'm afraid I don't think the color is the problem."

Helaine smiled.

"Perhaps it's the size—"

Helaine's eyes widened in horror.

"No, no!" he gasped before the baroness could say anything. "It's not the size. It's that . . . well . . ."

Helaine was mimicking something. Her hands were rising up. As if getting taller? Looking to the sky? Oh! Lifting off!

"Do you know, I believe no bows would be perfect. Can I see the gown without the bows?"

Helaine gifted him with a beaming smile. Good Lord, but she struck him dumb when she did that. Meanwhile, another woman began unpinning the bows, only to reveal a wrap of lace underneath.

"What about the lace, my lord?" asked the baroness.

He glanced at Helaine, who again mimicked taking something off.

"Oh, no," he drawled. "I'm afraid that's much too . . . too . . ."

"Too little?" asked the baroness hopefully.

Helaine was shaking her head.

"Too much," he said. "Pray remove that as well."

The baroness actually pouted a bit, but she dutifully lifted her arms while the lace was removed. And then there she stood, an elegant woman in a simple gown of deepest red.

"Absolutely stunning," he breathed. Only to be stopped short as Helaine furiously shook her head and pointed to the hat. "Oh, wait!" he cried. "Take off that hat. It's hideous, you know."

Helaine's mouth dropped open in shock. Beside him, Gwen gasped in horror. Even the ladies behind him tsked like clucking hens. He looked desperately at Helaine. Did she want him to say the hat was lovely?

"Er, perhaps it's growing on me."

If his love looked horrified before, now she was practically apoplectic.

"No, no! Not growing on me. I mean . . . well, I . . . I don't like hats! Not at all!"

Helaine stared at him as if he had lost his mind. As did, coincidentally, everyone else in the room. He didn't dare look behind him to see what the maids thought.

"That is, er . . ."

Thankfully, Helaine was able to help. "I believe his lordship is saying that as a rule, gentlemen don't like hats on ladies. They're usually taller, you know. And so spend a great deal of time avoiding the feathers and such."

"Yes," he said much too enthusiastically. "That's it exactly."

Then, lest he feel he had successfully navigated the treacherous waters of female fashion, Gwen was there to puncture his ego. "Oh, leave off, Robert. You have said quite enough, thank you."

Robert turned at his sister's sharp tone. It wasn't unusual for her to poke fun at him, but there was an extra bite to her words. "Gwen," he began, but she waved him away.

"Go, go. You have no business being here anyway."

"I . . . ," he began. He could hardly say that he wanted

to talk to Helaine. That he wanted to see her again, then whisk her away to another glorious night of exploration. In the end, he executed a stiff bow. "Ladies, I can see that I am de trop."

Meanwhile, the baroness turned back to him, her eyes as tragic as her tone. "Do you truly not like *any* hat, my lord?"

He glanced back to Helaine for guidance, but she was occupied with avoiding the flop of what he believed were ostrich feathers and so could not guide him. In the end, he opted for simple honesty.

"Baroness, your skin is clear, your eyes quite pretty. And even your mouth, if I may be so bold, is very expressive. Without you even saying a word, I can tell when you are happy or sad or disapproving or delighted. Why ever would I want to look at ostrich feathers or lace or bows when I could see your face?"

The baroness gaped at him. Helaine, too, straightened up with a look of shocked gratitude on her face. And even Gwen released a gasp of surprise. He didn't know if he had stuck his foot in it again or not, but he had done his best. So with another bow he took his leave, only to be called back a moment later by Helaine.

"My lord!"

He stopped and leaned back in the room. Nothing on earth would induce him to walk farther inside. "Mrs. Mortimer?"

"I'm afraid I was occupied last night and so missed our discussion. Would you perhaps be available tonight? I am, of course, at your service whatever time you need."

He almost grinned. Was there ever a more perfect woman? "Oh, yes. Directly after dinner would be ideal. Thank you for reminding me, Mrs. Mortimer."

Then he bowed again before escaping with all the other men in the household. Indeed, he found them all downstairs with Dribbs, discussing the latest horse races. Thank heaven at last for rational conversation!

Chapter 23

Helaine was dropping with fatigue. After countless hours of discussion and sketches and ridiculous changes, all the women had gone back to the original gown designs with the exception of a half dozen tiny bows. The dowager baroness did love bows, so Helaine had added the decoration to her gown for the wedding. And Penny had to add bows to all of the women's shoes.

But now it was done, the fabrics were put away, and unlike Wendy who now had to sew all those dresses, Helaine's work was finished. She could have her discussion with Robert, and was already thinking about other things they might do, when she was stopped cold in the hallway.

She was leaving the upper parlor, passing by what she was sure was Gwen's room. The sound was muffled because the door was shut, but some noises were hard to miss. The sound of a girl sobbing was quite distinct and all the more alarming because it was probably Gwen in there. Gwen of the sunny disposition. Gwen who was filled with love for her fiancé and excitement about their coming wedding. Gwen who was now sobbing as if her heart would break.

Helaine hesitated, unsure whether or not to intrude. But who else could the girl talk to? Not her mother, who was right now back in her bedroom and, by all accounts, had stopped bathing again. Not any of the future in-laws, who were well-meaning but as dense as rocks. Which left no other female but her or perhaps a maid. So Helaine took a chance and knocked on the door.

The gasping sobs stopped immediately. Then there was a long pause. And just as Helaine was tapping again, she heard Gwen speak.

"I'm fine, Robert, really. Just let me rest."

Well, if that wasn't a lie, then Helaine was deaf, blind, and dumb. The girl's voice was stiff with false cheer and had none of the life Helaine was accustomed to hearing from her. So, taking the risk, Helaine turned the knob and was pleased to find that it wasn't locked.

"Forgive me," she said as she entered the room. "But as your dressmaker, it's part of my job to make sure you're looking your best in my gowns. And right now, it sounds like you're not quite feeling the thing."

Gwen regarded her from the bed. The room was dark, but enough light spilled in from the hallway to illuminate her swollen nose and red eyes. And her hair was all askew, as if she had tried to pull out the pins and ended up grabbing the hair instead.

"Helen! Oh, shut the door! Quickly, before Robert sees."

Now, that wasn't at all what Helaine expected, but she did as she was told, stepping inside the room and quietly shutting the door behind her. Meanwhile, Gwen lit a lamp, and soon the room was bathed in a warm glow. Sadly, the golden color did very little to aid Gwen's looks. If anything, she appeared all the more miserable.

Helaine crossed to her side. "Oh, sweetheart, what has happened? Has Robert been pompous or dictatorial again?" It was a joke of sorts. Nothing could bring out a smile in Gwen faster than poking fun at her brother's high-handed ways.

It worked. Gwen released a snort that was almost a laugh.

"Better to ask when he hasn't been an ass." Then her smile faded. "But that's not it." She waved at the closed door. "It's a game of sorts that he and I have played since we were children. Whenever something terrible has happened, I shut the door and sob so that he can stand at the doorway and listen in misery. Then he has the maids bring me treats and the like until I come out. I did much the same thing for him, too, until he became old enough to disappear for days on end. Jack was the only one who could comfort me, but that was only because he was so young. He would come into my bedroom and just curl up beside me. Something about having a little brother sleeping beside me always eased the pain. But then he went away to school, and I've barely ever seen him since."

Helaine nodded slowly, knowing a little something about needing to cry one's eyes out. "But Robert would do anything for you. Surely you know that."

"Of course I do. But so many things cannot be changed. We could do nothing when Mother had one of her spells or Father was dunned for debt."

Helaine didn't answer. She'd never had a brother or sister to share such burdens with. But if she had, she couldn't imagine shutting them out. Gwen must have read her expression, because she simply shrugged.

"I know it's silly. Truly, I do. But it's the way it's always been. Besides, why make him see my tears when there's nothing he can do about them?"

"I suppose that makes sense," she said, though she wasn't sure it really did. "But what has happened to cause all this?"

That was obviously something Gwen wasn't as eager to share. Her gaze dropped away, and her hands began twisting in the pillowcase. Then she began biting her lower lip, but she didn't speak. In the end, Helaine did the only thing she could think of. She put her arm around the girl and hugged her tight. Gwen didn't resist. In a minute, she had wrapped her other arm tight around Helaine and the tears were flowing along with a few words, not that they made much sense.

"I c-can't do it! I j-just can't!"

"Can't do what, sweetheart?"

"I can't get married!"

The words came out as a loud wail that was followed by heart-wrenching sobs. If Gwen had been anyone else, Helaine would have taken it as simple prewedding jitters. But the girl was one of the most levelheaded she'd ever met. Hadn't she had the sole care of her mother and younger brother all these years? To see her so completely undone was alarming. Whatever had happened, it was obviously tearing her apart.

But there was nothing Helaine could do but hold the girl for a while, waiting until the worst of the storm passed. And then, when Gwen was finally gaining control of herself again, Helaine began to ask for details.

"Was it Edward? Did he do something terrible?"

Gwen vehemently shook her head. "No, no! He has been perfect! But he warned me before. He told me he needed a strong wife, and I tried. I really tried, but I just can't do it!"

"What are you talking about? You are one of the strongest women I have ever met!"

Gwen straightened up and shook her head. "That's because you have only seen me lately, when I have been trying. But it has been so hard! I can't do it much longer!"

Gwen's voice was getting higher, the panic about to break through again, so Helaine gripped the woman's hands and turned to face her square on.

"Start at the beginning. Tell me what has been so hard."

"Being nice to his mother!" Gwen wailed. "And his aunt is so much worse!"

Ah. Now, that made sense. "Yes, today's dress changes were tiring, but you can hardly—"

"That's only a part of it!" Gwen cried. "They want a say in everything. They aren't even living here and yet they have tried to tell Dribbs what wine to serve and what meals should be cooked."

Helaine couldn't resist a smile at the idea of that. "I'm sure Dribbs handled it just fine."

"Of course he did, but that's because he's Dribbs. They

also have opinions about flowers and wood paneling and reading material. And children. Oh, my God, you cannot know what they think about how to raise children! Especially since his aunt used to be a schoolteacher."

Yes, Helaine could well imagine that they had quite the opinions about that. "But what is that—"

"And do you know, they said my breasts were too small and that I should plump them because Edward likes big breasts."

"Well, that's certainly impertinent—"

"And the very next day they said my breasts were too large! That he preferred smaller ones and I should stop eating turnips!"

Helaine frowned. "Turnips?"

"One said it fills the chest, the other claimed it simply broadened the hips, and then they started to quarrel about the merits of turnips in stews. It was all I could do to keep myself from throwing every turnip in the cellar right at their heads!"

Helaine couldn't keep herself from laughing. "Is that why Dribbs was muttering about turnips? I heard him distinctly this afternoon saying he was going to be sure to serve them for dinner."

Gwen's eyes widened with shock. "Truly? Do you think they will eat a meal at their house then?"

"I'm sure that was Dribbs's hope."

"Mine, too!" she whispered. Then she dropped her head into her hands and moaned. "So you see why I can't get married. I just can't!"

Helaine leaned forward, gently pulling Gwen's hands away from her face. "No, sweetheart, I really don't understand. What has any of this to do with your marriage?"

It took a moment for Gwen to respond. Her body was so defeated that it seemed to take true effort for her to get the words out.

"They told me yesterday, but I didn't believe it until Edward said it was true."

"What was true?"

"I knew we might have care of his sister. Connie is very

sweet, you know, when she's away from them. And she'll be coming out soon. Maybe get married."

Helaine nodded. She had seen flashes of real understanding from Edward's sister. But the girl was often drowned out by her mother and aunt. "I do like Connie," she said. "But I don't understand what—"

"They're going to live with us! Not just his mother but his aunt, too! Both of them! *Forever!*"

"Oh!" gasped Helaine, at last understanding the problem. "Oh, my."

"I can't do it! I just can't. I can't stand having them next door—how will I manage with them in my own home? I won't be able to escape them ever. And I won't even have Dribbs to serve turnips!"

Gwen flung herself into her pillow again, releasing a full-fledged scream into the depths of the feather stuffing. Helaine rested her hand on the girl's back, her sympathies fully engaged. Gwen was indeed facing a rather difficult married life if a solution couldn't be found. But surely there was a logical answer to this dilemma. Even knowing that Gwen had probably already thought of everything, Helaine started at the beginning.

"Have you told Edward that you would prefer a separate household?"

Gwen rolled over in her bed. "Yes, it was the first thing I said, most delicately of course."

"Of course. And what did he say?"

"That he would, too, but the baronetcy cannot afford a separate establishment at present. And besides . . ." She heaved a dramatic sigh. "He loves his mother and wants to see her happy. Worse, he's a good English boy. He won't banish his mother. He's not that cruel."

"Even if it's a choice between you and her?"

Gwen stared glumly at the wall. "Would you ask the man you love to make that choice? Between you and his mother?"

Helaine shook her head. No, she could never force Robert to make that choice. It would tear him apart.

"Very well then, we shall have to think of something else.

Have you talked to his mother? Perhaps she could be persuaded—"

"I tried. All she could talk about was how she will be such a help once the babies are born."

"Hmm. And how large is Edward's home? Perhaps it could be separated somehow."

"Two floors, five bedrooms including the nursery."

"Oh, that does sound rather tight."

Helaine continued to ask questions, racking her brains for a solution, but none presented themselves. In the end, she was forced to concede defeat . . . of a sort. She gripped Gwen's hands and heaved a dramatic sigh. "Well, that's it then," she said. "I can see only one solution."

Gwen's shoulders drooped. "I cannot marry him."

"No, silly. You must talk with Edward."

"But I can't make him choose!"

"And it is better to simply decide for him? To end the engagement without allowing him the chance to find a solution?"

Gwen bit her lip. "No. Of course not."

"And there is one more thing," Helaine said slowly. "It is a great secret that I discovered only this morning."

"You are going to tell me something I already know, aren't you?"

Helaine smiled. "Yes, probably. It is that love can make the most terrible things acceptable. Things that I never thought I would do, choices I never thought I'd make—good and bad—they have happened because of love."

Gwen nodded, obviously thinking hard. Helaine hoped that she was taking the message to heart—that no matter what happened with Edward's mother and aunt, Gwen's love for him would make it all worthwhile. That was what she was trying to say, but a moment later, she realized that Gwen's mind had gone in a completely new direction.

"You have fallen in love with my brother, haven't you?"

"What?" Helaine gasped, shocked that Gwen was so perceptive.

"All my friends have, you know. One after another, they have pined after him."

Really? How terribly mortifying to discover that she was a cliché. "Well, he is rather handsome."

"I know he has been attentive to you." Gwen peered at her face. "So you and he . . . You have become his mistress?"

Helaine nodded. "Do you mind terribly?"

"Yes!" Gwen snapped. "I should like nothing better than for you to be my sister, but you deserve better than him!"

Helaine shook her head, her words solidifying her decision. "There is no one better than your brother. And I shall take what happiness I can with him now."

Gwen moaned and she gripped Helaine's hands. "But you deserve to marry! I think my mother has soured him on marriage. He doesn't want to be saddled with another like her."

Helaine understood that completely. If Robert were anything like her own father, she wouldn't have given him the time of day. "Perhaps that is why we suit. I shall never be a burden to him." That was the role of a mistress, after all. To pleasure a man while it was good, and to be set free when it was not.

"But you deserve better!" Gwen repeated, her vehemence surprising.

Helaine frowned. "I am only a dressmaker, Gwen. No one thinks I deserve better than exactly what I have."

Gwen pressed her lips together, her expression both sad and defiant at the same time. Helaine waited it out. She knew whatever it was would come out eventually. Still, when it finally did, she was surprised by the anger that throbbed in the words.

"I do not know who you were, Mrs. Mortimer, but I know you are more than just a dressmaker. Even if you had the most wretched past, I would not care. I like you. You are smart and talented. You have helped me when my own mother could not. So I say it again, my brother is an idiot and you deserve better!"

Helaine looked into Gwen's eyes, and more than anything in the world, she wanted a life she couldn't have. She wanted Gwen as her sister, and Robert as her husband. She wanted to be Lady Helaine again, and to have it possible to marry the man she loved. She wanted it all with a yearning that brought tears to her eyes. But in the end, she had to put all of that away. She had to forget what might have been and focus on what was. But it was hard. Perhaps the hardest thing she'd ever done.

"We cannot all have the love that you and Edward share," she said. "Some of us must be content as a mistress to the man we love. Or abandoned by him like my mother. Some of us never have a chance like you. So even if you have to live in the same bedroom with your mother-in-law, you will find a way to stay happy. Do you understand me, Lady Gwen? You will find a way to make it work for all of us!"

Gwen's eyes widened at Helaine's tone. Helaine waited, wondering if Gwen would descend into tears again, but her words seemed to sink in. Eventually Gwen's chin stiffened with resolve and she straightened up from her bed. "I will," she said quietly. "You are right. I absolutely will."

"Good. Now come sit down over here. I shall brush your hair and then you shall go have a discussion with Edward." Helaine grabbed the brush and held it aloft like a weapon.

Gwen didn't dare argue as she sat down at her dressing table and began pulling out pins. Helaine stepped close to help, but then paused.

"Shall I have Dribbs send a message next door? To tell Edward to come?"

Gwen looked up with a sheepish smile. "I shouldn't bother. Dribbs has probably already done it." Then she released a heavy sigh. "If only there were more butlers like Dribbs. Then everything would go so much simpler."

Helaine nodded, her thoughts on so much more than a single butler. "If wishes were horses . . ."

"Then Edward's current idiot of a butler could ride far, far away. And then I'd kidnap Dribbs and force him to work for me."

* * *

The women's laughter carried easily to Robert where he stood just outside Gwen's bedroom door. He had already finished the rhyme in his thoughts correctly. If wishes were horses, then beggars could ride. Sadly, those were not the words that stuck with him. No, what he heard over and over were Gwen's words.

My brother is an idiot and you deserve better.

She was right, of course. Helaine deserved much, much better than to be a mistress. Even mistress to a future earl. But could he bring himself to give her up? To let her seek the life she should have?

No. Absolutely, positively not.

He sighed and turned away from Gwen's doorway. He had to find Dribbs to make sure Edward had been summoned. He also had to have a word with the boy about his mother and aunt. If he remembered things correctly, Edward's baronetcy was nearby to Robert's mining town. Or rather near enough to be convenient but not so near as to make them easy neighbors.

What if he set up Edward's mother and aunt as schoolteachers to the miners' children? They could occupy themselves with running other people's children and not driving Gwen to distraction. He would have a ready spy for all the gossip in that town. And if Edward and he shared the expense of the household, then it would be less of a strain on them both.

It was an idea worth exploring at least. And a problem he had a prayer of resolving. Then once that problem was solved, perhaps the boy would have some magic solution for Robert's dilemma.

Maybe.

If only . . .

Chapter 24

~⚜~

The life of a mistress was certainly less . . . well, less mistress-y than Helaine had thought. After their miracle night together at the Chandler, Helaine had expected to spend a great many more nights with Robert. But before they could arrange it, Robert had to take a trip to discuss things at his mine. And then the Season started. With Gwen talking her up as the best dressmaker in town, Helaine was suddenly busy with a dozen new clients. Enough that she made Wendy hire an apprentice just to keep up with orders. Of course, the old problem of getting those very same clients to pay was still an issue. But thanks to Robert's interference, Irene was able to purchase things on credit.

And so, in general, life was better than ever. Busy, chaotic, and so lonely that Helaine thought she'd go mad. How had she thought her life complete before she'd allowed herself to be seduced? Whenever she had a spare moment, she thought of Robert. Whenever she dropped exhausted into her bed, she longed for his caress. And sometimes she even dreamed he was climbing into bed with her, only to open her eyes and stare into the yellow gaze of the workroom tabby cat. She loved the mangy rat catcher, but he was no substitute for Robert.

Fortunately there was always more work to keep her busy. And with Gwen's wedding a day away, she was hoping her nights of sleeping alone were over. Robert would never miss his sister's wedding, and so she waited anxiously for a message from him. By the end of the day, she was a wreck of nerves. Which made her angry. How had she changed from independent woman to a girl waiting anxiously by the door for a message from a man? What was wrong with her?

And yet no matter how much she railed at herself, she still ran to the door when a liveried footman rapped. He handed her a message. Helaine didn't even have to open the missive to know it wasn't an invitation from Robert. He would have sent a carriage for her, but the footman had apparently traveled to her on foot. And sure enough, when she slit open the letter, she saw that it was from Gwen.

The girl was in quite a state. Both anxious and nervous and excited. Her handwriting climbed all over the page in crooked lines and even the sentences weren't complete. The crux of the letter was that she begged Helaine to come to her wedding on the morrow. She wasn't at all sure she could be in her best looks without help, and even if her maid was a magician with hair, she was only average with dresses. Besides, Gwen hoped that she could call Helaine her friend. And if so, Gwen would be pleased to have her attend the ceremony and breakfast afterward.

Helaine was stunned to see that her eyes were welling up with tears. Gwen was so much more to her than a client. That the other woman felt the same was like a gift from God. No matter what happened—or didn't happen—with Robert, at least Helaine had a friend in Gwen.

She told the footman her answer: that she would indeed be there bright and early to assist Lady Gwen however she was needed. Then she paused, hoping that there was something else, like a message from Robert. But the man simply bowed and turned around while Helaine's heart plummeted.

Had he tired of her already? And if so, she told herself,

then lucky for him. Because she was so angry at that moment that if he showed up at her door she would slam it in his face. *Hard.*

But he didn't show up. Not until she had drawn his face and started putting spot marks all over it to make him look ugly. It was childish of her and really didn't make her feel any better, especially since she erased the spots, added shading, and drew him as handsome as she remembered him. Only then did the horrid man show up, knocking at the workroom door and pleading with her to open up.

"Helaine! Are you in there? Oh, God, please, it's Robert. Helaine?"

She meant to be reserved, perhaps even icy to him. But all her intentions flew away at the desperation in his tone. She flung open the back door and was immediately engulfed in his arms. It felt as marvelous as she remembered, wrapped in his full embrace, the scent of him filling her lungs.

"Robert," she breathed, "I'm very cross with you."

"And well you should be," he answered as he pressed tiny kisses into her hair. "But first let me kiss you. I have been dying—"

She didn't wait. She stretched up to his mouth and soon he was doing all the things to her that she'd longed for these last two weeks. He plundered her mouth, and she all but wrapped herself around him so that he could do more. He was the one to break it off so that they could both breathe. And while they stood there, their foreheads touching and their ragged breath heating the air between them, he stroked her arms and entwined their fingers.

"Where is everyone?" he asked as he backhanded the door closed.

"Bed. Upstairs asleep. Wendy's at her home. She's exhaust—"

He kissed her again and this time when she stretched up to meet him, his hands were in the way. He was stroking her breasts, lifting them and rubbing his thumbs across her nipples. The movement was quick and a little rough, but, oh, she liked it. How she had dreamed of having his hands on her.

She arched her back, thrusting her breasts deeper into his hands. And while he pleasured her, she reached behind her and undid what buttons she could on her gown. She hadn't realized how desperate she was for his touch until his kisses set her aflame. Never had she responded so quickly, so completely to a man.

"I have been trying to get here all damn day," he said as he began pressing kisses down her neck. "But you cannot imagine everything that had to be done to set up a single damn school! And then to come home only to be besieged by relatives. They were everywhere! I tried to hand them off on Jack, but the boy can't be everywhere. And that's where those people are—everywhere!"

She paused, abandoning her buttons to lift her eyes to his. "School? You are setting up a school?"

He nodded as he reached behind her to finish undoing her buttons. "For Edward's mother and aunt to run. Even the little sister can help them until she's of age. It'll give them all something to do—"

"And a place to live far away from Gwen."

He grinned. "Exactly."

"Oh, Robert, that is a marvelous idea."

"Edward thought so, too. Wonderful boy. Levelheaded and practical. Thank God Gwen's marrying him, because we need him in the family. If she cries off, I think I'd have to blood bond with him or something."

Helaine laughed. "Blood bond?"

He shook his head. "Never mind. It is something I read as a boy."

"Oh. But she's not changing her mind at this late date, is she?"

"Better not!" he said in a mock growl as he stroked the skin of her neck and shoulders. Her gown was drooping, but it hadn't fallen yet.

"Take me," she said against his lips. "Right here. Right now."

He paused, but she saw the wicked gleam in his eye. "In the workroom?"

"No one is here."

His eyes seemed to glitter in the lamplight as he scanned the room. Then he angled his chin toward the full mirror. "Ever wanted to watch, Helaine? I swear you are the most beautiful sight when you peak."

Her eyebrows shot up. It had never occurred to her to look in a mirror as they . . . when they . . . "Will I be able to see your bum, then?" she asked as she boldly leaned down to grip him.

"You can see whatever you want, my lady." Then he scooped her up and carried her the six steps to the bench set before the mirror. He set her down carefully on her feet, then slipped behind her, pushing the gown off her shoulders as he moved. The dress and inset shift fell easily, needing only the slightest shimmy to have it pool at her feet. He took in a deep breath as he looked at her reflection. He stood behind her, fully clothed, a stark contrast to her.

"You are even more beautiful than I remember. All pink skin and full body. Your lips alone could drive me insane."

"You promised I would see all of you," she said as she turned around and began tugging at his cravat. He helped her, stripping off everything in record time. And when his organ was at last set free, she was able to stroke it and listen to his breath hiss in pleasure.

"Now—," she began, but he pressed a finger to her mouth. Then, while she watched, he sat down on the bench facing the mirror.

"Come here," he said.

She moved forward, but he stopped her, slowly turning her around. A moment later, he had set her on his lap, slowly coaxing her legs apart such that they draped over his knees.

Her face flamed in embarrassment, but also with excitement. She had never looked at herself all plump and open. It was scandalous for sure, but she was a mistress now. Scandalous was supposed to be her stock-in-trade.

"It's not very pretty," she said.

He chuckled. "No, it's gorgeous. Now watch what happens

when I do this." So saying, he cupped her breasts, lifting them in the mirror and tweaking her nipples. She gasped at the sensation and her bottom tightened. His organ was thick and tall between them, and she realized that with a slight shift of her hips, her movements would torture him as well.

"Minx," he whispered, but he didn't stop her.

Her head was resting on his shoulder as he began to slide down on the bench. He didn't go far, just enough to lift her center higher, into better view, and one of his hands abandoned her breast to slide between her legs.

Her skin was afire with flashes of heat, but it didn't stop her from watching the slow progress of his hand down her belly. Large tan fingers against her white skin, slipping down until he slid into her curls. It was the most incredible sight, and to feel it as it was happening was beyond erotic.

"This is where I want to be," he said as he thrust a finger deep inside her. She gasped in reaction as he filled her, instinctively tightening around him. "But this is what you like," he said as he pulled his hand back and began to stroke her higher up.

Her thighs tightened, but she was draped across the outside of his knees. He was so much stronger than her, so he kept her open for view. And he continued to stroke her while she writhed on his lap.

She was close, so close. But this was not what she wanted. Not his fingers. And so she gripped his hand and pulled it away.

"I want to watch you enter me."

He looked at her. "Are you sure?"

She nodded. "I want to see it. Slowly."

He grinned. "As you wish."

She directed things this time, adjusting the bench for the best angle. She sat down, making sure to position them in the mirror. And then she leaned back, trying as coy a look as she could manage.

"What are you waiting for?" she asked.

His eyes darkened in hunger as he grabbed her legs and

placed them on his shoulders. "You wanted to watch? How is this?"

He placed himself at her entrance and she looked in awe at his large mushroom head and thick stalk. It amazed her that he could fit in her, and indeed as he slowly pressed inside, she felt her whole body stretch around him.

Inch by slow inch he entered her and she had the dual view in front of her and of his backside in the mirror. And then he was fully seated, and she completely impaled. Opened, pinned, and impaled. Never would she have thought it would excite her to feel this vulnerable, but she did. And looking in his eyes, she could see an answering hunger in him.

Then he withdrew slowly until he was fully out, his breath coming in shuddering gasps as he lowered her legs from his shoulders.

She frowned. "Robert?"

He bent down and pulled out a French letter from his pocket, opening it to show it to her. "I cannot do that again without risk," he said. "Do you—"

"Oh, God!" She'd forgotten it. Again!

He looked at her face. "I have been worried about the last time. I didn't remember then. I—"

"I know. But I had my courses last week, so we are fine. I mean, there is no baby."

He exhaled a heavy breath in relief. "Thank goodness. I would have cared for the babe. Made sure everything was as you wanted it. But—"

"It's better this way." She touched his hand and the condom he held.

"Yes," he agreed. Then he showed her how to put it on him. It was an amazing thing, really, and it warmed her to know that he had thought of this. And that warmth translated to desire. And love. Such love she felt for him.

This time when he entered her, there was no holding back. Though she thought he intended to go slow, her patience had already run out. She wanted him inside her. She wanted to grip him inside and out. And she wanted to feel him thrusting deep.

He gave her what she wanted. He rammed into her while she cried out at every impact. And she watched in the mirror as his buttocks tightened and his back bowed.

Her belly was tightening, her thighs were adding to his rhythm. Again and again.

Bliss!

She came back to herself in his arms. How he had managed to twist them around such that she now sat on his lap was beyond her. But he had, and now she rested full and still impaled in his arms.

"You are a marvel," she said as she kissed his beard-rough jaw.

"Hmm," he rumbled. "I was about to say the same to you." Then he straightened, his eyes serious as he looked into hers. "Helaine, I have something to ask you. This is not quite the way I'd envisioned, but—"

Thump, thump!

Helaine slapped a hand over Robert's mouth. He had heard it, too, so he kept himself very still. And there it was again. *Thump, thump* on the back stairs.

"Helaine?" came her mother's voice from the doorway. "I heard a noise."

Robert's eyes widened and his lips curved in laughter. Helaine glared him into silence as she called out to her mother.

"Don't come down!" she called. "I, uh, I dropped a glass and it broke. There are shards everywhere."

"Oh, dear. I'll get the broom—"

"No, no! I've got it!" Helaine pushed herself off Robert, silently mourning the loss of him inside her, but mortified by the idea of her mother finding her like this. She was hastily pulling on her gown as she tried to warn her mother away. "Pray go back to bed, Mama. I'm sorry I woke you."

"But you should go to bed, dear. You have to be up and dressed for the wedding ever so early tomorrow."

"I know, I know!" She had pulled on her gown, but was having trouble buttoning it. Robert helped her out, of course, his fingers much more sure. But the damned man did it while still sitting down. *Naked!*

"Were you drinking tea?" Her mother asked as she made it to the main floor, but not around the corner into the work-room. "Where is that mop?"

"Go upstairs, Mama!" Helaine cried in near panic. Then she had an inspiration. "Could you warm a pan for me? For my bed? And throw some more coal on the upstairs fire?"

The sounds from the closet stilled. "I suppose, though it's not that cold a night."

"I'm freezing, Mama," Helaine countered. "Please, would you do that for me?"

She heard her mother sigh. "All right. But I think it's a waste of coal. Come up soon."

"Right away."

Helaine waited a moment, listening to her mother's steady tread back up the stairs. When she heard the coal rattle in the pan, she exhaled a sigh of relief. Then she turned to Robert, who was still sitting on the bench completely at ease. At least he'd pulled on his pants, but his upper torso was still completely nude. "Get dressed!"

"But—"

"Good God, Robert, my mother could come back down here any minute."

He gave a worried glance up the stairs, then returned to look back at Helaine. "I would like to ask you something, my dear. As I said, it's not exactly the time."

"It's not the time at all!" she said as she tossed him his shirt. "Whatever it is will wait until tomorrow."

He grimaced as his shirt hit him in the face. But then he pulled it away and she was startled to see how very serious he had become. "That's too late, my dear. Really it will only take a moment."

"Which is all my mother needs to get worried and come back down here."

"Helaine!"

"No! I shall be there first thing in the morning to help

Gwen with her gown. She's invited me to the wedding, you know. I hope that doesn't upset you."

"Upset me? I asked her if she'd like you to come. If—"

"Ssst!" she hissed as her mother continued to thump around upstairs. They both waited as still as statues to see where her mother would go. She thought for a moment that the woman would come back down the stairs, but after a bit, there was a different creak in a different place. Helaine exhaled. Her mother had gone into a bedroom. Probably Helaine's to put the warming pan in. Which meant the woman would be back down in less than a minute to haul her daughter up to bed.

"My dear—," Robert began again, but Helaine rushed to the door and pulled it open.

"It can wait until morning."

Robert frowned, obviously hating that idea, but Helaine would have none of it.

"Go!" Then she grabbed his shoes, dropped them in his hands, and shoved him out the door. She felt bad seeing him stumble outside in bare feet and bare chested. But sure enough, she heard her mother's tread on the stairs again.

"Helaine?"

"Coming, Mama!" Then she shut and locked the door tight.

Chapter 25

꒰⊱꒱

Helaine was in the middle of a yawn when Dribbs
opened the door. Fortunately, she had enough warning to
hide it behind her gloved hand. He nodded gravely to her
and ushered her inside. Barely a minute later, she was upstairs in Gwen's room, where the girl was seated before her
mirror dabbing color onto her cheeks.

"Oh, no!" cried Helaine. "You don't need that. You are
perfect without—"

"You are here!" Gwen cried as she abandoned her paint
pot to engulf Helaine in a fierce hug. "I am so glad."

"And I am so glad you invited me. But come now. What
is this silliness? You don't need paint."

Gwen bit her lip, looking unsure. "I want to look perfect."

"But you do! You are a stunning bride." Helaine stepped
back to inspect the young woman. She was dressed in her
shift and hose, covered by a dressing gown. Her bridal dress
lay across the bed, a vision in purest white. It wasn't really
common for brides to marry in white, but Helaine had
thought the fabric the perfect accent to Gwen's flushed pink
skin. With pearl drops along the bodice and skirt, she would

appear like Venus emerged from the frothy sea. And Penny had made slippers to match, adding a trace of gold to flash beneath the skirt as Gwen stepped down the aisle.

"Come, come, let us get you into your gown."

Gwen agreed, her eyes shimmering with excitement as Helaine held out the dress. But before she could do more than put one foot inside the skirt, there was a knock at the door.

"Gwen? Did I hear Helaine come in?"

"Helaine?" Gwen mouthed. "I thought your name was Helen."

Helaine flushed and shrugged. She could think of no answer, not with the memory of everything that had happened the night before flashing through her mind.

The knock came again. "Gwen? Is she there?"

"For heaven's sake, Robert, I'm dressing!" Gwen said back through the door.

"But I should like—"

Helaine interrupted before he could finish. "Whatever it is, my lord, it can wait, can't it? Your sister is about to get married!"

He groaned. "I know that, but—"

"Later!" both women cried together.

He had no choice but to agree, though he did so with an audible grumble. A moment later, they heard him clump down the stairs and away. The two women exchanged equal looks of bafflement at Robert's bizarre behavior, then quickly descended into giggles. There was no fathoming the male brain at a time like this, so they addressed themselves to making Gwen beautiful.

They succeeded because Gwen was so very happy. She was lovely, of course, but with the happiness literally filling the air around her, she would have appeared gorgeous in sackcloth. And with her future in-laws now moving to that school in the mining town, Gwen had no reservations about her marriage at all. She was head over heels in love with Edward, and that was all that mattered.

They took too long with the dressing. Despite rising in

plenty of time, there were extra pearls to add to Gwen's hair and a dash of oil to give her lips a special shine. There were shoes and wraps to set just right. And gloves, of course, to protect the bride's most delicate hands. Helaine carried the veil, which they would add at the church.

Then they rushed downstairs filled with giddy laughter, only to see Robert pacing the hallway in front of Dribbs. The butler was in his best looks, his uniform pressed to a knife's crease, but he was nothing compared to Robert, who wore deepest black over crisp white linen. It had been Helaine's suggestion that his cravat be white shot with gold to match his gold waistcoat. And it was punctuated by a solitary pink diamond. Helaine had never seen its like before, but Gwen had told her it was a family gemstone worn by every earl at his wedding.

"There you are!" he said. "Helaine, I must ask—"

"Robert! Look at your hair!" cried Gwen. "It looks like you've been tugging it out by the roots!"

Robert looked over at his sister and frowned. "What are you talking about?"

"You, brother dear!" Gwen said with a laugh. Then she sent a maid rushing back upstairs for her brush.

"But we haven't time!" he huffed.

"There is time for you to be in your best looks at my wedding!"

The maid came downstairs with a brush, which Gwen plied, to Robert's mortification and Dribbs's amusement. Then, before Gwen was finished, Robert grabbed the brush and waved it at Helaine. "Please, could I—"

"Oh, Gwenie! You look like a vision!" That was Gwen and Robert's mother, descending the stairs in a gown of pale blue. It matched her watery eyes and gave her a joyous look that—thankfully—seemed to match her spirits today.

"Mama! You are beautiful!"

As the two women embraced, Robert stepped to Helaine, touching her arm as he tried to get her attention. "Please, Helaine. I beg of you—"

"My lord, my lady. The carriage awaits," Dribbs intoned

as he threw open the door. And indeed, there was the earl's carriage waiting at the base of the walk, cleaned to a gleaming shine. The servants lined the walkway, all there to give Gwen their well-wishes as she all but danced down the path. A moment later a hackney appeared and Gwen's father, the Earl of Willington, descended. The youngest son Jack was with him, and both had dressed in their finest.

There would have been more hugs and talking but at that very moment, Edward's mother came running out of their home. "Go! Go! Edward is almost to the door. He cannot see you!"

It was bad luck to see the bride before the wedding, and so everyone bustled Gwen into the carriage. Her parents and Jack followed next, with Robert lingering, one foot on the step while his eyes sought Helaine's. He started to open his mouth but she shook her head.

"Go! Edward is almost here!" she urged him, pointing to where both mother and aunt were physically blocking the doorway until Gwen could leave.

"At the church, then," he said as he ducked into the carriage.

"Of course!" she returned, holding up the veil. She was to follow in another carriage, along with Dribbs and two other special family retainers who were allowed to attend. She followed Dribbs's direction and was soon ensconced in another carriage, which followed the family in the slow, ponderous pace that befitted a lady's wedding. The carriage had barely stopped at the cathedral when its door was opened by none other than Robert himself.

"Robert!" Helaine cried. "Whatever are you doing?"

"It is imperative—"

"That you go inside and make sure everything is set to rights. Go! I need to help with her veil." To everyone's horror, Edward's carriage was arriving as well and they were still standing about like gawking urchins.

"Helaine—"

"Go!" She shoved Robert away and then dashed up the stairs after Gwen. Really, she would have to take that man to task for being such an idiot at his sister's wedding. But that would have to wait until later. Right now, Gwen needed her veil.

All was accomplished with much giggles and excited talk. Gwen's two attendants were there before them, chattering in the excited voices of best girlfriends. Connie joined them as soon as the groom's carriage stopped and she ran with all the joy of a girl thrilled to be gaining a new sister. Helaine faded into the background. In truth, she should not be here at all, but she could not resist watching Gwen's happiness. It was a joy she would never have, and so she wanted to soak up as much as she could. But in the end, she had to leave. She pressed a kiss to Gwen's cheek and shared another tight hug. Then she rushed away to find a seat at the back of the cathedral.

It took her a bit, but she found her own family also hiding in the back. Wendy would not miss a wedding when the bride was wearing a gown stitched by her hand. Penny, too, was there with Tommy. And Helaine's mother rounded out the four-some, a ribbon in one hand for Tommy to play with and a ker-chief in her other hand. Her mama liked to cry at weddings.

Helaine took her seat beside her mother, and then they watched with held breath as ushers seated the family members. Weddings were usually private family affairs, but this was the wedding of Lady Gwen, the daughter of the Earl of Willington. For many it marked the official opening of the Season, and people had been vying for months to get invitations. Those select few came now, dressed in finery better suited to a ballroom, but gorgeous nonetheless.

And then the event began.

Gwen was radiant, and Edward was grinning. It looked as if he couldn't believe his luck to be joined with his lady love. Robert stood as his best man, tall and proud. He could not have looked more handsome, and Helaine fell more deeply in love with him.

The priest was no less a person than the Archbishop of Canterbury. The service proceeded as was expected with Edward and Gwen speaking their vows in voices that carried to the back of the cathedral. It was clear to all that there was no doubt in their minds. The two were desperately in love. Helaine had to reach for her own handkerchief at that moment. Before long, they were pronounced man and wife. The organ music swelled, Edward kissed Gwen soundly, and the two were wed.

Then everything took a very bizarre turn.

It was time for the bride and groom to leave the cathedral together. Edward had his wife's hand and a look of utter joy on his face. But he did not actually take his bride down the aisle. Instead, he leaned in close and whispered something to her. She gasped in shock, putting her hand to her mouth as her gaze hopped to her brother, who gave her a rather sheepish shrug. She squealed in delight and stepped to the side, pulling Edward with her.

It was Robert who then stepped to the center to address the congregation.

"Friends and family, I am afraid this is rather awkward. Or at least it is for me. But a man will do quite a few very awkward things for love. And I am definitely such a man. A man in love."

His gaze then flowed across everyone there to land right on Helaine. Whatever could he be doing? Announcing this in front of everyone? Meanwhile, he was coming down the aisle, talking as he moved.

"If everyone could please bear with me a moment. There is something I have been trying to ask for a very long time now. But the stubborn woman has been difficult indeed."

He made it to her side and held out his hand. Helaine just stared at him, her mind numb with shock. It took her mother poking her in the ribs before she moved.

"Stand up!" the woman hissed. "Stand up!"

Helaine did, her eyes wide, her body stiff. And then she released a squeak of shock as Robert dropped down to one knee before her. Then he took her hand and gazed up into her eyes.

"I love you, my dear. Will you make me the happiest man in the world and say you will marry me?"

Helaine gaped at him. He could not be serious. No one

married their mistress! Then, before she could frame any words, he pulled out a folded piece of paper and pressed it into her hands.

"It is a special license. We can be married right now by the archbishop himself. Look at it."

She did as he bade, slowly unfolding the parchment. There in bold black letters was a special license allowing Robert with all his names and titles to marry one Lady Helaine, daughter of the Earl of Chelmorton. It was her name. Her *real* name.

"Oh, God," she whispered.

"I want to marry *you*," Robert said firmly. "The bishop will only name you Helen Mortimer," he said in an undertone, "but I will allow no legalities to negate our vows."

Helaine stared at him, her hands trembling where they gripped the paper. "But . . . but, Robert." She swallowed and leaned forward to whisper in his ear. "There is no baby. There is no need—"

He took her face in his hands, turning her so that she could look directly in his eyes as he spoke. "There is every need for me to marry the woman I love. I love you. And I want desperately to marry you."

Her heart melted. Indeed, it had fallen for him a long, long time ago. "I have loved you forever," she said.

"Tsk!" snapped Wendy from the seat beside her mother. "Then say yes and let him get off his knees!"

Helaine laughed and nodded, her heart in her throat. "Yes, Robert. Yes, I will marry you."

Her family erupted into cheers. There were likely other comments as well, whispers and confusion, but Helaine didn't hear them. She was too busy kissing Robert. And then he was pulling her forward down the aisle, back to the front of the church. It took her a moment to realize that he meant to marry her this very second.

She stumbled slightly as she looked at the grinning bishop. "What? You mean right *now*?"

"It is the best way," Robert whispered into her ear. "Quickly, before anyone can look too deeply into your past.

I don't care, Helaine. Understand that. I don't care, and your identity will come out eventually. But it is best to establish you as Lady Redhill first. There will be scandal either way, but this will minimize it."

She swallowed, understanding the logic behind his decision. But this was Gwen and Edward's day. She didn't want to intrude. "Surely we can't," she began, but Edward just shook his head.

"You can. In fact, it was my idea."

"Not the wedding," Robert hastily added. "Just the timing of it."

Helaine looked to Gwen. "You don't mind?"

"Mind?" Gwen gasped. "I get a husband and another sister on the very same day! I am thrilled!"

And so it was done. Robert took her hand and led her to the altar, where they knelt before the Archbishop of Canterbury. They spoke their vows and Robert slid a pink diamond onto her finger, one that perfectly matched the gem in his cravat.

"You are mine now," he said after he had kissed her silly right there in front of everyone. "Nothing can take you from my side ever."

"Nothing," she agreed. Because why would she ever want to leave?

"I love you," he said. And she laughed because she had said the exact same words at the exact same moment.

In the back of the church where Wendy misted up and Helaine's mother openly cried, Penny hugged her brother tight and whispered into his curls.

"That's love, Tommy. Real love the way it should be. And someday, if we're very lucky, we'll have it, too." She didn't really believe it would happen, but she wanted to pretend. And more than anything, she wanted it to be true for Tommy. So she said the words and clutched her brother tight.

Having no words, Tommy didn't answer except to gurgle happily and leave a sloppy wet kiss on his sister's cheek.

Turn the page for a special preview of
Jade Lee's next Bridal Favors novel

Wedded in Sin

Coming soon from Berkley Sensation!

Samuel Morrison's mind was racing, but that was not unusual. His mind was always racing. Even on this most beautiful morning as he strolled down Bond Street at the height of a shopping day. His thoughts wandered to Lady Pierson, who had just slipped a note to the flushed and very young Mr. Cooper. Then it hopped to Lord Simpleton, er, Simpson, who appeared to have left his home without his hat. Or a clean shirt. Ah, that was because he was coming from the brothel, Samuel realized, mainly from the unmistakable scent of smoke and perfume that trailed in the man's wake. And from the man's smile. Obviously, poor Lord Simpson was arrears in his funds, because he was walking down this side stretch of Bond Street rather than hailing a cab from Nightingale Street.

His mind wandered on, noting everything from the style of one person's clothing to the rubbish on the street. Samuel did his best to ignore his thoughts. It was really the only way to survive without complete lunacy, but his mind kept chattering away, this time about the dark-haired boy with the bad cough who was trying to get up the nerve to pick someone's pocket. About four yards away, a gypsy woman was watching closely, most likely as the boy's instructor. Not mother and son, he realized, because of the different facial features. More likely from the same gypsy family, though, because of a certain twist of the head. An aunt, he guessed.

Following their gazes, Samuel realized their victim was likely to be Lord Histlewight, who had obviously just returned from Northampton because his shoes were new. The fine stitching of his footwear proclaimed them as Northampton made. Unlike Samuel's own; his feet had lately begun to throb from his very cheap and poorly made shoes.

With a sudden veer, Samuel decided to turn left rather than suffer the moral choice of preventing a pickpocketing crime or keeping a silent witness. Normally he would have warned the child off, but the boy was thin and ill and would probably make better use of the coin than Histlewight ever would.

But a moment later, Samuel spun on his heel and turned back. His sense of justice prevented him from allowing any crime, even against an ass like Histlewight, to go unchecked. He made it to the street barely two feet ahead of the boy. Quick as he could, he grabbed the child's arm and hauled him up. It was pitifully easy. The boy was stick thin and too frightened even to scream, so Samuel had ample time to speak harshly into his ear.

"No thieving today, my boy. There's a butcher shop seven blocks that way." He jerked his head in the right direction. "Talk smart and polite to Mr. Braun, and compliment his smoked bacon. He's extraordinarily vain about his pork. The man's looking for a new apprentice, as the last one ran off. No matter what your aunt says, thieving leads to the gallows or worse. Not every man is blind or stupid. Someone always sees."

He held the child a moment longer. The boy was shaking in terror, but Samuel didn't release him until he had caught the aunt's eye a block away. The boy was too young to know better, but the older one would see that Samuel would not be crossed on this. It was a lie, of course. They could move their business two blocks over and he would not be there to prevent it. But perhaps it was an illusion that would hold. Perhaps the woman would make the right choice, apprentice the boy to the butcher, and turn from their life of thieving.

So he held the woman's dark gaze and whispered a quiet prayer on the child's behalf. And then he let the boy go. The kid dashed away on wobbly legs, catching up to his aunt before tugging the woman away down toward the butcher. Perhaps he had done a good deed, he thought, though he doubted the lesson would stick. Gypsies, as a rule, did not like to be tied to regular jobs or regular homes.

Meanwhile, his mind had tired of the gypsies and wandered off to notice other things. Mrs. Worthington had lost some weight. She had a new charge this season—two girls fresh from the nursery. One was pretty, the other canny. He gleaned that in an instant from their clothing, the way they moved, and the way the canny one kept her head down but her eyes always roving. Her gaze stopped on him and she flashed him a flirtatious smile, but he was already turning away down a side street to avoid having to chatter with the females. Meanwhile, he noticed that the meat pie cart had a weak spoke on its left side wheel. And perhaps he ought to check his own pocket to be sure it hadn't been picked while he was about his good deed.

He shoved his hand into his pocket and was relieved to feel that his few meager coins were safe. He had enough to last him until quarter day, but not much beyond that. Perhaps he ought to avail himself of his own advice, he thought. Find a regular job, focus on a regular task as so many younger sons were forced to do.

Then the most extraordinary thing happened. His mind noticed one thing more before falling absolutely silent. It was a woman with a too thin build and above average looks. She was carrying a child and a satchel while being bodily evicted from a shoemaker's shop. No one else noticed what he saw, though there were a dozen people watching the spectacle. She was arguing, the child was crying, and none of the constabulary appeared to care despite her large gestures and vehement protests. Only he saw that all her noise was for show, covering the fact that she had just tossed a small bag at a pile of rubbish.

It was a poorly tied bag with thin seams. As it landed, to wedge between the brick wall and leather scraps, the stitching burst and something distinctive tumbled out. Something that silenced the noise in his head and left his thoughts utterly speechless.

She'd just discarded Lord Winston's left foot.

Penny Shoemaker was furious. And not the kind of fury that made tears burn in her eyes. This anger was like a living thing under her skin that drove her to madness. If someone gave her a knife right then, she would have easily sunk it hilt deep in the constable's throat. A tiny part of her was horrified by that, but it was only a tiny part lost beneath the weight of anger fueled by humiliation.

She was being thrown out of her home. While she'd been quietly feeding Tommy a celebratory breakfast of bread and real eggs, armed men had banged on her door. She'd picked up her nine-month-old brother and answered the door. She'd been told in round flat tones that she was no longer owner of their home. That everything they owned—from the tools in the shoe store on the first floor to the clothes in their home right above—had been sold to that bastard Cordwain, a small-time hack of a shoemaker.

Well, she'd told them flatly that they were mistaken. She'd never sold anything, hadn't been paid a groat, and they could bloody well leave. Then she slammed the door in the constable's face.

She knew it wouldn't work. She recognized the face of Authority when it came in the guise of armed men and a constable's badge. It didn't matter that her eviction was wrong. That she hadn't sold their home or that for the first time since her parents' deaths, she'd found a way to support herself and her brother. It didn't matter to those bastards outside. To them, she was a woman alone with a babe. Her parents had been murdered more than two months ago, and she was now vulnerable to every kind of horror that the uncaring world could throw at her.

"Bleeding curs," she spat as she dashed for the workroom. There was only one thing of true value in her home and she would be damned if Cordwain got his hands on it. It was in a satchel because her father had been a slob. He had always planned to put everything on display or at least organize it in a closet, but it had never happened. And now Penny had cause to be thankful for his forgetfulness. She was able to grab the bag and her coin purse. Then she was back upstairs, Tommy crying in her arms as she stuffed clothing and the like into another bag.

But she was out of time. Their door burst open and the men tromped upstairs. Before she could do more than scream, rough hands wrapped around her waist. She kicked and screamed, but she had no purchase as she was lifted off the ground. The bastard was strong, his grip bruising, and his smell even worse. She knew without looking that the greasy head of hair belonged to Jobby, Cordwain's nephew and all-around brute. He flipped her over his shoulder and carried her outside. How she kept hold of both Tommy and her bags, she didn't know. Except that it was her life and her brother that she held and she'd be damned if she dropped either one.

Jobby banged her head three times on the way out of the house. She barely cared. She was more interested in protecting Tommy's head than her own. Still, the pain made her head throb and gave birth to that living fury just beneath her skin. Once outside, the constable made Jobby set her down. Normally she wouldn't have heard it, but the man had a whistle that he blew right in Jobby's face to get the idiot's attention.

"There's no cause for that!" the man bellowed. And so Jobby put her down, copping a feel of her bottom as he did.

She kicked him as hard as she could right in the privates just for that. Luck was with her. She connected. Not as hard as she would have liked, but enough that Jobby went down with a howl. Every man there winced in sympathy, and that gave her time to toss the satchel of important things to the side, where hopefully no one would notice. Then she started screeching like a madwoman by way of covering. If anyone had noticed what she'd dropped, hopefully they'd get distracted and forget.

She focused on the constable, as he was the authority here. His eyes had darkened as he watched Jobby writhing on the ground, but now he focused on her.

"There were no cause fer—"

"He had no cause to be doing what he was doing to me bum, either," she snapped, her language deteriorating as her fury grew stronger. "And you've no cause to throw me out of my home!"

The constable sighed, the sound coming from deep within him. If she were less furious, she might have felt sorry for him. He had the air of a man keeping doggedly on simply because there was nowhere else to go. A soldier, she thought, in a forced march. But then the image was gone as Cordwain blustered forward.

"Got the bill of sale right here, my girl. As of dawn this morning, yer property is mine."

She snatched it from his hands, all but ripping the document. She would not have him waving the thing in her face. Problem was, she still had Tommy wailing in her arms, clinging to her like he was terrified. Which he was. Just as she was, but she controlled it better than the toddler. And while she was struggling to control the boy, Cordwain turned to Jobby, who was just now getting to his knees, his face a pasty white.

"Get inside. Make sure she didn't steal nothing!"

"It's not yours!" Penny snapped in reflex, but the constable just shook his head, his hands shoved deep in his pockets.

"I'm afraid he's right, Miss Shoemaker. I made sure of it before I came. Everything's sold to him."

"By who? How can someone up and sell my home right out from under me?"

Cordwain rolled his eyes. "Aw, listen to the tart. Lying bitch. I paid you all my damn savings for this place. You're rich, you bloodsucking whore. And you won't be denying me what's mine!"

Penny gaped at him, her mind rebelling at all the things that were absolutely wrong with everything he'd just said. But before she could get a word past the dam of fury clogging her throat, another man sauntered up. A gentleman, by the looks of him, and a useless one at that, given the worn state of his clothing. He was tall and somewhat thin, and his dark curly hair went every which way about his head as if his brains were exploding by way of his hair.

"If I might have a word, Constable—"

The official all but groaned. "Sir, this is hardly the time."

"Yes, I know, but in the interest of the writ of law, I thought I'd point out something." He gestured with his hand, and in that one movement alarm bells began to ring in Penny's mind. He was looking at the satchel. He knew and was about to tell. Bloody hell.

"You want justice?" she snapped. "Here, hold Tommy for a moment." Her words made no sense, but she had to distract him somehow. And how better to distract a toff than to hand him a squirming, screaming toddler?

"What? No!"

Too late. She'd shoved the boy into his arms, much to both males' terror. And with her hands free, she could finally look at Cordwain's false bill of sale while keeping half an eye on whether the toff hurt Tommy or not. He didn't, thank heaven, but neither boy nor man was pleased with the situation.

"Can you read it?" sneered Cordwain.

"'Course I can. Enough to see that you didn't pay me for my property. And as I'm the one who owns this place, I'm the only one who can sell."

"I did too pay!" snapped Cordwain as he grabbed the bill out of her hand. "Right here. Payment to one Thomas Shoemaker."

"Tommy! That's Tommy!" She pointed at the squirming babe. "And he can't sell anything but his drool."

"Look, you lying piece of—" Cordwain's next words were drowned out as the constable blew one long shrill note on his whistle again. The noise was so loud that everyone stopped to clap their hands over their ears, Tommy included. Then, while their ears were still ringing, the constable stepped forward, speaking in a low, reasonable tone.

"It wasn't Tommy himself who sold your home, Miss Shoemaker. It was his guardian."

"I'm Tommy's guardian," she snapped.

"No, miss. You're not." As proof he lifted up the bill of sale and pointed at a signature. Right there in dark ink she saw the signature of Mr. Addicock, solicitor and trustee of Thomas Shoemaker.

"What's a trustee?" she asked.

"Legal term for guardian," inserted the toff from behind Tommy's head. Apparently during that shrill whistle blow, Tommy and the gentleman had come to some mutual agreement. Tommy was wrapped around the toff's neck like a monkey and he wasn't screaming anymore. Meanwhile, the man supported Tommy's bum with one hand while angling for a better view of the bill of sale.

"But I've never heard of him! And he can't sell my home!"

"He can and he did!" bellowed Cordwain.

"You've never even heard of him?" asked the gentleman. "How long have your parents been gone?"

"Two months! Don't you think that in two months, the man would have presented himself?"

"Well, yes, that would be typical, wouldn't it?" The man reached over and picked the bill of sale right out of Cordwain's hand. No one disagreed. He had that kind of confidence that people went along with. As if he had the right to step in and solve the problem. Which he didn't. But as he was working on her side, Penny saw no reason to stop him. Meanwhile, he was frowning down at the document. "It does look official, but—"

"'Course it is," said Cordwain. "It's this lying—"

"Call me names again, and I will scratch your eyes out!"

"You will not!" inserted the constable. "But I will blow this whistle until you are both too deaf to hear it. So stubble it, Cordwain. You got no cause to be saying things like that to her. Especially since you got the law on your side."

"His side!" Penny cried. "But none of it is true!"

The constable grimaced. "Everything I got is legal and true, Miss Shoemaker. It says he purchased your shop and everything in it."

"But how? I haven't received any money, I haven't talked to this solicitor person, I don't know anything about this at all!"

The constable just sighed again, and the sound seemed to pull his shoulders down. It was the look of a miserable individual, but one who would do his duty no matter if it were wrong or not.

"It's not *right*," she said.

"Don't matter," inserted the toff. "It looks right from his end. He's got no cause to stop it."

"But it's *wrong*," Penny repeated, trying desperately to find a way to stop this. "All of it is just . . ."

"*Legal*," said Cordwain with a sneer. "All legal. Now get gone from here, girl. And take your brat with you. I can't have the likes of you around my place of business."

That was the final insult. The living fury beneath her skin broke free. She launched herself at Cordwain with the only weapon she had—her nails and her fury. But she never connected. Before she even realized she'd leaped, the toff had her around the waist. It was no small feat, given that he still had Tommy wrapped around his neck. And for a too tall, no-good toff, he was damned strong.

"We'll have none of that," he scolded, not winded in the least despite the way she was flailing in his one-armed grasp. "It's too late; surely you can see that," he continued.

He was right. While she was trapped by the toff, the constable had stepped between her and the bastard Cordwain. Jobby, too, had recovered and was now looking as dark and violent as she felt. Still, she would have fought on if it weren't for Tommy. All her struggles were putting the toddler in danger. Apparently the stranger knew that, too, because he was quickly shoving the boy into her arms even as he set her back onto her feet.

"There, now, hold the boy before he gets hurt," he said.

"That's right, you b—"

"Enough, Cordwain," cut in the constable. "Damned if you don't know how to make a bad situation worse every time I see you."

The bastard puffed himself up, his face flushed and his mouth starting to open, but the toff was there beforehand, his manner somewhat bumbling but his eyes very keen.

"One question, Mr. Cordwain, if I may. Did you know this solicitor before the sale?"

"Wot? Why—"

"How close were the two of you?"

"I didn't know the damned man before he took my money!"

"Well, that's clearly not true," said the gentleman with an eye roll. "You don't just give a man money for a store out of the blue. How'd you know he was Tommy's guardian? 'Specially since the lad's sister didn't even know."

Cordwain's brows narrowed and he looked to the storefront. "Everybody knows I've wanted this property. Been trying to buy it, but her dad wouldn't sell."

"I see," said the gentleman, his brows drawn together in a frown. "But what has that to do with Mr. Addicock?"

"He contacted me. Said as he knew I wanted to buy it, would I do it now? And for a bloody high price, too!" Cordwain's face snapped around to glare in their direction. "Had to spend all my savings for it. Every last groat!"

"Well, every last groat except for the men you're paying right there." He gestured to the three sour-looking thugs loitering around the shop's front door. "Five men plus the constable to evict one woman and a babe? Seems rather excessive, doesn't it?"

"I knew she would be trouble," the bastard growled. "And I was right."

"Huh." That was it. Just a grunt more than a word, accompanied by a glance at the constable, who simply shrugged.

"No!" Penny cried. "No!"

"I'm afraid so, Miss Shoemaker. It's the law. Do you have someplace to go? A relative perhaps? Or a friend?"

Penny stared at them. Cordwain, the constable, Jobby and his henchmen, then the toff last of all. They all stared at her like mutton. Blank male faces of differing personality, but all dumb, all blind. "Can't you see . . . ," she began, praying that one of them would help her. After everything she'd done since her parents' murder, everything she'd survived, this final humiliation was too much. It was—

"I'll see to her, Constable," the gentleman said. "Just let me get my bag." Then, without so much as a by-your-leave, he strolled straight over to her satchel and flipped it over his shoulder.

"But—"

"Best go with him," the constable said, giving her a sad smile. "Nothing to be done here."

"But . . ." Her gaze traveled to her home. She'd been born in the upper story of that building there, as had her father. The shop had been her grandfather's pride and joy, and her father's after that. One month ago, she had found a way to save it. She'd just begun to dream of opening its doors again to show her wares just like a Shoemaker had for over fifty years. It couldn't be taken from her. Not without warning. Not like this.

"Come now," said the gentleman as he gently cupped her elbow. "There's stuff to be done and it isn't here."

"But—"

"Just walk," he ordered. Not harshly, but with enough authority that she obeyed. She spoke not a word, and to her added fury she found she was crying. Big, wet tears leaked down her face. She couldn't stop it, and she damn well couldn't hide it.

They were three blocks away when the toff finally said something that jolted her out of her misery.

"Tell me why I'm carrying a bag of body parts."